Praise for Chelsea Caslie and The Fantasia Series

"I was fully enthralled from the first page." —*Early Reader Review*

"The most fun I've had reading a book in a years. Chelsea Caslie seamlessly blends action, adventure, romance, drama, and fantasy in a whirlwind love letter to video games of all genres." —*Early Reader Review*

"An exciting take on video-game genres and multiverse storytelling with lovable characters, fun banter, and pace that makes it impossible to put down." —*Early Reader Review*

"An exciting thrill ride. Female led, it adds a new element to the LitRPG genre. Will leave you begging for more!" —*Early Reader Review*

"Extremely detailed and fantastic world-building and character development... If you love feisty, strong female characters, you're going to love Lost in Fantasia. All three novels deliver the same emotive entertainment we love to read while relaying the importance of friendship. I can't recommend it enough." —*Early Reader Review*

About the author Chelsea Caslie

Chelsea Caslie is an author, reader, and avid video game player who incorporated all of her passions into one project. A perfect day is when she plays video games with her dog next to her. When it comes to video games the longer and more immersive the better and you'd probably find her playing the same games as the main characters from her debut trilogy. Chelsea was born and raised in California and calls the Bay Area her home with her family and dog.

The Fantasia Series is a Sci-fi and Fantasy trilogy composed of Lost in Fantasia, Fatal Reset, and A Broken Game.

Please follow @chellycaz on Twitter!

The Fantasia Series

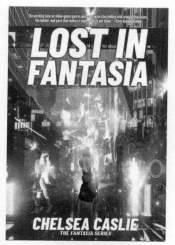

LOST IN FANTASIA

When virtual reality takes over, it's hard to tell the difference between what's real and what's a part of a game. After Tack's partner disappears, infected by a glitch, she is forced to find answers to determine if he is dead or alive. If Tack can't stop the glitch, she risks more than just losing her partner forever—everything she knows and loves might disappear.

FATAL RESET

Virtual reality has become the only way of life, and no one can tell the difference between what is virtual and what is real. So when a glitch began destroying Tack's reality, she stood up to save it. Rebelling against her typical intuition and traits, Tack trusts in what she's told. But when she is confronted with conflicting information regarding the Glitch, she is forced to choose who she trusts enough to fight with. If the only people who understand the Game aren't giving straight answers, who can Tack trust to help her save the world?

A BROKEN GAME

Virtual reality is a fun escape for everyone... unless you're forced to participate against your will. When the entire world thrives on augmented reality, how will it survive the destruction of the microchips that made it possible? When Tack confronts the Creator, she must determine what is real, what is a lie, and if any of it matters while she is trying to survive.

LOST IN FANTASIA

BOOK ONE
THE FANTASIA
SERIES

CHELSEA CASLIE

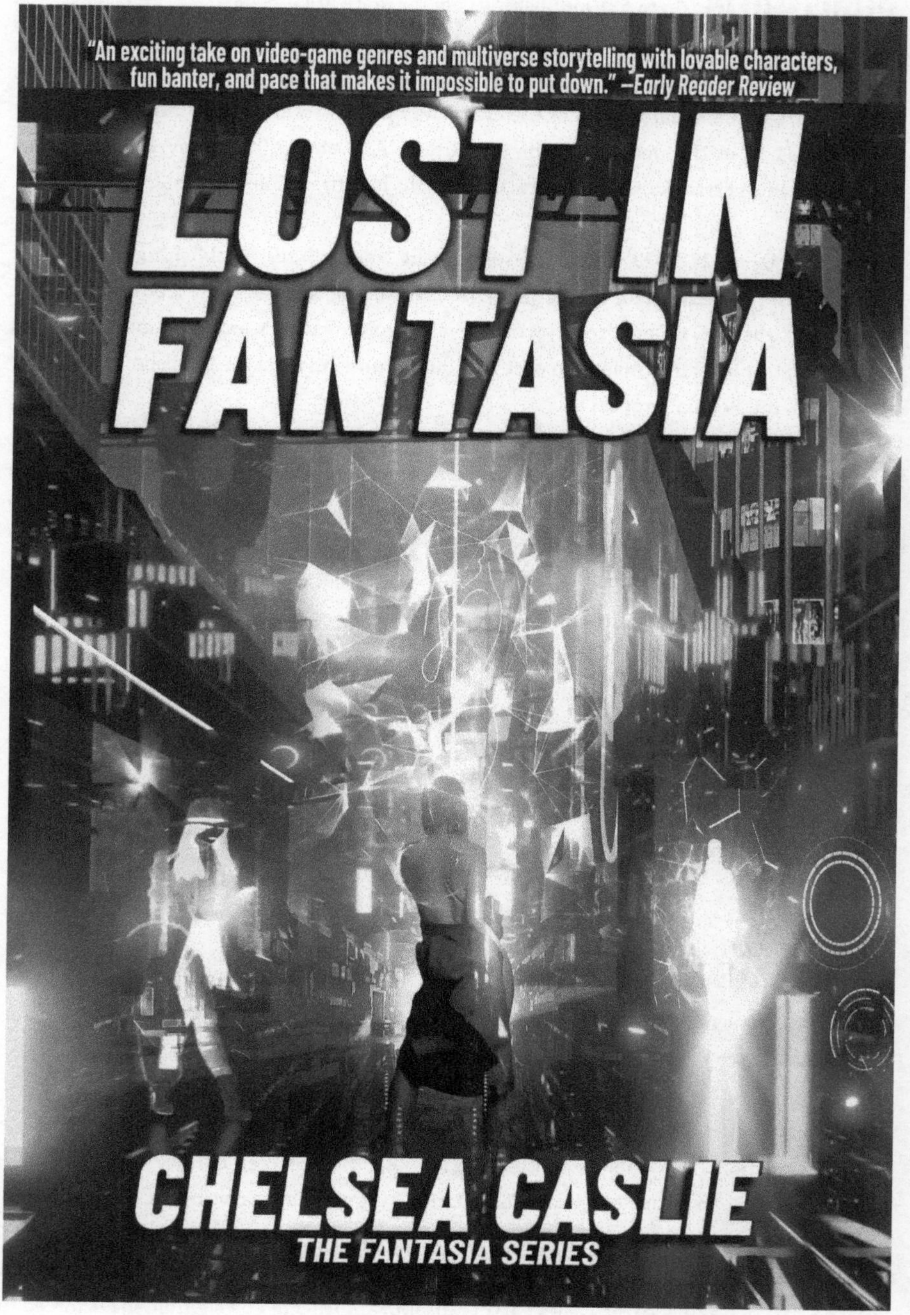
"An exciting take on video-game genres and multiverse storytelling with lovable characters, fun banter, and pace that makes it impossible to put down." –Early Reader Review
LOST IN FANTASIA
CHELSEA CASLIE
THE FANTASIA SERIES

5310
PUBLISHING

Published by
5310 Publishing Company
Go to 5310publishing.com for more great books!

SCAN ME

LOST IN FANTASIA (1ˢᵗ Edition) - ISBNs:
Hardcover: 9781990158872
Paperback: 9781990158889
Ebook / Kindle: 9781990158896

Author: Chelsea Caslie | Editor: Alex Williams | Cover Designer: Eric Williams

The first edition of *LOST IN FANTASIA* was released in February 2023.

ADULT FICTION (with Young Adult interest, 16+)
FICTION / Science Fiction / Cyberpunk
FICTION / Fantasy / Action & Adventure
FICTION / Science Fiction / Action & Adventure

Themes explored include: Science fiction; Cyberpunk; Contemporary/Futuristic Fantasy; Love and relationships; Themes of death, grief, loss; Interior life; Identity and belonging; Science fiction: near-future; Magical realism; LitRPG: Game-related; Dystopian/utopian fiction

When virtual reality takes over, it's hard to tell the difference between what's real and what's a part of a game. After Tack's partner disappears, infected by a glitch, she is forced to find answers to determine if he is dead or alive. If Tack can't stop the glitch, she risks more than just losing her partner forever—everything she knows and loves might disappear.

To my husband, Drew. Thank you for the constant support, late-night readings, and honest and direct feedback. You were my first fan. Without your push, this book would have remained "untitled book 1" on my computer, never to be read by another person.

To my parents. Your love and support throughout my life has been an amazing gift and one that I look forward to emulating with my own son.

Finally, to my sister, Katelyn. Being competitive and the younger sibling, I always wanted to copy you, which is what led me to writing. Your passion for stories encouraged my own. I am forever grateful for our relationship and all that you have taught me.

PROLOGUE
DECEMBER 2040

(NEWS1; San Jose, CA) Henry Fudders, the current CEO of the multi-billion dollar franchise, "Fudders," has announced his retirement today during a live stream. Henry Fudders was also the founder and CEO of "Gaming Science," the inventors of the augmented reality microchip used by billions of people worldwide.

Fudders thanked his employees, fans, and users of his proprietary microchip but offered no explanation for his abrupt departure from the world of gaming. For years, Fudders has been building and improving what is now known as "the Game" through innovative technology. As a result, Fudders is often referred to as the creator of what became known as "Everyday Gaming."

While NEWS1's requests for an interview fell silent, we are taking a moment to look back on Fudders' accomplishments throughout the years to highlight the innovations Fudders and both of his companies created.

Gaming Science, Henry Fudders' initial company, rose to power through their earliest innovation, virtual reality rooms. In the room, players engaged in a VR experience through single or multi-player mode without wearing traditional VR equipment, which was a requirement for most VR experiences at the time. The once unknown company, backed by private funding, quickly expanded its horizons by announcing its first augmented reality microchip. The visionary chip was backed by business conglomerates and healthcare professionals.

When first revealed, a company spokesperson stated that the product would allow users to experience video games like never before and incorporate players' favorite aspects of video games into their everyday life. The company's claims did not disappoint, as initial users could access a health meter, a virtual bank, and an online messaging system. In addition, all the menus and apps could be seen and navigated with their eyes, with no additional interruptions to users' daily lives.

These microchips helped solidify Gaming Science's success in the technology field. Companies, including Gaming Science, offered free downloads to employees who had the chips implanted to earn additional rewards at work, such as extra money for reaching productivity standards or additional bonuses for working overtime—it was the start of what the chips have grown into today. Within a year of its release, an estimated ninety percent of companies were on Gaming Science's microchip network and offering incentives to employees and customers.

The year before the chip's release, Gaming Science completed the construction of what they called "the Platform," the first spot where players arrived after technicians implanted a subdermal chip in the back of their neck. Gaming Science built the Platform in the epicenter of their 140-acre property.

Everyone who received the microchip was required to pass a medical exam and initial check of the microchip software to ensure it was working correctly, which was best done at the Platform, where the majority of the tech and supercomputers used to create the game were housed. Initially, only Gaming Science employees were allowed to live on the Platform, but nearby apartments were constructed shortly after.

The company's stocks skyrocketed upon the initial completion of the Platform and again after the press conference announcing the apartments.

When Henry realized after initial testing that the flow of people commuting to the Platform would be too much, he began a partnership with Teleport Transportation Services, or TTS. He announced that the chip would bring "additional forms of travel." The tease was given by Gaming Science only one month after TTS announced their first successful teleportation machine. This, again, caused an enormous boost to company stocks for both companies at the time.

Because of the perks associated with the chips, especially teleportation, most people, even those initially opposed to the idea, opted to implant the microchip in their brains.

Soon, new companies began joining in on Fudders' ideas and imitated his earliest VR rooms using his AR technology. Empty warehouses in once desolate locations were cheaply bought, bringing millions in revenue to businesses creating AR games.

Similar to previous gaming experiences, such as go-karting around a track inside or outside a building, chip users could teleport to those empty warehouses by paying for an annual or one-time pass. However, instead of traditional go-karting, one would see a world of clouds, jungles, or even race underwater, all while sitting in a go-kart in an empty warehouse. With the low cost of rent and cheaper insurance due to AR technology creating the experience, millions of companies popped up overnight, leading to a booming market, all utilizing Fudders' technology.

After separating from his wife and Gaming Science, many believe due to the disappointments of one of his first augmented reality games, Henry Fudders created a new company called "Fudders."

Within the first year, Henry bought a plot of land in the European countryside, which has since become known as the game of Fantasia. Before its institution as a game, Fudders developed the land with homes, a castle, and the surrounding area as if it were an amusement park. When the players teleported to Fantasia, they experienced a fantasy world like no other before it. It felt accurate and authentic because it was real. Players also experienced the augmented reality of monsters to battle or chests they could open with prizes inside, which existed only through their chips.

The idea of creating homes within the game also was a step up for Fudders as it allowed people to buy houses within Fantasia and pay their mortgage to the company through gold collected in-game. People began living in mixed augmented reality, much like what we see today. The success sparked further controversy after the initial release when the governments got involved in creating habitable and fun games within their country to increase revenue.

Slowly, many argue that the world forgot what life was like before the chips were created as the AR is too enticing. While the Platform initially built by Gaming Science still exists and provides the initial confirmation of software and medical check, many forgot the purpose of the teleportation as everything is done in the background without any interruptions to the user experience, unless the chip is determined to be faulty. Since its creation, the Platform has grown into an exciting and popular location to live due to the frequency of new and creative players joining the game every day.

The final progression of Fudders' work came with the invention of Characters. While playing retro games with virtual characters is fun, it was determined that playing a human being would be a penultimate endeavor. Consequently, those who weren't gaining popularity through streaming switched to becoming playable "Characters" as a way to gain fame and fortune.

While Fudders himself did not create any Characters, many believe it was inspired by augmented reality and aging video game technology. However, the ethical lines of playing human Characters were not easily overlooked, which led to the creation of Production, a team of individuals who help manage the Game and create safeguards for all Players and Characters.

Given his contributions to the Game, it's hard to imagine a more influential person in history, and Fudders' retirement will be something we will never forget. However, those old enough to remember the years without microchips are left to wonder: will our vision of reality continue to expand with the loss of Fudders? Both of his previous companies are still active in the Game.

It's hard to imagine that our experiences will be limited with Fudders out of the game. In fact, many younger generations have never experienced the world without AR and think of it as reality. So while Fudders may be gone, new and innovative ideas will always be on the horizon.

NEWS1 is thankful to Fudders, but we pose a question to our viewers and readers: will real life become lost to time, and if it does, what will that mean for humanity?

ONE
100 YEARS LATER
- 2140 -

Not everyone played the Game, but everyone was in it. Being in the Game was real life. The idea was thought up at a time when high technological advances were rife and was a response to the high demand for living a more fulfilling and adventurous life. Sure, I could work a nine-to-five desk job and *hate* my life. But, if I add some spice to it, such as exciting co-workers, fun graphics that say shit like "Cool!", "Awesome!", "Fantastic combo!", and a +1000 gold every time I file a simple stack of papers, then I wouldn't want to leave.

Well, I still would. But everyone and their mother loves the *Business Business* game, so they're doing something right. Maybe it's the average +12000 gold a day on top of their normal salary. For people like me, a job is more fulfilling when it's dangerous. Give me a dark setting, twenty-five hidden enemies, three minutes to kill them all without serious risk to my life, and +1000 gold for every combo any day. There's nothing I love more than drowning out the world and playing my game.

Now that's a life worth living.

Almost as soon as we are born, we are all implanted with a gaming chip that allows us to respawn, level up, and collect materials for any gaming journey. Playing the Game can be as simple as driving go-karts on any track you choose to teleport to or as complex as picking a genre and committing your life to it.

The most popular side effect for everyone, even those who didn't actively have a game, was the ability to protect themselves. Someone tried to rob me? Well, that was a horrible mistake, but mostly because I can kick their ass and get an extra +1000 gold for "winning" the fight. Safety came in the form of increased stats, fighting abilities without any real training, and, in some cases, the ability to go in slow motion mode to guarantee safety and success.

When I committed to the Game, I picked the First-Person Shooter genre. At least, that's what I was told. When you first joined, you could choose to keep your memories from before you joined with additional memories for your Character woven into your past or you could become fully immersed in your game with no memories of the past. I had no memories of my past; I only remember waking up in what looked like a doctor's office to some peppy good morning message informing me what was about to happen. It was the first message in my DMs, and it was the only one I couldn't delete. I tried.

All I had was built-in knowledge of the Game and everything I would have expected to know about life as if I still had my memories, but I couldn't even remember my name. I wasn't scared, which I assumed had something to do with the drugs they had given me before the procedure. Even so, the entire process was fast; I didn't have time to think about what any of it meant because, after I finished reading the message, I was immediately teleported to the Voting Forum.

Anyone could vote in the Voting Forum, including people outside of your chosen genre. My clothes quickly changed through colors, sizes, cuts, and fits as people vigorously voted for what I should look like. In typical gamer fashion, my defensive armor as a female was slim to none. I wore a slick black bodysuit that showed off way too much cleavage and a light vest that assisted in pushing up my boobs but not actually protecting me. My hair swirled around my face, changing colors, before settling into a brown ponytail.

Next came my weapon; my arms alternated in different positions for swords and guns before a tiny blip in the chat spiraled out of control. I watched as the weapon "thumbtacks" started getting Likes, HaHas, and Loves. The guns disappeared from my hands and, by making a pinching motion, a thumbtack appeared between my fingers. I threw the thumbtack at the empty space in front of me. For those watching, it cracked their screen, emphasizing the deadly nature of the unique weapon.

Most people assumed the number behind my name was a kill count, but it wasn't. The number behind my name was the speed at which I could throw my thumbtack straight through a person's heart. My kill count was much higher.

People voted on my abilities and even my personality. I stood still, feeling millions of invisible eyes judging me on looks alone. That was when I did it, the motion that dictated my entire Character profile. It was taking for-fucking-ever, so I let out a sigh and rolled my eyes. A flurry of voting began, then it was decided: stubborn, agile, and "loves to cook for her partner every year on his birthday."

Partner? Baking? Gross, all of it.

I didn't know if that thought came from the person I had been in the past, but that was my first thought after seeing what had been voted and decided on. I rolled my eyes again when I found out there was a special DLC pink apron that I could battle in if paid for and equipped by my Player.

When everyone finally finished voting, I woke up in the Platform. Those of us living in the Platform area can cross the street and see a grown man in combat uniform humping cows, which are crossing in front of racecars throwing bombs at each other before going to their game. The Platform is the epicenter of all gaming. Every new Character went through there.

Producers, popular Characters, and Players typically live there. And, at its core, is the computer system that runs all the games. It was treated like the main menu for every game and multiplayer interaction; from the Platform, you can choose to battle with people outside of your game, and if you don't want to live within your game, you can live in an apartment above one of the many buildings throughout the complex.

However, the Platform was the most desirable location. Some important guy made it a hundred years ago. No one really remembers *him*, but his original company, Gaming Science, was still around. It fought for the most popular Player/live streamer employer and was second place only to the company called Fudders. I guess he didn't like his first company anymore, so he made another one.

But that's none of my business.

The two competing companies continued to make the Platform a central hub, not just for the nostalgia of a man who's not even alive anymore, but because they had spent hundreds of billions of dollars making the Platform into the major metropolitan it is today. The number of apartments had grown well past the actual Platform. Sure, there were other worlds that you could live in Corporous, where the corporate types and bureaucrats lived, but those were typically reserved for specific themes. Like that annoying *Business Business* game. Producers that didn't live in the Platform lived in Corporous, along with a lot of gaming lawyers and CEOs of large streaming companies.

My partner, Ghost, and I chose to live in the Platform because a first-person shooter world isn't really one that you can make a comfortable home in. Ghost chose not to keep his memories as well, and the people in the Voting Forum prompted our Production team to give Ghost a mysterious backstory that no one knew. His abilities included strength and hand-to-hand combat, and his favorite food was obviously my cooking. People shipped us hard since we started.

Ghost was all I had. Without any memories of my past, I didn't know if I had a family, friends, or anyone that *cared* about the decision I made to join the Game. I let that thought fuck me up for a while, so did Ghost, but together we worked through it.

He cares.

That was why I focused so heavily on what I had now with Ghost; he grounded me. We joined at the same time, and our Production rep told me they spent days working on our story post-Voting Forum. They didn't allow me to remember that time; all I remembered was waking up, the Voting Forum experience, teleporting to the Platform, and finding Ghost, feeling an immediate connection with a person I might not have known before. Even though I had no memories of him either, he felt like home.

Our game started because we joined at the same time and one comment in the Voting Forum, just like my tacks, got traction because it said, "dude, two bad-ass Characters at once? How do you choose who to vote for right now?"

Production watched as our Characters were created in the Voting Forum, with voters starting our story for Production by combining our Characters in our Character profiles. Sure, Production could have separated us or given us non-playable characters to work with, but the popularity of those comments among the other voters, and Players with sway, caused Production to brainstorm how they could combine our two Characters into a single game. There was a romance between us, the drama of Ghost's mysterious past, comedy in our interactions, and a shit ton of action.

Being in the Game was fun for more than just the Characters and Players. Everyone can watch, and they did. Our game, *Duty Falls*, was long-standing and one of the best produced. In our weekly call with our Production rep, they said they have years of our story written out and waiting to be played. Our Characters had recently been separated from each other in an explosion that made the two-player game momentarily single-player and followed our Characters individually. This didn't bode well for Production when it wasn't well-received, with a sixty percent drop in viewership and increased lag time in connecting Players and Characters, so they brought our Characters back together and *everyone*, including Ghost and me, was happy about it.

I often complained when our game split the two of us; to Ghost, to my Production rep, to the non-existent people I imagined I was being interviewed by in the shower. I knew the risks of the Game going in, and I was sure I considered them before choosing my genre, as well, but the moment I was stabbed or shot and felt the crippling pain radiate through my body, it just made me angry, and I didn't know who to turn my anger to. The

Producers for inflicting the pain, the Players for not dodging, Ghost for not helping, or myself for not being better.

I didn't regret joining the Game itself: I just had this overwhelming need to be right, to be perfect, and getting injured was a sign of failure. Plus, it hurt like a bitch to die, and I wanted to avoid that.

No matter what happened in the Game, we were told it wasn't "real life." Our game was not us. Even though every scar on my body told a different story, we were told to keep working as if we weren't in pain—physically or emotionally. On *very* few occasions, I wondered if I picked the wrong genre. Would Ghost and I be happier if we lived as fitness instructors or people in dancing games?

Ha, yeah, right. Those people suck.

I didn't worry about any of that when I baked. I always felt better after baking, like I wasn't about to bitch out the next person who walked through the door. Baking turned into so much more than a Character trait for me; it was an escape, just like playing the Game. I'm alone, in control, and I get to decorate my cakes in themes that wouldn't fit my Character profile. My favorite cake to bake was a classic carrot cake with cream cheese frosting. It was exciting because carrots, as a vegetable, are unexpected in a dessert. Add some light pink flowers to the cream cheese frosting, and it was the perfect spring dessert.

I carefully spun a cake on its platform as I held a knife with icing up to the side of it, gently frosting the side. Then I stuck my finger in the leftover frosting and put it in my mouth.

Perfection.

I grabbed a spoon and dunked it in the frosting to get a bigger bite just as the door opened. I shoved the spoon into my mouth to hide the evidence as Ghost entered the apartment with two coffees in his hand. For people outside of the Platform, it would've been funny to see Ghost act so *normal*. He was wearing the military outfit picked by the voters, but he changed his hairstyle when he was outside our game. Instead of the strict army haircut, he had a fade and a five o'clock shadow on his face. He liked it better this way, but I liked him either way. We made eye contact, and he started laughing.

"Why are you stress baking?" he asked.

"Mhmm." I sucked on the spoon and put a finger up. "Not stress baking. Just baking."

"Is it my birthday?" He put the coffees down and smiled.

"No, you dork."

"Then why do I get a cake?"

"Who said the cake was for you?"

"Is it not?"

"Nope." I smiled. He dipped a finger in the frosting and put it in his mouth.

"Yum." He grabbed a spoon for himself and my spoon from me, then dipped both in frosting before handing mine back to me. "So, what's the deal with the cake?"

"I just got a feeling I wanted to bake all of a sudden. It felt relaxing. But." I stuck a finger up into the air, ready to defend myself. "I'm not stressed."

"So, the cake is for me." He was confused.

"No, the cake is for us," I corrected.

"Is there really a difference, Tack? You're just being sassy to be sassy."

"Don't call me sassy."

"Oh yeah, and what are you going to do about it?"

"Throw a tack through your heart and force you to respawn." I smiled.

"Hm," he groaned and stretched. "That doesn't sound like a lot of fun."

"It doesn't?"

"No, it really doesn't."

"I'll work on a barter system. What's in the cup?"

"Your usual." He smiled.

"I'll allow you to apologize with coffee. You're lucky this time."

"I get lucky a lot."

"That's because I love you."

"Oh, is it?"

"Yup, most people feel the wrath of Tack180."

"I feel like I still see that side of you." He laughed and then thought about it before poking me a few times in the stomach. "Especially when I push your buttons."

"I swear to god." I swiped at his hands.

"Tack, come here." He held out his arms and pulled me into a hug. He slapped my ass, winked, and then said, "I only keep you around because you're hot."

"Gross, you know I hate it when you say stuff like that." I threw up my hands and then walked out of the room. It was all I could do before I actually did throw a tack at Ghost.

That was one of the reasons I loved him; when everything else in my life felt like it was going wrong, especially when we were separated in our game, he was always waiting for me at home to make it better. He could crack a joke at any time, be the emotional support I needed, *and* be the only friend

I've had since joining the Game. It was just the two of us, and I wouldn't have it any other way.

"Wait," he called. I looked back as he took a sip of coffee before following me with my coffee in his other hand. He handed it to me. "Where do you want to go today?"

"Do you wanna battle?" I looked at the clock while I started quickly drinking my coffee.

"I don't want to deal with the fanservice NPCs today. We can play our game."

We were contractually obligated to give eight hours to our game either way, whether we played our campaign or chose the battle route. We could access the battle feature through the Platform then it was a free-for-all battle against anyone who wanted to play; even new Characters could try their luck.

On one occasion, we won twelve battles in a row before the Producers wrote in a famous retro NPC during the next round. The NPC was given unbeatable weapons and abilities, but buffs like that just ruined the fun of a good battle.

The only other way to join was the crossover feature. Producers preferred for Characters to play their own games, so playing in battles and crossovers typically brought in less money and less frequent item drops—and even lesser items in the drops, for that matter. Not much I could do with a mushroom outside of a crossover.

They didn't even taste good.

"We do make more money that way."

"Let's go online then."

Ghost reached down to a monitor on the side of his wrist, pressed a button, and teleported to our game. I rolled my eyes and teleported after him. One of the biggest problems about being the best was people always wanted to play us, especially new Players. I usually didn't mind it, I always won, but some days it just sucked dick.

There were days where I didn't move at all. I just stood there staring at the door as if I was waiting for someone to come in because, technically, I was. My Player for the day wasn't there; these Players that go AFK should be kicked the hell off the whole Game. Don't fight to get paired with a popular Character and then disappear. It's bad taste. My vision, also viewable by anyone watching on our game's channel, would fill with Thumbs Down and Angry emojis until the Producers booted my Player off and I was matched with a new one.

In a blink, I arrived at our last save point where Ghost was waiting for me. Above his name is his Player's name: GetSome69. I rolled my eyes as loud music played from above Ghost with the sound of laughter in the background.

"Yo, dude. I got Ghost." The sound of Ghost's Player echoed. "Shut up and turn off your music."

"What?" another voice asked.

"Fucking turn off the music. I got Ghost."

"Shit, man."

It didn't take long to get assigned a Player, especially for our game. Most people set alerts to go off every time we went online. Although, anyone could play us: the best and the worst. The name above mine said "Waiting" as Ghost started circling me, pushing up against my body as if the Player was trying to get Ghost to hump me.

"Sorry," Ghost whispered. "Horny teens."

"Fuck, dude, holy shit. Look who I'm playing with," Ghost's Player announced.

"Tack, look up," Ghost whispered again. I tracked his gaze above my head.

"What? You're playing with SmokeScreen. I'm recording this shit," Ghost's Player's friend screamed.

SmokeScreen never talked but always live-streamed. He, or she, was *the* top Player. We had never played together, but I'd watched their streams. I knew it was going to be a good day. With SmokeScreen playing, we would have more viewers, more loot to collect, and higher rewards. I just hoped Ghost's Player didn't fuck it up for us somehow. If Ghost died more than five times, we'd restart from our save point and his Player would be booted. Although SmokeScreen would have the choice to stay and try again, usually Players would decide against it. It was considered bad luck in the gaming community.

Now, one of the main rules in the Game was that a Character wasn't supposed to move on their own. I mean, that was the whole point of being in the Game: *to be played.* But it wasn't perfect, and I wasn't much of a fan of that rule. I would have been dead at least a hundred times had I not taken over at some point or another. Crashes, glitches, freezing. You can move all you fucking want and the Producers call it whatever they think of and make it look however they choose. Sure, I did it, but I followed my own code. I only glitched when it mattered—like almost dying, not AFK Players. Plus, it was easier to get away with smaller things, like a quick movement half a foot to the left. Although, Production would probably fire you for an obvious or extreme violation. Being stubborn and a perfectionist, I was more likely to "glitch" than Ghost, but I wouldn't need to with SmokeScreen.

SmokeScreen practiced all of my moves before we started the game. I jumped in the air, did a backflip, and shot a thumbtack all before gracefully landing back on the ground, where I continuously shot tacks at inanimate objects with precision and dodged non-existent attacks.

"Aw shit, man. He's so good."

Yeah, dumbass. It's fucking SmokeScreen—we are going to crush this campaign.

They lined us up at the save point, and the game started where it left off. Ghost and I had been working as undercover operatives for the past seven years with the game following us every step of the way. There were no fantasy elements; other than the unorthodox use of thumbtacks, we followed a pretty "typical" life.

"We have five minutes until extraction," Ghost said. He was reading from the script that we could both see. When you're a Character, you can see the same screen the Player sees in a tiny box on the top right of your field of vision; it was part of the implant. At the same time, we could see different forms of praise, such as emojis and thumbs-up, in our entire field of vision. The script covered our entire view in the same way but stayed near the bottom to avoid distracting us or covering up something important. "If we don't make it to the checkpoint by then, we're screwed."

"Well then, follow me," I said.

We began to run after a distant blue marker. The closer we got to the marker, the easier it was to see tiny blue dots in the distance that indicated eight NPCs were present. They were the rest of our team.

"Finally," one of them yelled. "We've been waiting for you two. We have a plane waiting in the field north of here. Follow our lead."

We started following the NPCs to an open field that looked ripe for an ambush. I could feel with every move that SmokeScreen was ready for it, just as I was. It felt nice to have a Player who knew what they were doing. Dying hurt like a bitch; there was no fun or poetic way to explain life actively leaving your body when you've had it happen over a dozen times. But the respawning process was instantaneous, and you spawned with three seconds of immunity, which was just enough time to fuck up the guy who killed you.

I looked over at Ghost, whose Player was making him roll the whole time instead of walking. Then I jumped and threw a thumbtack into the bushes ahead of us. Mini red dots began to fill the screen to indicate enemies. I looked over at Ghost, who was fading between fully visible and invisible; he had just respawned. He had four more respawns left before the race to connect with Ghost's Character began. Some Players just refreshed their connections while watching us in the hope that they are the first to press "play" as soon as our Character becomes "active."

SmokeScreen made quick progress as we dodged bullets, closing the gap between us and the red dots. I was throwing thumbtacks as fast as I could, taking out red dot after red dot. My kill count next to SmokeScreen's name raised to thirty-two. GetSome69 had one.

"Aw shit, I still can't believe I'm playing with SmokeScreen."

SmokeScreen had me look over and give Ghost a pity smile and a wink— my taunt. I was most known for two actions; my original taunt and rolling my eyes, which was offered in the same DLC as my pink apron when enough people complained that my signature move from the Voting Forum was missing.

"Dude, did you see that? He's fucking taunting me. He's so cool."

"I did, man. Shit. This is dope."

A new blue marker appeared in the distance, and we started running again, our NPCs following behind us. The sun started to set in the game as an orange glow began to fill the sky. I looked at Ghost; time shifts weren't a normal part of our game. Then Ghost glitched, actually glitched, he disappeared and then reappeared.

"Ghost," I whispered with fake surprise. "Did you just move yourself? I must be rubbing off on you."

"No, I don't know what it was. You did it, too."

"What?"

"It was like I blinked."

"New game change?" I asked.

"Odd to be done mid-game but not unheard of, I guess."

"Hmm," I hummed.

"Something's not right, Tack," he whispered.

I scanned the area and saw hostile forces in the distance but no red markers to indicate their appearance. We continued to run toward the hostiles, but our NPCs didn't make any comments about them. Nothing. Not even a "hostile forces incoming, be on your guard." They continued running like they didn't notice. But, as Ghost mentioned, something wasn't right. Though they were human in shape, their bodies were covered in black with a purple haze, almost like a flame, emanating from their bodies.

"Yo, are we supposed to fight these bitches?" It was Ghost's Player.

Always fight, dumbass. That's what our game is made for.

SmokeScreen pressed the X button, and I started attacking from a distance, staying behind as the NPCs and Ghost continued to run forward.

"Woah, did they add zombies? Shit, this game just keeps getting better and better."

That'd be stupid. I rolled my eyes.

Whatever they were, they weren't typical for our game. Our NPCs started auto-attacking, still strangely making no comment about the forces they were fighting. Our Captain, a strong woman and NPC with fifteen years of fighting experience in multiple fighting styles, engaged their leader. He knocked her gun away, and she took a fighting stance. SmokeScreen had me throw a tack at their leader, but the tack went through him without doing any damage, like a defective glitch. Our Captain made contact, and I watched as her body turned as black as theirs before disappearing. I looked around quickly but couldn't find where she had respawned.

Don't touch them, got it.

GetSome69 was holding his own with Ghost, but even Ghost's gun wasn't doing any damage.

"How are we supposed to kill them? This shit is hard," Ghost's Player said.

"Retreat!" Ghost yelled. I looked on my screen, but I didn't see a script to read. Ghost was going off-script. "Tack, get back!"

SmokeScreen took Ghost's advice, and my body started running backward while throwing tacks in an attempt to slow them down. When SmokeScreen finally turned me around, I saw why Ghost had gone off-script. Our NPCs weren't respawning, and there was only one left. NPCs always respawned, especially essential ones like our Captain. In some games, if your NPC died, you would have to go back to your previous checkpoint. Our game didn't follow that rule, but they had always respawned immediately. There was no reason for our game to lose all NPCs, with no script coming in and no directions.

I scanned the field and watched their leader kill the last of our NPCs. Ghost and I had created a good distance between us and the hostile forces, thanks to Ghost's warning. All we had to do was get back to the save point and either restart the campaign or save then end for the day. It seemed obvious to me that the Players would take us back. But, if they didn't, that was why we could take control of our bodies while in-game. I just happened to abuse that power more than others. It would be easy for Ghost and I to come up with a story to cover for the glitch until the Producers had time to fix it. We just had to get offline at a save point. Sure, glitches happen, but they aren't anything to be concerned about; Production has protocols in place for *any* system failure you could think of.

I guess there was a big blackout almost a hundred years ago when the Game was still new that forced them to put safeguards in place. While we all know it happened, the details surrounding the event were protected by

Production. No one knows what *really* happened unless they were there, and no one's alive anymore to give us an answer.

Ghost and I continued to sprint away from the hostile forces when I saw a flash, the same way Ghost glitched earlier, then the leader of the hostile forces was in front of me. SmokeScreen had me glance back to see the remainder of our adversaries still behind us. SmokeScreen faced me forward, toward the most urgent threat, again just as quickly as I had looked away. I dodged as the leader tried to grab me.

"Tack!" Ghost yelled, but I couldn't look at him. I was too busy dodging a barrage of attacks from the leader.

"Keep going," I yelled back. "I've got him."

The leader smiled as if he had won the fight already.

"Who are you?" I asked. He didn't answer. He just kept attacking me and, with SmokeScreen's help, I dodged with ease. "Our game's not open for crossovers."

"I'm not a crossover." He stopped attacking and looked at me. He tilted his head like he was confused by what I said.

"Okay, then what are you doing in our game?" I asked.

"I need to kill you."

"Respawn," I corrected, frowning slightly. "Did Production send you?"

If they did, there was a nicer way to reset us. Although, props to Production. This stunt would bring in lots of views. Hell, they probably did it to see how people would respond to adding zombies to our game. GetSome69 seemed to like it.

"I need to kill you." He reached forward again, and I flipped backward under SmokeScreen's guidance.

"Yo, Characters don't actually die. If you knew anything about the Game, you would know that," Ghost's Player chimed in as he brought him over.

Anyone who knew anything about our game would know better than to separate us for too long because our Characters had such a strong loyalty to each other. He continued to make Ghost dodge right and left to avoid being injured, even though no one was attacking him. The leader turned and looked at Ghost like he was analyzing him. The remainder of the hostile forces closed the gap.

GetSome69 was right. Characters didn't really die; even if we died in-game, we would just respawn. Or, if the producers wrote us out, we would go back to the Platform, and it's up to us if we want to battle, engage in crossovers, or just retire. That was another fun benefit of the world shifting to the Game: no one died of anything other than old age, and everyone could protect themselves with their own Character's abilities. With a quick movement, the leader lunged at Ghost, predicting where GetSome69 was going to have him land. SmokeScreen moved me forward, pushed Ghost out of the way, and turned me back to fight.

"Ghost, I think we should go," I said. I would never have taken over for SmokeScreen on any other occasion, but this psycho wasn't a part of our game, Production wasn't actively intervening, and our NPCs weren't respawning. Something was off, and if we didn't follow protocol by getting to a save point and going offline so our game could be fixed, then we would pay for it with large fines that made the day's loot worthless.

I started running again, but Ghost didn't move. There was no subtle way to tell him I had taken over, so I just yelled again. "Ghost, I'm moving. Let's go."

"Woah, dude, Ghost is moving on his own."

Good, he got it.

"What? Let me try to play."

"No, man. If you want to play him, you can get him when he comes back online. This is my turn."

"Shut up, both of you. This isn't a part of their game." It was SmokeScreen.

"Shit. You're a girl?" There was no response, so GetSome69 tried again: "Are you hot? How old are you? I bet I could show you a good time outside of the Game."

I looked over at Ghost and flipped his Player off. It wasn't either of my taunts, but GetSome69's response was the norm for girls who were in the Game, both Players and Characters.

I mean, look at my damn outfit.

"Thanks for the support, T," SmokeScreen said. "Now, let's get you out of this mess. Let me help."

We weren't far from the save point where we started. I looked back at the dark mob still following us. Before I looked forward, I felt Ghost slam into me, pushing me out of the way of their leader, who managed to get in front of us again. Ghost bumped me, then dodged back so we both ran past him as he laughed.

"T, I'm used to all types of games, including racing and jump scares. This doesn't seem to be your strong suit. Let me help," SmokeScreen said again.

"Just do it. You have a good Player, use her," Ghost said.

I took his advice and went limp. SmokeScreen took over. It was easy for her to dodge attacks while running. Ghost followed SmokeScreen's moves behind us perfectly. I could see the save point in the distance when I heard a loud crack, and the ground began to shake. I moved with perfectly timed jumps as the ground crumbled away underneath us. I let SmokeScreen have control of everything but my hand as I reached back for Ghost. He grabbed hold of me as he followed our jumps. Only a few yards away.

"I'm not going to make it, Tack. Just let me respawn," Ghost said.

"No, you're coming with me. Just like you always have. Let's go."

"Tack!"

Pain.

I looked back, SmokeScreen still moving me forward, as the leader grabbed Ghost. He turned black, with a purple haze, just like the leader. I felt a shooting pain through the hand he was holding onto. I looked down to see it turning black, and I let go. My hand remained black, but it didn't move any further up my arm. Ghost stayed frozen in the solid black bubble for a brief moment before disappearing in purple smoke.

"Don't touch anything with that black hand," SmokeScreen said. She continued to move me forward. "I'm getting you out right here. Your Producers will fix it from there. Just... a little... further. Made it!"

I touched the stone indicating our save spot with my healthy hand and went offline. I was teleported back to our apartment in the Platform.

"Ghost?" I stumbled around, trying to find any indication that he had respawned outside of the game. My glitched hand throbbed in pain, reminding me, with every sting, that I had let him go. "Ghost!"

Bang!

I looked outside my window, and it was absolute chaos. The sun remained perfectly in the middle of setting, it didn't even look like it had moved, and there was a melee in the Platform. People from different games were injured, battling, and unable to open the teleportation to their games. I looked down at my hand, still black with a purple aura around it, just like the weirdo who made it into *Duty Falls*, just like Ghost had looked before he died. But where did he respawn?

"Ghost?" I called again into the silence.

If he wasn't in *Duty Falls* and he wasn't home, then the only other place he could've possibly respawned was the actual Platform itself, where the brawl was occurring. I opened the door to the balcony overlooking the Platform and scanned the area. There were noobs, veteran Players, and NPCs fighting as if the battle option was offline and the only place for them to battle was the Platform.

"Tack!" I heard my name echo around me. It wasn't Ghost, and I couldn't be sure, but it sounded like SmokeScreen. "Get out!"

A giant bomb began to descend on the Platform. It moved in slow motion and was obviously part of another game, stuck in the Platform just like everyone else. There was something different about it, though; it was darker in coloring, with a... purple flame? *Shit.* I didn't have time to analyze it any further. As the bomb hit the Platform, it exploded, sending me back into the apartment. I threw my arms in front of me to block the blast.

I opened my eyes, and it was dark. The sun had finally set. I could see the moon perfectly, surrounded by trees. *Trees.* Not in my apartment. Panic set in as I pushed myself up to my feet.

How the hell did I end up in a forest?

I looked down at my hand, still glitched, which wasn't the only weird thing. My vision seemed different; the whole place looked like it had brighter colors, even in the darkness. I tried to teleport back home, but nothing worked. I tried testing several other systems, but they all seemed down. My health gauge was the only thing that appeared to be functioning.

"Who are you?" I turned around to find a group of eight people entering from an opening in the trees. They were holding weapons, without a name or Player name above them. I had a mini-map available, but there were no blue dots to indicate if they were friendly. There were no red dots either; so, I was either out of *Duty Falls* or they were like whatever that glitch was.

I went to turn myself online, but nothing registered. I knew it wouldn't, I had already tried, but I didn't trust anyone I didn't know. I pressed the button repeatedly as the group came closer while I kept my game face on and showed no fear. I couldn't deal with them—not at that moment. I just wanted to find Ghost and go home. Even without being online my instinct was to pinch my fingers, knowing damn well that a tack wouldn't appear if I was offline. And yet, a tack emerged in both hands, even the glitched hand.

"What game am I in?" I asked.

"You're in open-world territory, sweetie." A girl reached out a hand. "You seem to be out of your game."

"Okay, but where am I specifically? What game?"

"We encompass many different RPGs and MMORPGs in the largest open-world concept. You've ended up in a subset of Fantasia."

"I'm in fucking Fantasia? Gross. Look, I'm not interested in a crossover right now. Get out of Shadow mode and make your Player names visible."

"Haven't you heard?"

"Heard what?"

"This is The Night of the Never Setting Sun. The worlds are in chaos, and you don't need a Player to play the Game. We're playing right now but, then again, we could always do that." A different guy began sharpening an axe with a rock he picked up. "So, who are you? Some new mage? Hell of a time to be a new Character in the Game."

"I don't know what you're talking about. I'm not a magician. I'm just trying to find someone I've been separated from." I started looking around for the quickest escape route without turning my back to them. They continued to stare at me with their weapons exposed. The guy who asked the question looked down at my glitched hand.

"Do you have some kind of blight then?" They all took a step back like *I* was the dangerous one.

"Blight?"

"Are you diseased or not?"

"Look, I'm over this conversation. I'm just going to go now."

"Wait." The same girl from earlier reached for me again. I moved back to avoid her reach, the pain in my hand a reminder of what would happen if I let them touch me. I threw a tack at the girl, and an archer from their group quickly sent an arrow at me in response. I dodged and threw a tack taking out the archer before he could shoot again. While I was at it, I threw a tack at the man with the axe. Three down, five to go. I pinched my fingers and more tacks appeared.

"Stop, please!" one of them yelled with his arms up. I stopped and stared at him. A tack in each hand, ready to be flicked at any moment. "Please, you don't die in our game. Even when you are low on health, the most you do is faint. You just wiped them out. You *killed* them."

"I didn't kill anyone. You know that." I put my good hand on my hip. Who did this guy think he was? *I'm not stupid.*

"Then, where are they?" He was crying. The others had taken the opportunity to run away.

"I don't know. This isn't my game."

"You killed them."

"I didn't *kill* anyone," I yelled back.

"Please don't kill me. Take all my loot." He threw his entire stash on the ground. Laying over a hundred items on the ground around him, from shields to potions.

"Look, I think there is some misunderstanding. I need to get back to *my* game. Or to the Platform. How can I get there?"

"I don't know. Everything's down. I'm sorry." He stood up and started slowly backing away.

"Wait, please, I need to get out of here."

"I'm sorry." He moved in a zigzagged pattern as he ran away from me, leaving his stash on the ground still.

I grabbed a potion and poured it on my hand. It paused the feeling of excruciating pain but did nothing to remove the glitch. I threw the empty bottle, grabbed one of the cloaks, and headed in the direction away from where the remainder of the group ran off. I was stuck in Fantasia, of all places, and, as shitty as it was, it wouldn't be long until I ran into someone who could hopefully help me back to *Duty Falls*. My adrenaline kicked in, and I felt invincible, ready to find help so that I could get *home*.

I wrapped the cloak around my glitched hand and started adventuring like I was born to play in RPGs. I looked under rocks to see if any creature was hiding that could help me, looked into trees, checked near any and all bodies of water. It was the typical stuff I had seen live streamers do, although I had no idea if it would help me in Fantasia.

Thunk.

I turned my head to see an arrow stuck in a tree, right where my head had been a second before. I spun around and prepared two tacks. The crying guy had brought back up of at least ten men.

"There she is, men. She's the one who killed the members of our guild."

"Like I said, that's not what happened. I didn't *kill* anyone," I argued.

Instead of shooting at me, he waved his hand, and an archer turned on the other men and shot them. It would have been considered kill shots in *Duty Falls*. They would disappear and then have three seconds of invincibility. But these men just fell to the ground. They lay there for five seconds without either of us saying anything. And then they stood up like they had never been injured.

"You killed our friends." He wasn't crying anymore. Now, he was pissed.

I looked down at my glitch. Did I really *kill* them? If I killed them, did that mean that Ghost was really dead?

No, I won't accept that.

I was shaking, regardless. It was impossible to suppress, but I tried to remain as still as possible, not showing them my fear.

"If she can kill us, can we kill her?" the archer asked. "For the Immortal Hell Crushers guild!"

They advanced. I threw a tack, purposefully aimed to slow them down rather than kill them, and ran. I stumbled through unfamiliar terrain: woods purposely meant to confuse, filled with mud pits that came out of nowhere. But everywhere I turned, I still saw them following me, knowing the woods much better than myself. I finally emerged from the woods to see a giant walled city surrounding an ornate and grand castle on a hill. *Safety*. On the outskirts of the wall, there were many soldiers guarding the city. Even closer than those soldiers were three walking the perimeter.

"Help, please!" I yelled. The three guards closer to me readied for a fight. "There are people following me. They want to kill me."

"Halt," one of the three yelled. He was holding his sword and stood in a fighting stance. I stopped running. "Not you, girl. The men behind you."

"She's a murderer," the man I'd now dubbed the "crying man" yelled.

"You don't understand," I pleaded back to the guards. "There is a huge misunderstanding. I'm just trying to get back to my own game."

"She killed them. *Actually* killed them. Now it's our turn to kill her."

"I said halt," the man with the sword yelled again as he and the other two stepped in between the men and me.

"We don't have to listen to you," another man replied.

"You'll listen when you are in the presence of royalty. That is the law laid out in the Fantasia treaty. Or did you forget?" That one spoke more like a royal than the other soldier as he stared the men down.

"Blood for blood is also in the treaty."

"If you want to fight, then I am more than happy to oblige." His hand made a fist and began to glow a light blue color.

Gross, magic.

"It... It's the prince." The crying man started to back up slowly before all the guild members began to run.

"Ha! Scared them off before we even got the chance to fight," the man with the sword said as he turned back to me. He mouthed the word "oh" and nodded when he finally got a good look at me. He seemed to recognize me, which would be helpful.

"And who exactly are you?" the last soldier asked as he joined the conversation. He held onto a spear. At least their different weapons would make them easier to differentiate; there was the prince, Spear Soldier, and Sword Guy. "You don't look like you are from this game. I would love to show you around."

"That's..." Sword Guy started. "Never mind."

I stiff-armed Spear Soldier as he advanced on me and directed my comments to the prince, "Sir, I request your help."

"Didn't we just help you?" Sword Guy asked.

"Who even are you?" I looked above their head and saw nothing, not even a Character name. "If you're an NPC, you have to tell me. It's the law across worlds."

"No, it's not."

"How do you know?" I asked him.

"Is it?" He looked at the prince.

"She's messing with you," he replied.

"Well, we aren't NPCs. Why would you think that?" Sword Guy asked.

"You don't have Character names."

He looked up and then back at me. "Neither do you."

"Yes, I do."

"No, you don't."

I glanced up, and it was gone, just like my ability to go online. "Oh."

"Who looks stupid now?"

"Still you," said the prince, looking at Sword Guy. "Well, what's your name?"

"I'm Tack One Eighty." I pronounced it carefully, knowing most people outside of *Duty Falls* wouldn't understand me the first time if I said it quickly.

"Tack what?" Still didn't get it.

Why did I even try?

"My game's not like yours. Just call me Ta—" I stopped myself. Ghost was the only one who called me Tack. Everyone else just called me by my full name. Tack was special. They didn't deserve Tack. "T."

"T, what a lovely name." Spear Soldier came closer to me again. "You can call me Nathaniel, defender of the prince."

"I'm Alton," Sword Guy said. "And this is Prince Kaspian, crowned prince of the royal capital of Fantasia, and home of Her Majesty the Queen Seraphina."

"Great, that was way more information than I needed. Look, I'm just—"

"Do you dabble in magic, Lady T?" Nathaniel asked. He looked down at my glitched hand.

"This isn't magic."

"Looks like magic to me," Alton said.

"It's not magic."

"Then what is it?" Alton asked.

"None of your business."

"Both of you stop," Prince Kaspian said. "T, what exactly did those men mean when they called you a murderer?"

"They attacked me first," I defended.

"I still don't understand."

"They think I actually killed their friends."

"Did they not faint?"

"No. They respawned, I think. Well, not in their current location and I'm sure they're around here somewhere. But, again, they attacked me first. I didn't realize that I would have that kind of effect. I never had before this thing." I raised my hand and removed the cloak.

"Ah, you're blighted. We have healers. However, if you did, in fact, *kill* those people." Prince Kaspian smiled as if he didn't believe it was possible. Sure, he had to say it out of duty, but he didn't actually mean it. I smiled with him, agreeing that the thought was absurd. "You will need to answer for your crimes, not just in Fantasia, but with the greater Production team."

"I didn't mean—" No. Why was I apologizing? That insinuated guilt, and I wasn't guilty. "I didn't kill them. Look, you don't understand. I'm not from your game, so I'm not going to answer for any crimes, intentional or otherwise. I need to get home. I need to find Ghost."

"Who is Ghost?" Nathaniel asked. Alton put his head in his hand as if he couldn't be more embarrassed by his friend's lack of knowledge.

"He's my partner. Our game glitched while we were online. It was weird: he was there one second, and then he turned black, like my hand, and disappeared. He didn't respawn in game, I couldn't find him on the Platform, and he wasn't at home."

"So, there is a chance that Ghost is dead, just as the others?" Prince Kaspian suggested. His tone changed. He questioned me rather than laughing it off like his previous statement.

"He's not dead. Just like they aren't dead. They can't be."

"I guess it would make sense they aren't dead if you're still present," Alton said, and I felt myself relax a fraction. Then, he came closer to examine my hand. "They could've ended up in a different game, as well. How are you here?"

"Don't touch it," I snapped and pulled away, worried about what might happen to him if he touched my hand. All three of them took a step back. The two with weapons held them in front as if they were afraid I would attack their precious prince.

Fuck, I needed their help. I can't have them assume the worst and turn on me. If I'm stuck in a stupid dungeon, I can't get back home to try to find Ghost. I tried again: "Listen, I *won't* hurt you. My hand looks like this because I was holding Ghost's hand when he was attacked. I've never been in so much pain before; I can only imagine what it felt like coursing through his whole body. It was the pain that shocked me, and I let go of him. It stopped climbing up my hand when I did, but that was also when he disappeared. I—"

"You don't need to tell us any more if you do not wish to," Prince Kaspian stopped me. I had tears in my eyes and rolling down my cheeks. I instinctively went to wipe my face with both hands.

"Don't!" they all yelled at the same time.

"Here," Nathaniel pulled off a glove and handed it to me. "Protect your beautiful face."

"I'm not accepting anything that comes from you."

"Why not?"

"Because you talk like you moonlight in a dating sim."

"Take mine then," Prince Kaspian took off his glove and handed it to me. I put the glove on my hand, which covered the black color but did not stop my hand from glowing purple. "Until we determine if your hand is blighted by design or by a kill-inducing glitch, it will remain covered."

"I understand." I nodded. From their responses to my movement, it was obvious at least some part of them believed my hand could be dangerous, regardless of how impossible killing someone actually is. Either way, they were my best bet at getting out of this place, and I had to trust them. "Can you help me get home?"

"We can bring you to the queen. She knows more about out-of-world dynamics than we do," Alton suggested. "Especially since the teleportation feature is down. She might also know where everyone is respawning."

Prince Kaspian stared at me and then back down at my hand, covered in his glove. He looked in the direction he was originally walking and then back at my hand.

Yeah, I get it. You don't trust me.

"I will escort you to the castle, but I do have other matters to attend to. I won't be able to stay around to see what my sister decides of you." With that said, Prince Kaspian started walking toward the gates and the others followed. I jogged to catch up to them. "You are not allowed to fight or use your weapons while within the game of Fantasia. For the safety of all involved."

"That's fine with me. I don't play multiplayer anyway."

"We aren't playing right now. This is our home."

"You live in your game?"

"You don't?"

"No. But I guess it would make sense for you guys. I'm in a shooting game, so I'm either playing my main campaign or in battle when I play. It's not really a place to live."

"And you live with Ghost?" Nathaniel asked.

"Yes."

"What exactly is your relationship with him?" Nathaniel continued to ask.

"None of your business."

"You're feisty. I can be feisty, too. If you know what I mean."

"Talk to me again and so help me. I will take this glove off of my hand and shove it up your ass."

"Don't tempt me."

"Nathaniel," Prince Kaspian chided.

"Sir." Nathaniel pulled ahead and talked to the guards blocking the gate. They moved away, opened the gate, and bowed for the prince.

I entered the gates, and soft music began to play in the background. I looked around, but I couldn't see anyone playing music. I rolled my eyes at the thought of playing music as part of their Player experience. I missed the silence of *Duty Falls*.

Although it was night, the city surrounding the castle was still lively. People were in bars drinking, out on the streets selling the last of their wares before cleaning up for the night and taking leisurely strolls. The bars matched the theme of Fantasia. There were no large screens or beers on tap. At least, none were visibly present to pull from the mood. It was just a cottage-looking building, with people sitting around wooden tables on benches. There was no gunfire or violence, people lived *peacefully*. I was jealous of them, living life in their own world without any consequences from the glitch that just devastated my own. I would give anything to be in their shoes, enjoying time with Ghost, rather than stuck in some ridiculous fantasy game.

"Welcome to Fantasia's Castle Town," Alton said. "The largest, and dare I say greatest, in all of Fantasia."

"Why is there music playing?"

"There's always music playing in Castle Town. Doesn't it make you feel at home?" Alton asked.

"No," I replied, a little too bluntly. That won't do. I need to try and get them to like me. "I mean, this isn't like *my* home. I live in the Platform, so I'm used to bright lights, loud sounds, and all kinds of different people. It does feel homey, though."

"That's what I like to hear!" Alton smiled.

"You have a lot of pride for your game."

"It's my home as well as my game. I wasn't accepted where I came from before. I was always the kid that everyone made fun of in and out of school and even at work as I got older. I used to be a Player to get away from it all. But streaming only made so much money unless you were famous, like SmokeScreen. So, I decided to join the Game about two years ago and worked my way up to Prince Kaspian's retainer. I have nothing but love for my new home."

"You kept your memories?"

"Of course! I still write home, too. It's all a part of who I am and why I chose this game. I don't think I would have worked so hard without that knowledge. You didn't?"

"I don't know. I don't have any memories, so I assume I didn't."

"So, you really don't know anything about yourself, like your name?"

"I know plenty about my backstory and my name's Tack180, or T."

"I'm sorry."

"For what?"

"Because you don't know who you *were*."

"I have Ghost. It doesn't bother me."

"Whatever you say," he threw his hands up. I rolled my eyes. How could I miss something I never knew I had? I must have hated it if I didn't want to remember it. I couldn't even dream about forgetting Ghost. If something's not worth fighting for, maybe it's better that I didn't remember it. But, if I missed someone that I was *created* to love, shouldn't I miss something I've actually lost, as well? It didn't bother me that I had no memories of my past with such a solid future with Ghost.

Now, without him with me, I just didn't know anymore. I've never lived without him.

"It doesn't bother me," I repeated because I didn't want him to be right. Although, I was a little less sure than the last time I had answered.

I can't let them get in my head.

"Alton," Prince Kaspian chided again.

"Sir."

As we walked further into Castle Town, I noticed Fantasia was not what I expected. I thought I would see old run-down cottages and no running water; I definitely didn't expect to see electricity. However, the houses seemed to be a combination of fantasy homes and something you'd see in the Platform; sure, there were some small cottages, but judging from what I could see through the windows, most were larger homes that just *looked* like a cottage on the outside. They almost seemed like dollhouses with their light-colored doors, colorful roofs, and dark-wood-trimmed windows with flowers in every windowsill. While everyone looked to be the same style on the outside, they all seemed unique. In one house there was even a screen that took up the entire side of the wall.

"I thought this game was supposed to be based on medieval times," I said. "The screen in that house was bigger than some you see back home at the Platform."

"We live in a highly technical world," Prince Kaspian remarked. "If given a choice, not many would choose to live here if the basic necessities, and I say that word loosely, were taken away. There is a theme to Fantasia, but what people choose to do inside their own homes is their choice."

"If I'm stuck here, I need to confirm that you have running water," I said. Alton started laughing. "What's funny about that?"

"I worried about the same thing before joining Fantasia, too. You're fine. Toilets, washing machines, screens to watch gaming—the works."

"Right. I know *of* Fantasia, but I don't know how you guys operate," I hedged. If I wanted to get out of here without them giving the forest incident a second thought, I needed to gain their trust. I needed to be their friend. I felt like an idiot just thinking about it, but I knew what needed to be done; I took a deep breath and then started the necessary small talk. "Anyway, Kaspian—"

"Prince Kaspian," Alton corrected me.

"*Prince Kaspian*," I tried again, "when did you join the Game?"

"28 years ago," he answered.

"Huh?"

"He was born into it. He comes from a long line of actual royalty. His family has been playing this game for decades," Alton answered for him.

"Oh." To be in one game for all your life, to grow up in it, with people watching you love, grieve, and live. I felt sorry for him for a moment, but that feeling quickly went away. It hardly seemed like he was suffering in this life. Hell, he was the Prince of Fantasia. "You must be a popular game to have been going on for so long. What's your Player rating?"

"It's not like that." Alton shook his head. "We are the Characters and Players of our own game. Our Producers only add side quests, special promotions every other week, and fun new costumes and gear every month. In exchange, we go online for official business, you know—war, parties, side quests, and such. I still get to stream, which is pretty cool."

"Our people do well when we do well," Prince Kaspian added. "Seraphina and I stream so our people can live in harmony without the outside world's influence if they desire. The more viewers we have, the more gold we receive for quests and other streaming events. While comms and other Game features are currently down, our people can live in the comfort that Fantasia is mostly run through actual government regardless of a Production blackout. They will not notice a difference in their quality of life while we await further instructions from Production."

"There aren't many other games that can say the same." Alton smiled widely, looking overly pleased with himself and his choice of game.

We were getting closer to the castle. Although it was large, it wasn't overly ominous. Just as the rest of Castle Town had, there was a fantasy vibe to it. Long spires protruded from the top, and rotundas kept the castle from feeling like a box and gave the perfect viewpoints from higher within. The light color felt welcoming, like anyone could enter and talk to the queen. Not that I wanted to, but I bet her people did.

"Your city is huge," I said after a moment's silence.

Kaspian looked back at me. "We are almost there."

"Oh, I'm not tired—you just have quite a lot of people to care for in here." I looked around. Given our location from the castle and how far we had walked, it was about a mile to the castle from the gate.

"You're only seeing the people within the city limits. We are in charge of a few other fractions outside of the wall and the entire game as a whole. Although individual leaders within their games manage their own Players. We do our best." He smiled and walked further ahead to the soldiers blocking the gate that led to the castle.

"Queen Seraphina is strong, beautiful, and a fair ruler. If anyone knows how to get you back into your game and how to fix your hand, it would be her," Alton said as we walked through the gate.

The grounds were beautifully maintained with a perfect rose garden, light purple and yellow roses, and elaborate fountains for the short walk from the castle gate to the actual doors. Inside, the palace was decorated excessively, with large purple and gold floor-length curtains, statues, and glasses made of gold used for decoration. Busts of people, who I'm assuming were the royal family, were lingering everywhere. The same light coloring I had seen on the outside of the castle was found inside, and there was a strong floral scent in the air, probably due to the number of vases surrounding the hallway with fresh-cut roses, presumably from their garden. It was pretty but overly showy.

Not my style.

Guards lined the initial room we entered as well as every entry and exit point within it, such as the stairs and doors. We walked past the guards and up the prominent flight of stairs in front of us. At the top of the stairs were a set of double doors with another two guards on the outside. The two guards took one look at me, then moved in synchronization to cross their spears and restrict access to the room.

"She's with me. We are here to speak to the queen," Kaspian said.

The guards returned to their original position, standing still next to the doors. Alton reached a hand forward and knocked twice before we heard a faint, "Come in." He opened the door. In the room, there was only a beautiful woman with long, blonde hair that touched the floor. A large golden crown encircled her head as she sat on an oversized, golden chair with purple cushioning. The room itself was mostly empty; there were two steps up to her throne from where everyone else would stand and the area behind her was shrouded in purple curtains, creating a dark backdrop behind the glowing gold of her hair, crown, and chair. She had a resting bitch face, but everything else about her, from her relaxed position to the decorations around the room, made her seem approachable.

Kaspian and Nathaniel were about to walk away, having delivered me to the queen, when I felt a pull into the room like a gust of wind blowing me inside. My feet stumbled against the feeling. The prince made a groaning sound before leading the way inside. We walked about ten feet toward the throne before the doors shut behind us. We were only halfway to the queen when all three of them knelt in front of her.

"Alton. Nathaniel." She smiled. "It's always a pleasure."

"As always, My Queen, your radiance is astounding." I rolled my eyes at Nathaniel's response.

"While on our nightly patrol," Kaspian began, "we ran into someone outside of their game."

"I see." The queen looked at me, her blue eyes blended in with the purple curtains around her for a brief moment. "And who are you?"

"My name is Ta-, T. Please, call me T."

"Tea? I should call you a beverage?"

"My full name is Tack180. I'm trying to get back to my game, *Duty Falls*. I'm hoping you can help."

"And why would I help someone who didn't even kneel before me? While you are in my game, should you not follow our rules?"

"I'm sorry," I quickly knelt next to Alton.

"How did you find your way here?" She looked down at my glitched hand, or maybe it was Kaspian's glove that she noticed.

"My partner and I were in our game when it glitched, and some crazy person showed up. My partner has been lost since the glitch and I've been injured." I removed Kaspian's glove to show my hand. "After exiting my game to escape the crazy person, I checked my apartment and the Platform, but I couldn't find where my partner respawned. The Platform was chaotic, and I was looking for my partner when a bomb exploded. But, when I opened my eyes after the explosion, I wasn't in the Platform anymore; I was in your world."

"I see. Do you practice magic?" she nodded at the glitch.

"No, this isn't magic. Didn't you just listen?" Just as quickly as I said it, I felt the wind slap me across the face. Her eyes were glowing purple and my face felt hot where her magic touched me.

So, the first time wasn't just a product of the lighting in the room then.

"You will speak to your queen with more respect than that."

"You're not *my* queen," I spat back. Alton nudged me. *Fine.* "Please, excuse me. I'm not familiar with your game and your rules."

"Clearly. Now, *T*, one of my guards on duty tonight at the castle walls made it back here before you did. I've heard members of a guild who hail from a nearby game have been murdered. Would you know anything about that?" she asked it in the same way Prince Kaspian had at first, like the thought of actually killing someone was laughable, but she still needed to ask.

"I didn't kill anyone."

"So, you *were* involved?" Her eyes widened in a quick moment of weakness. She glanced briefly at her brother and then back at me, any sign of concern now gone from her face as her passive mask slipped back on.

"Yes, but, like I said, I didn't kill anyone. No one actually dies. We all just respawn. I don't know where they respawned, but they are here, somewhere." I sighed at the challenge ahead of me. No one believed me, and I didn't blame them, but niceties and fake relationships were annoying.

"I see. If I were to tell you that during the daytime, the sky in our world was green instead of blue, would you believe me?"

"No."

"Why not?"

"Because the sky is blue."

"Yes, but you have never been in our game before and therefore have not seen our sky in the daytime and I *strongly* believe that the sky is green. Using your logic regarding respawning, the sky is green."

"They aren't dead."

"I will send my men to search the world of Fantasia for you. However, I will also acknowledge the possibility that they may have respawned outside of Fantasia. With that in mind, it is true that we won't know if they are truly dead or not until we resolve your problem, as well. So, it looks like I must help you to either clear your name or prove you a murderer. You look like a capable fighter. You will serve as my retainer, where I will keep a close eye on you."

"What?" I asked. I didn't even attempt to look at the others in the room. The queen was supposed to help me get out of the mess I was in, not make it worse.

"I recommend you align yourself with my brother to familiarize yourself with your own magical abilities. With his assistance, you may be able to open a portal back to your world. However, his magic is not strong enough on its own."

"She doesn't possess any magical abilities," Prince Kaspian answered for me.

"We shall see." She smiled. "Olivia?"

"Yes." The voice was familiar, but I didn't recognize the girl who came into the room. She had short, brown hair, a short stature, and was adorned in jewelry just as fancy as the queens. We made eye contact, and her eyes widened. "Tack180?"

"SmokeScreen?" I made the connection to the voice.

"But I watched a bomb blow you up!"

"How? I was offline."

"When you hit your save stone the feed didn't end. Your game was still streaming to me while you were at home. I think it was part of the glitch."

The queen cleared her throat. "I see you two are already acquainted. Olivia, please show *T* to our servants' quarters. She will be joining us for the time being as another of my retainers."

"Huh?" Olivia had the same response I had. Confusion flooded the room as we all stared at the queen, waiting for an answer.

"You do fight, don't you, T?" the queen asked.

"I'm one of the best distance fighters, with or without a Player. Ghost and I train all the time."

Seraphina looked over at Olivia for approval. She nodded enthusiastically. The queen waved her arm forward. "Then my statement stands."

"My Queen, if I may, you've never seen her in battle." If Alton bent down any further, he would have been kissing the ground.

"You overstep your bounds, Alton. But I trust your judgment. T, please, give us a demonstration."

"No." Prince Kaspian stood up to stare at his sister.

"Do you intend to protest?" she asked.

"If she can kill?" he asked her. "We cannot risk that threat to our kingdom to prove to you that a stranger should spend her time by your side rather than a dungeon."

"She won't kill me." The queen stared at me as if she was challenging me to try. I watched her eyes change from blue to purple and back to blue again. She nodded and I took that as my cue, but I hesitated. I didn't want to be her retainer; I didn't even know what that meant. I wasn't about to settle into their picture-perfect Castle Town. *I have a partner to find.* She sighed after a moment and then added, "It's either this or the dungeons."

That's all I needed to hear. I can't help Ghost if I'm locked up. Regardless of how I felt about this queen, I needed to have her on my side. I put Kaspian's glove back on, and with a quick pinch, I was holding tacks in both hands. With a quick flick of my wrists, they went flying to either side of the queen's head. I threw in some acrobatics for show; backflips, front flips, basically anything to show off my flexibility and speed.

"That's enough, thank you," she said as I was in the middle of flipping and throwing a tack at the same time—my signature move. "You will spend your days working under Alton to learn necessities of close encounter battle. You will be most useful here."

"I'm good up close and personal, too." I defended myself. I didn't need *their* training. "Ghost trained me, although my combat style is probably different from your game."

"All the more reason to learn a sword technique to make you more comfortable here."

"Your Majesty, she might *actually* kill someone," Alton raised his voice at the same time I said, "I'm not planning on staying here."

"Silence, both of you. You heard what I said. Olivia?"

"Right. Wow, I still can't believe you're here," she said. "I can't wait to show you around!"

"Olivia?" Prince Kaspian called after her. The queen stared at her brother but allowed him to speak. "Be sure to compose yourself. T has not been cleared of crimes against the people of Fantasia."

"Right," she repeated herself. "Well then, follow me."

"Alton," Prince Kaspian said. Alton stood up as if to join us, or more to *protect* Olivia.

"That will be unnecessary." The queen shook her head. Alton immediately knelt back down. I stood up to follow Olivia. She led us out a back door and down a flight of stairs. That part of the castle was not as beautiful and elegant as the previous areas had been; stone lined the hallways without additional decorative flowers or gold. The only similarities were the purple and gold curtains. It was obvious visitors typically didn't walk through these halls.

"This is where I live, and you will, too. It's the servant quarters, but I promise Lady Seraphina keeps us well taken care of."

"I don't plan on staying here for long."

"Of course, you still have to find Ghost!"

"Do you believe he is alive, too?"

"I'm a *very* optimistic person. If you believe he is out there somewhere, then so do I, and I will do whatever I can to help you find him."

"Thanks."

"You have an ally in me, T, and not just because I was the last one to play you. You are stuck here, for now, so you should probably enjoy it."

"I know teleportation is down, but can't I just use your backup machine to gain entrance to the Platform?"

"Oh, no! You really have no idea what's going on, do you? After you hit your save stone, I still had access to you on my feed. So, you know, I saw the bomb."

"Yeah, I thought I heard you shouting my name," I acknowledged.

"Well, after the bomb went off, your screen went blank, so I tried to see who else I could play. But here's the catch." She dramatically got uncomfortably close to my ear and started whispering as if she was afraid someone would hear us. I took a step back and she kept talking normally. "*Everything* is offline. No one can connect to the mainframe, the Platform's gone dark, and no one is playing. We can't. No one can teleport, send communications, or anything. It's some really freaky lockdown shit."

"Lockdown, like the Producers did this?"

"Well, I don't really know. I'm just guessing. Anyway, this is my room, and yours is going to be right across the way from me. Mostly because it's the only one still available and also because we would make the best across-the-way pseudo roomies. In the mornings, we make Queen Seraphina breakfast, sometimes we have to do her laundry—"

"No," I cut her off. "I'm not doing any of that."

"This. Is. Not. Your. Game." She emphasized every word while she clapped at me. "You will need to follow the rules if you want Queen Seraphina's help to get back home. By the way, what kinda situation are you in?"

"I killed some people in the forest nearby."

"So?"

"That's what I'm saying."

"But really, what's the catch?"

"They didn't respawn, like Ghost."

She cleared her throat but didn't move away from me. If she did think it was possible, she knew I didn't intend to harm her. "I'm sure we'll find them. *All of them.* Anyway, do you wanna see my gaming throne room?"

"Your what?"

"Come inside!" She grabbed my arm and pulled me inside. "This is my heaven."

Inside, her room looked like a modern room you would find in an apartment by the Platform. Large screen mounted onto the wall, keyboards, controllers, state-of-the-art chairs that you could only order on specialty sites, and the highest quality streaming gear. It didn't fit into the medieval world I was thrown into.

"You don't have to hide your excitement. It's awesome, isn't it?"

"Yes, of course, it is. But how?" Sure, the houses in Castle Town were decked out, but the castle didn't seem like it would allow for others to personalize it.

"I was SmokeScreen before I decided to join the Game. I'm sponsored by a lot of companies and games, but I wanted a more immersive experience, so I joined Fantasia. I mean, I'm obviously good, so I worked my way to be being Queen Seraphina's retainer, and she allowed me to keep all of my gaming things. You'd be able to make your room your own, as well. She's honestly the best."

"That's nice of her."

"Anyway, can I see it?" she asked, pointing at my hand.

"I really don't think I should take the glove off." She was the only one who didn't pull away when she found out I could kill; I didn't want to give her a reason to. As the best Player, SmokeScreen was someone I wanted to have on my side.

"I'm a Healer class. Just let me take a look at it." She grabbed the top of my arm and pulled off the glove. Then she reached for a staff that was leaning against the wall and waved it over my hand. I felt a cooling sensation. "How does that feel?"

"Honestly, better. But it's not going away."

"Yeah, well, one thing at a time. Now, I bet if I get Prince Kaspian's help, we could give you a glove that relieves the pain and might aid in the healing process, if possible."

"You could fix it?"

"I can't promise anything, but if it feels better, then that's a good sign, right?"

"You really are optimistic," I smirked while I put the glove back on.

"It's one of my Character traits! Alright, let's get you hooked up in your new room, and then I recommend you get some sleep. We have to get up at dawn. And don't worry, I have clothes you can borrow."

"I'm not changing my clothes."

"This. Is. Not—"

"I get it. This is not my game."

"But if it was, and you were on a mission, blending in would be the best course of action, would it not?"

"Fine, fine."

"And there are a bunch of really cool people here that you might actually become friends with. Like me!"

I glared at her, and she smiled back. I was in the wrong fucking game. I walked across the hall and found my room to be a complete shithole compared to Olivia's. It had the basic necessities, a bed, sheets, a wardrobe, and a mirror. But that was all I needed. I fell onto the bed and stretched out my arms. What did I get myself into? It had been such a normal day until the glitch happened.

What the fuck, Ghost? Where are you?

Damn. I can't even process what's happening. It was so unusual from anything that I was used to. Glitches are normal, easy—nothing to be too concerned about. I was supposed to touch my save stone, teleport home, and everything would be fixed by Production. How the hell did following protocol make things worse? I'm in fucking Fantasia, of all places. I could've ended up in any other world, literally any other world, and I'd be happier than I am now. But most of all, I just wanted to know where Ghost was. I took off the glove and stared at my glitched hand. It was painful now, and it hurt when it first happened. To have this glitch course through his entire body was probably the most painful thing he's ever been through.

Wherever you are, I hope you're ok.

My thoughts continued to race for what seemed like hours. Every time I closed my eyes, I saw Ghost disappear. Even if I didn't think about Ghost for a second, the pain in my hand was constantly throbbing.

Fuck.

What about those people today from the guild? Every time I thought about them, I felt guilty. It was impossible to kill, I knew that, but it didn't make sense; none of it did. After a while, I just got out of bed and looked out the bedroom window, hoping that something out there could give me peace of mind. Or maybe Olivia's optimism was rubbing off on me already, but what if there was a chance, if I ended up in this hellhole of a world, so did Ghost.

It didn't take long for me to notice the dark outline of what looked like a person climbing over the castle's closest gate. While I didn't need to get involved with royal affairs, I kept watching the person, but the closer they got, the easier it was for me to determine that their body type was too petite to be Ghost. They knew exactly how to avoid the guard's gaze as they hid behind bushes and climbed walls until they were nearing the building I was in. There were plenty of guards walking the castle grounds; one of them had to see the intruder. There was no way Fantasia's security is *that* lax. The intruder looked up, and it seemed as though they were looking at me. I pinched my fingers and readied two tacks.

Game on.

THREE

With the intruder focused on me, they weren't paying attention to the guard nearest them. The guard readied his spear, and I felt instant relief. Probably better that way. I didn't actually want to get involved, anyway. The spear flew through the air and landed about three feet short. The intruder took notice, taking a moment to hide behind the nearest bush as the soldier ran after the spear. The guard made it to the spear, picked it up, looked around, and, upon finding no one in his sight, returned to his spot as if he never saw anything. If that was the best a guard of Fantasia could do, they were screwed.

I opened my window and climbed onto the nearest tree while the intruder continued through the castle, unfazed by the incident with the spear.

Hell, I wouldn't be fazed by it either.

I climbed down the tree and faced a petite figure staring at me, only a hundred yards away. They ran toward me, but I stood my ground. I pinched my fingers to ready two tacks. I took a deep breath, aimed, and right before I released the tacks, I felt sick to my stomach.

What happened to those guild members? Where did they go?

I shook my hands, making the tacks disappear. I didn't need to fight with tacks to win a battle. Ghost was my hand-to-hand combat instructor and taught me all the non-lethal ways to stop someone.

She moved quickly and quietly, attempting to gain the advantage by throwing a shuriken at me before we made contact. I dodged, unaffected by her fighting style since it was similar to my own. I closed the gap, knowing that most distance fighters, myself included, aren't programmed for close combat. Ghost's training gave me an advantage, one that proved rather useful. She was thrown off by the proximity of the battle, attempting to dodge back to a safer distance. I continued my assault, not letting her get far enough away to feel comfortable throwing another shuriken. She ran backward, barely dodging my punches, but I wasn't about to give up. I was in the perfect position to force her a little further back and she'd crash into a few barrels. That'd get the guard's attention, and I could be free of this mess and, as a bonus, in the good graces of the royals for catching an intruder on castle grounds that their guards would've missed. As she collided with the barrels, I could see the lighting change around us. I looked back, and a guard was shining a lantern in our direction.

Right on time.

"Hey!" the guard yelled. I looked back, and the intruder was running away. I lunged after her and tackled her to the ground.

"You will pay for what you did to my guild members," she said right before she spat in my face. I swung my head forward and aimed for her nose. I felt the crack of her cartilage under the force of my forehead.

"I didn't do anything to your guild members, and I'm sick of people thinking I did." I stood up as the guard approached us.

"She killed my guild." The intruder pointed at me with one hand as she nursed her nose with the other. "And now she's trying to kill me."

Lying bitch.

"That's not what happened," I tried to explain. The guard looked between the two of us and lifted his spear. "She snuck onto castle grounds and—"

I felt the sharp pain as the guard made a quick jab with his spear to my right shoulder. I reached instinctively for the pain with my glitched hand, still covered in the glove. The guard looked at my hand then lunged for me with the spear again. I dodged. The intruder stood up and took her opportunity to sneak away. The guard looked between the two of us without moving. I stood where I was.

I'm not a threat.

"Are you going to let her get away?" I yelled. He looked at me and then we both looked in the direction of the intruder. A different spear, thrown with great force, plunged into her thigh. She fell to the ground.

"What are you doing?" Nathaniel yelled at the guard in front of me. Nathaniel ran toward the intruder, placed his foot on the intruder's thigh, and pulled his spear out. He whistled and a few guards joined him. I couldn't hear what he said, but they took the girl away. He ran back toward us. "Did you hear me?"

"Sir?" the guard asked. Nathaniel reached for a bottle in his pouch and grabbed my hand in an attempt to move it from the stab wound. I pulled away from him.

"Why are you harassing a guest in our kingdom?" He focused his attention back on the guard.

"The other girl said she murdered her guild members."

"And that overrides the message relayed to you by your prince and queen earlier? You're lucky it was me who found you and not royalty. Get out of my sight. I'll deal with you later."

"I'm sorry, sir." The guard bowed multiple times.

"I said, get out of my sight," Nathaniel repeated. The guard ran away, and Nathaniel brought his attention back to me. "Let me look at it."

"It'll heal after a couple of minutes." Ghost and I had a slow-healing ability. If we are attacked, we can hide behind a wall to gain some HP back prior to engaging in battle. I looked down at the stab wound. According to my HP, I was healing, but not healed yet.

"I can heal it now."

"What can you do?" I laughed.

"I'm an apothecary; Olivia's not the only one with the ability to help heal you." He held up a bottle and shook it in his hand. "Half a bottle will heal you right up."

"Fine," I sighed. No need to be in pain if he could help me. He pointed to a garden bench in the middle of light purple roses. I followed where he was pointing and sat down.

"Deep breath," he said as he opened the bottle. He poured the liquid, and I exhaled as the pain slowly dissipated.

"Your security is lacking," I said.

"Is that my thank you?"

"No. Thanks, but my statement stands."

"It's part of our game to allow people the opportunity to sneak onto castle grounds."

"That sounds stupid."

"Our people receive quest points for sneaking onto castle grounds."

"So?"

"And our guards receive quest points for catching an intruder."

"And what of the safety of your queen and prince?"

"No one ever gets that close. Our defenses increase as you get closer to the royal family. It's impossible to actually get to them." He patted the once stabbed shoulder. "You're all good. Either way, they weren't attempting to kill our queen."

"And why didn't you let them kill me?"

"I couldn't let them kill a pretty face like yours. It would be a sin."

"Say something so cringeworthy again, and I'll respawn you."

"I'd like to see you try." He stared at me, challenging me. If it were any other day, I'd have respawned him long before now. I couldn't even pinch my fingers to form a tack because the thought of killing him terrified me. He was annoying, but that wasn't a crime punishable by death. "What? All talk and no action?"

"I don't want to kill you," I muttered under my breath.

"What was that? I couldn't hear you."

"I don't want to actually kill you." I shook my head. "I don't know what the hell is going on, it seems like no one does, but that doesn't make me the bad guy in this scenario. If I can kill, then we need to consider the implications of a serious Game-altering glitch out there. If they are dead, which I don't think they are, then it should *never* have happened. It hasn't in a hundred years. I'd be the least of your problems in that scenario. I'm just a girl, trying to get home to find her *missing* partner."

"I'm sorry."

"Huh?" *That was easy.*

"I'm showing you compassion. Unlike you, I have a dynamic personality," he laughed, showing that he wasn't serious.

"I have a great personality."

"It's a little off-putting."

"Mine? Or are we talking about yours again?" I asked. He laughed again.

"Fair enough. We both got dealt some shitty Character traits, but also some awesome ones. I'll try not to judge yours so harshly if you do the same for mine."

"I'm still going to call you out when you're being gross," I said.

"Fair. And I will call you out when you have a stick up your ass."

I didn't plan on staying in Fantasia but, until I found a way out, I needed to blend in, just like Olivia suggested. My plan needed to include getting the royals and their retainers on my side. They had more sway, which would help when someone actually got in contact with Production.

"Agreed." I held out my good hand for him to shake. He shook my hand and then put his arm around me. I lifted my shoulder and bumped his arm, "You're already being weird."

He removed his arm but kept it outstretched on the back of the bench rather than around me. I nodded in approval.

"I'm trying to understand how you might be feeling—waking up in a foreign game, unable to return to your own game, losing your only friend and lover?" He paused, waiting for me to correct the word "lover." I just ignored him. "And killing people in a truly murder-less world. That sounds terrifying."

"Thank you?" I asked. I couldn't tell if he was being genuine or not, not after he added the part about my lover in there.

"I actually mean that. I can't put myself in your shoes, no matter how much I try. I didn't consider your side of things until you pointed it out. I'm sorry you're going through this."

"I honestly appreciate that."

"You can stay out here to clear your head for as long as you like. I can also keep you company." He winked.

And there it was. "That's not necessary."

"Fair enough. If you want to sleep, I recommend you take some of this." He handed me a plant. "Soak it in some water and drink it. The results have a soporific effect."

"Thanks."

"Although." He smiled. "The guards standing outside your room would be quite surprised and angry if they saw you entering from the door."

"What guards?"

"The ones meant to keep you inside your room. If I were them, I'd throw you in the dungeon for sneaking out. Anyway, I gotta go now. See ya." With that bombshell, he winked then started walking off as if what happened to me didn't bother him at all.

"Are you kidding me?" I yelled. I stood up and ran after him. If I was with the prince's retainer, they couldn't be angry at me. "You're coming with me."

"If you want me to go to your room, all you had to do was ask." He smiled at me. I let out a heavy sigh. I had reached my limit with him. He laughed before continuing, "Relax, I'm just pushing your buttons. I was planning on escorting you to your room anyway."

I looked away; his phrase reminded me of what Ghost would say when he teased me in the same way. Maybe that's why, no matter how annoying Nathaniel was, I didn't hate him. A part of him was so similar to Ghost, and that familiarity was comforting. Annoying but *comforting*.

He stopped us at a kitchen before heading back to my room and I started soaking the plants he gave me. The kitchen was beautiful and gigantic; there were five different ovens, at least three different sized mixers, and two blast chillers. It was a baker's paradise. After a certain amount of time had passed, Nathaniel grabbed the cup, drained the plants, nodded toward the door, and we headed back to my room. I was unsure of the full effects of the plant, but I just wanted to stop seeing Ghost's face long enough to forget that I missed him, to stop feeling the pain in my hand, and to use sleep as a way to forget.

I didn't remember falling asleep, but the pounding on the door at dawn was jarring.

"T, time to get up," Olivia called from the other side of the door. "We've gotta make breakfast for Queen Seraphina and get our chores started before your training. I also brought you clothes."

"Come in," I yelled. She slowly opened the door and smiled. "Whatever it is, I'm not wearing it."

"Actually, I think you'll like this! Queen Seraphina approved that you could wear clothes that you can feel comfortable in as long as they match the overarching world of Fantasia. I just figured you would want a clean change of clothes."

It wasn't *my* suit, but I wish it had been from the start. It was a black bodysuit, similar to my own, but it had armor, less cleavage, and, best of all, it wasn't girly in any way. It was something that could probably have been found in one of the games within Fantasia, but not necessarily Castle Town.

Olivia carried on trying to convince me, even though I was already sold. "This was a free gift from one of my sponsors after completing a difficult final boss from one of the RPG games. But, since I'm not open about being SmokeScreen in public, it hasn't seen much use. I guess you deserve it more than I do."

"I love you *so* much," I said it slowly while analyzing the beautiful fabric in front of me.

"What? Me?" she questioned with a laugh. Then threw her hand around and said, "No, I don't deserve such praise."

"I literally might not be here if you weren't playing me. You deserve all of my praise. And, I'll admit, I'm a fan of your work, too."

"T, and I don't want this to come across the wrong way, but you are in a *really* good mood this morning, all things considered." She sat down on the edge of my bed, truly unafraid that I would have any negative reaction to the comment she made. I instinctively smiled at her familiarity. At the end of this whole event, Olivia was the only one out of this place that I would actually want to keep in contact with. She was *amazing*, and I know Ghost would love her, too.

"Nathaniel gave me some plant last night that put me to sleep. I don't even remember what happened after I drank it. It, thankfully, knocked me out."

"Oh, I should have thought of that! Damn Nathaniel and his forward-thinking. Well, either way, I brought you a badass warrior princess outfit, according to the item description, that is. So, I win, right?"

"If it were a competition, there would be no competition. Thank you."

"See, I knew you'd like it. It's skin-tight like your other outfit, but the armor keeps you covered, and it's got a tactical belt, which I wouldn't use much as a healer, but you could use it."

"You're the best," I confirmed.

"Honestly, stop flattering me." She raised her hands under her chin and smiled at me. "Anyway, change, and then let's get cooking."

"I'm not cooking for her." Could I cook for her? Sure. Did I want to? Hell no. *I'm a warrior, not some personal chef for a queen I barely know.*

"Wait, T, no. We were having such a good moment. Let's keep it up."

"No. My time would be better spent finding a way back to the Platform."

"You need to give the Producers time to fix whatever's going on with the Platform. That's *protocol*. Who knows? Ghost might even show up after the Producers fix it. And remember, this. Is. Not. Your. Game. Now, get up and get going." She grabbed my arm and pulled me out of bed.

"Okay, damn. You're kind of scary when you're angry."

"Me? Never! Now get yourself dressed and meet me outside. I'll be waiting by the door."

I got up and did as she asked, making sure to wave at the guards by my door as I was leaving. She talked relentlessly while we walked down the hall to the same kitchen from last night. I could've sworn I heard someone yell "shut up, Olivia!" as we walked by. Apparently, not everyone had to get up at dawn.

"T, you stopped listening to me, huh?"

"What?" I didn't even realize we had finished making breakfast for the queen.

"It's ok, I get that a lot. I mean, *a lot*, I like to talk."

"That's not what I would expect from SmokeScreen," I laughed.

"Yes, well, SmokeScreen wasn't my first shot at building a live streaming personality. I learned a lot from my time at Gaming Science and now at Fudders. There are successful patterns and unsuccessful ones." She stopped for a second and then cleared her throat. "Anyway, I'll bring this to the queen, and you can go over and get your training started with Alton. He should be up by now."

She waved me out of the room and nodded to the right. I wonder if she had told me how to get there earlier when I wasn't listening to her. I wasn't purposely ignoring her; it was just hard to keep up. She jumped from idea to idea and I sure as hell wasn't fully awake yet. I walked down the hallway to the right and saw a light coming from another hallway to the left. I followed the light until I was out in what seemed the be a training ground for the soldiers. Kaspian, Alton, and Nathaniel were all standing, talking away.

"Good morning," Nathaniel said, interrupting whatever conversation they were having.

"Don't talk to me."

"Someone's not a morning person. I figured we would be on much better terms after, well, last night." Nathaniel was so suggestive in the way he phrased the last part that even I thought we did more than just talk.

"Nathaniel," Kaspian chided, yet again.

"It's not what it sounds like," I defended myself. "Really, nothing happened."

Nathaniel winked.

"We know better than to take him seriously. No one is judging you. Anyway," Kaspian smoothly transitioned the conversation. "You will train with Alton until noon. After that, we can reconvene to review the basics of magic."

I looked away and resisted the urge to roll my eyes.

"I understand that you do not want to be here. However, after Nathaniel's report from last night, it's important that we ensure you can continue to protect yourself against the weapons of our game in a non-lethal way."

"I already know how to do that," I groaned, giving in and rolling my eyes.

"For the safety of our game, the worlds, and all the citizens of Fantasia, I'd like to make that decision myself."

"Okay." I chose not to fight it any longer. It wasn't a fight worth having because, if I were in the same situation, I wouldn't trust me either. I folded my arms and looked straight ahead at the training area in front of us.

"We have dealt with the intruder," he said. I looked up at him. "And the guard."

"Thank you."

"It won't happen again." He was about to step aside and let me get started, but then he stopped. "Also, please do try to control your attitude. My sister was forgiving last night."

I nodded, acknowledging that a slap across the face was a warning and the actual punishment would be much worse. Kaspian nudged me as he walked past me to stand next to Nathaniel, giving Alton and I space for our training. I wanted to say something back, but Nathaniel gave me a look as though to say, "You were in the wrong." I didn't think so, but I wasn't going to die on that hill. I sighed.

"Understood. I will try to hide it a little better." A half-apology was the best I could go.

"I'll take it from here," Alton grabbed my arm and dragged me away. I pulled my arm away from his grasp and resisted the urge to snap at him for grabbing me. "I'm sorry about all of them. We honestly aren't like this as a people. We know you aren't the bad guy. I think we are all on edge with everything that has happened, and we have forgotten to treat you like the guest that you are to our world. None of us are showing you our best sides, myself included."

"I would act the same if the roles were reversed." I shrugged it off.

I don't want their pity. I just want answers.

"Cool, then let's get started. I've seen you play before, so I already know you're great at dodging attacks. Let's work on teaching you how to fight and defend yourself a little better for our gameplay. Ever held a sword?"

Training with Alton wasn't horrible. Since Alton had experienced the broader world outside of Fantasia before joining, he was easier to get along with and could use references that were easy for me to understand. We walked through the basics of sword training, which I performed horribly at, and then some hand-to-hand combat, similar to what I had done with Ghost in my own game. Kaspian and Nathaniel watched us the whole time. I wondered if the queen forced them to keep an eye on me in the same way I was forced to engage with them. But, then again, the queen seemed a little more accepting of me than the prince had the night before, so maybe it was just the snooty prince's own decision not to trust me.

"Alton, why is Seraphina ruling and not Kaspian?" I asked as we took a water break.

He looked at me for a moment, seeming to weigh how to answer. "Well, the simplest explanation is that she is the older sibling by two years. Her magic and Prince Kaspian's magic are very different, though, and I think that is another reason."

"How so?"

"When she learned magic, it was dark magic that called to her. She can revive fallen allies, break bones by just looking at people, and some say she can read your future." He paused for dramatic effect. Though I'm not sure how it worked, maybe that was how she knew I wouldn't kill her last night. I didn't make any comments, so he continued, "Prince Kaspian's magic is light, and he calls upon the elements to assist him. His is more typical to those who practice magic in our game. The only thing that sets him apart is his family could afford to give him the best training and weapons that money could buy. So, Prince Kaspian's been raised to fight, and Seraphina was raised to rule."

"Alton," Kaspian called from afar. Another soldier was talking to Nathaniel as Kaspian came up to us. "We need to end your training early. We have visitors from another Kingdom. T, we will need to move our training until after dinner. You have been summoned to this meeting, as well."

"Why am I needed?"

"My sister wants both of her retainers present. Olivia is on her way to your quarters to assist you in getting more presentable for a diplomatic meeting." He didn't even try to put it nicely.

"I only just got here. It seems a little odd to be acting as a diplomatic envoy within your game." It was a weird request, but if schmoozing with the queen and her guests meant getting answers about Ghost, then I would play along.

"I feel the same way. However, neither of us outrank the queen, so my best recommendation for you is not to speak and seat yourself as far away from our visitors as possible. Be present without actually being seen. I will also be there and keep my distance. You can watch me if you want a model for the appropriate behavior."

"You can sit by me," Nathaniel suggested. I rolled my eyes.

"That." Kaspian stopped me, narrowing his eyes at my own. "That is exactly what you cannot do in the presence of our guests. Am I clear?"

"Crystal."

"Then proceed to your quarters. They should be here soon, and you need to be waiting by the queen's side before they arrive."

"And you." Kaspian turned toward Nathaniel. "I've had enough of—"

I walked away with a smile, knowing Nathaniel was going to get in trouble. I hurried back to my room to find Olivia waiting for me with a dress that matched hers. She forced me to wear jewelry and head adornments. She didn't even let me protest before she got that same angry voice that she had earlier. I was given white gloves to cover up my hands, but the purple haze still lingered around my left. Then she took my hair down. Even when outside of *Duty Falls*, I always worked my hair in a ponytail. She tousled it, trying to get the perfect look before she pointed me to a mirror. I looked at myself; I didn't look or feel like myself in the outfit. She clapped at her handiwork and then grabbed my hand, leading me back up the stairs to the throne room I had been in the night before. She pushed her way through some curtains and pointed at the spot next to the queen's left side as she stood by the queen's right.

"Cutting it a little close, Olivia."

"I'm sorry, Your Majesty. But we made it."

"Yes, you did." I swear I saw the briefest smile pass on the queen's face. "Tack180, I need you to understand that our visitors do not know of Oliva's identity. Our people don't often play the Game outside of Fantasia. While you are very well-known, when you look like that, they likely will not easily identify you. Let's keep it that way."

"Yes, Your Majesty."

"I appreciate your tone today." She glanced back at me. "You look nice."

"Thank you."

There was a knock on the large double doors followed by Kaspian's voice, "Your Majesty?"

"Come in," she called.

Kaspian was flanked by Alton and Nathaniel. Behind them were two men I didn't recognize: the visitors. They were highly trouped; one wore a long cape with a large collar and had unbelievably pale skin, the other was burly with dark, hairy skin, guns in holsters on his body, and a crossbow attached to his back. They assessed me just as heavily as I assessed them before kneeling before the queen.

"Queen Seraphina, ruler of Castle Town, Capital of all of Fantasia, and Queen to the Game of Fantasia, we send greetings from Vampira."

Ah yes, Vampira—that made sense for their outfits. They were the ones that liked that kinky stuff. From what I had heard, Vampira started as a typical colony that enjoyed games relating to vampires and their hunters, both of whom were represented in the room. But then it got a reputation as the red-light district. The thing was, "I want to suck your blood" made a lot of great puns for establishment owners. So, the once escape for those interested in the fantasy of monsters became the poster child for dens of sin and ecstasy.

"To what do I owe the honor?"

"We come with concerns of the citizens, of many worlds, not just our own. I'm sure you are familiar with the never-setting sun."

"Yes, we, too, experienced the phenomenon."

"Our patrons are stuck. Those who were enjoying the Player experience were blacked out of the games they were watching. Those who were visiting cannot connect to the teleportation service. And, while we have plenty of rooms to house those affected, it seems as though this issue is larger than the Producers can handle. The longest Production blackout on record is one week. An average blackout is less than twelve hours. Even more—"

He hesitated.

"You may continue," Seraphina prodded.

"It seems as though a fair number of games experienced the exact same glitch." Although their movements were small, this notably caught the attention of everyone in our party. Kaspian clenched his fists. Nathaniel, who had been looking at the floor with his arms crossed in front of his chest, was suddenly attentive again. I actually don't think Alton changed what he was doing; he was already paying attention with one hand ready on his sword and the other on his hip. "Blackouts, as you know, are usually localized in a world. However, four of the largest games, each from different worlds, glitched at the same time. And those are only the ones currently reported to us by our people. Our sources indicate that all playable Characters of the games, as well as NPCs, did not respawn. The games were wiped out completely, except for one."

"And?" It almost seemed as if Seraphina was holding her breath. I was.

"That is all we know," he said. I exhaled. "Since no one can communicate with anyone in the Game, outside of Fantasia, we do not know if this particular Character actually survived the escape from their game. Nor do we know of the larger implications of the Platform, Producers, or fate of the Characters lost to the glitch."

"I understand your concerns. I already have a team gathering as much information as possible on communicating, not only with other games but with the Platform and Producers, as well. Operations and safeguards were put into the Game in case of blackouts, as you may know. While the experience can be concerning, it is not out of the ordinary and well planned for. However, when I have more information, I would be glad to share it with all games within Fantasia."

"Thank you, Your Majesty."

"Prince Kaspian, please inform the general to deploy soldiers to all communities within Fantasia to share that we are working on a solution and following Production guidelines for blackouts. No one should feel as though they have been left out of this important information."

"Yes, My Queen."

"Then, return to join us for dinner." Kaspian, Alton, and Nathaniel left the room without saying another word. The queen directed her next words to the visitors. "Please, do us the honor of having dinner with us. You traveled far to come here. We will also have rooms made available for the night."

"We would be honored."

The queen stood up and Olivia followed her a few steps behind. I looked over at her and she nodded for me to follow, as well. The vampire and hunter waited for the queen to pass them before standing up and following behind Olivia and me. The queen led us to a large dining room and seated herself at the end of the table. Olivia sat on her right, and I followed suit and sat on her left. Instead of sitting at the far end of the table, they sat down on either side of Olivia and me.

"Ambrosio, Hawthorn, please take your proper seats. This is highly inappropriate behavior," the queen said. "Even for Vampirans."

"My Queen, we only wish to court your maidens," the vampire responded.

"Ambrosio, I will not say it again. Whatever you choose to do to the females in your establishments will not be tolerated when you visit *my* castle and with *my* retainers. You will keep your hands and appendages to yourself, lest you have them chopped off."

As Ambrosio and Hawthorn stood up to move, Kaspian, Alton, and Nathaniel returned. Ambrosio, who had been sitting next to me, grabbed the back of my chair and then leaned in close. He inhaled deeply as he smelled my hair.

I should've insisted it stay up in the ponytail.

I flinched at his behavior, ready to get up and punch him in the face, but stopped myself knowing that I needed to blend in.

"My Queen, I humbly apologize," Ambrosio said, still hovering over me. Olivia shook her head at me, ever so briefly, and I knew I shouldn't stand up and smack him, no matter how much I wanted to. "Your new maiden, I just can't shake this feeling that I know her. Her smell, so familiar."

Gross.

"Ambrosio." The queen was curt.

"Do I know you?" he asked, getting closer and whispering in my ear. He ran his fingers through my hair. "Have you come to visit me before?"

I slammed my fists on the table and stood up at the same time that the two visitors went flying back to their appropriate spots at the edge of the table. The purple haze resonated strongly from my left hand.

"I said *enough*." I looked up at the queen, whose eyes looked the same shade of purple as my hand, just as they had when I saw them in the throne room.

"Your dark magic is hauntingly beautiful, Your Majesty," Nathaniel said as he sat down next to me. Kaspian sat next to Olivia and Alton sat on his right side.

"Please forgive my friend, Your Majesty." Hawthorn stood up and bowed his head. "It has been years since you possessed a second retainer. It was mere curiosity."

"You will have to ask my retainer, *Thea*, if she will accept your apology. If she rejects it, then I will break every bone in your body, even the flaccid one." I looked at the queen, whose eyes continued to glow purple. She was more amazing than I had initially given her credit for. "Thea?"

I waited a little too long before I realized that I was Thea. *It's so unfamiliar.* I looked at Olivia, Alton, and Kaspian to read for their approval. All three refused to make eye contact with me.

"It's all right," I said, sitting back down and wishing to be as invisible as Kaspian warned me to be.

"Then, so be it." The queen waved, and a servant came forward with food for us to eat.

"If I may," Ambrosio started.

"What?" The queen's eyes flashed purple again.

"Never mind."

No one spoke for the remainder of the dinner. It was one of the most awkward situations I had ever had to sit through. Seraphina continued to stare daggers at the visitors at the other end of the table anytime one of them looked up from their food, which was almost always to look at me.

"You may be excused," the queen said when everyone finished eating. "Alton, please show them to their guest quarters."

"Yes, Your Majesty." Alton stood up and waited at the door for the visitors, who slowly excused themselves from the table.

"I appreciate you holding it in as long as you did," the queen said when they were finally gone. "However—"

"I know, I'm sorry." I cut her off before she could finish. I was out of line blah, blah, blah.

"*T*," Olivia chided me. Yeah, I already knew. *This. Is. Not. My. Game.*

"It's a breath of fresh air, actually." Everyone looked over at the queen. Did she have too much wine with dinner?

"Your Majesty?" I asked.

"Having someone from another game come visit us in an informal manner. It's surprisingly comical to watch, and I truly am enjoying it."

"I'm not here to stay."

"Yes, I know, and, just as I said to our visitors, we will find a way to communicate with the outside world and get you back to your game. For now, continue to go by Thea when in the company of anyone outside of this room and don't kill the visitors."

"I can't really guarantee that last one."

"Neither can I." She smiled, and we all laughed, although I wasn't convinced the others hadn't only laughed out of duty. But I truly laughed because that shit was the most hilarious thing she had said yet. Then, she looked around the room and took a deep breath. She looked back at me and smiled slightly. It seemed like she was relieved we had made it through the dinner without getting caught. I know I was. She reached forward and grabbed my hand. Then patted it with a smile before I had the chance to pull away from her. "Now, back to your training."

"I have to grab a few of my personal books. Nathaniel, Will you show T to the library?" Kaspian stood up to excuse himself. Nathaniel nodded and Kaspian ran off.

"Milady?" Nathaniel stood up and extended a hand. I stood up and walked past him without acknowledging his outstretched arm. He jogged after me. "Wait, you don't even know where you're going."

"I'm sure I can find it without you. The 'milady' thing weirds me out."

"Fine, just know that I will be ready and waiting for you when you show up late." He winked and walked off.

"Okay, wait, no, I'm sorry." I ran after him.

"No, it's too late. Now I get to watch you squirm under both Prince Kaspian and Queen Seraphina's wrath. The thought is more delicious than our dinner was."

"Nathaniel," I groaned. "Please, what more do you want from me?"

"For you to grovel, of course."

"I grovel to no one. I will find the library by myself."

"Suit yourself." He threw his hands in the air and walked away.

I waited for him to round the corner before I just started following him. If he genuinely was going to be ready and waiting in the room for Kaspian to punish me, then he'd lead me straight to the library. But when I rounded the corner, he was already gone, and the window was open. I looked outside for any sign of him, but there was none; that asshole. My pride prevented me from returning to Olivia and the queen, so I started walking around. The royal library would be grand, so it would need a big room. It was also none of the rooms we had already walked past so there were some rooms already eliminated.

"That smell." I heard as I walked past one door. "My *precious* Tack180. Let's talk."

FOUR

The door opened and Ambrosio and Hawthorn stepped out. Ambrosio stayed back, but Hawthorn took a step toward me, exhaled, and crossed his arms over his chest as if he were trying to exert power over me.

"Let's talk, shall we?" Ambrosio asked from behind his defensive barrier.

"No." I folded my arms across my chest, mirroring Hawthorn. Although, I don't fully know why that was my response. I owed the royals no loyalty. Maybe it was just the way they creeped me out, but I knew, without a doubt, I didn't want anything to do with them.

"I'm certain you'll change your mind once you come join us in Vampira. We have quite a lot to discuss with you." Ambrosio pushed lightly on Hawthorn, who nodded like he knew what his boss wanted without him having to say it. He reached in his pocket and pulled out a tiny object that I didn't have enough time to analyze before it opened a portal.

My way out.

I instinctively took a step forward, acknowledging that they might have some useful information.

"What's going on here?" Alton asked. I looked back as he rounded the corner with Olivia. Ambrosio pushed Hawthorn who walked through the portal. I lunged forward, but it closed behind him. Ambrosio winked at me.

"Hey! What did the queen say about wooing her retainers?" Olivia demanded.

"You know where to find me." Ambrosio bowed before returning to his room. I made sure to note where I was in the castle in case I did decide to talk with Ambrosio. I didn't trust him, but trust wasn't required to find Ghost. Power and information were, however, and Ambrosio displayed more in those few moments than Seraphina had. I just needed some sort of assurance that it wasn't all smoke and mirrors. Betraying the queen to join the "Sex King" in his game would need more thought prior to action.

"Aren't you supposed to be with Nathaniel?" Olivia asked when we were alone.

"Yeah, well, that asshole—"

"Say no more," Alton stopped me. "Where do you need to go?"

"Library, come on, you two," Olivia answered for me. She grabbed both our arms and led us through the castle.

When we made it to the library, Nathaniel was already waiting there with Kaspian.

"Ah, there you are." Nathaniel smiled.

"Dude," Alton groaned. "Ambrosio had her cornered."

"What?" Kaspian demanded.

"Exactly what *do* you do on your weekends, *milady*?" Nathaniel smiled.

"I don't know that man." I defended myself. "I never needed to go to Vampira. I had Ghost. But he seems to know me—really know me, as Tack180. He acts like he has answers."

"Opening a portal back to his game isn't 'answers.' " Alton shook his head.

I looked up to the ceiling. Seemed like he could teleport when no one else could.

"He could watch a stream?" Olivia suggested at the same time as Alton spoke. "If he spends more money, he can have the full experience, including the one that completely envelops all your senses. And, if he's the king of the sex den, I'm sure he has the cash for it. Not to mention, once he knows what T's like, he could always make a sex clone that is just like her. To be honest, I wouldn't be surprised. You're hot, and you smell good, T, even when you're gross and sweaty."

I didn't remove my eyes from the ceiling, trying to hold in any emotion they could use against me. I wasn't interested in their excuses.

"It's vanilla." Nathaniel took a big whiff of me. "So soft and subtle for someone so strong and stubborn."

"Back off, Nathaniel." I shook my head and pushed him away.

"Enough, everyone," Kaspian commanded the room. "It was only a matter of time before word would get out that we have a new retainer in the castle. No one needs to know how famous you are, and we will all try to keep it that way. Especially if the guild who accused you finds out exactly who you are. I will make sure Queen Seraphina handles this before they leave. Now, you're late."

"I'm only late because of Nathaniel."

"You're still late." Nathaniel smiled.

"But you're not off the hook either, Nathaniel," Kaspian said.

"Of course not, sir. My deepest apologies."

"Make him the guinea pig," Alton said.

"Sir, that's not necessary. Twelve years of friendship should dictate that I have seniority over Alton," Nathaniel protested.

"Great suggestion, Alton." Kaspian smiled. "Nathaniel, twelve years of friendship grants you many things, but you've been pushing your limits since T arrived."

"She's just fun to tease," Nathaniel tried again.

"I'm certain she will find your pain rather humorous, too." Kaspian stretched exaggeratedly. Nathaniel lowered his head in defeat as he began walking to the library balcony.

"Fuck yeah, in your face, Nathaniel." Alton shot his hands into the air in triumph. "And you were just bragging about it, too."

I smothered my own laugh, trying to not go overboard with smugness, unlike Alton.

"That's what you get for bragging," Kaspian agreed.

"What's happening?" I whispered to Olivia as we stepped outside.

"I have no idea." Her eyes were wide. "I usually don't spend this much personal time with the prince and his retainers. Well, at least not in two years."

"Why not?" I tried, but Kaspian raised a hand to stop us. Two years was such an oddly specific amount of time to mention that she hadn't spent that much time with them. SmokeScreen had been around for longer than that amount of time, so what happened two years ago?

Nah, it didn't matter anyway.

"T," Kaspian started. "There are two types of magic in our world, light magic and dark magic. I practice light magic, while my sister practices dark magic."

Nathaniel sat down in a chair on the balcony and Kaspian started to circle him. He flipped his palm up, made a fist, and it began to glow a light-blue color, the same color I had seen the night before. He opened his palm and flicked it up. Nathaniel tensed his body as a gust of wind slapped him across the face.

"Oh, this is going to be great," Olivia laughed as she took a seat in the chair Alton had pulled up for her.

"My magic pulls from the elements."

Kaspian's hands were held as though they clutched a giant invisible ball. After a moment, a flame ignited between his palms. He held his right palm up, the flame followed his lead and traveled across, staying in his right palm.

He snapped his fingers to his palm and the flame hovered under Nathaniel's chair. Nathaniel wasn't looking so cocky anymore.

Kaspian then held both hands above his head and pulled them down with force as a torrent of water crashed over Nathaniel's head, then rushed down his body to extinguish the flame. Olivia and Alton laughed from the doorway of the balcony. A crack of thunder rumbled, I looked up and saw clouds forming above us. Kaspian raised a fist again, and his hand looked like it electrified; little sparks of lightning danced around his fist. He then brought his hand down and offered it to me.

"What happens if I touch it?" I asked.

"Try it with both hands separately," he advised, without really answering my question.

I tried with my good hand, my right, first. With my game face on, I reached forward and touched his outstretched fist. An electric current lightly zapped me. He was, thankfully, holding back. I looked at my glitched hand, glowing the same purple as the queen's eyes, and reached forward. I didn't feel anything.

"What does it mean?"

"You possess magical ability," he suggested.

"But I don't."

"Your left hand does."

"That's not how magic works."

"How would you know? You come from a land without magic."

"Okay, fine. Is that how magic works?"

"No," he admitted.

"Then, it's not magic."

"I don't know what else it would mean. Watch." He zapped Nathaniel with the remaining electricity, and he shook for a second before cursing his precious prince. "Next time, follow orders. Understood, Nathaniel?"

"Yes, sir."

"I need to hang out with you guys more if this is how we treat Nathaniel. Now come here, Nathaniel." Olivia waved her staff over Nathaniel to heal him of all his status ailments.

"T." Kaspian outstretched his arm, inviting me back into the library. He stood by a table filled with books, which I'm assuming were some of the ones he grabbed before meeting us here.

"Magical Mutations?" I read the label of one of the books I picked up. He grabbed it back from me and placed it on the table in the exact spot I had taken it from.

"Try to calm your body. Use the anger you feel about Ghost, and force that energy into your hands." Kaspian grabbed my arms, maneuvered my hands, careful not to touch my left, and placed them into the same position he had previously been in with the invisible ball.

"I don't feel anything."

"Focus, a moment longer." I tried to send my energy, whatever that meant, to my hands—nothing. His face scrunched together. "But I swear I saw it earlier. When Seraphina used her magic."

"The intensified glow?" Alton asked. "Yeah, I saw it, too."

"That glow is not mine, though; that's the glitch."

"May I?" Kaspian stretched out his hand and hovered it just under my glitched one. I took off the glove and extended my hand so Kaspian could look at it. "Does it hurt?"

"It's a constant light throb. If I'm distracted, then I don't notice it. But it's a bitch when I try to sleep."

"Olivia?"

"On it!" Olivia jumped up and hovered her staff over my hand. "I tried this with her last night. It relieves the pain, but the discoloration doesn't go away. You think we could imbue a glove to ease some of the pain?"

"Shouldn't be too hard. I can work on it tonight," Kaspian mused as he continued to analyze my hand under Olivia's staff.

"I'm not a test subject." I finally pulled my hand away from them. "I'm just trying to find my way home. This..." I gestured my arms around to encompass all of them. "All of this. None of it helps me get home. Seraphina said you could do that."

"I can open a portal."

"What? Why wouldn't you say that to begin with?" I'd rather have the royals open a portal for me than Ambrosio. If I didn't have to partner with the annoying leader of the red-light district, that would be great. "Let's go now!"

"My portals use magic and are limited to the surrounding games within Fantasia. Although Ambrosio possesses no magic, there are items that have the same effect. I can't get you out of the overarching world of Fantasia. However, if you feel like your time would be better spent elsewhere, as in another game within Fantasia, maybe with your friends in Vampira? Then I am more than happy to send you there."

He laughed at his own joke, and I felt like we had a breakthrough moment. Even if he was making fun of me, opening up in this way gave me some hope that he was less suspicious of me than he had been. Here was hoping he was being genuine.

"That's not what I meant." I gave a small laugh, playing on the moment.

He smiled. "Then I promise we won't treat you like a test subject. But we will try to help cure you of your blight and get you home."

"Fine. Just don't take it to Nathaniel's level," I agreed.

"Then I recommend you don't show up late again."

"Deal," I laughed. I looked down at all the books laid across the table: *Magical Mutations, Dark Sorcery and Necromancy, Latent Magical Abilities in Fantasian Youths: A Case Study.* It was laughable, all of it. I had no magic. I just needed to appease these people long enough to survive until I get in touch with Production and get out of this mess. "Damn, I need a drink."

"Me, too." Nathaniel raised his hand.

"To the alehouse?" Alton suggested.

"To the alehouse!" Olivia cheered.

"To the alehouse," Kaspian agreed.

"My Lord?" Alton asked while gaping at Kaspian. "Are you really going to join us?"

"I think we all deserve it after dealing with Vampira's finest."

"I'll take that as a yes." Alton grabbed Olivia's hand and started walking out of the room.

"Are they a thing?" I asked Nathaniel as I followed him out of the room.

"They usually hide it a bit better in front of the prince," he answered.

"I think he's still chasing the high of watching Nathaniel get embarrassed," Kaspian joined in.

"Is it usually Alton? Do you guys gang up on him?"

"Us? Never." Nathaniel's heavy sarcasm and hand flapping in front of his face gave a very different answer. I looked at Kaspian and he looked down, embarrassed to admit it.

"Well, I think you deserve it, Nathaniel," I joked back.

"I'm a glutton for punishment." He put an arm around my shoulder and the prince's as he walked between us. This time I didn't shrug him off. If I wanted to be trusted, I had to be liked. There needed to be some give and take in the relationship, however fake, in order to get my answers. Besides, the similarity to Ghost made it easy to pretend it was Ghost's arm around my shoulder and I felt my stress disappear.

We were with royalty, so, of course, we didn't go down to the bustling bars I remembered walking by in Castle Town. We went off to the side of the training area to a small square building. Outside were soldiers half-drunk trying to battle each other. Inside was no different, it was just a bunch of rowdy soldiers that filled the bar. Decorations were non-existent. The bar was filled with large tables and benches surrounding them to cram in as many soldiers as possible. In the corner was a basic bar with very few bottles on the wall and beer on tap; unlike the places I'd seen in Castle Town, this place stuck to the theme of Fantasia inside as well as out. Very minimalist. Ghost would like it; maybe I'll bring him here when I finally find him. The soldiers quieted down when Kaspian walked in, probably not used to seeing their prince in such an informal capacity. Not to mention, all of us were still dressed in fancy garments fit to meet and greet the visitors to the castle. Nathaniel went up to sweet-talk the woman walking around the bar with an apron on, and the bubble of comfort I had made for myself disappeared. I felt more comfortable in the alehouse than any other place in the castle, and yet, I still felt so out of place with my company and attire. It was a sobering, lonely feeling.

Within a few seconds, Nathaniel came back with the woman who brought a pitcher of pale brown liquid to the table—beer. I wanted something a little stronger. I *needed* something a little bit stronger after what I had been through. Whiskey, vodka, anything to help me forget the mess I was in.

"I'll be back." I got up and found the closest bottle of alcohol, opened it, and took a big whiff. Rum. I could work with rum. The waitress, bar maiden, whatever they wanted to call her, brought over empty glasses. Olivia placed a glass in front of each person after I poured the rum in. "Okay, Nathaniel, Kaspian—"

"Prince Kaspian," Alton corrected me. *Whatever.* I would get it sooner or later and technically it didn't matter. I didn't plan on staying longer than I had to.

I need to complete my mission.

"*Prince* Kaspian, let me teach you guys some games to make this a little more fun."

The Production teams were filled with large party animals. Anytime we had to wine and dine with Production reps, Ghost and I always had to put on a show. With the right crowd, any social gathering could be made into a hell of a party. I used to hate the rep parties, but the more we did them and the more we learned their games, it became kinda fun. But I'd never admitted that to them or Ghost. Now was my time to put on my Production rep persona and schmooze the shit out of some royals.

We raised our glasses, clinked them together, and downed the rum. After a couple of those, the night started to get a little blurry. We had more shots, more beers, and just had fun. No one treated me the way they had that first night. If they did still worry about what I *could* do to them, they at least knew that I *wouldn't* do it.

Making the prince and his retainers drink was a mutually beneficial arrangement. It built rapport with the royals, which strengthened their trust in me and, in turn, would help them fight for me when Production became available. It also numbed the pain of Ghost, still missing, and the recent feelings of helplessness. I was at the mercy of people who didn't have answers and no one had been in contact with Production, the people who *could* have answers.

I didn't want to feel helpless. I didn't like ever feeling that way, even when I was playing the Game, hence why I would take matters into my own hands and move for my Players. When I played the Game, I was more in control; if my Player sucked, it didn't matter. Now, I was stuck without control, no answers to where Ghost was or what happened to him, and no way to get home.

Still, I couldn't leave. The royals held the most power in Fantasia. If Production got in contact with this world, they would reach out to Seraphina. Based on all of my training, I was following the best path I could. And yet, I still felt helpless.

The next morning, I changed back into my new warrior princess outfit that Olivia gave me, which was much more comfortable than those Fantasian dresses. I threw on Kaspian's glove and walked outside to wait for Olivia in the hallway.

"What's up?" I asked one of the guards standing outside of my door. He continued to look ahead as if I hadn't said anything.

"T?" Olivia opened the door. "You're up early! I was going to swing by Alton's quickly, and then we can get started on our chores for the queen."

I nodded and we walked a few doors down. Olivia quietly knocked on Alton's door. No answer. She tried again. Still nothing.

"Alton?" she said quietly. "It's Olivia."

Still no response, so she just opened the door like it was her room. She walked in, looked around, and then walked back out.

"Well?" I asked.

"He's not there. To Nathaniel's!" She grabbed my hand and pulled me next door. She knocked again, but it was less gentle and more of a pound. No response. Olivia was braver than I was. She opened the door to walk in, but I stopped her.

"He might have someone in there."

"So?"

"I'm thinking fully naked bar maiden from last night."

She pulled her arm away and walked in with her eyes covered. "Nathaniel, wake up!"

No response. She uncovered her eyes, looked at me, and shook her head.

"Ok, well, next logical question is: did they even make it back last night?" I asked. We looked back down the hall at the soldiers blocking my door. The one closest to us shook his head no.

"Well, I'd like to find him to make sure he's okay. Since comms are down, I can't just message him. Do you mind helping me search after we get started on our chores?"

I shrugged. Until they found a way to get me out of here or someone got in contact with Production, I was stuck in my current mission. *Helpless.* So, we started our chores for the queen and then Olivia gave me a tour of the castle while attempting to find her missing boyfriend. She didn't seem too worried that we couldn't find him, so I worried for her. But there were also no obvious signs of the glitched man anywhere within the castle, so that fear didn't last for long.

"This is the library, as you know, since, you know, you saw it last night and all." She opened the double doors to the library where Alton, Nathaniel, and Kaspian were spread throughout the room. Alton was on the floor, Nathaniel on a pile of books, and Kaspian was slouched over a table.

"Alton?" Olivia laughed. The boys stirred, acknowledged there was another person in the room and then realized that they were in a public location. Well, at least, Kaspian and Alton did. Nathaniel didn't move much. "Do you realize what time it is? We have breakfast with visiting guests in a few minutes."

"Tack180." Kaspian stood up, cleared his throat, and straightened himself out. "I'm glad you're here. I'd like to provide you with something you might find helpful."

I folded my arms across my chest. "Helpful" to the royals didn't mean much to me. The past thirty-six hours seemed more like a waste of my time versus a journey to find answers. I was doing *everything* I could to gain their trust, make them happy, and blend in. I didn't trust their version of "helpful," but I felt my stomach turn anyway.

"Here." He was holding something in his hand and handed it over to me. I unfolded my arms and grabbed it. "We spent all night working on it. It's a glove imbued with healing properties. Nathaniel found the best herbs to mix into potions, and we used my magic to maintain the effect over extended periods of time. We will need to refill it after about a month's worth of use."

"What?" I looked over to see a pile of broken glass and spilled potions. I didn't know what to say, so I focused on the pile. Was it answers to Ghost's whereabouts? No, but it was *helpful.* They had spent all night working on a solution for my glitched hand. These were people I had just met; they owed me nothing. Hell, they barely trusted me. But they put me first when I had only been putting Ghost and my mission to find him first. It was nice. It made me feel all warm and happy, and yet, at the same time, it made me miss Ghost and home even more because that kind of care was something Ghost would've done for any random stranger he met, as well.

"There were a few missteps considering how inebriated we were." Alton took a step toward the mess, attempting to block it. I looked back up at them and they kept talking.

"Alton insisted that he does his best work while drunk." Kaspian looked at Olivia for approval. She shook her head.

I put the glove on my hand, and the pain was immediately relieved. I shook my head in disbelief that these people worked so hard to make me comfortable before I was finally able to say the words I wanted to say from the beginning, "Thank you."

"No need to thank us. That is our token of appreciation for all the fun we had last night. It was actually Nathaniel's idea to work on it."

I smiled a slightly surprised smile at him, "Nathaniel, thank you." He grumbled from where he remained, half-asleep on the books.

"Okay, thank you aside. We've gotta get ready, people. Our guests are expecting breakfast before they leave." Olivia clapped.

With the new glove, I felt renewed confidence. Help in my mission came in different forms and, while I still wanted the more direct help of answers, providing me a way to safely navigate the new world I found myself in was the best item I could receive. I wondered what other help I could find if I opened up to others outside of the royals. There were people all over Fantasia who might be helpful. I just needed to find them.

I went through the whole process of putting on the gown again, but I didn't put the fancy gloves on. I kept my new blue glove on my left hand and nothing on my right. I looked down at it and smirked—this was a game-changer. Olivia was waiting for me outside when I was finished before we ran off to the throne room to meet with the queen.

"You all were up late last night." The queen smiled when we entered.

"Did we keep you up? I'm so sorry, Your Majesty." Olivia knelt to the ground.

"Not at all. I'm glad you had fun."

"Thank you!"

"Thea, your new glove looks to be rather useful. Please thank my brother for me."

"Yes, Your Majesty," I said. She was definitely growing on me.

There was a knock on the door, Seraphina called them in, and then Kaspian, Nathaniel, and Alton entered the room, followed by Ambrosio and Hawthorn. Except they weren't alone; at least ten more people were behind them, all in different clothing. Most of them looked to be wearing the traditional clothing of their game, which didn't make any of them stand out in the same way as Ambrosio and Hawthorn. However, there were another two that stood out to me, only because of the way they acted. The rest of the people entered with confidence, staring at the queen. The guy I was raking a judgmental glance over wore an eyepatch over one eye as if it were missing, a crow sat on his shoulder, and he wasn't looking at the queen. His eye focused slightly to the side of her, at Olivia.

How do they know each other?

Alton stood directly next to him, with his hand on his sword as if at any moment he was ready to attack. Although, there was no way to know if Alton's stance was due to the one-eyed man or the mob of people in general.

Next to the one-eyed man was a beautiful woman, wearing a skin-tight dress with a deep plunging V-neck. Her make-up shimmered in the light as if she had a gold dusting across her face. She was looking everywhere else in the room as though she was trying to avoid making eye contact with Seraphina. A gold teardrop fell down her face when she finally looked at the queen. Seraphina held up a hand, and the oncoming group stopped.

"I already know why you are here," she said.

That started the long and rough Council of Fantasia. Everyone new also came in the name of their people bearing the same concerns as Ambrosio and Hawthorn. Since it was well past twelve hours, they were concerned that no one had heard from Production, citing the longest blackout in nearly a hundred years. One person cited history even further by announcing that the longest blackout in history, one week long, occurred when Henry Fudders still worked at his original company, Gaming Science. No one could remember the exact date, so a comment that was supposed to help people understand the severity of the situation turned into a bunch of people arguing over dates in an already escalated environment. People were angry, expecting Seraphina to know the answers to everything. I wondered if they expected that of her because of her position of power and relationship to Production as ruler of Fantasia or because of her supposed power to see into the future.

"Enough," Seraphina finally announced after hours of fighting, at times, with weapons, over what to do regarding the inability to communicate with the Platform, Producers, and games which were glitched. Her eyes were purple, but it didn't look like she had used her powers yet. "I have no answers for you right now. However, I will do the best in my ability to keep the people of Fantasia safe. That includes continuing to follow the protocol given to us by Production. Yes, this is a long blackout, but our Protocol allows for the worst-case scenarios, including months without communication with Production. Continue as I have told you and please make sure that all visitors to your kingdoms are well taken care of until we can establish communication to the outside worlds."

"But you do have answers," Ambrosio rebutted. "Or is that not Tack180, a Character from one of the glitched games?"

There were gasps as people followed Ambrosio's pointed finger to where I stood on the left side of the queen. Then the whispers started.

"I knew she was familiar."

"How did she get here if her game glitched during play?"

"Why is she parading in such a formal position with the queen?"

"Explain yourself, Queen Seraphina," Ambrosio continued. Seraphina stared at the group in front of her with wide eyes, and I could tell she didn't have an answer for them. She tried not to show it, but I saw it. *Fear.*

She looked at me just as an out-of-breath soldier ran into the room without knocking like she knew he was coming. She grabbed my hand just before he started speaking. I wanted to pull it away because the motion and intent seemed foreign to do with someone I didn't entirely know, but she gripped onto me so tightly; that I let her hold my hand anyway.

"Your Majesty." She turned her head to the well-timed interruption. "There are reports from the coast. The sun is not setting."

Fear spread through people in the room as more whispers of confusion started again. Seraphina looked at Kaspian, who nodded, stood up, and headed for the door with Nathaniel and Alton on his heels. It was my opportunity; if the same glitched man was present, then I could potentially get answers to where Ghost went. He may even be there, with the Glitch, in which case, I *needed* to go with them.

"Your Majesty?" I asked. She looked back at me and patted the hand she was holding as I said, "I know the enemy."

"Fine." She let go of me and I followed them. "Olivia?"

"On it," she yelled as she followed behind me. We passed two guards on their way to take our place beside the queen.

"What do I need to know?" Kaspian asked me as we started walking out of the room.

"Don't engage."

"That's not an option."

"You don't understand. If you touch them, then what happened to my hand will happen to you. If any part of you still believes that I can kill, then don't engage. Weapons go straight through their bodies, anyway."

Kaspian didn't need any further explanation. "Alton, Nathaniel, when I open the portal, I need you to go evacuate the nearby areas. Make sure the people get out safely. Clearing the area of civilians will be our priority. You heard T! Do not engage."

When we were safely out of the room and into the hallway, Kaspian started spinning his hands. The hallway in front of me disappeared as I saw a mesmerizing ocean behind a sea of royal soldiers engaged in battle with blacked-out enemies, glowing the same purple as my glitched hand. Whatever they were, they took Ghost from me. In the distance, I spotted their leader. His back was toward the portal but, as if he could sense the portal open, his head turned around as his body continued to fight. His head cocked to the side as if he could tell it was me and was just as confused as I was as to how I got there. I ripped off the fancy dress to display my warrior princess gear underneath.

"T, what the hell?" Olivia said. "You wore your outfit underneath?"

"You always need to be ready for battle," I said as I walked through the portal. That *thing* took Ghost, and I needed to figure out where he was hiding him. Time to get him back. I pinched my fingers, and tacks appeared just as they always did.

"You need to wait for orders," Kaspian yelled after me.

Olivia ran after me first, followed by Alton, Nathaniel, and Kaspian last as he closed the portal behind him. Alton and Nathaniel immediately ran in separate directions to get people to safety. Olivia raised her staff in the air and healed as many people in the vicinity as she could. Those who were touched by the Glitch disappeared, so she was only healing the people who were injured as they were trying to leave. Buildings were on fire, there were stampedes of people trampling over one another, and the whole scene was chaotic as the sound of Kaspian's thunder cracked in the sky.

"T, I can't reach them all, cover me," Olivia said as she started moving forward.

"I need you to stay by Kaspian," I replied. I was watching the leader just as intently as he was watching me. He slowly turned his body in the same direction as his head and began walking toward me.

"Don't tell me what to do! Hey, are you listening to me? T?" If she was trying to do something to get my attention, I didn't see it. My focus was on the one person, *or thing*, that knew what the hell was going on.

"It's the leader; he's here." I nodded in his direction.

"I'm not leaving you, especially if you are engaging in battle. Which, by the way, is precisely what you just told Prince Kaspian not to do."

"He has Ghost."

"He'll take you."

"Then I will be able to save Ghost."

"Not if Ghost is dead."

"He's not."

I knew he wasn't, but the potential was there. Olivia's words stopped me for a brief second. If I let the leader, no the Glitch, touch me, and it genuinely did kill, no one would get answers for Ghost and avenge his death. I needed to live for Ghost. The Glitch malfunctioned as he made his way over to us—disappearing and then reappearing closer than he had been before. I needed to get as much out of him as I could while I engaged him in battle. I threw a tack that went straight through his heart. Nothing happened. Then he glitched and was in front of me, I dodged a blow as he tried to punch me. He looked down at my hand, covered in a glove but still glowing the same light purple as him. His head tilted again.

"Where's Ghost?" I asked him.

"How are you here?"

"Who are you?"

"Stop it," he shouted and everyone he controlled stopped moving. He raised his hands in the air and opened his own portal, just like Kaspian, except his was in the sky. More dark shadow figures fell out of it; I liked Kaspian's version of a portal better.

"Oh, sorry, I thought we were answering questions with questions," I said, smirking at him. He had just summoned a shit ton of fighters for himself, so I was trying to sound cocky, but I didn't really feel that way. A bolt of lightning struck straight through his body doing no damage.

Focus, T. You have one mission.

"Now, where's Ghost?"

"Is this 'Ghost?' " His body morphed into a copy of my partner.

"That's not possible," I said.

He was an exact copy of Ghost. This *thing* had Ghost's code which would mean he had everything, including his fighting style. I was angry, beyond angry, that instead of getting answers, this Glitch used my concern for my partner to intimidate me. I won't let him win. Ghost was great at hand-to-hand combat and the use of guns, so the Glitch threw a couple of punches in my direction before he reached for his gun. I didn't want to ruin the glove Kaspian and the others had worked hard on, so I pulled it off my hand and grabbed the gun out of his hand, taking him by surprise. I screamed as my left hand felt like it was on fire, the glitch slowly creeping farther up to cover my wrist until I threw the gun into the distance.

"I got you, T," Olivia yelled as she raised her staff again.

The Glitch disappeared and then he was in front of Olivia.

"Liv," I heard Alton scream somewhere in the distance.

My body was already moving, my arms outstretched as I pushed the Glitch. Both hands were engulfed in darkness and purple fire as I shoved him to the side, the knife he was going to stab Olivia with hitting only air next to her. Alton pulled her back and took a fighting stance. Thanks to Kaspian, fire engulfed the area around us as a barrier to the other shadows.

"Back off, Alton. I'm already glitched," I yelled. The Glitch looked down at my hands as if he was trying to process what I meant. I waved my left hand at him. "This was a present from you last time."

He continued to stare at my hands. I needed to capitalize on his distraction. I pinched my fingers quickly and shot a constant stream of tacks at him, all making contact and still doing no damage.

"Retreat," I heard Kaspian yell.

I took a step backward, and the Glitch disappeared. I turned and then dodged an attack from behind.

Yeah, Kaspian, it would be so fucking easy to retreat.

I was exhausted, dodging punch after punch from someone who looked exactly like Ghost. The only benefit I had on my side was knowing Ghost's fighting style so well. But, as we fought, he was learning my fighting style, too, anticipating my dodges and following my patterns. I landed roughly on the ground, without enough energy to get myself back up.

This can't be how I die.

I slammed my hands on the ground and rolled over, dodging a kick from the Glitch.

"Get up!" Olivia was yelling as Alton held her back. Kaspian was trying every element on the Glitch and all of them went straight through his body. A throwing spear landed in front of the Glitch as Nathaniel ran to grab it and readied himself for combat.

"Now, I know you aren't giving up when I just spent all night trying to help you." He looked back.

"Nathaniel, no!" I yelled as the Glitch went straight for his head with a gun.

FIVE

It felt like everything froze. No, it didn't just feel that way; everything was frozen in a purple mist. My outstretched hands were glowing purple, and no one was moving, not even the Glitch.

What kind of magic is this?

A heavy weight filled my body as I stood up and looked at Nathaniel and the Glitch. A bullet was just shy of piercing Nathaniel's skull. The world glowed purple just as though it was glitched, and maybe it was. Regardless, I needed to take advantage of the situation and save Nathaniel's *pretty face*, just as he would my own. I could worry about the how and why later. I struggled against the weight of the glitch, running towards Nathaniel as fast as the resistance would allow me. I tucked my shoulder down and shoved him out of the way without touching him with my hands. The heavy feeling slowly disappeared as we landed on the ground.

The bullet meant for Nathaniel flew through the empty air. The Glitch looked at me briefly before he disappeared along with the rest of his followers. The sun set as I rolled on the ground. I could feel the flesh on my hands burning—more than they ever had before whatever just happened to the Game. I tried digging my hands into the dirt beneath us as if the coolness of the soil could alleviate some of my pain. I felt Nathaniel pull me up by hooking his arms under my chest. Olivia waved her staff over my hands, and I felt instant relief. If they were talking, I didn't hear any of it. Kaspian handed me the magical glove I had taken off, and Alton offered me one of his gloves for my newly glitched right hand.

"The city's cleared, sir," Alton said to Kaspian. "The soldier's confirmed that he's not here."

"What of the people?" Kaspian asked.

"Those who made it out have been healed, either by Liv or the city's healers. They've made an encampment outside of town. The soldiers offered to stay and help them rebuild since instant purchase is down. Shouldn't take more than a few days with the manpower offering to help."

"How many casualties?"

"Still unknown."

"I see. We need to return home and inform Queen Seraphina."

"T! What happened? Tack180? T, are you listening?" I focused on the voice as the weight continued to lessen. It was Olivia. "Can you move?"

Nathaniel was still holding onto me, and we hadn't moved in… I don't know how long. I looked around and rolled my wrists, opened and closed my fingers, and pulled away from Nathaniel. I took a step; everything seemed to be in working order.

"Great," she said, then slapped me across the face. She immediately waved her staff at me. "You won't feel that; I promise. But what were you thinking? You were the one who told us not to engage with the enemy. You weren't following *your own* orders."

"Liv," Alton said.

"No, she's not some fragile flower. Prince Kaspian, what would you do if Alton or Nathaniel didn't follow an order and almost got themselves, and others, killed?"

"I'd do more than slap them," Kaspian replied. I thought back to Nathaniel's punishment from the night before. It wasn't *that* bad. Then again, Kaspian didn't seem too mad.

"Exactly. T, are you listening?" She waved a hand in front of my face. The weighted feeling fully left my body, and it seemed like my vision cleared, as well. I focused on Olivia as she continued to yell at me. "This. Is. Not. Your. Game. You can't fight like it is either. We are a *team*. T-E-A-M. Team! Now we have to get you two gloves. Two! Well, at least you'll be matching now."

I listened to Olivia, but I wasn't really paying attention. I was still trying to understand what happened.

What the fuck is going on?

I don't even know what that was and what I did to do it in the first place. It seemed like I froze everything, but I've never done anything like that before. It could have been the Glitch, but I'm sure he would've moved as well if it were. The only other option I could think of, if it wasn't me, was that it was a side effect of the glitch on the Game.

But still, it was like magic.

I didn't know about magic, I'd made that obvious to everyone, and they still believed the glitch was related to magic. Maybe they were right. After all that time bitching that my glitch wasn't magic and then it acts like magic. Well, magic or not, without it, Nathaniel would be dead.

"Nathaniel?" I turned to Nathaniel and analyzed his face. Not a single fucking scratch. *Duty Falls* prepared me for quick thinking in dangerous scenarios. I did good, but now wasn't the time to gloat. I saved Nathaniel, but it was luck that the Glitch left. "I'm sorry. To all of you, I'm sorry."

"You're sorry, that's it?" Olivia started going off again and then stopped. "Oh. Wait, you're sorry, really? It's not in your Character profile to apologize so easily. Are you hurt somewhere else?"

"I'm fine." She reached for my glitched hands, covered in gloves. I brushed away her hands from grabbing at me. "I'm fine."

"Good, then let's get out of here. We need to report what happened to my sister," Kaspian said.

He opened another portal before anyone could say another word. Nathaniel helped support me as we walked through the portal where Seraphina was already waiting for us in the throne room. She outstretched her arms as she walked toward me. Nathaniel backed away, and Seraphina went straight in for a hug; I felt uncomfortable with her arms around me. I tapped her back twice, and she held on for a few seconds longer before letting go and looking at the whole group, assessing them for injuries.

"Our kingdom owes you a great deal. I'm sorry I couldn't tell you what would happen," she finally said.

"You knew?" I asked. "Why didn't you tell anyone?"

"If I did, it may have changed the outcome, changed the future away from the version I saw. There were other potential outcomes; someone could have actually died, including you."

"How long have you known?" Kaspian asked.

"I got the vision right before you entered the throne room with Tack180 for the first time. I don't control how or when I get my visions, T, but I can at least assure that the vision I see plays out the way it was meant to."

"Do you know more about what is going on?" I asked. "How I ended up here, anything?"

"No." She shook her head. "I just saw you stating that you knew the enemy and following Prince Kaspian into battle and, later, another vision of your safe return. Thank you again. This magic you possess is overwhelming."

"It's not magic," Kaspian and I both said at the same time.

"Well then, what is it?"

"I don't know," I answered. I guess it *could* be magic, but I'm not going to tell her that.

"Very well." She shrugged it off. "Thank you for saving all of Fantasia. We owe you so much more than we can offer."

"I need a way home. You said you could help me find one."

"Certainly. You must continue to hone your power. It is greater than mine and Kaspian's combined. If there is a way back to your world, it is through you."

"That doesn't help."

My gut instinct was to roll my eyes at such a stupid answer. I looked down instead, feeling the weight of the tears as they blurred my vision. That was the shittiest response she could've given me. All that schmoozing and time spent with them was time away from saving Ghost. It was supposed to help me, but all it did was keep me from reaching my target earlier. I held in the tears for as long as I could, but once I blinked, I felt the liquid roll down my face. It wasn't just Seraphina's comment that bothered me. It was everything; having to fight a copy of my partner, not knowing what the fuck was going on, remembering the feeling of the weight on my body, and the realization that there was a possibility that I wouldn't see Ghost ever again. Not if their leader took his form so easily, like he had retained all of Ghost's powers somehow, as though he had downloaded his code. It was like Ghost was the Character and the Glitch was his Player. Did I not save him in time?

Fuck this.

"T." Olivia extended her arm out.

"Don't." I pushed her away as I felt the same heavy weight from before taking hold of my body. "I don't want to be here anymore. I just want to go home and go back to *Duty Falls*."

She reached again, and I took a step back, shoving my hands forward to keep the distance.

Frozen.

A purple mist enveloped everyone, freezing them in place. I looked down and my whole body was glowing in the purple haze that had once only covered my hand. Was the purple haze the weight I felt? I noticed a flicker behind the queen; what looked like a portal began to stabilize behind her. Was this my way out? It could be a message, Ghost even, helping me get home. I looked into the portal and saw darkness; if it was home then it would've been dark since the Platform had been bombed and, subsequently, so had my apartment.

I tried to move my body, but it was like I was stuck in a nightmare when you try to move, and maybe you do, but only in slow motion. My HP was draining as I was forcing my body forward. I reached out my arm to stabilize myself on Olivia. She immediately grabbed me, her body moving again, while everyone else remained frozen.

"What's going on?" she asked.

"I don't know. But we need to act fast. Do your little wave thing on me, please." She aimed her staff toward me, and I felt the weight begin to lift. "Can you keep it going on me? I'm going through that portal."

"What the hell, where did that come from?"

"I can't answer that, but it looks like home."

"Then I'm coming with you. You don't know what to expect there, and I think you are going to need my help."

"I won't fight you on that." Olivia was the only one who would be helpful regardless of the battle. As a healer, we wouldn't have to worry about injury and, as the best ranked Player SmokeScreen, she'd have a great strategy for any situation we were thrown into.

"Oh, T. You flatter me," she laughed. Although, I could tell she really was excited that I chose for her to come with me, even though we didn't know what was waiting for us on the other side.

The portal started blinking again and I wasn't about to miss my chance. I grabbed Olivia's arm as we rushed through it, into the darkness. I looked around; we weren't home, at least, we weren't in my home. Wherever we were, I had never been there before. I looked back at the portal as it continued to flicker. I walked toward it again, reaching out a hand to analyze it; how did it open? As my hand made contact with the portal, the people we had left behind started to move again. Four bodies rushed to the portal after us as the flickers gained speed. We were hit full force as the portal closed, tackling us to the ground. In the darkness, I couldn't tell who had made it through and who was left behind.

Olivia's staff no longer focused its healing power on me, but my body stuck to the ground underneath the heavy weight, which still hadn't been released from my body. A light flame glowed in the distance, and I knew Kaspian had made it through the portal. The flame illuminated the rest of the room, and I could see that Nathaniel and Alton made it, as well. So, Seraphina was the only one who didn't and maybe she didn't on purpose.

As I stood back up, I assessed my body: the purple haze had returned to its rightful spot on my hands only. Whatever the purple mist was, I needed to find a way to stop it. If I couldn't, then I risked whatever happened to Ghost happening to me as well. *Ghost.* Was this some kind of message? I looked around again as the others gathered themselves.

Where the fuck are we?

There were deserted-looking buildings, flickering lights, and we seemed to be in the middle of the street. There was no one around and nothing in the sky. When I looked up, it was just darkness; no stars, no moon, nothing.

"I thought you lived at the Platform," Olivia said.

"I do."

"Then how did we end up in the last place any of us would want to be?"

"Wait, you know where we are?"

"Yeah, we're in one of those horror games. I think we're in the one with the clowns that jump out and scare you. God, what's it called, Clowns of Terror? No, Killer Clowns? Something like that. I've personally never played it because it scares the shit out of me."

"Oh shit," Alton said under his breath.

"Can someone explain what just happened?" Kaspian asked.

Everyone looked at me. I shrugged. I didn't want to think about how I did it, *if* I did it. Just because I was glitched didn't mean I knew what was going on any more than they did. We're stuck in yet another game, even farther away from answers than I had been. I was hopeful that the portal was some sort of message for me, but I had no fucking clue. My voice would've faltered if I had tried to say something and I would've ended up crying in front of them, so I looked away.

"T, come on. Something happened in there," Olivia touched my arm as a form of comfort. "You touched me then we were moving when no one else could. Is it you? Is it the glitch? Do you hurt anywhere?"

I took a deep breath and tried to concentrate as I spoke so that they wouldn't hear the helplessness in my voice.

"Back with Nathaniel and again with Seraphina, I got this weird, heavy sensation like I couldn't move my body. It's like time's frozen and I should be frozen too, but for some reason, I can move. When it happened with Nathaniel, I didn't take the time to think about it. I knew I had to save him. I don't know about what just happened; if I opened the portal or if it's some kind of message from Production or Ghost, but that same thing happened. I also don't know how you started moving."

"I think it was you, to be honest." She coughed out a small laugh like it was obvious. "You touched me and I felt like I had just woken up. It was really weird. The portal here must have been you, too. Just like magic. I mean, you landed in our world with magic during the middle of a glitch. There's a possibility you ended up as a Character in our game. Maybe you have magical powers now, you know, like the queen suggested. We just need to help you figure out how to control it, okay? We've just got to make it fast. You know, *before* we run into clowns."

"What's so terrifying about a jester?" Nathaniel asked.

"You can ask that question again when one is chasing you with a knife or a chainsaw," I said. "It's not necessarily the clown itself, but how they have been portrayed."

"These guys are worse than most." Olivia raised her hands to her mouth and dragged them down. "They foam at the mouth, they're rabid, and all of them have different types of weapons or torture devices. It's terrifying. They are also all NPCs. This game is a single-player or multiplayer experience, but there is no Character to play. The Player comes in as themselves."

"So, there's no help here?" I asked. I already knew the answer. I just wanted the confirmation. I had never played a jump-scare game, nor did I have a crossover with one. I didn't want to be here for multiple reasons, waste of time being the most important, but killer clowns were a close second.

My chest hurt at the thought of being stuck with these people in an unknown game. I wanted to be at home, baking and venting to my imaginary shower audience, they'd be getting an earful with the new shit I'd had to deal with.

"Yeah, if we have no access to the Platform or Producers, then neither does this game. It's full of NPCs programmed to chase the Players that enter the game and that's currently us," Olivia said. She thought for a second and then continued. "I think we need someone facing every direction. With any jump-scare game, they aren't supposed to move if you keep an eye on them. You can't blink or look away, or they start moving. If one of them gets out of our sight, then we are done for. But we've been in here long enough that they know we are here. They must be planning something for us."

"What will they do when they catch us?" Kaspian asked.

"They kill you." Olivia said it so matter of fact that the action of killing didn't seem as intrusive as it was.

"Are you sure they're all NPCs?" Kaspian asked.

"Should be."

"Regardless," he said. "We should avoid deadly force in case it's not an NPC. Try not to get yourselves killed."

"That's easy to say when you aren't scared of clowns," Olivia said.

"I'll keep you safe, Olivia," Nathaniel said as he put his arm around her.

"Keep your paws off me, Nathaniel." She pushed him off. "We'll see how you do with this clown game and whether you are in any condition to protect anyone."

"Well, just know that I offered, and Alton didn't." Nathaniel threw his hands in the air and stepped away from her.

"Dude, I don't mess around with clowns," Alton said. "It's everyone for themselves in this scenario. Even Olivia. Plus, she kicks ass, even in these jump-scare games. Do you even realize who you're talking about?"

A sound in the distance of something crashing caught our attention. And so, the game began. Nathaniel took the lead with his spear and Alton took up the rear with his sword. Kaspian and I, as distance fighters, remained on the sides while Olivia stayed in the middle to easily heal anyone that needed it. And, regardless of what Alton said, she had no weapon other than her staff. How was she going to take out a clown with a staff that heals people?

"I think I see something," Nathaniel said. "Olivia, can you confirm that what's ahead of us is actually a clown?"

"Yes," Olivia grumbled under her breath.

"I don't know why that's so scary." Out of the corner of my eye, I could see Nathaniel look back at Olivia, who had turned her head to scan the rest of the area.

"No, Nathaniel!" Olivia yelled. Nathaniel turned his head back and stopped. All of us ran into him. "No one else turn away from your positions."

"What happened?" Kaspian asked. "Why did we stop?"

"It moved." Nathaniel was barely whispering, speaking through gritted teeth.

"What do you mean?"

"I mean, the thing is right in front of me."

I knew without having to look that Kaspian turned his head. Anyone curious enough in that scenario would look, I got it, but goddammit, Kaspian. I heard him groan seconds later and my best guess was that there were two clowns, with the new one standing in front of the prince.

"Son of a bitch," Nathaniel cursed. I could hear rustling behind us, but I knew better than to turn around.

"Stop fighting it, Nathaniel," Olivia said.

"It stabbed me."

"More clowns have shown up in your direction since you've been distracted."

"They won't move if you keep looking at them," Alton reminded everyone. "Stop looking away, Nathaniel."

"Resume formation," Kaspian ordered. "Engaging in combat compromises the rest of the team. Stand down."

"So, how do we move around them?" Nathaniel asked.

"We could move backward. I'm clear back here," Alton suggested.

So, Alton took the lead and Nathaniel the rear. But it didn't end there. At some point, every single one of us fucked up enough to make a clown move, either slightly or enough to entirely block us. We were tired, hungry, and getting angry with each other. Tensions only continued to rise as no one knew of a way to get out. No matter what we did, we were still stuck in the game.

"For fucks sake, stop looking," I yelled.

"You messed up, too, T," Olivia yelled back.

"Both of you shut up. I'm trying to think," Kaspian snapped.

"If Liv and T hadn't rushed into the portal without consulting anyone, we wouldn't be in this mess," Alton joined in.

"No one asked any of you guys to follow us." I stood my ground.

"Like we were just going to let you leave," Nathaniel joined the conversation. "We like Olivia, and we all owe you the safety of our kingdom."

"Right, but none of you like me." I rolled my eyes, and a clown appeared in the distance. My sight returning to the position in front of me paused its movement. It was a tall, lanky clown with a purple top hat, large shoes, colorful get up, and a mace, straight out of Fantasia. Initially, it looked like it had a painted white face and red make-up, but the more I looked at it, the more I realized that it wasn't make-up, but red blood smeared across its face and dripping down its neck.

Note to self: no more rolling your eyes.

"We don't even know you," Alton shouted back.

"I said, shut up," Kaspian's voice echoed throughout the street. "We don't know how long we will be stuck here. We need to find food and make a shelter so that these godforsaken clowns stop popping up on us."

"There was a deserted-looking restaurant in the distance about thirty minutes ago," I said. "But, if this game is built for people to play for long amounts of time, then I'm sure, given the game's algorithms, it's filled with clowns."

"Okay, and I take back what I said before, engage when you see the enemy and use all the excessive force you want; they are NPCs, they aren't real, so it's probably better if they don't respawn."

We walked the thirty minutes back to the restaurant, where there was a line of clowns waiting outside. So, it was one of *those* games; the ones that listen to you and adjust for "better" gameplay. Although, I'm not sure why killer clowns blocking our idea of safety made for better gameplay. Then again, I would never have played this game by my own choosing anyway. Olivia covered Kaspian's direction as he tried to take them all out with magic. Every single one respawned.

"T, I'll cover your side," Olivia offered.

She pushed me out of the circle and into the street in the direction of the clowns. This was the real test; was I a killer? I pinched my fingers, and two trusty tacks spawned in between them. With a simple flick, I sent one flying at the middle clown, bullseye—straight through the heart. I watched as the clown blinked out of existence and then waited for it to reappear. Alton, who was in the lead and could see the whole thing, put a hand on my shoulder. I dropped to the ground and put my head in my hands.

"Son of a bitch," I cursed.

"What happened?" Olivia asked.

"He—um, he didn't respawn," I choked out the response, feeling an immense sense of guilt for what I had done to the people in the forest.

I looked down at my hands, hidden under gloves, they were black, but the purple haze was glowing brightly around them. Was I a killer or did they just respawn somewhere else? If I was a killer, then I was guilty of murdering people in the land of Fantasia. If it was because of the glitch, did that confirm Ghost was dead since he was glitched, too? I didn't want to accept that answer—not without a fight. Ghost was strong, so there was still a chance that I just needed to defeat the Glitch to release him.

This would be so much easier to figure out if I could talk it over with Ghost.

He was never supposed to leave me, so why was he suddenly gone? I took a deep breath and held back the tears that I wanted to let out.

I will not let these people see me so vulnerable... again.

I stood back up.

"Take 'em out, killer," Olivia said. "I'm done with this clown bullshit."

I pinched my fingers and sent tacks flying as the remaining clowns began to attack. New clowns spawned to continue the tirade before they stopped coming, but it seemed a little too soon; a well-known game such as this would have more than a dozen clowns set for attack. I turned in a circle, trying to look for any indication of more clowns coming. In the distance, I could hear a clown laugh but that was it. There were no clowns in sight.

"Did you get them, T?" Olivia asked.

"She kicked ass," Alton answered for me.

" 'Atta girl!"

"They aren't showing up anymore. Olivia, what does that mean?" I questioned.

"I've never seen anything like that. Assuming there's a respawn algorithm and points based on killing clowns, who typically respawn, there is a chance that we've unlocked a special endgame that people usually don't get to."

"Is it safe to get out of formation?" Kaspian asked.

"Hell if I know."

"Alton, look away," Nathaniel suggested.

"No, dude, you look away!"

"Childish, both of you," Kaspian chided.

"Oh, I'll do it," Olivia offered. She quickly looked away and then back again. "It's clear."

Everyone let out a deep breath and started walking toward the restaurant. Unfortunately for us, there were no fresh food items inside. Olivia, Alton, and I started grabbing any canned food we could find. Kaspian and Nathaniel looked out of their element, or should I say, out of their game. It was easy to forget that they hadn't been out of their game until that moment. I handed them a few cans each and then grabbed more for myself.

"Where do we go from here, Olivia?" I asked.

"Kaspian said we need to set up camp. So, let's break into one of these buildings, find a windowless room, and keep an eye on the door. That's what most Players would do when they want to last a long time. Follow me!"

We left the restaurant then followed Olivia as she led us down a series of streets and alleys, proving that she had played this game at least once before, regardless of her previous statement. She found a perfect room, big enough to comfortably fit us all, that didn't have a single window—just the door. We blockaded the entrance with what little items we could find around the room, and then Kaspian raised his hands over the lock.

"What did that do?" I asked.

"Hopefully created an indestructible lock on the door. I'm not sure how well this world takes to my magic."

"Something's better than nothing." I jiggled the door handle, but it wouldn't open. "Seems to have done something."

Alton pierced a can with his sword and handed it to Kaspian. "Can you heat this up?"

Kaspian lit a flame in his hands and held it under the can until it started to bubble. We didn't know how long we would be stuck there, so we shared the one can of beans between the five of us. Given that there was no access to the Producers, Platform, or any Players, we didn't know if any of the items would respawn after a couple of hours or not.

"You need to rest," Kaspian said to his retainers. "I will watch the door."

"No, my lord, you need to rest! Not us!" Alton argued.

"I am your prince. I am to protect my people in times of war. This might be a little different, but this is still war. Get some rest and I will take first watch."

"I'll stay up, too," I offered. "I got us into this mess, and we all know that I can stop them better than anyone else here."

"We can also take the time to train," Kaspian suggested. "Your glitch acts so similarly to magic, even though it's not."

"You won't hear a complaint from me!" Olivia seemed a little too happy considering the condition we were in. "This day has been crazy. But also, one of my best."

"Your best, really?" Alton asked.

"Don't act like this drama hasn't been fun. As long as no one gets hurt, this is a blast. I've brought some of my favorite people into a new game, and we are all playing together. This is the best multiplayer team I have played on. With one of the Characters I didn't think I would ever meet in person. I hope T never goes back to her game! Wait, no, that was super insensitive. Sorry, T."

I let the initial sting of her words pass before I replied, "It has been fun and a relief to not be stuck with incompetent or horny Players, Nathaniel's company excluded. I'll feel better when *this* is all over. You're all capable fighters to have on my side, except for when it comes to dodging clowns."

"In both of their defenses," Alton started. We all knew Kaspian and Nathaniel had been the worst offenders, even if we all messed up once or twice. "This is their first time out of Fantasia."

"And you brought us here," Nathaniel joked. "Couldn't you have brought us somewhere a little more, what's the word I'm looking for, romantic?"

I didn't do it. At least, I didn't think I did it. Olivia thought I did, and I trusted her judgment more than anyone else. So, maybe I did do it. But what did I do and how did I do it? If it wasn't the Game that glitched, that means that I glitched.

I'm broken.

I couldn't think like that, not if I was holding out hope that Ghost was alive. Still, if I can get us out of this mess then I need to try something, anything, to get us out of here. That would include treating the glitch like some sort of magic I inherited while ending up in Fantasia.

"Okay, we're putting you to sleep," Kaspian said as he pushed Nathaniel into a corner.

"Putting him to sleep?"

"Not the way you think. Even if we could use our herbs here, I wouldn't want to. We need them to be ready to battle at a moment's notice and some soporific items might leave them drowsy," Kaspian replied.

Nathaniel sat down, leaned his head up against the wall, and gave me a wink before Kaspian waved a hand over his head. Unlike his usual light-blue magic, purple magic emanated from his hand, and then Nathaniel's eyes were shut, and he was snoring softly. Alton and Olivia sat down as they followed suit, waiting for Kaspian to put them to sleep.

"What exactly did you do?" I asked when they were all out.

"I have a mild affinity for dark magic, and that was one of the tricks my sister taught me. It's rather useful in the field to put them to sleep and wake them up as needed. While they rest, they also regain health and stamina. They won't dream, and they won't wake up on their own. So, regardless of how loud it gets, they will get a full rest. That can also be a downside though if we're suddenly attacked, so it's meant to be used with caution."

"Can you put yourself out?" I asked, wondering about the next shift.

"No."

"So, you will just have to try to sleep and fail miserably?"

"Perhaps." He looked over at the three sleeping in the corner. "But keeping them safe and healthy is my first priority."

"You do a good job." We sat down, leaning up against the wall and facing the door. I wanted to practice because I wanted to get out of this damn place, but I needed a mental break. I couldn't focus on practicing and what that meant for me or Ghost right this minute.

"I appreciate the compliment."

We could hear loud laughter and banging coming from above.

"Sorry this is the first game you ended up in outside of your own. I was sure this was the Platform when I saw the portal."

"If the Platform looks anything like this, then I don't think I will ever visit you when this is done."

I snorted a laugh, "No, it's not. At least, not usually. The Platform is filled with people from different games, brand new Characters, and veteran Characters alike. It's beautiful and bright with ads and shiny billboards everywhere."

"Then why would you think this was it?"

"Well, after *Duty Falls* was infiltrated by that Glitch you met earlier on the battlefield, I got to my save stone. I saved and was sent back to the Platform, but it wasn't like normal. There was this bomb and it hit the entire Platform. I don't know how I ended up in your game, but given everything I know, it just seems like the Platform is in ruins right now."

"What if the Platform is gone? If this darkness and purple haze, this glitch, erases or deletes things, then wouldn't the Platform be gone?"

"Wouldn't I be gone, too, then?"

"Not if you opened a portal without realizing it."

"I don't think so."

"You already have. That's how we are here."

"But—" He looked at me and smiled. I sighed. "Okay, fine. That's a valid option. Not the one I'm choosing to accept, but a valid one. When you use magic do you drain HP?"

"No, well, I don't. However, there are other magical abilities, like some of Seraphina's, which take from the spell caster's HP rather than SP to be used, like a payment of sorts. Are you losing HP?"

"I don't really know. It just happened, but it seemed like my gauge was constantly draining. Not a set amount for payment or anything like that. What about when you use it. Does it feel heavy?"

"Heavy is not a word I would use to describe magic. I would almost say the opposite—I feel light, almost like flying."

A loud bang, much closer than any of the previous ones, caught our attention. We looked at each other and then back at the barricaded door. We heard the doorknob jiggle followed by that same maniacal laughter we had always heard in the distance.

"Peek-a-boo, I found you," the clown waiting on the other side of the door sang.

Kaspian looked at me and shook his head. Neither of us moved and I'm pretty sure we were both holding our breaths.

"Mary had a little axe, little axe, little axe. Mary had a little axe; its blades were sharp as knives."

A knock on the door.

"Little pigs, little pigs, please let me in?"

There was another eerie laugh followed by what sounded like a heavy object scraping along the floor. The sound got quieter as the clown walked away. When I was sure the creepy clown was gone, I looked at Kaspian, who seemed way too calm given the situation.

"You don't look even a little scared."

"Well, if they aren't going to attack, then what's the point?" he asked.

"Oh, I'm sure that *thing* will be back and will attack when it's ready. So, please, teach me your magic mojo or whatever so I can get us back home."

"Magic mojo?" he laughed at my phrasing.

"Now is not the time to joke. I don't want to be around when that clown decides to use that axe to bust in here. I'd much rather be in Fantasia. Or looking for Ghost and finding a way home."

"So, that's your plan? After we get back to Fantasia, that is."

"Yeah. Finding a way home. Saving Ghost."

"Yes, but if Ghost is dead, which a part of you seems to suspect, what is your plan?"

"I won't know he's dead until I defeat that Glitch. He could be under some weird Player and Character control. I need to do everything I can to find that Glitch and get more answers, including accessing resources from your sister. I will do what she wants me to do if it helps me achieve that goal."

"I'm sure my sister, although she was using you earlier, would love to have you serve as her retainer. If you, well... if you want to stay with us, we are more than happy to have you join us."

"I appreciate that, but that's not really what I had in mind."

I hadn't thought about what would happen when we made it back. Obviously, my plan had always been to find Ghost if he was alive. Even if Ghost was dead, which I didn't fully accept, then the plan would be to get revenge on the thing that did this and its creator. But I didn't want to think about an alternative where Fantasia was my only option. Getting back to Fantasia was step one. Honing the glitch, if that's something I can even do, to get into other games was a whole different scenario that I needed to tackle. I took a deep breath and looked over at Kaspian, even though a normal person would shit themselves in this scenario, he was smiling.

"She's having a lot of fun." He nodded at Olivia.

"It makes sense. She's the *best* Player out there. Playing any game would be fun."

"Sure," he said like he didn't believe me, or maybe like there was more to the story that I wouldn't get to hear. "My sister would be happy to see her now, ordering us around in the same way she used to."

"She used to order *you* around?" I laughed.

"Myself and my sister. Things were different back then, in many ways."

"How so?" I asked.

"It's not important." He said, trying to shut down the conversation.

"What? Were you previously the king? Did your sister usurp your throne, and now you don't get along?" I prodded. I was more curious about it now since he didn't want to talk about it. I didn't overly care either way, but some good Fantasian drama could take my mind off everything else I was dealing with.

"It's not that." He adjusted the way he was sitting. "To say that I didn't want to be king would be a lie, but I know that the people love Seraphina. They infantilize her; saying, 'oh look, Seraphina is talking!' or 'Wow, she's walking through the city!' "

"Don't know what that's like," I said with a flair of melodrama, smiling at him. "I was just as popular as, if not more popular, than Ghost."

"Okay," he laughed and nudged my arm. "I'm not saying people hate me."

"No, I get that. It's just that they don't throw gold confetti at you for existing."

"How did you find out about the golden confetti? I thought we did a good job of keeping that one a secret." I shook my head with a laugh, turning him down. "Anyway, I know that it must be hard for her to see the future and not be able to talk about it, lest she changes it for the worse. It's even harder when the outcome is not as fortunate as our run-in earlier."

"Like what?"

"Some time ago, my ex-fiancé stole prized jewels. Seraphina knew it was coming but didn't say anything."

"What? Wait, I need more information than that. What happened to the jewels? To the fiancé?" Hell yes—this was exactly the escape I needed.

I want to know more.

"We got them back. That was all Alton's doing, actually. It was how he worked himself up to become my retainer. She left the game. I guess, according to Olivia, she became some fitness game instructor."

"Really? Which one?" I thought about the top three most popular ones. "QuadraStrength?"

Kaspian raised an eyebrow like he had no idea what I was talking about. Not her.

"Carmen? That only dance instructor that teaches ballroom?"

Still no response.

"Becky?"

He clenched his fists like he had when Ambrosio unmasked me in the throne room. *Got him.*

"Oh my god. Were you engaged to ButtBusterBecky?" Kaspian grimaced. "Oh wow, you were. 'And one, and two, keep it up, everyone!' "

"Okay, you don't need to pretend to be her." He nudged me.

"But this is gold. You two are so—" I paused, thinking about the perky redhead whose class I took a couple of times. "Different."

"Yes, well, I guess she was unhappy in Fantasia and wanted a change. That quest was her way out."

"Okay, but ButtBusterBecky has been around for at least two years. You've been uncomfortable and pissy around your sister for two years? You haven't made up yet?"

"No, we were always really close, even after Rebecca and I broke up. I didn't know about her knowledge on the subject until recently. I guess, if it had played out any other way, Alton wouldn't be where he is."

He looked back at his friend. Sure, it was shitty what ButtBusterBecky had done and the fact that his sister didn't tell him, but he didn't seem to realize how happy he was.

"It looks like you are happy with how life turned out."

"It was humiliating and heartbreaking. She's my sister, and she knew the pain I was going to go through and said nothing."

"I'm sure that hurts her just as much as it hurts you," I offered. He looked over at me. I could tell he was trying hard not to be angry with me for not stroking his ego like his retainers did. I shrugged. "It's true."

"You're already a good retainer, protecting the queen even when she's not your queen."

"It just so happened to work out that way. I'm just trying to show you another perspective. I'm not purposely protecting anyone." I tried to backtrack. This was not my game, and I was not staying.

It's time to get back to Ghost.

"Anyway, teach me magic; I'm over this clown-infested hellhole."

We tried. We tried for hours, and nothing happened. I spun my arms like he did, tried to feel weightless, tried to feel heavy, tried to feel anything, but nothing happened at all—not even a little flicker from the purple haze permeating my hands. The same creepy-ass clown continued to return, taunting us with new phrases every time he passed our door. We stayed as quiet as possible every time he went by, neither of us wanting to engage in battle with the others resting. I sat down, ready to call it a night with the practice since we were getting nowhere.

"Did you miss me?" The clown asked from the other side of the door. It was as though he knew to come taunt me when I felt defeated. "I have a present for you. Happy Birthday, Kaspian."

Kaspian and I looked at each other without moving. Another jiggle of the door handle as the clown tried to enter. I made a face at Kaspian. "Is it your birthday?" He shook his head.

"Do you want a balloon animal, Tack180?" Then it sounded like he honked some sort of horn three times.

We stayed silent and looked at our allies in the corner, checking they were all right.

"I said to let—" A loud bang on the door.

"Me." Silver metal pierced the middle of the door as the clown finally started to come for us.

"In." The clown looked through the crack he created in the door and grinned.

"T, get behind me," Kaspian tried to command me. I readied myself to throw a tack, but Kaspian held out a hand to stop me as if I was one of his subjects. "I don't want to accidentally hurt you. Stay back."

He used a gust of wind to push the clown away from the door. The clown just laughed and then started whacking away at the door. Kaspian swung his hand again. This time water flooded the clown's mouth and the clown started to drown. I looked over at Kaspian, amazed at how dark his light magic could be. The clown gagged as he continued to try and chop his way into the room. He made the hole in the door big enough to get through and began to charge in. I threw a tack that landed on the floor in front of the clown as a warning shot. The clown gagged and water fell out of his mouth. The clown raised his axe over his head as ice began to crawl up his body, freezing him in place. A fire started on the handle of the axe, burning it away as the blade fell down onto the clown's head and lodged itself there. The clown flickered, a maniacal laugh echoed the hall, and then the clown in front of us warped away.

Kaspian rushed over to our sleeping allies.

"What happened?" Olivia asked.

"Sir, are you alright?" Alton asked.

"We need to move rooms." I threw the bags of canned food in their hands and readied more tacks. If he just let me handle things, we wouldn't have to move again. "We know that Kaspian doesn't kill like I do. So that clown just respawned somewhere, and we need a new place to call camp."

"I really hate clowns," Olivia scoffed. "Follow me again."

Olivia led us through more corridors until we ended up in another windowless room. We moved furniture against the door and protected the refuge in the same way we had the other one, with Kaspian finishing it off with a spell over the lock. He debriefed the others as we shared another can of beans. Kaspian and I agreed to sleep while the others stood guard for the next round. I watched as he waved a hand over me, unsure of what it would feel like to be put into a state of rest, and then everything went black. Well, black for a second. Something pulled me awake, and Kaspian was standing back over me.

Blink.

"Kill it, T!" Olivia yelled.

Blink.

Nathaniel was being strangled by the largest clown we'd fought so far. Alton took a swing at it with his sword and the clown backhanded him. Kaspian froze the clown, who immediately defrosted.

"Now, please," Olivia screeched from the corner of the room.

The clown released Nathaniel then began stomping in her direction. I pinched my fingers and sent a tack flying. He deflected it. Literally backhanded it the same way he had Alton. Alton stood up and ran full force at the clown, jumping on his back and stabbing his sword down until the clown flickered and warped away again.

"They are getting bigger," Olivia said as she took a breath.

"And stronger," Kaspian agreed as he grabbed my glove-covered hand and pulled me out of the room. "Let's go."

"What happened while I was asleep? I thought I was out for a second," I said, following the group into another room.

"You've been asleep for a couple hours," Kaspian began catching me up on what I'd missed. "Olivia has informed us they'll be respawning with higher levels now. It seems she is correct; this one was larger and stronger than the one we fought."

"Weren't you supposed to be sleeping, too?"

"It was hard to sleep when the clown kept making his rounds and banging on the door."

"Okay, I can stay up, and we can do more training to try and get out of here."

This went on for a week. A whole, fucking, week based on my implant's calendar system. Kaspian started putting only one of us to sleep at a time as the clowns continued to grow. We were tired, running out of food, and getting beat up faster than Olivia could heal us. Worst of all, each new clown metallicized, so my tacks just bounced off them in the same way that Alton's sword and Nathaniel's spear did. That left Kaspian to be the only fighter doing actual damage, with Olivia heavily focusing on healing the three of us taking the beating on the front lines while protecting them.

"If they get any bigger, then I'm going to murder you when we get home, T," Olivia breathed heavily as we settled in from our most recent clown battle. "You brought us to this game."

"You good, sir?" Alton asked, assessing Kaspian.

"I'm good." Kaspian swatted him away and sat down next to me.

"You look like you just finished a butt-busting workout with ButtBusterBecky," I joked.

"Jokes on her for having a shitty name." Olivia was beaming as she sat down across from me. "I helped persuade people on the Voting Forum to vote for ButtBusterBecky; before SmokeScreen got involved, it was going to be something cute and normal for a girl who always wears yoga pants, like Becks or something like that. It was my revenge. We had the perfect number of people in our group for quests before she started dating Kaspian. I got the boot, and she took my spot. So, I made sure to be there during her Voting Forum. That's what she gets for making me Player five in the lineup and essentially knocking me out of any limited number Player quests."

"The good old days." Nathaniel smiled.

"Which times, with me or without me?" Olivia gave him a look that could kill.

"Of course, with you," Kaspian stopped Nathaniel from saying anything.

"That's what I thought! You, me, Seraphina, and Nathaniel. The best multiplayer combo ever."

"Didn't you say that about us when we first got here?" I asked. She ignored me.

"I mean, I'm right here." Alton sat down next to her.

"Oh, I know and no offense to you. You're my favorite two-player combo." She placed a hand on his arm and winked. "Hm, wait, unless T stays and wants to join me in battle. I might like that, too. But I also had four years with them before you even came into the picture. Nothing can beat my original crew."

"Don't worry. I'm not taking your spot," I said to Alton. "I need to get back home, salvage the Platform area if I can, and, most importantly, find Ghost."

The chitchat was brought to a halt when the lights in the room started flickering before the building started shaking. We quickly unbarricaded the door and ran from the room, then Kaspian stopped to look out of the hallway window.

"Get out of the building," he yelled, his eyes wide.

"Why?" Olivia asked as we all started running toward the closest exit.

"It got bigger."

"It's massive!" Olivia yelled as we exited the building. Olivia raised her staff as we assessed the giant, golden clown in front of us. It wielded multiple weapons from axes to chainsaws and was taller than any building in the game.

I pinched my fingers and flicked a tack at it. As with the more recent clowns, I couldn't penetrate it, so Nathaniel and Alton stayed back with me as we acted as distractions for Kaspian, who started with the same water attack he had used on the first clown. He swirled his hands around, and water came from nowhere; it filled the clown's mouth and poured out as the clown gagged. As the giant clown started gargling the water, he flailed, knocking into the buildings around him. We all scattered, dodging the debris and the gigantic clown feet stomping around.

"T!" I heard my name yelled and I didn't need to look to know I was about to get hit by something big. I saw the shadow on the floor, then it was as if time had frozen, and it had. The Game glitched again.

My body was heavy as I looked around. Above me, I was about to be stomped on by a ridiculously large shoe. On the other side of the street: Olivia held her staff over Nathaniel, who leaned against the wall for support. Kaspian was the one who had yelled my name. I looked over at him, and a bolt of lightning, frozen in time, rushed from his hand to the foot above me. I couldn't see Alton.

I started moving, as fast as the weight would allow me, toward Kaspian, my closest ally. There wasn't any time to waste or doubt myself. I had to assume that I did this, and that Olivia was right, I opened the portal before and, since I did, I could do it again. I just needed to touch Kaspian, and he could help me find Alton and figure out how to open the portal. I grabbed his outstretched hand, and he started moving, and so did the lightning. It zapped the clown's foot without doing damage. He looked around, took a moment to realize what was happening, and then handed me a potion.

"Is your HP draining still?" he asked.

"Yup." I looked at my gauge as it depleted while the world remained frozen. I'm not stupid. There's obviously an actual correlation between myself and when the Game glitches. I just don't want to accept that answer. It's easier to hold out hope if I don't.

"Let me know if you feel weak and I can give you another. We need to get to Olivia." He practically pulled me as we started toward Olivia and Nathaniel.

"I can't see Alton," I said.

"He was by me. We can look for him after we get you to Olivia."

I touched Olivia first, who immediately pointed her staff at me, then Nathaniel, who cursed in pain. Kaspian offered him one of his potions. Nathaniel nodded back toward where we had gotten Kaspian, and Alton was there, lying on the floor hidden under some debris. Nathaniel and Kaspian ran after him, picked him up, and brought him back to us.

"Open the portal," Olivia said as Nathaniel and Kaspian returned with Alton's limp body.

I touched him. "Is he dead?"

"No, he's breathing." Kaspian's words sent relief through my body. The world flickered as if it tried to move, as though time wanted to keep going. It hadn't been frozen this long before.

"Now, T," Olivia tried again.

"I'm trying. I don't know how this works." I don't want it to work just as much as I do want it to work.

"Think of home," Kaspian offered. "Our home," he added. "We can get you back to Ghost after. Picture the castle, the grounds, the library."

"I'm trying."

"Close your eyes, take a deep breath, and try again. Picture them: the castle, the grounds, the library. You can also think of events, like the party in the bar or getting your glove. Okay, great. Now, open your eyes."

I opened my eyes, and there it was: a portal straight to Seraphina.

SIX

We crashed through the portal, smashing into the ground, and Olivia immediately left my side to wave her staff over Alton. I looked up and Seraphina was still waiting in the same spot we had left her. She looked at us, blinked, and then ran over to assess the damage.

"What happened?" she asked as she watched Olivia and Alton.

"Monstrous clowns," I said as I sprawled my body out on the ground, drained. It felt so comforting and safe to be back in Fantasia. Kaspian sat up and rolled a potion in my direction. I rolled it back. "I'm good."

"Drink it anyway." Kaspian rolled it right back.

"I'll take it." Nathaniel's hand intercepted the bottle and downed it. "Oh, I think I still have some on my lips."

Nathaniel leaned over in my direction and a rush of wind slapped him back. Both Kaspian and Seraphina were glowing their respective colors, so I wasn't sure who got the kill shot in.

"Please tell me we're home and I'm not imagining this?" Alton asked as he sat up.

"We're home. Are you okay? Do you hurt anywhere?" Olivia asked. "I can heal you again."

"Olivia, I'm okay. Thanks to you." You could tell he wanted to hug her, but all he did was grab her shoulder and squeeze it. Obviously, Seraphina wasn't in on the relationship, or maybe she wasn't as calm about it as Kaspian was. No dating your coworker or whatever. Ghost and I were a couple from the beginning, but other games had put in that stipulation in the past.

"Kaspian, debrief me," Seraphina ordered.

Kaspian gave her a brief run-down of what had happened. The days we spent with sleepless nights, the ones where we got some respite, and the continuously growing clowns. Olivia interrupted with her own theories about defeating one endgame boss and how that only brought about higher-level bosses. The last one, the top dog, being the most difficult, being giant and golden and all. Seraphina looked at us in shock, surely that wasn't the most outrageous story she had heard or thing she had experienced.

"That's not possible," she finally said after we had finished telling the story.

"I mean, it happened. We all experienced it," I said.

"No, no, it's not that. You only left just a moment ago."

"Huh?" Olivia asked.

"No time has passed since you left."

"But that was a week's worth of hell," Alton defended.

"I believe you. You just returned at the same time that you left. I will inform the Council of Fantasia of your safe return and success battling the darkness. I will say nothing about what transpired with the, um... clowns. All of you are relieved for the day. Please, rest up and eat."

"Seraphina," Kaspian said. She looked over at him and, for a brief moment, you could see they were both relieved that the other was safe and healthy.

"I'm glad you're safe," she said when he didn't say anything else.

We all went our separate ways after that. A week together in hell was too long, and we all needed a break. To have a space that I could call my own was bliss. Well, at first. Every time I tried to close my eyes, it was something new; flashes of clowns, the Glitch, Ghost. It all haunted me, but, most of all, Ghost haunted me. I've let him down. In accepting that I killed people due to the glitch, I was accepting that Ghost was dead.

"I'll avenge you," I whispered.

I won't let him down again.

I rolled over in bed and pulled the blankets over my head. I hated feeling so helpless, so *lonely*.

I lay in the darkness, and my chest tightened. I tried to take deep breaths, but it felt as though there was a rock on my chest, restricting my ability to breathe. I can't use my tacks anymore, not until this was straightened out. But, if I can't use my tacks, my namesake, then *who am I?* I have no memories, no partner, and no name. I am no one. I started sweating, gasping for air. I reached over in the bed to where Ghost would have been. I needed his reassurance. I needed to hear him tell me it was all going to be okay. My hand hit nothing but an empty pillow next to me. I picked up the pillow and threw it across the room.

I fucking hate this.

The only hope I clung to was that maybe the guards in front of my door had some of those herbs Nathaniel gave me. I opened the door, but they were gone; I guess a week together in that shitty clown town was enough to build trust. I went to his room and knocked on the door, but there was no answer. There was no answer for Alton or Olivia either. I didn't know where they would be, but I decided to wander around the castle, with the hope I'd into one of them. In the hallways, along with the typical purple and gold decorations, there were painted portraits of the royals, either alone or with their family, hung on the walls. My favorite was one that was off on its own, down a hallway that led to the kitchen. In the painting, the royals were maybe five and seven. Seraphina had such a cheesy smile, and Kaspian had the chubbiest cheeks. They looked happy, together with their family.

I wondered if I had a family. I mean, Ghost was, and always will be, my family. But, before Ghost, before I joined the Game and agreed to remove my memories, did I have a family? Hell, I was twenty-two when I joined; I could've had a child. Were they mad at me for erasing my memories? Did they even care? In the middle of a crisis across worlds, would they want to know I was still alive? Looking at their picture had me fucked up even more than I had been when I was alone in my room.

"Fuck that," I mumbled, passing by another picture of a happy family. There were over fifty pictures spread throughout the castle: the previous king and queen joining the royals for a yearly family painting and individual pictures, as well. I probably didn't have any *paintings* with my family, but I was missing out on years of memories with loved ones. People who loved me regardless of Character traits, game rating, or social status. Ghost is the only person to love me despite those things, well, *programmed* to love me.

"Thea?" I heard my name. I took a few steps backward and peeked into the library I had just walked by. I looked back inside, and Kaspian was there, sitting at the chess table off to the side. I sat down across from him.

"You should be sleeping," I observed. He was the only one who didn't get to "sleep" like the rest of us did.

"You're up, too."

"Not by choice."

"I could help with that, with magic or potions."

"I was actually coming to find that. But it's okay. I feel like my mind has a lot it needs to figure out right now."

"Are you repenting for something? Don't blame yourself for what happened with the clowns."

"It's not just the clowns."

102

"What else could you blame yourself for?"

"I just," I stopped, thinking about what to say. Ghost was on my mind, but at that moment, my identity was the first thing that came out of my mouth, "Wonder if anyone cares that I survived the Glitch. If there are people out there who I knew before I erased my memories, were they trying to get answers to see if I survived like I'm doing for Ghost? If Ghost is gone, what do I do with the rest of *my* life?"

"Well, I can't speak for anyone in your past. However, if you were to disappear tomorrow, without even a goodbye, I can name at least five people who would be upset, myself included. Regardless, if the roles were reversed, I'm sure your partner would be searching for you, as well."

"Ghost," I groaned. I rubbed my hands on my face. "I feel like I let him down in the clown game. By accepting that I murder people, does that mean that I have to accept that Ghost is dead? Oh god, and does that mean I actually murdered people?"

"Disregard what I said previously and anything my sister has said to you. We, of course, took the report with a grain of salt. No one, and I mean *no one*, expected that to be possible. You will not be tried here for any crime."

"How do you know that?"

"You saved Fantasia. My sister owes you one. Now, do you feel better?"

"No."

"No? That's not the answer I was expecting."

"Well, that did alleviate some stress, but if he really is dead, then I want to avenge him. And, if he's not dead, I won't know until I defeat the Glitch. I don't know if I'll feel better until we fix the glitch."

"I'm sure Ghost—" He made a face when he said Ghost's name like it was weird.

"Hey, now. It's better than ButtBusterBecky." And Kaspian. Who was he to make fun of Ghost's name?

"She didn't go by that name when she was here," he defended himself. "And is Tack180 that much better?"

"I find it harder to respond to *Thea*."

"It's a beautiful name—never mind, we're off track. I'm sure Ghost will appreciate the effort you are putting into finding him, regardless of the outcome. You are more than welcome to stay in Fantasia if the outcome is anything less than desirable."

"I'll think about it." I didn't want to be rude but staying long-term in Fantasia was my backup plan if literally everything else failed.

"No one will force you to stay here. I think we would all like it if you did, but if you choose to travel to different provinces in Fantasia, like Vampira," he stopped and smiled knowingly at me. "Then I won't stop you. But we may try to coax you back. I'm sure I could find some gold confetti for you, and you still need to see the dragons."

"Now you're talking." I laughed, then I sighed. "I'm just really confused."

"I imagine anyone in your position would be." He nodded.

"I really need to bake."

"You bake?" He snorted with laughter.

"Don't judge me, Kaspian. You've never tried my cooking, so how would you know?"

"Okay, fine. Bake me a cake."

"Maybe I will, and it will be the best damn cake you've ever had."

"Let me guess, Ghost thought so? I'm sure he felt obligated to give you that answer."

"No!"

"Was it written in his bio?"

"Olivia told you, didn't she?"

"I don't know what you're talking about."

"You're totally lying." I pointed at him, and he laughed. "Can I use the kitchen or not?"

"I'm sure you could bake in the kitchen tomorrow." Then he smiled and handed me what looked like the same herbs Nathaniel had the first night. "Get some sleep."

"You deserve some, too."

"You aren't the only one atoning tonight."

"Oh. Well, you can share with me, too." I stayed seated. Although, I couldn't tell what he might've felt bad for. He wasn't a bad guy; he maintained composure as much as anyone would've in the clown game, he worked with the others to make me a glove, and he was trying to help me. I could repay the kindness I had received so far.

"Alton and Nathaniel have already told me to stop worrying about it." He shook his head. "Sometimes you just need to sit and think about it."

I stayed where I was and moved a pawn forward. Kaspian looked up at me, shook his head again, and moved his own pawn. We sat in silence, playing chess, for hours. When one game ended, a new one started. It wasn't until the sun started to rise that Alton came in to find the prince. He grabbed Kaspian and shuffled him away over some diplomatic thing that I didn't really care to pay enough attention to. I took that as my own opportunity to return to my room and finally sleep.

"T." A knock at my door. "T?"

I grumbled as I rolled over. Why would anyone be waking me up? Wouldn't I get the day off after saving Fantasia and fighting killer clowns?

"T!" The knock, louder, was followed by Olivia's angry voice. I could only imagine the look in her eyes on the other side of the door.

"Come in," I called, staying in bed.

"I've got a surprise for you!" She entered the room in her typical perky manner.

"What?"

"An empty shop in Castle Town that needs a shop owner."

"So?"

"It's already set up to be a bakery. We bought it for you!"

"You what?"

"Well, Kaspian told Alton, who told me, that you missed baking and I just kind of bought it for you. Stay with us! Be a baker here in Castle Town. The place even has an upper unit set up to be living quarters. You could live there if that would make you more comfortable."

"I'm not moving." I shook my head. The minute Production resumed communications, especially if only with leaders of different worlds, I needed to be in the castle, ready to hear what was said. "And you bought me a bakery?"

"Well, I figured since we don't use the same currency and the communications are down, meaning the currency exchange is down, there would be no way for you to afford anything, even your own breakfast. But I never thought about how you might miss baking. I mean, I know you like it based on your bio, but I just assumed it was one of those Character traits that you might not care about since it didn't really seem like you and—"

"Olivia," I sighed, interrupting her rant. "Okay, this isn't exactly what I wanted, and I can't say I'm not appreciative, but damn. You're clingier than ButtBusterBecky is with SquatsWithSteve."

"Oh, that's a great analogy. Does that mean you took their combo class?"

"Once or twice. Enough to be grossed out by how obsessed she was with him. I stopped going after that. It was a good workout, though. But, anyway, you just bought me a bakery. I don't know how to repay you."

"Well, I may feel slightly guilty," she whispered.

"Why?"

"Well, this thing that you do." She paused and looked at me as if she waited for me to correct her. I wanted to, but I couldn't. She placed a hand on my arm when she noticed I wasn't going to say anything. Or maybe I had some other tell that she caught onto. I sighed but let her keep her hand there.

"It seems to happen during moments of high-stress and near-death experiences."

I nodded.

"Well, I was still playing you when you went back to the Platform that day, and I screamed at you to get out. So, when the glitch kicked in maybe it sent you here because of me."

"Okay…" Pretty sound logic, given the circumstances. But, if that was what happened, I should be thanking her. "I don't think you should feel guilty, then. In regard to Ghost, I'm trying to think of different scenarios, from he is dead to he is being played by a demented Player. What I do know is that the Platform was about to be destroyed by some glitched-out bomb. Given what we have seen of the Glitch so far, right now, there might not be a Platform. Maybe that's why no one can communicate with any Producers because most of them were taken out with the bomb, too. So, if you hadn't called my name, I could have died. Or the portal would have taken me somewhere else. Would I have been just as lucky there as I have been here? I don't know, but I reckon I got lucky with this RPG 'friends are everything' crap."

"T!" She hugged me. "Friends are everything! You're going to be so happy here. This makes me feel so much better. So, are you ready to look at your new bakery?"

"Hell yes, let's go." I smiled, getting a new burst of energy at the idea of baking again.

The bakery was in the southwest corner of Castle Town. The music rang in my ears as we walked through the streets to the bakery, and I noticed the town was livelier than the first night we walked through it. The area was mostly residential, but there was a florist across the way, the beautiful flowers attracting people walking through the streets of Castle Town. The people stopped to smell the flowers, making the area more crowded than the surrounding areas. The bakery itself was perfect. The double doors outside were rounded and the turquoise color made them seem inviting. All the seating for the bakery would be outside, with tables and chairs already set up. Vines were growing up the side of the building, which looked like the perfect place for a romantic date with a fresh-baked cookie for dessert. The oven was immediately on the left side after entering the building. The right side offered a ladder to the upper level, loft-style living, and additional living space.

Ghost would like it.

"This is—" I started.

"Beautiful? Yours? All of the above?"

"Yes, to all."

"You wanna break it in?"

I nodded, trying not to add a little skip, and we got started. I looked at what we had available and got started with Olivia as my apprentice. Usually, I made carrot cake for Ghost, it was his favorite, but I had to work with the materials available to me at the closest market. A light and sweet strawberry cake would do the trick. Plus, it would be a great thank-you cake for Olivia and the rest of the crew. A bakery might not be what I wanted, and it also might be their way of trying to keep me here, but I could use it to help me, as well. Word of my bakery could spread throughout Fantasia and there might be other people stuck out of their games, who might be able to help me. There were a lot of 'might's in that statement, but I'll accept any chance at getting answers as a step in the right direction. We baked the cake and we let it set while I started making the homemade whipped cream.

"Knock," Nathaniel called as he looked inside the door.

"I'm glad you guys came to support T," Olivia said as she beamed then jumped off the counter she was sitting on. The prince and his retainers showing up solidified my idea that they were trying to find a way to keep me here. It showed me that they cared, just like Kaspian said last night. I mattered to them; regardless of my past, regardless of what happens to Ghost, regardless of my freaking Character traits that can be off-putting, these people cared about me. I felt the urge to cry even though I wasn't sad. Was I about to happy-cry?

That's embarrassing.

I focused my attention on the crowd past them, trying to ignore the feeling.

Through the windows and open doors, I could see the people whispering about Kaspian's presence in Castle Town. There was one group that stuck out more than others, sitting across the way. I didn't know Fantasia that well, but at least one of them looked like he was out of his game. He had blue hair and seemed to be wearing a sort of military outfit that wasn't the same as any of the guards and it seemed to be more futuristic than the theme Fantasia had going.

"I'm almost done with the cake if you guys don't mind waiting a little bit," I said. I turned my attention to the cake as I spread the whipped cream across the top.

"You made us a cake?" Alton asked.

"Yes, I owe you all for your hospitality and concern for me, not just during the clown incident but since I got here. Plus, I seriously do love baking. It weirdly relaxes me."

"Fantasia owes you just as much thanks," Kaspian said as he held out a pair of gloves. Just like my original one, the new ones were a perfect pair to protect myself and others from the spread of the darkness. I took off the white ones I had on that matched my fancy castle dress and put the new ones on. "They look good on you."

"Thank you, Kaspian. I really appreciate this." The music in Castle Town started to change. The addition of a piano riff and a faster beat joined in. "Woah."

"Woah, what?" Olivia asked.

"Did you notice the change in music? Can that happen?"

"Your music changed?" Nathaniel asked as he stepped closer. He put an arm around my shoulders.

"Did you do it, Nathaniel?"

"That depends on what the music sounds like."

"What do you mean? Is this a thing, or are you just joking with me?"

"It's very much a thing," Olivia offered more information than Nathaniel. "Castle Town's music is set to intertwine with a Character's experience. Obviously, you have heard the battle music and castle music. But there are other everyday experiences that this world helps accentuate through music."

"Okay, like what?" I asked.

"Love," Nathaniel whispered in my ear.

"Stop it, Nathaniel." I pushed him away.

"Actually, Nathaniel is right this time," Alton offered. "There are a number of variations to the music you will hear ranging from love, friendship, and even those sneaking suspicions that something is wrong. Right now, I hear my music with the friendship riff since all of my friends are around. I would hear the romance riff if it were just Liv and me."

"So, Prince Kaspian changed your music?" Nathaniel squeezed my shoulders.

"What?" I asked as I looked at Kaspian. Kaspian looked away. I don't love him; I love Ghost. "No! Now how do I change it back?"

"Assuming its romance, it won't change until Kaspian's gone." Alton shrugged.

"It's not Kaspian," I reaffirmed.

"Okay, so if it's friendship, then you are stuck with it because it's going to play any time we are around."

"What does it sound like?" Nathaniel asked. "I can solve this in a second if you just let me know. Do you hear the violins?"

"No, I'm not telling you anything."

"Too embarrassed?"

The blue-haired guy and his group were on the move again, pulling my attention away from the group. He looked into the bakery as he was passing by. We made eye contact, and I looked away.

"Is it suspicion?" Nathaniel looked in the same direction I was. Everyone else followed suit like a lame version of 'don't look now.'

"I don't think so. I think he just caught my attention since it's obvious he's out of his game."

"Alright, fine." Nathaniel brought his attention back to the cake; he brought his finger too close, and I smacked his hand just before he touched it. "You really won't tell me what it sounds like?"

"You're acting like a child," Kaspian chimed in. He flicked his hand and Nathaniel's face turned quickly to the side as if he had been slapped.

"So, anyway..." Nathaniel decided to change the topic as I cut the cake then passed around slices of it. "Are you going to live here?"

"No." I was firm in my answer. The loft upstairs was furnished already, so I easily could've, but it wasn't right. Being close to the royals meant answers. Ghost and I also lived together since joining the Game, and I didn't know what it was like to live alone. I didn't sleep well as it was when I had a room to myself; what would happen when I didn't have the crutch of the royal's retainers to fall back on? Besides, it could've been the music with a friendship riff that enhanced my Player experience but being with these people felt a little bit like *home*. "But this place is ready to go, so I would like to get this opened up and selling tomorrow."

Was it necessary to start selling items tomorrow? No, but there was nothing stopping me. The sooner people heard rumors that I was around, the faster I could get answers from other people stuck outside of their game. With comms down, I might not be able to reach out to others, but I can make myself available for others to reach me. Finding and tracking down each individual person in Fantasia who might help me would take too long.

I offered Kaspian a piece, but he turned me down. "I don't enjoy sweets."

"You wanted a cake last night, and you don't even eat sweets? You disappoint me." I shook my head. I turned and handed the cake to Olivia; she immediately shoved it in her mouth.

"Oh my god! I've wanted to try your cakes since I read Ghost's Player description for the first time, and I have to say that you did not disappoint." Olivia ate the cake in two bites and then grabbed another piece. "You're missing out, Prince Kaspian!"

We only stayed there long enough for me to pack the remainder of the cake and bring it back to the castle with me. As we were leaving, Nathaniel and Alton started pimping out the bakery, calling me "The Personal Baker of the Prince and Queen" and begging anyone who walked by to "come to the grand opening tomorrow" because "the prince will be there!" The riff, which I rightfully assumed was for friendship, stayed with my music while I spent the remainder of my night with them, drinking in the alehouse.

***

I woke up early and headed to the kitchen to grab as many supplies as I could before heading to the bakery. Seraphina's grand opening gift was to let me have access to some leftover castle supplies since I decided to open in such a short amount of time. There were already soldiers waiting for me, two of which were my previous guards from my door, that Kaspian and I, after a few drinks, had enlisted in helping me carry supplies to the bakery. We carried wagons full of ingredients down the streets to the bakery. The soldiers helped me unload and then I started baking, doing what I knew best other than fighting, and getting lost in the moment. Drowning out the thoughts of Ghost and how strangely alone I felt outside of the castle.

I decided to make six different options, from sweet to savory, knowing now that the prince wasn't a big fan of sweets. There was: The Queen, which was a sugar cookie with royal icing in the shape of a crown; The Olivia, which was the light strawberry cake I had made the day before; The Prince, which was a quiche with tomato and basil topped with melted mozzarella; The Alton, which was an artichoke and lemon bread pudding; The Nathaniel, a cinnamon roll with cream cheese frosting; and finally, the sixth, The Original, which was my carrot cake. My first customer showed up at dawn and, by the time Olivia and the others made it to me, I had already sold out of half my stock.

As Seraphina joined Kaspian and his retainers, they were followed by a shit ton of royal guards. Seraphina started shaking the hands of the people seated at the bakery, making it a mini meet-and-greet event. The music sped up as the beat changed to intertwine the friendship melody with the Castle Town music. It made me feel warm inside. I was starting to feel just as comfortable with these people as I had been with Ghost. I'd never really tried to make friends earlier; it was in my Character to avoid making friends. Because of that, no one tried to be friends with me either, but I never felt lonely because Ghost was always there. I only tried out of necessity with the royals, but, unlike previously, they are also trying. Hell, they were trying before I was. I want Ghost to meet them and care for them as much as I'm starting to.

I don't want to lose them when this is over.

The streets buzzed with gossip of the queen and the prince visiting a bakery in town. The queen continued to make her way toward me while smiling and waving at her subjects. Their presence boosted customer morale immediately, so I was happy I had saved them all a piece of their own baked goods earlier, so I wouldn't sell out without them getting a chance to try some. I readied their pieces while Seraphina's grand entrance continued.

"What a lovely shop," Seraphina said as she greeted me.

"Thank you, Your Majesty." I bowed down for her.

"I'm proud of you, Thea. I hope you have success with your endeavor."

"You named them after us?" Olivia asked, jumping up and down. She took a seat outside at the closest table to the doors. "Mmm, wow, this carrot cake is to die for. I understand why it gets all the credit."

"You made me a quiche?" Kaspian asked.

"I'm not going to name something after you if you won't eat it. You said you don't like sweets."

"T," Olivia said. "That's really thoughtful."

"So?" I laughed. She hugged me and I didn't push her off.

"I'm just happy you're here," she said. "We all are."

"Okay, okay." I tapped her shoulders. I liked the feeling of being hugged and truly meaning it. But it was so foreign that it still felt uncomfortable; it made me feel nauseous, with a tingling feeling running through my body. I felt myself smile. "I tap out. I gotta get back to work."

"We'll leave you to it," Kaspian said.

"See you tonight, T!" Olivia waved. "Games at the alehouse?"

"Sure." I waved back, the friendship riff fading as they disappeared.

I sold out after that: seating people as fast as I could, rushing to fulfill orders without angering customers. It felt great to bake again; it was comforting and exactly what I needed to keep myself grounded when I felt so confused. The only thing missing was Ghost taste testing everything I made. I was closing the shop, ready to head back home, when I heard a sound upstairs, and my music changed.

It was fast, frantic, and spine-tingling. I climbed the ladder to the top floor and instinctively pinched my fingers; fresh tacks appeared in their rightful place as I looked around. A red cape flashed in my peripheral vision. I flicked the tacks, perfectly outlining the intruder's body and prepared two new ones in my hands as he stopped and looked at me.

"Who are you?" I asked the man with blue hair. It was the same guy from the day before.

"I'm Eros, God of—"

"That's a weird name." I stopped him. I didn't need to hear his spiel. "If we were going to fight, let's get this over with."

"Actually, it's Greek and if you didn't cut me off, you would have heard my whole introduction."

"Fine." I sighed. Maybe we weren't fighting. Maybe he came with information as I had hoped. "What are you doing here?"

"I'm here to kill you." Maybe not.

He lunged forward, pulling out what looked like a stick that then expanded into a sword in a quick, bright light. I dodged as he sliced through the bed. He tried again, pinning me in the tight corner, with his weird sword to my neck. The heavy weight took over as the Game glitched again. I blinked as Eros's head slowly tilted. Time was slowing down until it froze completely. I carefully tried not to touch him, it was the only action that I knew definitively changed things, as I wiggled out of the corner. I didn't know how much time I had, so I moved swiftly as I grabbed his sword out of his hand and wrapped his legs in rope. Nothing happened after I finished tying him up, even though I was safe. I remembered back to the clown game and Kaspian's advice; I took a deep breath, thought of the castle, of Olivia, of Ghost, and of Kaspian handing me the gloves. It didn't work and I needed to finish it before my HP dropped to zero. Getting him out of my bakery would help, so I just touched the guy who unfroze with me.

"What the hell?" He looked around at the world with a purple tint to it. "What's going on?"

"Watch your step," I suggested as he tried to step forward. He fell to the ground. I pointed his sword at him. "Whoever sent you didn't debrief you well enough."

"Obviously not." He looked around, still confused.

"Calm down. It will stop." Sooner or later, *I think.*

"Are we in a parallel world?"

"Dude, you just tried to kill me. I'm not about to tell you shit. Now, why are you here?"

"I'm not going to tell you anything either," he countered.

"I want to be very clear when I say this." I got down to his level on the ground, using his sword to help keep me stable while squatting. "I can kill you right now. Literally kill you, and you won't respawn. I bet you didn't get that intel either."

I threw his sword out of both our reach and pulled off my gloves to expose my glitched hands. The purple haze glowed powerfully as the frozen world around us glitched with it. The darkness covered my hands like a plague as I threatened to touch him. He wiggled his body away, terrified. He clearly wasn't sent by the guild from my first night; surely, they would have warned him of my glitch and ability to kill.

Who sent him?

"Now, what are you doing here, Eros?"

"I'm an assassin from an indie game." He answered me quickly, without stumbling.

"How did you get here? There is no communication with the Platform or other games right now."

"I don't know."

I rolled my eyes. "Okay, then, who sent you?"

"I don't know his name." I reached toward him with my exposed glitched hand. "No, really—it was weird, and I don't remember it. He paid me a lot of money to kill you but always sent a messenger."

"How much did he pay you?"

"A million platinum." Platinum was the only currency that was usable across all games. The exchange rate was different for each game but, either way, it was an extremely generous sum of money.

"Return the money, let this go, and you can go free."

"What?"

"I won't kill you."

I don't want to be a murderer if I don't have to be. I could totally beat this guy in one-to-one combat, anyway.

"I won't report you to the royals. Get out, return the money, and never come back. But, if you do come back, know that I will kill you without a second thought."

He stared at me.

I stood up, grabbed his sword, handed it back to him, and nodded at the window. "Now, go."

He took the sword I extended to him and cut off the rope, watching me carefully. He started to back away slowly, but when he realized I was genuinely letting him go, he ran. He looked out the window and I was sure he saw people frozen in the walkway. He looked back at me in horror. I waved him off, and he opened a window and jumped out. The relief of him leaving, along with the overwhelming weight that I couldn't hold anymore, released from my body and time unfroze. I fell back onto the half-destroyed bed while Nathaniel entered through a different window with his spear ready. When he realized he was too late, he grabbed my gloves and brought them over to me.

"I came as soon as I saw him enter. I'm guessing at one point, time stopped because it didn't feel like it to me, but you look like you've lived a full week in a clown's game."

"What are you doing here, Nathaniel?" I sat up on the bed, and he sat down next to me.

"I came to congratulate you on your first day and escort you home." He handed me a potion. "Didn't think you'd actually need my help."

"I'm not a murderer," I sighed, feeling the need to say that out loud, and then drank the concoction. I didn't want to look weak in front of Eros, because he was trying to kill me, but Nathaniel reminded me so much of Ghost. He put an arm around me. Using my ability to kill to threaten Eros had made me feel the guilt from before all over again. Even as I said it, I hoped it wasn't true. I hoped *none* of it was true. I didn't want to be a murderer.

"I know."

"I don't want Ghost to be dead, either."

"I know," he repeated himself. "I'll stay here in case he comes back. We can head back when you're ready."

"He won't come back."

"You sound confident."

"I'm pretty sure that if we weren't on the same side, and I used my glitched hands to threaten you, that you would be scared, as well."

"Regardless, you need a friend. I'm not going anywhere." The friendship riff filled the void as the music returned to the original Castle Town melody.

"Yeah, I do." I smiled. "Let's just go home now."

Nathaniel helped me close the bakery before we went back to the castle. Before we headed to the alehouse, he insisted we stop by the throne room first, where Seraphina was. Nathaniel explained his version of what happened, and then I explained my version.

"I'm glad to see you are well, Tack180," Seraphina said when we finished talking. "This could've ended differently."

I wondered if she really knew that based on a future she saw or was just speaking about hypotheticals.

"Nothing I can't handle," I said.

"It may not seem like it since you aren't actively pursuing quests, but you are currently *playing* our game in the same way you would yours," she said. "Except, this time, no one is here to play you. You are fully in control of your own actions, and those actions will affect others who are playing this game."

"But the Game is down right now. No one is playing," I countered.

"Living your life is playing our game. You are your own Character and Player," she clarified. "The actions you take, such as letting that man go, could affect others. The man you let get away could attempt to kill another person, and we are still unsure of whether or not those people will respawn."

"But—" I tried to come back with a rebuttal, but I didn't have one. Since I didn't live in *Duty Falls*, situations like these weren't obvious. My actions outside of *Duty Falls* didn't affect those in it. I didn't feel like I was playing a game in Fantasia; it felt like I was living my life. Maybe that's why I hadn't thought of it that way yet.

Is this why people like these types of games?

Every decision I had made affected how the game progressed for me, from running into the prince and his retainers that night to letting Eros go. How did my decision to let Eros live affect the game? Would I be held responsible for his future actions because I didn't have him locked in the dungeons? I took a deep breath.

"You're not in trouble." Seraphina smiled. "I will send my guard after the blue-haired man who did this, and he will be brought to justice. I will also have our guards provide stricter checks to those entering Castle Town. You shouldn't have to worry about an assassin within the castle gates or our town. I will ensure that our city security standards protect not only your life within its walls but the lives of all my citizens."

"Thank you." I nodded.

There was a knock on the door, and Seraphina looked up at the sound and then back to us. Her eyes flashed purple, and there were tears in her eyes that she was holding back.

"If you will excuse me, I'm still dealing with members of the Council of Fantasia." She stood up. "Please see yourselves out."

We bowed and headed out of the room. When Nathaniel opened the door, the woman who cried golden tears and had stood next to the one-eyed man in the throne room was waiting to talk with the queen.

SEVEN

I didn't let anything change my plans the next day. I still opened the bakery and hoped for answers in the process. More people came to visit me the second day, including additional members of the royal guard as protection, but the pool was still limited mostly to residents of Castle Town and the surrounding areas. I won't get answers any time soon at this rate, which was frustrating, but I won't let it hold me back. Eros's attack gave me hope that at least someone out there knew I was stuck here and that I shouldn't be. I couldn't give up yet.

The royal guard walked the streets of Castle Town frequently, still searching for Eros, but the royals themselves didn't visit. I was disappointed they didn't come. It was weird to feel so dependent on people other than Ghost. Even weirder was I wasn't programmed to like these people and yet, here I was, missing people I wasn't programmed to miss. Did that mean I actually liked them, *genuinely* liked them? Would that make the feelings I had for these people more real than the feelings I had for Ghost? No. After seven years with him, my feelings for Ghost became real at some point. But I can't overlook the fact that I, without any interference from the Production team, care about these people.

They're friends.

At the end of the day, I was just as excited to go back to the castle as I had been to go to the bakery in the morning. I was halfway to the castle when the sound of distant screaming caught my attention. I paused to listen. There was a loud bang, followed by crashing sounds. I scaled the roof of a nearby building to get a better view. From there, I could see it; near a bar, so as not to be too noticeable, were two people fighting. One with an obvious, weird, and familiar mechanical sword that was not from Fantasia. *Fucking Eros.*

Every decision I made was important, including the one to let him go. If he was harassing Castle Town civilians, then it was *my* duty to stop him. I jumped down, not fully knowing what to expect or even thinking about what side I would be on.

"Tack180?" Eros asked in disbelief as he saw me.

I didn't say anything back as I assessed the area around me. I was standing in between Eros and a petite female figure. Her skin was green, and her hair made of snakes, she hissed at my inclusion. She wasn't Fantasian.

"Sssorry," she drew out the word. "Too many people."

She twisted her hands, the same way that Kaspian had, and opened a portal. The spinning circle started nearby her, and she pushed it toward me. Eros charged at me, and I dodged him, which put me in the path of the portal. As the portal engulfed me, Eros leaped—making it through the portal with me before it closed. I checked my mini-map, and we were still in Fantasia, just far away from the castle in the middle of an open field. Eros immediately readied for battle again and positioned himself in front of me. Except, he wasn't looking at me. About a hundred yards away, she showed up again.

"Sneaky son of a bitch," she yelled at Eros.

"I prefer resourceful," he yelled back. Then he looked at me. "Don't leave my side or else she will keep sending you to other places."

"Who is she?" I asked, looking around, but there wasn't much in terms of coverage, for her or us.

I can use that to my advantage.

With my dexterity stats, she won't even be able to get a hit in, with or without shelter.

"Medusa. She's from my game originally but had a crossover with a game in Fantasia a few months back. They seem to have given her some new attacks."

"And why are you fighting?"

"Actually, it's because of my failed contract in killing you. But Medusa is just low-hanging fruit in the operation. Another contract killer out of our game is being offered Platinum, so she's just blindly following her orders. I thought staying in Castle Town would trip her up, but she's smarter than I gave her credit for. I could use someone like you on my side. You wanna help?"

No. But, knowing who Eros's boss is could help get some sort of answers about Ghost or even how to get in touch with Production. They had intel on me or at least thought they did, and they got it from somewhere or *someone.*

"If it gives me answers, I guess so."

"Like I said, she's not up there in the operation, so you won't be able to get much out of her, but you can definitely try."

"Then, let's do it," I agreed.

He smiled and then ran at her. I came at her from the other side as she tried to hit me with a stream of white lightning. I easily dodged the attack as Eros got closer to her. She turned on him, and I took the opportunity to advance. By the way she responded, she hadn't been prepared for us to team up. She switched to a defensive approach. Her hands spun as she opened another portal; a roar came through the portal and, in the small area I could see, there was one leg and side body of what I could only assume was a dragon based on the scales on its skin and wings protruding from its body. *Hell no.* Not ready for that shit. She sent the portal straight at me, as she had before, but I dodged it this time. Then I ran forward to close the gap between us. She looked at me when I ran, and her eyes shined a possessed red.

"Don't make eye contact," Eros warned, but it was too late. I was frozen, unable to move. She raised her hand, ready to strike me with white lightning at the same time Eros lunged at her, his sword piercing her chest from behind. He pulled out his sword, and I could feel myself move again. If I kept fighting, I could risk serious injury, and Olivia wasn't here to heal me. With Medusa's power to incapacitate her opponents, it was time for a strategic retreat. I checked my map, verified Castle Town's location in relation to my own, and started running. Eros pulled up on my side, keeping pace with me. I looked back, and Medusa had stood up at the exact moment we made it to the edge of a nearby forest. Eros looked at me. "Don't look back; she can freeze you from far away. Focus on what's in front of you."

We kept running through a dense part of the forest before Eros stuck out his hand. I thought about running past him anyway, but he knew the enemy best. I slowed down with him.

"Why are you stopping?" I asked. Then I laughed. "Are you tired?"

"No," he said, even though he was out of breath. "She wouldn't follow us this far. She'll be waiting for us closer to Castle Town. You sure you want to go back there?"

"Yes." I didn't want to go back there; I *needed* to go back there, even if they couldn't get me the answers I wanted. I cared for them, which was a scarier feeling than the lonely feeling I had when I first wound up in Fantasia.

"Fine," he sighed. "Let's at least rest for a second."

"I'm not traveling with you," I declined. "If you want to rest, then that's on you."

"Let me make sure you get home in one piece. I owe you one, anyway."

"What?"

"After you let me loose instead of killing me, which I truly believe you can do, I decided that I owed you one. So, let me help you get home."

I stopped and looked him in the eye. His face was gentle, but a few visible scars on his face, neck, and hands showed that he had been in many fights in his game and didn't have a healer, like Olivia. I didn't have healers in *Duty Falls* either, so my body was also covered in scars from the more difficult battles; bullets, knives, and the worst from the time my helicopter was blown up mid-flight. At that moment, I felt an odd connection to him.

"You're not scared of me?" I laughed.

"Don't get me wrong, I threw up after I got away from you. But, if you were going to kill people, you would've done it already, right?" I stared at him. I'd stay the hell away from a murderous glitched person. Well, I say that, but I'm actively pursuing the Glitch for answers, so maybe his logic wasn't as flawed as I had originally thought. He kept going, "Besides, after what I saw, you're probably my best bet at getting back home to my world. With your little freezing thing, you're far more powerful than the people who sent me to kill you. So, I'm going to stick with you for a while. Can't have you actually dying on me either, so I need you to stay safe, as well. Let's consider this a mutually beneficial arrangement of protection."

"That just sounds like you're using me."

"Tomato-tomat-o," he said the words in two different ways. "You can expect to see a lot of me."

I started walking away.

"Hey, wait up." He ran after me.

"We're wasting time, and I want to get home. Keep up."

"What should we talk about?" he asked as we kept walking toward Castle Town. I didn't want to talk about anything with him. But, if he was feeling chatty, maybe I could get some answers from him now that he wanted to be friendly.

"Who paid you to kill me?"

"I really didn't pay attention. It was a weird name, and I was focused on the money."

"That's usually all it is for you mercenaries, isn't it?" I laughed. "The royals aren't going to pay you for helping me right now."

"I don't expect them to. But I do have a code that I follow and helping others is part of my code."

"Having a hero-type personality kinda contradicts the fact that you tried to kill me yesterday."

"It's more complicated than that. I'm not a hero; besides, even heroes do whatever they think would be better for the greater good, and sometimes that includes making difficult decisions. I obviously wasn't given the correct intel on you. But the money was nice, and the story they gave me seemed legit. I was told that if I off you, I get the money, sure, but they said that it would help me get home, too. Get everyone home. I was doing what was best for *all* people. I didn't know, and I would never have guessed that you would die. I'm trying to make up for that because I feel guilty. So, let me."

He didn't need to help me with Medusa, especially if she worked for the same person who sent him the first time. He could've turned on me and collected the money again if he wanted to. Instead, he helped me stop Medusa and get away. He didn't seem like a murderer; he was just following orders. My beef wasn't with him but the person who hired him. Besides, making friends with the royals turned out to be such a positive experience. Maybe extending an offer of friendship to Eros would be just as rewarding.

"Fine," I sighed. "And, if you want money, you know, since you lost the reward for me. I need help at the bakery."

"What now?" he asked.

"It would be nice to have a helping hand."

"No, I don't bake." He laughed.

"I can teach you."

"You're serious?"

"If you want to spend time with me, you are going to have to help. I'm not going to wait on you at the corner table every day."

"I actually wanted the spot by the door. It smells the best." I stared at him, waiting for his reply. "Fine. I can help."

"But I swear to God, if this is just a way for you to try to kill me again, then I won't hesitate like I did at the bakery. I'll kill you on the spot," I warned. I wouldn't, but I didn't want him to think I was soft. I took a step toward him and took off my glove to expose my glitch. "Have I made myself clear?"

"Crystal." I smiled, hearing a bit of myself in him. He lifted up a hand and raised it next to his face then put the other hand on his chest, over his heart. "Let's make a pact. I vow not to kill you."

It would be good to have another ally on my side. Not that the royals aren't helpful, but there was something about Eros. He didn't remind me of Ghost, like Nathaniel. Maybe it's that he reminds me of myself a little bit. I didn't know. But it was nice having him around. *Shit.* Maybe this is the product of spending too much time in friendship-happy Fantasia. Maybe I want to make friends now.

"Okay, I won't kill you either," I agreed.

"Let's get moving, then, partner." He smiled.

"Don't call me that." I rolled my eyes.

Ghost is my only partner.

We jogged for an hour or two, fighting off ogres, wolves, and imps easily between the two of us before we stopped to rest. I sat down on a log, and Eros sat across from me. Fighting alongside Eros was easy; he didn't try to tell me what to do, like Kaspian or Olivia. He saw my moves and adapted. Fighting in a two-player system was normal for me; it felt like I was fighting with Ghost again. I only had to worry about myself and one other person, not a group of other people. I was stuck with him, but at least he knew what he was doing. It made running through this world a hell of a lot more *fun*.

Eros took out his sword, opened and closed it in a flash of blue light before officially sheathing it again on the side of his hip. Show off. It was an interesting weapon, though, not just in the way it looked, but as a choice for his Character. Most Characters who were representing the Greek god, Eros, all used a bow and arrow combo as their weapon. Not that Eros was similar in any way to other representations that I had seen, but personalities were always different between Characters— weapon choices, not as much.

"So, if you're supposed to be Eros, why don't you use a bow and arrow?" I asked.

"I do." He shrugged.

"You've only used a sword when I've seen you."

"I have my preferences and my reasons." He shook his head as he rolled his shoulders back and stretched his arms out. "So, where's Ghost?"

"I don't know." I knew he was trying to divert the conversation, but a feeling of loneliness rushed through my body, regardless.

Guess it worked.

My chest tightened at the sound of his name. I turned away, trying not to let him see the outward effect his question had on me. Even if he was on my side, for now, I didn't want him to have anything to use against me in the future. The real way to get under my skin was to bring up Ghost and the fact he was gone. I bent down to stretch my legs, so I didn't have to look back up at him. "I'm still trying to figure that out."

"I'm sorry. I know how it feels to lose someone."

"You lost someone to the Glitch?" I looked up at him.

"No. But it's basically the same thing. My dad joined the Game and my—" He stopped himself. "Well, my dad joined the Game."

"Oh, he chose not to keep his memories?" I caught onto the moment of vulnerability he showed me. I didn't want him to use my vulnerabilities against me, so I'd give him the same courtesy. He wanted to talk about his dad, not the other scenario and I wasn't going to pry. Besides, I didn't know him well enough to tease him like I would with the others.

"He was my best friend. I tried to keep going as if I didn't care, but I missed him. The Character they made him into... It's so much like him, it's as if he's still there. They didn't let me join his game directly, so I joined a different game in his world. I see him every day in my game and it's as if he sees right through me."

I wondered how much of my past self I retained. I rolled my eyes instinctively while waiting for the Voting Forum and everyone voted on that action but were they just solidifying a trait I already had?

"I'm so sorry. I had no idea—" I tried to say something. I couldn't shake the implications of not keeping my memories. Those close to you are forced to sign a non-disclosure agreement. So, even if Eros wanted to tell his father how they were related, he couldn't. Would his father even believe him? If someone came up to me right now and said they were related to me, I would probably laugh and think they were trying to get their fifteen minutes of fame. Eros was just as lonely as I was.

"I wouldn't expect you to. We just met."

We were silent for a few minutes, and I realized Eros wasn't going to go out of his way to talk about it anymore. I felt for him more than I wanted to admit. Our backgrounds weren't exactly alike, but he seemed to pull me in. Not only that, but he had me questioning my relationship with a family I could have had before and no longer knew. As he was on the opposite side of the situation than me, he could help me understand if I was screwed or not with my own family. It reminded me of my own concerns: was there anyone out there worrying if I had survived or not?

"Do you worry if he survived the glitch or not?" I asked, finally breaking the silence.

"Of course."

"You don't hate him enough to forget about him?" I asked.

"I might be mad at him, but I still love him. I'll check up on him and the rest of my family when comms are back up. I take it you didn't keep your memories?" he asked.

I slowly nodded. "It didn't bother me before. But..."

"But... now you're alone in the middle of a crisis, without anyone you know, you're left wondering if there's anyone who even cares that you made it out of the glitch that day?"

"Is that how you feel?" I turned it back on him. I wasn't going to admit anything that easily.

"I think anyone stuck out of their game feels that way, especially with comms down. But it seems like your friends care a lot about you," he offered.

"Yeah," I laughed as I stood up. *My friends.* "I'm loyal to more than just Ghost now. That's why I'm trying to get back to them. Let's get moving."

"You got it, boss."

We continued the trek back to Fantasia through the night. We were completely in sync as we took out the low-level monsters that had extremely obvious and easy weaknesses. Even though I was stuck in unfamiliar terrain with a complete stranger, I was more confident in myself than I had been that first night in Fantasia. I was aware of how Fantasia operated, and I knew that, regardless of what he had tried previously, the guy I was with wasn't trying to kill me at the moment. It was dusk as we made it to the edge of the forest at the outskirts of Castle Town. Just before we exited the woods, he grabbed my arm and slowed me down. We left the forest completely and had an unobstructed view of the castle and Castle Town. Waiting just shy of the gates was Medusa, just as Eros said she would be. Eros and I looked at each other.

"You ready for another round?" he asked.

"Yup." I nodded. She started attacking before we closed the gap. The guards at the Castle Town entrance locked the gates then looked over at what was happening. As long as one of them could get the word out that the blue-haired guy they had been looking for was found, we'd have back up momentarily. Even better, as he was with me, they would hopefully call on the royals or their retainers. We just needed to hold her off and let the royals deal with her however they wanted once they showed up. Eros and I charged, dodging her attacks just as we had the first time. This time, however, she wasn't fazed by the fact we were working as a team. She expected it and adjusted her fighting style to keep us both back.

I focused on her hands as we ran forward, not making eye contact with her to avoid being frozen. I might not see where she was looking, but I could tell when she was trying to open a portal or raise her fist to rain lightning down on us.

"T," I heard Olivia yell.

Medusa looked back at Olivia and raised her hand. Alton ran into Olivia, pushing her out of the way of the lightning strike. Just as I had hoped, the guards called the royals in for backup. Well, everyone but Seraphina, but I didn't expect the queen to come out when she had other shit to deal with. Medusa was ill-equipped to battle all of us; her magic didn't even begin to compare to Kaspian's. He struck her with ice, freezing her in place, as they closed in on her. Guards followed behind Kaspian as he stopped to take Medusa into custody.

"We need more guards over here," Alton called out as he came running toward us. I stood in front of Eros; they didn't know we were cool now.

"Wait," I said. Eros stuck up his hands. "I need to ask you to pardon him."

"You want us to pardon him?" Kaspian asked as he joined us.

"T, this guy tried to kill you," Olivia said.

"Actually," Eros popped his head out from behind me. "We've come to an arrangement. She won't kill me, and I won't kill her. So, we good?"

"No, we're most certainly not good." Kaspian stood his ground.

Eros slowly took a step out from behind me and closer to the group before finally kneeling down on one knee in front of Kaspian. I didn't know what he was about to do, but he was confident in his motions like he knew how to gain a royal's trust.

"Prince Kaspian of Castle Town and—whatever, Prince of Fantasia," he started. "I pledge my life to Tack180. I will protect her in the same way that your retainers pledge their lives to you. Yes, I was contracted to kill her, but I had no idea of the implications of my actions. I mean, who would? I think the most important questions, and your wrath, are better directed at the people who hired me."

"You're a smooth-talker," Kaspian offered. He looked at me and raised an eyebrow. I nodded. "Cross her or anyone in my kingdom, and I assure you, I will make sure you suffer a fate worse than respawning."

"You got it, boss." Eros smiled and stood back up.

The royals prepped a room for Eros and let us rest before training again. It was midday when we reconvened in the library. No one messed with Eros while we slept, and I appreciated their trust in my decision. He genuinely seemed like a nice guy who was caught up in something he didn't mean to be and talking with him gave me hope. I wondered if what he said about his father was true and, if it was, did that mean that there was hope for me? After getting answers for Ghost, should I pursue answers about my family? Maybe, in meeting them, I'd get more answers as to why I joined the Game to begin with and, when given the option to keep my memories, why I chose to erase them. I was staring at Eros, thinking about what he had said about his father and his missing memories. We were all seated in the library. Kaspian and Alton were, in fact, reading books on magic, which is what the rest of us were supposed to be doing, as well, but we were talking instead. Although, after he noticed we weren't doing anything, Kaspian pulled me aside and started our practice.

While we trained, the others focused on researching magic, as they tried to link similarities from the magic Kaspian and Seraphina used to the glitch. Training went on for hours as Kaspian tried to help me open a portal by swirling my hands. The movement felt so foreign and stupid that I couldn't try any harder, even if I wanted to. There were times when I threw my hands up and walked away for a moment, collected myself, and then returned. Usually, the others would try to give Kaspian updates whenever I threw a fit and rage-quit. It seemed like they hadn't gotten anywhere either: there wasn't much to connect the glitch to magic, other than the color and the portals. As much as I wanted to say the whole thing was pointless and keeping me away from doing real work that would help me find answers, I knew it wasn't true. There was nothing else I could do and maybe it *was* something I could control. I didn't want to stop practicing; it was just extremely frustrating.

"I don't want to practice anymore," I said after the others gave their most recent update to the prince. "I'm done for today."

"Wait." Kaspian followed me as I started walking toward the door. "You'll get the hang of it."

"I don't want to hear RPG positivity right now," I said. "I just want to be angry and that's ok."

"How about a game of chess?" he offered. "You can be as mad as you want, and no one has to talk about it."

I sighed. It was a tempting offer. Playing chess with Kaspian previously helped me alleviate some of the stress I had felt thinking about Ghost, my past, and killer clowns at night. I nodded, and we walked toward the chess table.

"I'll let you be white," he offered.

"Are you serious?" I laughed.

"What?"

"You want me to go first, giving me an advantage, so I don't feel as bad?"

"That—" He tried not to laugh. He knew he was caught. "That was not my intent."

"Oh my god." I laughed again. "Now you're lying about it."

"Okay, okay. You can be black. I'll be white."

"Now *you* want to have an advantage," I teased him further.

"Tack180, please sit down and play the game." He tried to be serious. "I should've offered the dragons instead."

"You chose to offer me chess over dragons?" I moved a white pawn forward, and he shook his head with a smile. "Prince Kaspian—"

"Kaspian is fine," he interrupted.

"Good. It felt weird still speaking to you so formally. Now, Kaspian, you don't have to make me feel better. It's not your job."

"I don't think of it as a job. Besides, I don't like it when you're upset." I looked up at him as he moved his pawn forward. He had blonde hair and blue eyes, just like his sister. His hair had this wave in it like it wanted to curl. It added a softness to his overall muscular build; it was kinda cute. Just briefly, it seemed like my music changed. Instead of the usual friendship riff, there were violins for a short moment before he said, "None of us do."

"Right." I smiled. "Ghost used to complain about the wrath of Tack180 all the time. I get it. I just feel like we are so close to answers and still so far away from them. We think we know something, like the similarity of the glitch to magic, and we can't capitalize on it."

"If you want answers, why don't you try Vampira?" Eros asked from the table he sat at with the others. We all looked over at him.

"I do love a good trip to Vampira," Nathaniel sighed.

"Yeah, T, to tell you the truth, I was actually in Vampira when the Glitch hit." Eros was leaning so far back in his chair–I expected him to fall over. "I didn't tell you earlier because I was there to kill you, you were scary, and it didn't seem appropriate to tell you how I actually got here. Especially since I was living there."

"How would Vampira help us?" I asked.

"Medusa, yours truly, and a few others from my game make frequent visits to Vampira, which are typically paid for by our employer back home. There are a lot of out-of-gamers stuck there. Not just Characters, either. I once got a lap dance while sitting next to a Producer from a different game. I'm just saying it might be worth a visit."

"Producers?" I stood up quickly, knocking over some of the chess pieces.

"That's very astute of you, Eros," Olivia said. "We could ask the queen about a trip to Vampira. I think Ambrosio might still be around here somewhere, as well."

"Let's go now," I said. "This could be our big break. We could finally find some answers."

"Alton," Kaspian said. "See if my sister is available to talk to us."

"Yes, sir." Alton nodded and headed off.

"I'll join him." Olivia ran after him.

"Ambrosio's a unique name," Eros said. "I feel like I've heard it before."

"He's this annoying guy from Vampira," I said. "He was staying in the castle for a few days with his muscle, Hawthorn."

"Hawthorn?" Eros asked. Then he moved his hands in a way to outline a person of large stature. "Big, tall, ripped, vampire hunter, whose so hairy he's probably a werewolf, who walks around with an axe?"

"Do you know him?" I laughed.

"The names were familiar, but if I just described the right guy, then he's the one that contracted me to kill T."

"To my sister—now," Kaspian demanded.

We immediately turned around and rushed to the throne room, beating Alton and Olivia who ended up running after us.

"Thea," Queen Seraphina greeted, then turned to Eros. "And you are?"

"Thea?" Eros asked.

"Well, I certainly don't believe your name is also Thea," she laughed to herself.

"Thea is my normal people name here so that I blend in better," I clarified for Eros, then turned back to Seraphina, "this is Eros; he just said Hawthorn was the one who contracted him to kill me."

"What?" Her eyes flashed purple for a split second. "Kaspian."

Kaspian opened a portal immediately without questioning what Seraphina wanted. She turned to Olivia and gave her a nod. Olivia started toward the portal, and I followed. When Eros got close, Seraphina held out her hand. "We don't need you."

"But—" Eros tried.

"Begone." She waved him off. Kaspian stepped closer to the portal, ready to follow us and Seraphina shot him a look I never wanted to be on the receiving end of. "We also don't need you."

"But—" Kaspian parroted Eros.

"*We* don't need you. Let's go, ladies."

EIGHT

She pushed us forward, and we stumbled through the portal into an office area where a receptionist was working behind a desk. The receptionist worked under a black light and wore a neon dress, which was emphasized with the lighting. There was a potent but soft floral smell, like jasmine, wafting through the room. The music, unlike Castle Town's fast beat, was a sensual single instrument saxophone melody.

"Welcome to Vampira. How may I help you?" The young woman asked before looking up from a computer screen. "Oh, Queen Seraphina! How may I help you today? Male? Female? Both? At the same time?"

Seraphina ignored her as she began to walk past the desk.

"He's not in right now." The receptionist stood up.

"We both know he is."

Seraphina swiped her hand in the air, and the girl went flying backward. She walked forward, with Olivia and I on her heels, and stuck her hand out. The door behind the receptionist flew open, exposing Ambrosio behind a desk, writing something down with Hawthorn standing over him. Ambrosio stood up, and Hawthorn swung an axe over his shoulder.

"Queen Seraphina," Ambrosio acknowledged.

"Cut the small talk." She snapped her fingers, and the two men's mouths glued shut. "I will let one of you, and only one of you, talk at a time. You will answer me truthfully, or you will pay. Now, I know Hawthorn wouldn't make any decisions like this on his own. So, Ambrosio, why did you put a hit out on Tack180?"

She swung her hand, and Ambrosio answered. "I just wanted to scare her, that's all. A little respawn never hurt anyone."

"But it does, does it not?" She squinted her eyes and a cut spread across Ambrosio's face. Olivia immediately healed him. "Did you feel that pain?"

He nodded.

"Did you feel it?" she demanded again.

"Yes, My Queen."

"Respawn or not, Tack180 would have felt a significant deal of pain. Hawthorn, I'll ask you, why did you do it?"

Hawthorn stayed silent and stared at Seraphina. Her eyes tightened and Hawthorn groaned.

"We have two members of Production here. They were visiting when the glitch happened," he finally gave away.

Members of Production, just like Eros said could happen. We needed to find them. If I could only explain the situation to them: I could get answers about what happened to Ghost and find out for real if he was dead or alive.

"They asked for you to place a hit on Tack180?" Seraphina closed Hawthorn's mouth again and moved back to Ambrosio.

"No. One of them mentioned it might be helpful. We took matters into our own hands at that point," he answered. "Of course, we tried to avoid harming our relationship with Fantasia by sending a contract killer, but they ended up returning the money."

"Where are they?" Seraphina asked.

"I'll show you. Just let me go."

She let them go, and both Ambrosio and Hawthorn started out of the room. We followed them down a series of corridors, twisting and turning through hallways lined with doors with moaning behind them. Finally, they stopped and knocked on a door.

"It's us," Hawthorn mumbled.

"Come in," a female's voice called.

They opened the door, and a man and woman were sitting on a bed. The man was reading a book, and the woman was staring at a computer screen. They stopped and looked at who entered the room. When they realized it was more than just Ambrosio and Hawthorn, they put down their work.

"So, you *are* alive," the man said, staring at me.

"Can you tell us more about that day? Look at your hand!" The woman started looking at my hands. "How does it affect your day-to-day life? Can you still function?"

"Hardly," the man answered before any of us could say anything. "Looks like she needs a reset like I said."

"I don't know," the woman said. But the man had already grabbed a computer and started typing. They were moving and talking faster than I could process.

"This shouldn't hurt," he said to me. "And when it's done, you'll be reset, and so should your entire game, even Ghost."

"No," I finally had the chance to say. He had lifted his finger in an exaggerated motion as if pressing that next button would reset me. I didn't have time to explain, so I shouted, "Don't reset me."

He scrunched his face as if he didn't understand and started moving again. Seraphina waved her hand, and he rolled on the bed, away from the computer. He laughed and then pulled out a smaller tablet-like item from his pocket. He did something on the tablet then reached for his computer again. Seraphina flung her arm a second time, but nothing happened.

"You forget, I'm a Producer," he said.

"What did you do to me?" Seraphina yelled.

"I turned off your powers. Don't worry. It's just a dampener that works while I'm around."

I took a fighting stance, and then I felt a heavy arm grab me from behind. I could still see Ambrosia out of the corner of my eyes, so it had to be Hawthorn. If they reset me, then I would die; actually die, not reset like they think would happen. I wasn't about to let that happen. I threw my head back as hard as I could and heard Hawthorn groan. Warm liquid splattered on my head from wherever I hit Hawthorn as a feeling of heaviness began to take over. It was the perfect time for the Game to glitch again.

I turned around, and frozen Hawthorn was nursing a bloody nose. Good, he deserved it. I took a moment to look at the room. Hawthorn was the muscle, so I used some rope I found around the room to tie his legs together. I took one of the fuzzy cheetah print blindfolds that I found in the room and put it over Ambrosio's eyes. The woman was sitting comfortably on the bed. I still threw a blanket over her just in case. For the guy, I closed his computer and held onto it. I returned to a defensive position in front of Seraphina and Olivia, where I felt a little more comfortable and tried to calm my body down. Just like with Eros, I couldn't control the glitch, and I watched as my HP continued to drain. I touched Olivia and, when she realized what was happening, she waved her staff over me.

"I got you, T," she said. But nothing happened. Whatever dampener the man used on Seraphina also worked on Olivia. I tried to produce a tack, but that didn't work either. She handed me a potion instead. "Don't let your HP drop too low."

"I can't get it to unfreeze," I said. My heart rate increased as I thought about the glitch, slowly killing me, in front of a healer whose powers were dampened.

Just my luck.

"You got this," she offered. "Think about the things that make you happy, the same way you did last time."

I thought about frosting a cake, watching the frosting swirl as it mixed. It helped but didn't bring it down completely. Deep breath. The faster we finished this, the faster I could get back to my bakery, to my friends, to my safety, to Nathaniel, Alton, and Eros. To Kaspian and playing chess with him. They all started moving again at once: confusion and yelling replacing the once frozen scene.

"What the hell?" the man asked as his hands went to type on nothing but the bed in front of him.

"Looking for this?" I held up his computer.

"How did you do that?" The woman asked in amazement. Her hair was messy from pulling the blanket off.

"If you guys gave me a chance to explain things, you would have known. But one pump over here was a little premature." I took off one glove to expose a glitched hand.

"Would you look at that!" The female stood up and walked closer to me.

"He touched me."

"Who touched you?"

"Ghost, while the Glitch got him."

"That would be consistent with the reports," the man said, joining the woman examining my hand after he adjusted his shoelaces. "But still doesn't answer what happened."

"We will continue this conversation at our castle," Seraphina interrupted.

"My Queen," Ambrosio started.

"No." Seraphina shot him a look that could kill if her powers weren't dampened. "You have been privy to more information than you both deserve. We will be taking the rest of this conversation to the privacy of our castle, where the Producers are more than welcome to stay. You may send their items via portal by no later than the end of the day."

"Of course," the woman said. "I think we'd both like to look into this further."

"Understood, Your Majesty," Ambrosio bowed.

The Producers packed up the necessities they didn't want to leave behind and then followed us back to the reception area. Seraphina looked at the man until he fumbled around on his controls so the receptionist could open a portal for us back to the castle. The portal opened to the throne room, where all the boys were waiting for us. As we walked through the portal, Nathaniel straightened out his appearance and then took a step toward the female member of Production we brought back with us.

"My lady," he bowed.

"You're not my type," she answered without even looking at him. Nathaniel looked devastated.

"Let me try again. That really wasn't my best line."

"I would, but you would just be making a fool of yourself, and that's not fair to you. You're not my type, and that should be enough."

"What is your type? I'm sure I can—"

"Long, blonde hair." The girl looked at the queen.

"I mean, that's a simple change." Nathaniel's eyes darted back and forth as he attempted to adjust his controls.

"She's not into guys," the man finally said, placing a hand on Nathaniel's shoulder. The woman just laughed, happy that she almost got Nathaniel to change his whole appearance.

"You got a little blood on your—" Eros pointed to his head as he looked at me.

"Who's injured?" Kaspian asked.

"Hawthorn." I smiled. Eros held up a hand indicating he wanted a high-five, and I met it with my own. "I just need to clean up."

"Meet our newest guests," Seraphina announced as she displayed her open arms at the Producers. "They will be staying with us and helping us determine the cause of the Glitch and how to resolve the issue."

"Technically," the girl started, "we didn't really agree to anything yet, but are very curious about the incident that occurred and would like to determine a workable solution for all people involved."

"Including ourselves, since we are stuck," the guy agreed.

"And you are?" Alton asked.

"I'm Isabella," the girl said, with an accent that accentuated the "e" sound at the beginning of her name. "But you can call me Isa. I'm in technical support for the Production team on several games."

"I'm Bryce," the other said. "I'm a lead Producer on Tack180's game."

I looked over at him, surprised and a little more understanding of the fact that he wanted to reset me less than five minutes ago. He knew me almost as well as I knew myself; he could have even helped create the person I am.

"Tell me," Eros asked. "Was she always meant to be so pig-headed, or did something go wrong in production?"

"She was always like that, even before joining the Game." He winked at Eros.

"That's not fair," I said. "My past is off-limits for anyone who has questions about it, especially nosy people in this room."

If anyone deserved to know about my past, it was me.

Hell, I wanted to ask him a million questions. But all of them came flooding to my head at the same time, and I couldn't keep track of what questions were important and others that I was curious about more than anything else. *No.* I wanted to know all of them, important or not. I just didn't want to do it with everyone else around. I didn't want to do it without Ghost. I was in the middle of one trauma; I couldn't deal with another one until the first book was closed, whether that meant I actually found Ghost or just got confirmation of my suspicions.

"Agreed." Bryce stuck out a hand and, right before we shook, he pulled back. "Is it safe?"

"With a glove, yes, but don't touch the glitch without one."

"You call it a glitch." Isa held out her hands, and I took off a glove and hovered it over hers. "Can you tell me more?"

I partially filled in our companions. I didn't trust them, so I didn't tell them everything and tried to skim over the finer details.

"And the gloves help?" Isa asked, caring more about the story than Bryce.

"It doesn't hurt when I wear them because they have healing properties, but other than that, any glove could act as a barrier."

"I wonder if the relation to your weapon and your hands has anything to do with the whole killing people thing," she mused out loud. "You produce unlimited tacks from your hands with the way your code is written, but your hands are glitched. If your weapon were a solid object, like a sword or spear, would the outcome still be the same?"

"I don't know if I'm willing to kill more people," I declined, not wanting to give her ideas about testing her theories.

"No, just a computer-generated NPC. Watch." She flipped open a tablet and pressed on the screen before a copy of Bryce showed up in front of us. He opened his mouth to talk, and a "moo" came out instead. "No feelings, no emotions, murder friendly."

"Wait." Eros stopped me before I made any movement. He took out his sword and stabbed the NPC straight through the heart. The NPC fell to the floor, flashed a few times, and then reappeared. He had a look of satisfaction on his face. "Go ahead."

"Was that necessary?" Bryce asked.

"We needed a control condition in the experiment." Eros smiled.

I pinched my fingers, two tacks, one in each hand, appeared. I threw one out with a flick of my wrist as it shot straight through the NPC's head. The NPC disappeared. "Interesting," was all Isa said under her breath as she created another copy of Bryce. Alton stepped up and handed me his sword; I stabbed the NPC through the heart. The NPC fell to the ground, flashed, and then reappeared – as it had when Eros stabbed him. Isa smiled, and Olivia clapped.

"Congratulations. You're not broken, Tack180—just your hands." Bryce patted me on the back.

"So, would I still die?"

"Well, technically, since you are glitched, there is still a possibility of that, and I can't test that theory without the risk of actually killing you. So, I'm just going to say err on the side of caution and try not to let your HP fall too low." Isa was not as confident in her answer as she was the first time. "Can I continue to study you?"

"She's not a science experiment, Isa," Bryce intervened. "She's a lethal killing machine, and she needs a new weapon."

Bryce looked at me like he could see through my clothes, observe my muscles and their limits, and my new outfit's necessary modifications. He took out a tablet and started messing around with it. I felt my arms fly up into a T shape, the feeling similar to when I was in the Voting Forum.

"Hey," Eros said, taking a step toward him with his sword. "What are you doing?"

"Calm down, lover boy. I'm upgrading your friend here."

"I'm not her—whatever, just don't hurt her."

My warrior princess outfit changed to a darker shade of black, a cross-body belt with pockets for potions and other small items showed up in addition to the tactical belt, and then I was holding throwing knives. My body's stance changed, my arms holding the knives in my hand as if I were going to throw them. Isa, understanding what Bryce was going for, brought up another NPC. I threw the knife, the NPC fell, blinked, and then reappeared. Bryce smiled at his work, then held up a finger to indicate he wasn't done. I felt my hair fall, then pull back up, two knives assisting my hair to stay in place.

"Alright, Tack180. You're rigged up to hold six throwing knives. You got two in the new pocket attachments on your thighs, two in the belt, and two in your hair. They are not linked to your person as an unlimited item because then they would be considered 'hand weapons.' " He made quotation marks with his hands. "So, if I set them up to respawn after a throw, if broken, or what have you, then you will be in the same situation as you were with your tacks. The ones you have on now are technically cosmetic but still sharp as fuck, so they will do the job. I also added an update that should be sending any second now to upgrade your fighting style slightly, you can still fight with your tacks, but I also added throwing knives in there. Since that isn't a big change from your previous fighting style, you didn't need a reset for it."

"Can you upgrade me?" Olivia asked in amazement.

"No, I'm a Producer for Tack180's game. I know her code like the back of my hand and have unlimited access to it."

"Give it a shot, T. I want to take some data," Isa said.

She set up a few more NPCs for me to shoot at. I pulled out the throwing knives from my thighs first. I spun them around in my hands then, just as I had with my tacks, flicked my wrists and sent them flying. Dodging, athleticism, and acrobatics seemed the same. I did a couple of flips, pulled knives from my hair next, and threw a knife while upside down. After I landed, I threw the other two left. I grabbed them out of the belt and held onto them. I felt a hand on my arm—Bryce. He pulled my arm up and examined the knife I was holding, still holding onto my arm the whole time. He took the knife out of my hand and put it in the belt holster. He pulled it in and out a few times, testing its speed. He nodded in approval. Then, with the same knife, he tested the thigh holsters.

"I think you've done enough," Seraphina finally said. Bryce backed away. She turned to Isa, "Did you get the testing done that you needed?"

"Enough for now. We can call it a night."

"Very well. I ask that next time you test Tack180, please do so in our designated training area. Although she has impeccable aim, I would prefer nothing in my castle is broken in the process. Olivia, show our guests to their quarters, please."

"Yes, Your Majesty." Olivia bowed and then started walking. "Please, follow me."

"Well?" Seraphina asked after they left the room. "You seem to have more answers than you did previously."

"Some," I answered.

"Is that all?"

She eyed me, and I looked away. I didn't know how to process any of what had just happened. I felt more comfortable than I had since waking up in Fantasia. Finding Bryce and Isa meant that I was one step closer to my goal of figuring out what happened to Ghost. I should have been happy. I *was* happy, but I also felt guilty. Getting answers about Ghost meant leaving my new friends. But how much of what I felt for them was real? How much of what I felt for Ghost was real, for that matter? Did I truly love him, or was I only programmed to love him? Since he was gone, would that love fade? I had too many questions and wanted to be alone—instead, I had five people staring at me, wanting to know what I was thinking and to talk about how this *changed* things.

"I need to go," I finally said, unable to accept the silence any longer.

"That's it?" Alton asked.

"Yes," Eros answered for me. "We're leaving."

"No," I stopped him. "*I'm* leaving."

"Are you leaving Fantasia?" Nathaniel asked. There was concern in his voice that made me feel happy that he cared whether I stayed.

"I want to be by myself, and I want you all to respect that." I stuck my hands up and started walking backward. No one made any indication that they would follow me, so I turned around and kept walking out of the room, out of the castle, and out of Castle Town. I had been looking forward to getting answers and, now that I was at the cusp of getting those answers, I didn't want them anymore. Based on what I had seen with the NPC and how Bryce said my hands were broken, I felt like it was the worst-case scenario, and that terrified me more than no answers at all. At least without answers, I could still hold hope that I'd be able to find Ghost or fix this. Things seemed a little more final now.

Once I made it out of Castle Town's front gates, I just kept walking along an unmarked path. Most monsters stayed away from the path, and I passed by a few other travelers, like merchants going to Castle Town. The first place along the path was a little city by the water. There were quite a few large ships in the port, considering how small the city was. There were three different shops for weapons, armory, and items, two inns, a couple of houses, and one bar. I walked through the town, and barely anyone looked at me. I was out of place, but so were many of the other people staying there.

I entered the bar; it was full of pirates who all cheered when I walked in and began singing a shanty. I pushed my way through the singing seamen to the bartender, I raised a finger, and he poured me something. I grabbed it, threw some spare gold on the countertop, and found a corner. Another person entered and the pirates cheered again, beginning a new song. I had avoided the bakery because I didn't want anyone to find and bother me, so I hunkered down in the corner of the bar and drank alone.

The pirates cheered again, and I mockingly lifted my glass. *So annoying,*

"That's the stuff, lassie." A nearby pirate banged his cup against mine, spilling some of its contents. "Sing with us."

I smiled, but I didn't know their songs, so I just nodded along.

"I'm Captain Baldassare of the *Obsidian Rose*." I nodded in acknowledgment. He cheered and handed me another cup. "Drink."

The more I participated with the pirates, the more they provided me with drink and, the more I drank, the more I genuinely *wanted* to participate. In no time, I was cheering along with the rest of them. The pirates were a good distraction. But they were just that—a distraction. I needed to go back and figure out what this meant for me. Or at least talk it out with someone more level-headed than myself, like Kaspian.

"To Tack180," they cheered for me. It felt so good to be myself. I wasn't pretending to be Thea, and I didn't need to worry about how my actions affected others. I could just drink, and that felt *damn* good.

"To the pirates." I raised my glass.

"We be heading out now, lassie. Will ya be joining us?"

"I've got my own treasure to find," I declined.

"If ya find yourself roamin' the seas, give us a holler. Off we go, men!" Captain Baldassare yelled. "The sea waits for no man."

The men cheered as they left the bar, which left just me and a passed-out patron. *Time to go.* I shook my head, downed the new drink, and started the walk back to Castle Town. Except, it was nighttime in an RPG world, so it wasn't guaranteed to be a peaceful walk. I didn't really feel like battling any monsters, so I started and used the go-to method of run the fuck away, especially if you see a high-level monster that you aren't equipped to battle. Running got me to the outskirts of Castle Town in record time. Castle Town's music rang in my ears as I found my way to the castle. I found Nathaniel and Eros in the alehouse. I gave them a wave but didn't stay. That's not what I *need* right now. I walked to the library next, where Kaspian was studying the books we were looking at before going to Vampira.

"Hey." I knocked on the library doors. He looked up from the books.

"Tack180, to what do I owe the honor?"

"I was hoping you would play a game of chess with me. I could use a friend right now."

"I'd never turn you down." He smiled and joined me at the chess table. The same violins from before intertwined with the music, adding a softer melody instead of the usual friendship riff. This time the music played fully and, whatever the melody was, it was beautiful.

"Thanks for your help earlier," I said.

"Anytime. How are you feeling?" he asked.

"Not good," I answered. My throat began to tighten as I held back tears. He reached over the table, grabbed my hand, and squeezed it.

"Kaspian, can you—" Seraphina entered and stopped talking when she saw us. Kaspian pulled his hand away. She smiled as she continued walking into the room. "I hope I'm not interrupting."

"No," I said.

"Good. There's plenty of work that my brother should be doing." It took every effort I could muster not to roll my eyes at her answer. She looked at me, her eyes flashing purple. She sighed and changed her tone. "Did you get the answers you were seeking?"

"Not yet," I answered.

"Know that you have our support, regardless of the outcome." She put her hand on mine just as Kaspian had.

It was the moment our hands touched that I was no longer in the library with the others. I was standing at the head of the table in the strategy room as someone gently touched my hand. I looked over and it was Isa. It made me feel happy. I turned to look back at the table, but *I* was sitting there. I wasn't looking through my eyes; I was seeing from Seraphina's.

"It's been two years," I said from my spot in between Eros and Olivia, who was directly next to Seraphina on the side that Isa wasn't. Nathaniel sat next to Eros, and Kaspian was sandwiched in between Nathaniel and Alton. "Why is he back now?"

"I don't know the answer to that," Isa answered. "But so far, he hasn't affected any of our comms in the same way he did last time."

"T," Seraphina said. I looked at myself. I looked different and yet the same. I had taken on more aspects of the Fantasia lifestyle, including my style, and wore a circlet on my head just as I had the first time Olivia dressed me up. But it was elaborate, more elaborate than the one I'd worn before. Olivia also looked different. Was that a wedding band? I felt my gaze pull again to me as if Seraphina had taken over what we were looking at. "I understand if you don't want to fight."

"I'll smack Ghost's face off that Glitch if it's the last thing I do."

Then I was back in the library, looking at Seraphina, who was still touching me. Our eyes met and I watched her eyes return from a light purple back to normal.

"Did you just?" Seraphina asked, not fully finishing her sentence.

"See that? Yes, what was that?"

"The future," she answered.

NINE

"That was the future?" I asked. "But—"

"No!" Seraphina and Kaspian both yelled, and then Seraphina finished, "you can't discuss what you saw in front of others. I'm not sure how you saw that; I've never shared a vision before. Discussing it could change the outcome we saw. It is one of many and any of them could come true."

Seraphina looked down at my glitched hands. Was this another side effect of the glitch? I hid my hands, rubbing them on my legs, trying to ignore what happened.

"What did you need, Seraphina?" Kaspian asked.

"Can you take a look at these documents? They were provided to us by the Production members as their credentials. I want to cross-reference their names with information in our library."

"I will look into it," he agreed. Seraphina nodded and left the room. Kaspian looked back at me. "Would you like to help? It might get your mind off everything, and I wouldn't mind some company."

"Sure," I laughed. We searched through the library for a few hours, talking about random things to keep me distracted. We finally found one helpful document, which was a huge book titled "Character and Game Audit" from the previous year. If Bryce was a listed member of my Production team, he would be listed under *Duty Falls*.

"Here." Kaspian pointed to *Duty Falls*. There was Ghost's Character description, my own, and our listed Producers. Bryce's name was on there.

"So, he's legit." I nodded. "Makes sense considering he could make changes to my code."

"What about Isa?" Kaspian asked. He dropped the thousand-page manual, which made a loud thud, on the table. "I can't find her anywhere in here. As a member of IT, she wouldn't be listed, so there's no way to check her credentials when our system's down."

"I trust Isa," I said. *She* was there two years from the last time we saw the Glitch, Bryce wasn't. She seemed special when she touched Seraphina; I felt warm in my chest. Honestly, I felt like I loved her in that moment.

"Wh—" Kaspian stopped himself as he looked at me. I'm pretty sure his question was 'why?' but he knew better than to ask it. I just nodded.

"Tack180," Eros sang as he entered the library. "Oh, hey, Kaspian. What's up?"

"Eros." Kaspian acknowledged. "You may call me Prince Kaspian."

"You got it, boss. Anyway, T," Eros started again. "Wait, am I interrupting something?"

"No," we both said a little too quickly. We were loud and *obvious*. I looked at Kaspian; I liked spending time with him. I purposefully sought him out when the others were also available.

But I love Ghost, not Kaspian.

"Right," Eros nodded, trying to hide his smirk. "Well, I came to check on you. I even brought a gift from Nathaniel, but it looks like you're fine."

"What do you have from Nathaniel?" I asked. He pulled out the same herbs from the first night. I nodded and smiled. *Just what I need.*

"It is getting late," Kaspian said. "I'll wrap up the research for my sister. You go get some rest."

"Are you sure?" I asked. "I can stay and help."

"It's fine. I've got it covered here."

I followed Eros and left Kaspian there, alone, even though I wanted to go back and help him. I wanted to spend more time with *him*.

***

Bryce and Isa continued to monitor me for about a month. It had officially become the longest blackout in Production history, but no one in Fantasia really saw the extent of it. Just like the royals had explained to me that first night, Fantasia was created with royalty running their game without heavy Production influence. The glitch could go on for years and they wouldn't notice or care.

That must be nice.

Eros and I would work at the bakery in the morning, and then we'd go back to the castle for training in the afternoon. Bryce and Isa watched me when they could, and things felt like a new normal, whatever that meant. I hoped that the more I performed for Bryce and Isa, the more answers we could get in the future. Going to training became more exciting now there was hope that one day, Bryce and Isa would tell me they figured out what the problem was.

When Eros and I arrived at the training grounds that day, something seemed off. Maybe it was Olivia's, especially, high level of excitement, Isa's determination in the way she was talking with Kaspian, or the way Alton and Nathaniel were fucking around while waiting for us.

"T," Isa greeted me. "You'll never guess what happened last night."

"What?" I asked, not nearly as excited as she was.

"I think I set up a way to get everyone's comms back online. This would improve current communications and expand them across worlds. Since the blackout has lasted over a month now, leaders are running on the last stages of the protocol. Fixing this is essential to ensure a better quality of life for all games. So, even though we can't teleport, play the Game, or stream, we can communicate via DMs with our loved ones in different games and worlds. Producers would be able to send patches and updates in their games to help the worlds prosper in this weird new setting, and the internet would be back up."

"Isn't it amazing, T?" Olivia asked.

"Yeah, as long as other worlds weren't taken out by the Glitch."

"Yes, well, that's what we need you for," Isa continued. "There is a slight, but necessary, adjustment that needs to be made, and it can't be made here in Fantasia."

"You didn't mention this earlier," Kaspian interrupted.

"How else do I get people that don't really know me on board for something so grandiose?"

"Haven't you heard of the saying, it's easier to beg for forgiveness than to ask for permission?" Bryce added.

I looked at Eros, who looked back at me. In the past month, we had become inseparable. The annoying contract killer was a hit with the ladies at the bakery, bringing in more customers than I had my first few days without him. Just like he promised, he followed me everywhere, making sure I was safe from potential dangers. He became a part of my daily life, so much so that I didn't want him to leave and go back to his game. I wanted him to stay in Fantasia. He was my friend. Not only that, but he wasn't from this friendship-happy game. He was from a completely different world, and he *still* liked me. At least, I hoped he liked me as a friend and not just a way back home.

"I'll follow you, boss," he said.

"What do you need from me, Isa?" I asked.

"Well, your apartment in the Platform would be closest to our target destination."

"Which is?"

"Underneath the actual Platform itself is the central processing for all comms. I need to get there."

"Oh, you aren't coming," I laughed.

"Well, I wasn't asking. Consider it more of a mission to get me there than asking you to do it for me. I'm the only one of us technologically savvy enough to do it."

"Fair point," Eros offered.

"Fine," I agreed.

"You can't be seriously considering this?" Alton asked.

"I'm not considering it; I'm agreeing to it."

"That's the Tack180 I know," Bryce cheered me on.

"No one asked you." Alton shot him a look.

"Alton," Kaspian chided.

"Sorry, sir."

"We will come, too," Kaspian said.

"We what?" Alton asked.

"We can't let T go without us," Nathaniel agreed.

"This is becoming a large group," Isa tried to argue.

"You don't know how much help you will need," I offered. "If the Platform is destroyed, then we will have to try and fight off the Glitch, and honestly, the more the merrier there. If the Platform isn't destroyed, then it's going to be a shitshow. That's what it was before I got sent here."

"How did you know that?" Eros asked.

"Because I live in the Platform."

"Me, too. Where do you live?"

"Like, right above a coffee shop that's in the Platform."

"Seriously? You're one of *those* people?"

"What? Where do you live?" I asked.

"Like forty-five minutes away!"

"I mean, *Duty Falls* is a lot bigger than your game."

"You rich people enjoying your lavish things." He rolled his eyes.

"Can we get back to the subject at hand? This got off-topic really fast," Isa tried to rope us back in. "T, can you open a portal?"

"No. Well, I don't know. They've only ever appeared when I'm under high levels of stress or near-death experiences for myself or others."

"Hmm," Isa hummed. "Getting comms set up again is a rather urgent matter for everyone. I was hoping the connection to the glitch was a little stronger than that."

"I've got an idea," Bryce offered. "But you won't like it."

I knew his idea; I think we all did. We just didn't want to say it out loud. He opened his tablet and started typing things–I felt my body moving under his guidance. I started to pull off my gloves.

"I understand the logic, but I'm sure there's another way," Isa said. "T, what are your thoughts?"

"It's a glitch. I'm still not fully convinced I'm the one who is actually opening portals. I've never willfully opened a portal in practice yet," I rephrased what I had said previously. I looked down at the glitch, my hands ready to move under Bryce's guidance.

"This could be done within a matter of seconds," Bryce tried one more time. "A momentary scare for the entire comms system being set up. You can hate it all you want, but we're in a time crunch and this will get results."

"Okay," I agreed.

Everyone stared at me, unsure of what Bryce was going to make me do. Eros took a step toward me. My hand shot out in his direction, almost touching him.

"Stay back!" I yelled. I turned to Bryce. "I don't want to hurt them."

Everyone took a few steps back and, when there were no open targets, Bryce took control. My glitched hands went straight for my own body. Without my gloves on, the process was excruciating; my hands throbbed in the frozen state and the purple haze intensified.

It worked.

I still hoped it didn't because, at some point, I knew I needed to just accept that I was glitched and that glitch affected the Game. Still, that had larger implications for Ghost than it did for me, and I don't want to accept it, even when it seemed so obvious. I hurried to put on my gloves and ease the pain, then I touched Olivia, who immediately started healing me. I touched Eros next, followed by Isa. Her eyes were wide as she realized what was happening, but she was also trying to actively calm herself down. She then started feverishly jotting notes down on her tablet.

"They don't *need* to come," Isa said, looking at the group of frozen guys.

"No, but Kaspian undoubtedly helps me focus since it's similar to his magic." I touched Kaspian. I hovered my hands over Alton and Nathaniel but left them there. No, they didn't *need* to come. Bryce wasn't needed either and no one needed to know how much it hurt that this worked, so I powered through it. "Bear with me, guys. The last time I tried to get to the Platform, we ended up in a clown game."

"The jump-scare one?" Isa asked.

"That's the one."

"I regret this decision," she mumbled under her breath.

I took a deep breath, closed my eyes, and started thinking about the Platform; its eccentric lights and people, loud music, fighting. My apartment, sitting just above the Platform; looking down and watching the noobs, me and Ghost training in the living room, eating dinner together after a long day. Ghost's smile. Ghost. I felt a warm tear fall down my face, and a hand reached out for mine. I opened my eyes and looked down at the hand holding mine. Kaspian.

"You did it," he said.

I looked over my shoulder, and there it was: a portal. The room that it led to was dark and hard to see, but there was a purple haze emanating from specific areas within the room—the glitch. I looked harder and saw a picture of Ghost and me with the frame cracked; it was my apartment.

"Be careful when you enter," Olivia said. "I can't guarantee that I will be able to heal you if you touch anything glitched."

"Let me go first," I held out an arm to stop everyone. "It could be in the air, and I'm already glitched."

"Okay, but how would that help us?" Eros asked. "If you're already glitched, then it might not affect you the same way. I will go, too. Everyone else can stay back to see if I fall to my death or not."

"Let's go, then." I grabbed Eros's hand as we walked through the portal before he could take it back.

Walking through the portal was like walking into a warzone. The front room of my apartment was gone, and I could see straight onto the Platform. That's how the glitch got into the rest of the apartment. I looked back at Eros, who was breathing just fine, his body remaining the same color it always was. It was safe. I waved into the portal behind us, and the rest of the group walked through.

"You had a nice place," Kaspian acknowledged.

"Bitch," Eros muttered.

"Aw, is someone jealous of a destroyed apartment?" Olivia teased him.

"You've got to admit," Isa said, looking at the picture of Ghost and me hanging on the wall. "You two did make a beautiful couple. I was team Ghost180, even though you were never officially shipped in *Duty Falls*."

"Right?" Olivia fangirled. "They were my OTP. When they kept them separated, it was the worst."

"Oh, the Producers paid heavily for that," Isa said.

I grabbed a different picture from the side table in the living room. I stared at the happy picture of us; Ghost had his out-of-game haircut and stubble, and I looked just like I always did before the glitch.

I miss him.

I smiled and touched it. I'd changed so much in just a month and a half. I had worn the same outfit for seven years and now I had a different outfit, weapons, and friends. I'm so different now, that while I look the same, I can hardly recognize the person I was in that picture.

"He'd be proud of you." Kaspian placed a hand on my shoulder.

"I don't know." I shook my head. "I haven't got any answers."

"We're in the middle of the Platform when teleportation services are down," Eros joined in. "You might not have answers, but you can do some crazy shit."

"Hell yeah." I laughed. He held up a hand, and I high-fived him.

"Let's roll out." Eros made a circular motion with his fingers.

I kicked down my front door and led everyone down a hall and then a flight of stairs until we came out onto the street in front of the coffee shop. There was no sign of life. There were empty go-karts that crashed as though their drivers had disappeared. No one said anything as we walked to the middle of the Platform. The buildings surrounding the flat metallic structure were built in a circle to emphasize the shape of the Platform. The sound of our footsteps changed as we moved from the metallic section to a portion covered in LED lights. Usually, it lit up beautifully, but the once bright lights weren't working. At the very center of the circle was another area covered in metal. That's where Isa stopped.

"A little help, T?" Isa asked, looking down at the glitched area surrounding the part of the Platform she wanted to look at.

"Why isn't this whole place a glitch?" Eros asked. "How is it just sitting there on the surface?"

I wasn't sure how to go about moving it, but luckily, I could easily slide the glitch, which felt a lot like slime that people played with in ASMR videos, over for Isa. I hadn't seen it pool up like that before. *Gross.*

"Actually, that's a pretty simple answer," Isa started. "You see, the glitch doesn't seem to affect *real* matter; buildings are made of real wood, steel, and such. Whereas we are humans, yes, but we are highly infused with technological matter at birth. That's why, when T stopped touching the Glitch, it stopped spreading through her body because it couldn't continue through her without a host. Half and half. With me, so far?"

Eros nodded.

"Good. Look around—I don't see many weapons. Some, like that wooden sword over there, are made with real materials, while others, like T's tacks, are in the technological part of us. Therefore, if T were to fully glitch out on us, she wouldn't leave behind a bag of tacks in the same way a person left behind that training sword. The technical is the difference between what you think you are holding or feeling versus what is really happening to your body. Prince Kaspian? Do me a favor, I'd like to test something. Can you hold a fireball?"

He followed her instructions.

"Great, now, T. Can you touch it?"

"I know the answer to this one!" Olivia said enthusiastically. "We already tried it."

"Well, I want to see for myself."

I took off my glove and let my glitched hand hover as the flames danced around it. Eros touched the flame with a finger, immediately pulled it away, and then sucked on the finger. With his free hand, Kaspian smacked Eros's hand out of his mouth and flicked his fingers. Water splashed over Eros's burn. Olivia then slapped Kaspian's hand out of the way and waved her staff over Eros.

"Just as I thought," Isa hummed. "The glitch is only destroying *Game* technology. Prince Kaspian's magic, obviously technical, doesn't affect the glitched areas of T in the same way it does others. However, I can't guarantee the effect would be the same if I were to make a fire right now out of sticks and matches. That's something we can test another day. Any questions?"

"What about T's gloves?" Kaspian asked. "The magic can't heal the glitch; however, they still relieve the pain."

"I assume you used magic *and* herbs? The herbs within your game are real medicinal herbs; hence the real medicine alleviates the real pain. Also, the gloves themselves are made of leather, so the material is not technical."

"Can we just walk on it then?" Eros asked.

"Depends on the materials of your boots. Better to be safe than sorry and just avoid it."

"What about the portals?" Eros asked.

"Well, my best guess is, since the glitch attacks the technical, and teleportation and portals are technical, then T's glitch is attacking the nearby code, which is invisible to the naked eye, and it attacks it in the way she wants. I'm sure there's more she can do; she just hasn't played around with the glitch enough to learn all it can do yet."

"Why does it feel heavy?" I asked.

"It's an energy drain. It's not heavy as much as you are losing your life at such a quick rate that you don't have enough energy coming in to match the energy going out. So, basically, you're exhausted and dying, so keep Olivia around. I can't confirm, but I think the only thing stopping it from instantly killing you when you use the power is the slow self-heal ability from your game."

"Will we ever be able to heal her?" Olivia asked.

"I don't have the answer to that one," she said. Then she looked at me. "You might stay like this forever. But, if we think of this as a technological problem, then I could look into getting everyone anti-virus software installed and, if I knew it wouldn't kill you, we could try a reset to factory conditions."

"Factory conditions?" Kaspian asked.

"It would erase everything about T and bring her back to the way she was exactly after the Voting Forum. But that comes with large downsides as well, you know. It could kill her and, if it doesn't, she would be a completely empty slate for Production to work with. So, no memories of Ghost."

"Or us," Olivia said.

"Or you," she agreed.

"No," I said. I didn't want to lose the memories I had created with people. Even though I was sad and missed Ghost, I didn't want to forget him entirely. He helped make me who I was today. And my new group; I'd have been lost, potentially dead, had it not been for the kindness they showed me, even looking past my Character traits to help me grow in a new environment. I never wanted to forget them; they had become like a family to me.

"Yes," Isa acknowledged. "I would say that option is extreme. If the glitch spreads or the pain of the glitch on your hands becomes too unbearable, then that would be an option. Right now, though, you are a fully functioning Character."

I nodded. She typed a code into her tablet, and a pillar started to rise out of the Platform. Her fingers moved quickly as she began typing on a keyboard that popped out of the pillar. She then plugged her tablet into a cable, linking it to the pillar, and moved her hand in a motion that expressed "hurry the fuck up" as she waited for something. A minute later, she made a fist and pulled it down in excitement, unplugged the tablet, and looked up.

"T?"

"Yeah."

"Did the Glitch look like an all-black version of Ghost?"

Isa pointed behind me; we all turned and saw what looked like Ghost rising out of a pile of leftover glitch hanging around the platform. Then, the army formed around him and around us.

"Are you done?" I asked.

"Yes, open the portal. Open the portal. Open the portal," she started repeating.

Isa was the only one of us who wasn't a Character; she had no sort of fighting advantage against the Glitch. But, since everyone had the implant, she was just as screwed as the rest of us if it touched her. I focused for a second, trying to open a portal, but nothing worked as the Glitch kept advancing. Kaspian and I started attacking from afar, I kept the throwing knives in place, knowing they wouldn't affect them, so I just used my tacks as always.

"I've got this, T," Kaspian said. "Focus on opening the portal."

At that point, the Glitch was only a few feet away, so I stepped in front of everyone to keep them back. I was glitched already; they didn't need to be. I couldn't lose them in the same way I lost Ghost. The Glitch looked past me and straight at the others. I looked back and he seemed to be focusing on Isa. When I turned back to him, his head tilted as he *analyzed* her. Hell no, I wouldn't let him get to the only person who seemed to be giving me any sort of answers to work with.

"I'm the one you care about, right?" I asked, gaining his attention back.

"I don't *care* for you," he said. He looked down at my glitched hand. "But I have started to download your code."

Then he quickly reached for my arm. I dodged his grab, almost running into one of his followers before it turned into him, well, Ghost. He pulled out two guns, one in each hand, and aimed them at me. I heard the *bang* but didn't feel anything. I looked down, and surrounding me was a purple shield, its appearance technical, nearly invisible with a hexagonal pattern. Who could produce a shield that worked against the glitch's leader? I looked around, but there was no one new there. He tilted his head as he looked at me. Then I watched the shield that surrounded me begin to break apart. The Glitch's eyes, piercingly purple, stared at me as if he could kill me by making eye contact, and maybe he could.

"Enough games!" The Glitch finally yelled.

All of his followers froze where they were. Then, the Glitch multiplied, an army of Ghosts appearing behind him, and I didn't know how to defeat him. I quickly looked back at my group. Time wasn't frozen, but it felt as if they were yelling at me in slow motion. Olivia's arms moved in an exaggerated circular motion prompting me to step away from the Glitch. And then he was there, the Glitch, standing right next to Isa.

No, *I need her*.

Their slow-motion actions came to a halt as the world around froze. I went into action and shifted my attention to opening a portal by thinking about the castle. I thought about Isa and the support she gave in finding answers to Ghost's disappearance, the bakery and my time spent with the royals, and of spending time playing chess with Kaspian. Once the portal opened, I touched the others and shuffled them through the portal, quickly and without question. I was the last one to go through the portal, taking one long last look at my apartment before I jumped through.

"Let's hurry this up, Tack180," Bryce said, moving my arms again.

"Wait, are we back at the same time we left?" Isa asked.

"Yup, forgot to mention that," I said. "And you can stop controlling me, Bryce."

"Interesting," she said, jotting the notes down on her tablet. I felt my body go limp as Bryce's control stopped. "I—wow, the things we saw, Bryce. You would have been amazed. This Glitch is no joke. It speaks, interacts, it's basically an intelligent creature. Imagine all of the plausible causes—someone who wants to actually commit murder, fanatic groups who don't like the Game, an innocent accident gone wrong?"

"Calm down there, Isa," Bryce laughed.

She laughed and then started crying. Olivia reached out to hug her, and Isa shook her head before taking a deep breath. After a moment, she gave out an intense "It worked!" and looked around at the rest of us. I could tell by the message notification blinking at me from the top left of my view that our comms were back up, which meant my DMs were blowing up. I tried to ignore the red dot notification dancing in my vision.

"Currency exchange is back up, as well," Isa acknowledged. "It wasn't hard to add in there, and I was low."

I looked at my bank account, which automatically exchanged my old currency for the gold of Fantasia. I was no longer broke. The first thing I did was transfer the funds back into Olivia's account for what I thought was the price of the bakery.

"T!" She yelled. "It was a gift. You aren't supposed to pay back gifts."

"So, then, how rich are you?" Eros asked me.

"She is probably the equivalent of Prince Kaspian," Bryce answered. "She made less than Ghost but is still one of the top paid Characters in the industry."

"I was paid less than Ghost?" I scoffed.

"Just the way it worked out." He shrugged.

"That's some bullshit."

"Sorry," Bryce said in a way that indicated he could care less.

"No, don't gloss over this," Olivia demanded. "T's stats are all better than Ghost's. There were higher notification rates when she became available for play than when Ghost did. Not to mention, when the game split, more

Players were intent on playing T's individual story than Ghost's, on all satisfaction surveys."

"Down, tiger," Alton squeezed Olivia's shoulders.

"Get off me." She shook her arms. "This is so typical in the field. That's why I refuse to answer that stupid male or female question."

"How do you know those types of stats?" Bryce asked.

"I like games." Her response was slow and calculated.

"Did you all get a message?" Isa asked, diverting everyone's attention.

"I have at least a thousand DMs to look through," I said, watching the number rise. Everyone else agreed.

"Look at the most recent one from me. It should be a message that Seraphina and I worked out before going to the Platform. I set it to auto-send."

We all sifted through our DMs. The first one at the top came from Isabella Rodriguez, Technical Specialist for the Production Team. In short, it said not to freak out. There was a glitch that shut down everyone's systems for a few weeks, and communications with some worlds may still be limited, which created a nice, convenient cover for the fact that their loved ones may be dead. *Diplomatic.* They were still working on ways to get the Teleportation System up and running, but, until then, worlds with visitors were asked to help house the refugees. It ended with a call for all heads of worlds, Producers, or main Characters who received this DM to follow blackout protocol and message Isa directly for further instructions.

"I plan to document which worlds, or parts of worlds, are glitched based on who contacts me. We should get a good map of how the glitch has been spreading to see if there are any patterns," Isa said. "Ah! I already have a message."

"I'd be happy to show you to a room where you can map things out, Isa," Kaspian offered.

"And another! Yes, please do."

Kaspian, Isa, and Bryce ran off to be with Seraphina and do royal and diplomatic shit, based on those messages. Olivia and Alton both chose to privately reach out to their families and see if they were alive. That left me with Nathaniel and Eros.

We did it. These messages were confirmed to be post-glitch messages, meaning people were alive, seeking aid from Production, and reaching out to loved ones. The red dot continued to dance at the top of my vision. I had hundreds of unread messages. Was, at least, one of them from Ghost? Was there a message from someone else, someone I didn't remember, just making sure I was alive?

"Let's check our comms over a beer," Nathaniel suggested.

He didn't need to ask more than once. We got situated in the alehouse and started skimming through. My DMs were filled with messages from the day the glitch arrived. A couple hundred unsolicited dick pics that were *immediately* trashed, people praising my skills, and others sending me death threats. I deleted all the messages as I scrolled through them; I didn't care about any of them anyway. I deleted them until I got to the DMs between Ghost and me. No unread messages. I hovered over his name before I opened them up.

"Are you out there?" I messaged. If he was alive, he wouldn't keep me waiting, especially considering the state of the world. *Nothing.*

"How's your family, Eros?" I asked when I couldn't stand waiting anymore.

"Looks like everyone is safe, those who remember me and otherwise. No sightings of the Glitch there."

"That's amazing. I'm happy to hear that. Nathaniel?"

"Well, all my family are here in Fantasia, so my DMs are just full of men and women who want me."

"Keep telling yourself that, man, one of these days, you'll find someone," Eros teased.

"You can slide into my DMs any day."

"Only in your dreams, Nathaniel."

"On a more serious note, T," Nathaniel started. "Did *you* get anything?"

I shook my head. No. But I wouldn't let that stop me. I opened my messages to my Production rep and demanded answers, then I messaged our mentor, Cap. Cap was originally a Character with 30-years-experience in the Game. He was about to retire when they pulled him into *Duty Falls* for a crossover event, and the new game, *Duty Rises*, was born as a new first-person shooter game in our world. If Ghost didn't respond to me, Cap would. Then I stood up. It was time to get to business; there was no use waiting around for a response from someone that might not even respond. I needed to take action. Our comms were back up, and that meant I was finally going to get the answers I very much deserved.

"I'm not waiting anymore. I'm getting answers," I said.

"Sign me up, boss." Eros stood up with a smile and then stretched.

"What are you doing?" I heard Kaspian ask. We turned to see him filling the doorway of the alehouse.

"I'm ready to get answers."

"Well, your timing couldn't be better. We need you in the strategy room."

TEN

Eros and I followed Kaspian to the door, and he stopped Eros short at the doorway. *Just me.* I nodded to Eros, and he walked back to sit with Nathaniel. I was too afraid to ask what we were going to talk about, especially if I wasn't going to be happy with the answers I was about to get, so we didn't say anything as we walked to the strategy room. Once there, Isa, Seraphina, and Bryce were waiting at the table already. Kaspian shut the door and motioned for me to sit down. I sat in a chair at the end of the table and stared back at them.

"Tack180," Seraphina started. "Bryce is the only Producer still alive from your game. You two are the last living remnants of *Duty Falls.*"

"How do you know that?" I asked. I looked at Bryce; his eyes were red as if he had been crying, and he avoided eye contact with me. My right leg started to shake in anticipation of their answers. The table shook with me.

"Blackout protocol indicates that all world leaders must message their Production reps, or alternative liaison if one is determined, which I made myself when I sent out that email, within one hour of communications being brought online," Isa said. "Sure, there will be a few stragglers. However, given the current map that I've created based on location data from the messages already received and Bryce's corresponding location data for other members of your team; well, we all saw what happened to the Platform."

"You are the sole survivor of your entire world," Kaspian said, sympathy lacing his voice. Or was it pity?

"No." I shook my head. "I just messaged everyone. They'll respond."

"They're gone, T," Bryce said. I looked over at him. "All of them."

"Stop lying." I slammed my fists on the table. This glitch couldn't be *that* big. There was no way it devastated my entire world, the Platform, and countless other games and worlds. Nothing that big was easily fixable with a patch. Getting answers meant I was supposed to figure out a way to bring Ghost back from the dead. If I had learned anything from this stupid RPG world, it was that friendship and love could save anyone. So why can't I save Ghost?

"Your game was—" Kaspian tried.

"I know what happened to it," I cut him off.

"No one has contacted us from the other games within your world, either," he said.

"At this point, to move forward and create a plan, we must assume that you are the last remaining member of your entire world," Seraphina said. "We will need your feedback and support in determining ways to create a new world, operating as the new leader for your world."

"But Cap's the leader," I said. Cap's experience and military rank within his game made him the perfect option for our leader.

I'm sure he will message me back.

Cap always replied to me, no matter what I needed help with.

"Cap was playing at the same time you were and there's been no response," Bryce said. He rubbed his hands over his face, then looked at me. "You'll get a lot of answers this way."

"Okay," I said. "Then someone tell me; what the hell is going on? How do we bring back the people who were glitched?"

Isa sighed and looked at me.

"Realistically?" she asked. "The damage is widespread, and that's just based on current reports. The glitch infiltrated most worlds; some were only minor, but a few seem to be completely devastated. I don't have an accurate estimate of how many games it's infiltrated yet. I want to be transparent with you, it's not fair to get anyone's hopes up. This may change, but if I had to work with just the data I have right now? The files, games, and Characters that are completely destroyed are unsalvageable."

A part of me had already assumed that was the answer, and I'm not sure if that was the reason why I didn't cry, or if I didn't cry at that moment because I was still shocked by the severity of it all. I stared forward at Seraphina, who was sitting directly across from me.

"We need your help." She smiled softly at me. "We need to continue the implementation of the blackout protocol."

"I don't care about the protocol if I'm the last one alive in *Duty Falls*. I want more direct answers. Who can I talk to in Production?" I looked at Isa and Bryce for the answers to that last one.

"We are still determining the hierarchy within Production based on who is still alive," Bryce said. "It could be a bit until they determine answers and then, based on the answers, how and what information to disseminate to the larger populace."

"So, are we going to do this off the books then?" I asked Bryce. "I've waited long enough for answers."

"That's my Tack180." He smiled. "But I don't have that kind of access. I know your game, and the other games I'm a Producer for, only. Most of my equipment for looking into your game is back at my headquarters in Corporous. Even then, it's specific for your game. I won't have any additional information on the glitch for you."

"So, after all this time, I'm still stuck waiting?"

"Not necessarily," Seraphina offered. "We are spearheading the research. Isa is one of the most knowledgeable members of IT and has been asked to look into this matter."

"My research from studying you has already helped exponentially. We can help each other," Isa offered. "Especially now we've determined there are other partially glitched people, like you, out there."

"There are?" I asked. I knew it wasn't Ghost, not after what they had said, but if there were others like me, then maybe it wasn't as deadly as they thought. I wasn't the only one, there was nothing inherently special about me, but there was something about all of us that kept us alive. If we can just figure that out, we can begin to fix this, right?

"I'll update you when I know more."

"Who are they? Do I know them? Are they from other worlds? Big games or small games?" I continued to ask.

"Like I said, I'll update you as soon as I know more."

More? I want more information now. What is happening across the worlds?

"What else changed with the comms coming back online?" I asked.

"Blackout protocol orders that we must keep to our way of living prior to the incident as strictly as possible to ensure that people don't notice any intense differences to the lives they once lived," Bryce said. Then he laughed. It was an uncomfortable laugh like the whole situation was fucked up, but he couldn't help but laugh despite that. "I think that's a little different for us."

"Yeah." I nodded.

"We won't be able to pull in as much money as you had been as Tack180, a playable Character in a popular first-person shooter. However, in order to maintain our day-to-day life, we will have to bring in some form of income for eight hours a day, in which I, as your Producer, will get a cut of your pay."

I knew that was in my contract and something that had always been done on the backend of my paycheck, but to hear it now, in a moment of confusion and immense change, made me angry. I started to roll my eyes and then closed them, trying not to let anyone see that I had actually rolled them. I took a deep breath.

"Until we get in contact with a lawyer to look things over, we will have to do the best with what is available to us. We don't have an active cross-over here, so battling monsters, which probably could've been our biggest source of income, is out of the question for now. I'd like to re-examine that once we get you set up in this game."

"So, we have to capitalize on the bakery?" I asked. I didn't want to use the bakery in that way. It was my place to separate myself from all the madness around me, my reprieve from the stresses which now plagued my life. I didn't want to change that. "It doesn't make that much money."

"That was before. Comms are up, so it's easier to spread the word. We are going to make it well known that Tack180 is here and ready to battle. Just that action alone could increase our base income by fifty percent. You're famous. You're Tack180! Let's use that to our advantage. We have to adapt; we're the only ones left, you and I. I understand what you're going through better than anyone else in this room and vice versa."

I sighed. He was right; we were the only ones left in a billion-dollar franchise that had lasted seven years. To have it end so abruptly, without a goodbye to anyone, was jarring. As it was, I had dealt with it for a while already, but Bryce was just now faced with the death of everything he once knew. No one else in this room understood that, but that didn't mean he was the only one I could fall back on. He just felt like I was the only one he could fall back on.

"This won't change our mission to find our friends," he added. I looked up at him. "Ghost, Cap, everyone from your world and my Production friends. This fight isn't over yet, Tack180. It's just the beginning, and we need to work together to find answers."

I saw movement out of the corner of my eyes, and I glanced at Seraphina. It looked as though she had just finished rolling her eyes. *How uncharacteristic.* I looked back at Bryce. He offered a weak smile, also uncharacteristic. I didn't want to be Tack180, the first-person shooter, here. That was a life with Ghost that didn't exist anymore and trying to bring it back was only reinviting pain that I've been trying to overcome. But I also didn't feel like a Thea, either. Somehow there had to be a way to make both options a reality.

"I'm thinking out loud here, but what about a battle option?" He continued. "Anyone who beats you gets a free carrot cake as a prize."

"No one's going to beat me," I laughed. "No one would get a free cake, then."

He smiled. "And that's the whole point. The challenge would draw in more customers than ever before. If they wanted your carrot cake and failed to defeat you, they would have to pay full price, and that would be on top of the entry fee."

I stared at Bryce. I had no immediate answers for him. I didn't want to agree to anything I would regret, even though I liked how the idea sounded.

"How about you take time to think about this," Seraphina said. "We've presented you with a lot of information, and I don't think you've fully processed it."

I nodded in agreement. I stopped my leg from shaking, stood up, and looked over at Bryce, "I'll get back to you."

When I walked out of the room, Eros was standing there waiting for me. He was leaning against the wall with his arms crossed and head down. He looked up and straightened himself out as I closed the door behind me.

"T," he said. "Alton and Olivia heard back about their families."

I could tell from the way he phrased it, something awful had happened. I started in the direction of their rooms.

"What happened?" I asked.

"Alton's family is fine. Liv's didn't make it. She lost both her parents."

I started running. I ran for Olivia, and I ran for myself. No one was supposed to die. What was the point of a deathless world if people ended up dying anyway? Who did Henry Fudders think he was? Some guy with a God complex pretending to create some perfect utopia that couldn't even hold up to its name after he died. No one knew how to deal with sudden death anymore because we were told we didn't have to worry about it. But, if death was back, what did that mean for this world we had created? Would it even be possible to play the Game anymore? I couldn't imagine throwing a tack at someone right now, even if someone swore to me that they would respawn as they always had. How could I trust that they really would? We had to face it; the Game, as we once knew it, was over. Death was back, and it was going to destroy our peaceful utopia. It already had.

I opened Olivia's door without knocking. Alton had his arms around her as they sat on the edge of the bed. They both looked up at me, Olivia's eyes rimmed red, and I sat down on the bed next to her; I didn't know what to say. I wanted to reach out to her, but all I could do was sit there, with Alton comforting her, as my right leg began to shake again. Olivia finally placed her hand on my leg, and I reached for her hand with my own. She squeezed it, and I squeezed back. I heard a hiccup and looked at her, but the sound hadn't come from her. It came from me; I was crying, and so was she. She pulled away from Alton and hugged me. We both sunk to the bed, an unfamiliar heaviness soaking over us. *Grief.*

***

I don't know how long we stayed there, but no one moved us. I just remember that at one point, Seraphina came. She didn't say a word, she just held out her hands to us, and Olivia grabbed one, and I grabbed the other. I wasn't sure why I took her hand, but I wanted to stay close to Olivia, and I felt like I needed to follow the queen, too. She moved with confidence like she was going to provide me with some kind of answer to all of my problems, a meaning for continuing with life as we knew it. She brought us out to a graveyard overlooking the water on the backside of the castle. She waved, and soldiers came over with heavy rocks and lay them in front of us. Seraphina stood in front of the rocks and lowered her head.

"May those who have lost their lives, rest in peace and know that their deaths will be avenged," she said firmly.

I pinched my fingers, dug a small hole next to Ghost's new gravestone, and placed the two tacks in the hole.

I'll find answers for you. For us. I will avenge you.

If that's the only reason I'm still alive today, I won't waste it. Olivia lay on her parents' gravestone; her body heaved as she cried. Alton sat down next to her and put one hand on her back. My tears were gone, but my feelings were just as strong. I took a deep breath and stood up.

"Tack180," Bryce said. I didn't even realize he was there. He probably knew what Seraphina had planned since they were both in the strategy room. I looked around, and the whole group was there, Isa included. "I feel like some exercise might actually make you feel better."

I nodded and left without another word to the others in the area. I felt so heavy inside, and none of it was due to the glitch. I needed to run it off. I needed to train, and I wanted to do it harder than I ever had before. Eros followed Bryce and me to the castle training area. Eros wasn't ready for my training routine. Bryce wasn't even ready for the energy I put into training. I needed to push myself. I was not weak; I won't succumb to the glitch. I won't die. I will keep pushing myself to be faster, stronger, and better than I have ever been. The glitch was unprecedented, but so was I. I will protect my friends. I will protect myself. I will protect the life I knew, whatever was left of it. I will destroy the Glitch until nothing is left.

"You can do better."

"Do it again but add a flip at the end."

"Tighter on the landing."

"Aim better."

I pushed myself harder every time Bryce yelled at me. The number of times he threatened to hang me by my feet until I hit a bullseye on a moving target while flipping was uncountable. I reckoned he needed new material. I kept going until I missed a landing from exhaustion. I lay on the ground, my breathing erratic.

"You working hard or hardly working?" Bryce tried to joke.

"I can keep going." I stood up.

"No, you can't."

"Let's run it again." I clapped. "I can do it."

"T." Eros put a hand on my shoulder. "Time to call it a night."

"We have an early morning, Tack180," Bryce agreed. "We've got prep to do for the battle bakery. That is... if you want to do it."

"Sure." I hadn't thought about it since earlier, but I did like the idea.

I took a step forward, my legs wobbled after the brief moment of rest. I stopped myself, stretching to ease some of the pain. A foam roller appeared next to me, and I nodded at Bryce. I rolled out my muscles, feeling the pain of even the slightest amount of pressure.

"You should get some sleep," Bryce said when we wrapped up.

It's what I intended to do anyway, but I didn't need him to tell me what to do. Especially when I watched my friends walk by. The first one I saw was Nathaniel; the friendship riff began to play as he entered my field of vision. Alton and Kaspian followed him, and the light-yet-beautiful violin riff started playing again. I wanted to keep listening to it. Eros looked at me and then tracked my eyes to the group. He smiled and then started walking toward them.

"Nathaniel," he yelled. Nathaniel turned his head and nodded at us.

"Let's go, Tack180. To your room," Bryce said.

We started walking toward Kaspian and his retainers since we were all going in the same direction.

"Eros." Nathaniel nudged him.

"How are you, T?" Alton asked.

"She's grieving," Bryce answered for me. I nodded. *He's not wrong.* But I also felt stronger emotions. The answers I got today only solidified what I had thought for a while. It wasn't a shock to me, so I didn't feel as sad as I expected to. It didn't mean it didn't hurt; it was just a dull pain versus an intense jolt. I would use that pain, just as I always have, to fight. That was the emotion I felt, *vengeful.*

"I'm reinvigorated," I said after a moment.

"I'm glad to hear you're doing well," Kaspian said.

"Kaspian, are you a fan of carrot cake?" Eros asked.

"I don't think I've had it before."

"T makes the best. You should stop by tomorrow. If you fight her, then you can get a piece for free."

"Come to think of it, that wouldn't be bad for business," Bryce mused.

"He doesn't like sweets," I answered at the same time Kaspian said, "I can swing by."

"You're going to battle me?" I laughed.

"He's got the home-field advantage," Alton said.

"He won't beat Tack180. None of you would," Bryce said. "But it would boost sales tremendously."

"I think the two of them would be a pretty even match," Alton said. "T's got great defense stats, sure. But Prince Kaspian's magic is the best in all of Fantasia. If he were to go all out, I think he'd win."

"Get off it, nerd," Bryce said. "My Tack180 would beat anyone in this MMORPG shit."

"Did you just call my retainer a nerd?" Kaspian asked. He tried not to laugh.

"I think he's right, to be honest," Nathaniel answered.

"You're all nerds here," Bryce tried again. "Everyone knows your worlds are full of nerds. Leave Tack180 out of it; she doesn't belong here."

I rolled my eyes.

I belong wherever I choose.

These people have been here for me through some crazy shit and didn't even blink when I sent them to a scary ass clown game for a week. Ghost probably would've stopped talking to me for at least a week if I had done that to him. I cared about them, all of them, and I never would've expected that. I'd changed since the glitch; whether that was because of actual change or the Game mechanics of being in Fantasia so long, I didn't know. But that didn't matter to me either way—if it was Game mechanics forcing my happiness, then I didn't want to lose it. I liked the sound of violins and the piano riff. I missed both when I was alone, and I would be even lonelier if I lost that music in the background altogether.

"Weren't you visiting Vampira?" Kaspian asked.

"That would make him a promiscuous nerd," Alton clarified. "That's why you're confused."

"Well, then, I'm offended. I think I'd be classified as a promiscuous nerd, too," Nathaniel offered to Bryce.

"All of you are fucking nerds," Bryce scoffed. "Come on, Tack180."

"No," I defended them. "These are some of the strongest fighters I've come across. I've been honored to fight alongside them."

"Whatever. Let's go." Bryce huffed as he walked off.

Shove it up your ass, Bryce.

Except, with everything going on, I didn't feel completely safe saying that to someone I didn't fully trust who could alter my code and reset me at any moment. I bit my tongue instead.

"We'll see you tomorrow, T," Kaspian said. "I look forward to trying your carrot cake."

"You'll have to buy it then." I gave him a smile and a wink, my original taunt. It was so fluid, as if someone was playing me and pressed the Y button. Except, *I* was playing, and it felt damn good to play as myself.

"Tack180," Bryce yelled, not turning around. He was really starting to piss me off.

"Come on, Eros." I sighed.

"What's going on with you and the prince?" Eros asked when we were far enough away. He wasn't hiding his smirk well at all.

"I don't know what you're talking about."

"I bet he changes your music."

"You all change my music."

"Not like he does."

"Okay, that's enough." I laughed as I pushed him.

Ghost was still programmed into my code as someone I love, regardless of whether he was alive. I don't ever think I could lose the love I felt for him, even though he was gone. I needed answers as to what happened to him, and that mission would never disappear because Ghost was, and always would be, a large part of my life.

But my music did change when Kaspian was around, and it was *beautiful.* It didn't make sense. How was it possible to love someone if it wasn't written into my code? Did that make my feelings for Kaspian more genuine than my feelings for Ghost? I felt guilty even considering it.

"How am I supposed to have feelings for someone else?" I asked out loud.

"I don't know, but you do, don't you?"

"I don't know." I took a deep breath. "I'm just confused. A lot has happened today, and I don't feel like I'm in a good headspace. The only thing I know right now is it's the right choice keeping you around. Thanks for being an awesome sidekick."

"What did you call me?" He elbowed me.

"You've turned out to be a pretty good one. Well, you'll do for now anyway."

"Yeah, you're not too shabby yourself."

Had I been the person I was when the glitch hit, I think Bryce and I would've been an amazing team. I would have appreciated his *my Tack180* bullshit. Hell, it would've pushed me to show off more. But hearing it now made me feel gross–dirty even. I was no one's property, especially not some stranger's plaything to show off. Hell, I wasn't even the same Tack180 that he thought I was. I didn't think it was possible to change so dramatically in such a short time. Were these my real feelings coming out since I'd been separated from *Duty Falls* for so long? Am I now closer to the person I was before erasing my memories or was my original Tack180 persona closer to that person? Regardless, I liked who I'd become; this Tack180's pretty lucky to have so many people who care about her.

As I lay in bed that night, ignoring messages from Bryce about how early he wanted to meet at the bakery, I started flicking through my DMs and follows. I searched for my new friends' names.

Kaspian, Prince of Fantasia, had about three-and-a-half million followers. I had over six million, so, regardless of how nerdy Bryce thought he was, Kaspian was still a well-liked and followed Character. I looked up Eros next; he only had four-hundred-thousand followers. The number was still nothing to laugh at, but I understood why he lived forty-five minutes away from the Platform now. You couldn't compete with high-level games if your numbers are *that* low. I pressed "follow" for Eros, and then I searched for Kaspian again and did the same. Under "suggested" I found Nathaniel, Alton, Seraphina, and Olivia. Then, from Olivia, I searched for SmokeScreen specifically. It must have been tiring to uphold two separate accounts that are both relatively popular, with SmokeScreen being the far more popular account, rivaling my own in likes. I followed all of them, but Kaspian was the first to follow me back, almost immediately. I felt my face flush with excitement and tried to ignore it.

I've got a job to do and a partner to avenge.

The next morning was a whirlwind. Bryce was promptly waiting in front of the bakery for me at four in the morning. When Eros and I rolled up, he looked at me, shook his head, and got out his tablet. He started typing, and I felt myself changing. I looked down and was wearing the pink apron DLC. I rolled my eyes at the pink fabric hugging my body. Of course, Bryce would make me wear it, the apron was a huge fan service, especially if we would be pulling in visitors from Vampira. The first guests showed up at six, then I non-stop battled all morning. We had long lines, some of the people just wanting to see me. It felt normal and uncomfortable at the same time. I was used to people wanting to see me, but these people were crying at the sight of me, even yelling, about how blessed they were to be in my presence or how thankful they were that I was alive.

Those who wanted to battle me were prioritized over other customers because the price to battle paid more. From magicians to vampire hunters, the best fighters across Fantasia showed up to fight me for a free slice of carrot cake. That, or they missed the battle option only accessible from the Platform. Training with Alton and Kaspian set me up to take on the different Character types I'd run into in Fantasia. It wasn't like I wouldn't have been prepared without their help, I still would've beat these fighters in the battle setting with Ghost, but without the actual Game mechanics or battle rules, people were fighting dirty. Bryce had already called out a few obvious cheaters, like those using magic from the crowd to assist a Character fighting against me, but that didn't mean he caught them all.

The first challenger came in hot, and all the subsequent battles followed a pretty similar pattern. They'd always charge at me first–surely, they must have forgotten I had great agility stats. Either way, they rushed, I dodged, like a perfectly choreographed dance. Then the real battle would start. If they were a one-on-one combat type of fighter, they'd try to overpower me, back me into a corner where it was harder to dodge.

I'd keep myself as centered as possible. Distance fighters of the group tried to make sure I didn't get too close. Unlike me, not all distance fighters knew hand-to-hand combat. So, while the whole thing was a great stress reliever, it got a little repetitive. Those sitting in the crowd enjoyed watching the battle while they ate their food. Given our turnout, and those who opted for the more expensive battle *and* a baked good afterward, we more than quadrupled our typical income.

The last challenger of the day was a warrior with wings on his back. I'm assuming he was some kind of fallen angel type Character; his dark wings got a little annoying as they kept hitting objects around the bakery. I rolled my eyes and pointed outside, expecting a better and larger space to battle. Except, the area outside the bakery was packed: lines weaving through the street so that people could still see the fights instead of being stuck away from the action.

"Hold on, Blessed One." The guy scooped me into his arms and flew up into the sky. *Son of a bitch.* I raised a brow at him and resisted the urge to stab him with a knife.

"No cheating," Bryce yelled. "The battle hasn't started yet."

"Find us in the western field outside of Castle Town," the fallen angel yelled back. A fall from this height would be a respawn, so I didn't move as he began flying over the wall surrounding the town and then stopped in the open field. Those who used magic created a portal, immediately showing up before we landed. One of them was nice enough to bring Eros and Bryce.

"Alright," Bryce called out when we got settled. "We've got ourselves a match."

"Honor me, Holy One, Tack180, with a battle." There was something about the way he spoke, as if he was mocking me. Or at least mocking the people who had been yelling at me all day. I looked around the field with nothing to protect me and nothing to protect him. It'd be pretty evenly matched. I nodded and pulled out two knives from my thigh holsters.

Let's fight.

As expected, he charged me first, and I dodged. He flew into the air, probably only ten feet, and then dive-bombed down. I backflipped away from his attack before he engaged in military-style combat moves, like Ghost. He continued to push an offensive onslaught, and I blocked, dodged, and parried every attack.

"I can do this all day." I laughed. I *have* been doing this all day.

"Divine Restitution," he yelled.

A warm, white light beamed down, and I barely dodged it. So, he was distance and hand-to-hand. I admit; I wasn't expecting that, but it didn't make him any more of a challenge to me. I ran forward, dodging as he yelled "Divine Restitution" repeatedly. I knew it was coming every time he did it, so it's not like he was going to surprise me with it. He reached forward to punch me, and, in a fluid motion, I blocked and pushed his hands down. I shoved forward with my shoulder on his dominant side, which knocked him off-balance, forcing him to swing with his left hand. I locked his arm with my own, planted my left foot, and swung my right. He fell, and I landed on top of him, still locked to his arm. I pushed my body down on his, the weight keeping him from wiggling.

Just as every battle started the same way, they also ended the same. I brought a knife up to his throat and asked him the same question they all got, "Do you know anything about the Glitch?"

"No," they all replied. And, just as with every time before, I stared at him; knife on his throat, provocation in his eyes, and a reputation on the line. But I couldn't do it. Just the thought of killing any of them terrified me. What if he didn't come back? Sure, Isa and Bryce had me test the knives out on NPCs, but these were *real* people with *real* lives. I couldn't risk it; *who am I anymore?*

"Finish him," the crowd yelled.

I tapped his shoulder, indicating that I had won and the battle was over.

"That's it," Bryce called out. "Tack180's won another one."

I stood up and felt the stab of metal near my ankle, ripping its way through my Achilles tendon. The snap of the tendon dropped me to the floor. The crowd murmured in shock as I rolled my body away from the angel while he continued to stab at me with a hidden blade he had pulled out from who knows where? Eros ran over and jumped in between the attacker and me. I reached for my bloodied foot and applied pressure, decreasing the rate at which my HP was falling. My body began to feel heavy as I tried to get to my messages to notify Olivia. I looked back just as Eros stabbed the fallen angel in the throat. He choked out a bloodied cough before falling to the ground and respawning.

"Holy One, I can heal you." Someone came up to my side.

"She can re-heal." Eros ran over to me and pushed the other person away. He turned to me and applied pressure, as well. "I don't trust anyone we don't know, and Liv's on her way."

I nodded, withholding the heavy feeling as much as I could. I didn't want to freeze the world before my healer got to me.

"Give us a break," Bryce yelled out and raised his hands. The group didn't move as they continued to circle us. Most people began harassing the fallen angel, who, finally fed up with the angry fans, got up and flew off. No one liked a cheater. The others, however, made a circle around me and began praying out loud for my safety.

"Move out of the way," I heard Olivia yell as she pushed her way through the crowd. She fell to the ground beside me and held her staff over my entire leg. I let go and looked away, feeling immediate relief from the pain. She looked back at Bryce and yelled, "That's it for the day."

"You can't tell me what to do," Bryce countered.

"Yes, I can. You need to determine safeguards to prevent this in case T really gets hurt in the future." Then she started to whisper, "Unless you want her to actually die?"

"That's it for today, folks. Thanks for swinging by for the battle. The kind person who opens a portal back to the bakery for us, where we will continue to sell our goods, will get a free slice of carrot cake." Bryce waved. A few people left the crowd, but most were ready to follow us back to the bakery. There were at least a dozen different portals back to the bakery, all wanting a free slice of cake.

"You're good now." Olivia nodded. I stood up and it felt as if nothing had happened.

"I let my guard down." I shook my head. How could I be so stupid? The game was called; I should've been safe, but this wasn't normal life anymore. In the past, he'd have been kicked out of any game for a cheap shot like that. Now, he faced no repercussions other than if someone caught it on video and it went viral, but he won't be the only one to do shit like that. It was just the beginning. Lawfulness be damned if there was no Game mechanics to prohibit it and no way to monitor or confirm cheating to the point of taking action. It wasn't the same Game we knew before. I can't expect people to play by the rules. I don't even know if I want to play by the rules: who says I have to be Bryce's bitch? I don't *want* to be someone's Character anymore, especially if it gets me stabbed in the back, well, Achilles tendon.

"You were safe," Olivia said. "Cheaters like that always bugged me. He'll get what he deserves. I'll make sure the queen knows about this."

We went through a random portal back to the bakery, and it was like nothing had changed. Bryce started a sign-up sheet to accurately determine what our days would look like. Within thirty minutes, we were booked for two months-worth of battles. It was an exhausting page to look at. I didn't want to do this for two months. I was hoping to find some sort of lead to follow, in which I could travel with my friends and get answers—long before two months from now. I heard something and ignored it as I scanned through the list of people. I sighed and placed the sign-up sheet on the counter in front of me.

"T!" Olivia's hand was waving in front of my face. Behind her stood Kaspian, Alton, and Nathaniel. "Earth to T."

"Sorry." I took off my pink apron and put it on the counter so I could take a break with my crew.

"You were a zombie there for a second; I didn't think we'd be able to get you out of your trance. You missed Nathaniel's not-so-subtle comments about your apron, and that's when we realized something was off," Olivia said. Nathaniel just winked at me.

"We heard what happened," Kaspian said. "Know that we will find the perpetrator and make sure they are dealt with accordingly. Fantasia will *not* allow disarray during this time. Our citizens and games within our world will be made aware, and this man, if you can even call him that, will be made an example of."

"Make that another Ghost," Bryce yelled from the front. I looked up at the sound of Ghost's name as if I thought he'd be there, knowing damn well he wasn't. It was such an instinctive motion.

"Has Isa got any more information?" I asked.

"She's still mapping things out right now. It doesn't seem like anyone has any answers at this time. Or, if they do know what is happening, they aren't talking," Kaspian said. "I tried to find out more about those who are like you, and I was given a similar answer that you were."

"It's a waiting game—we all know how Production works," Alton sighed.

I nodded.

"Guess you're off the hook then, Kaspian." Eros punched him on the shoulder. Kaspian wiped off the area where Eros hit and then took a step away.

"He wasn't ready for the disappointment of defeat today anyway," I laughed.

"I might not have the sweet taste of victory today, but a slice of your cake should hold me over," he countered.

"Only winners get free cake." I slid any readily available cakes away from him. He pulled out a pouch of coins, grabbed a few, and threw them on the counter.

"Tack180, let's go," Bryce yelled from the front. "Every minute you're late is another ten reps of your least favorite exercise today."

I slid a slice of carrot cake in his direction and winked. Then I grabbed another one to bring to the front.

"If you aren't going to battle, then they need to go away," Bryce said when I got there.

"Some would say they're boosting our sales," I countered.

"Not if you're distracted."

"Fine, fine," I agreed.

Bryce kept true to his promise and made me pay for it during training. Eros wasn't allowed to stay, and, instead of going to the castle, we trained outside of Castle Town, including, but not limited to, battling actual monsters. My side effects from the battles were real; burns, cuts, short-lasting poisons—the works. New scars formed on my body since I didn't have Olivia to heal me. But nothing was as bad as the Achilles tendon, I had to be thankful for that, I guess. Every day I spent training was another day stronger, another day ready for revenge.

"Stop making that face, or you'll give yourself more wrinkles," Bryce said as we walked back to the castle.

"Excuse me? More wrinkles?"

"Relax, it's a joke because you don't have any. When I stop making comments, that means you actually have wrinkles."

"That is," I stopped to think carefully, "rude."

"It's Producer humor; I guess you wouldn't get it."

"I think I hate you," I sighed.

"That's my Tack180. Today was amazing for sales and our reputation. We're making great progress here. It's not our end goal, but it has potential."

"We aren't doing this any longer than it takes to get answers."

"I agree to that. We're going to Corporous when this shit finally lifts."

"Hell no," I said. Corporous was for people like Alton and the Producers, it would be hell on earth for me. Sure, I wasn't happy I ended up in Fantasia, but at least it was known for adventure and fighting. Corporous had that stupid *Business Business* game and other "work" games. That wasn't somewhere for a warrior to live.

"What? What exactly do you expect us to do?"

"I'm chasing that Glitch until it's gone, and, once it's eradicated from all the worlds, I'm going to come back here," I said. "I want to stay with my friends."

"These people aren't your friends, Tack180. They're taking care of you as a person stuck out of their game. They don't understand the complexity of who you are and what is expected of you. You can't return here when the Glitch is gone. We've got a game to return to, a legacy to claim."

"Eros is my friend. Regardless of if the royals are only being nice. Eros and Smo—livia are my friends." I quickly caught myself before I called Olivia by her Player name.

"Nicknames, huh?" he laughed. It had only become a nickname because I almost outed her frequently. "It's all for show. Everyone wants to be associated with *the* Tack180. No one wanted you before you were famous but us. Pro-duc-tion. We're all you have."

"That's not true," I said.

"You didn't want your memories for a reason. Now, trust me. Production will keep you happy. These people don't truly care about you; they care about your status and what it can do for their game when this whole glitch is over."

I felt so lonely. I wanted to think that the friendships I made were real, but it was unusual. No one usually liked me; they were all turned away by my "off-putting" behavior. Ghost was *literally* all I had, past and present. Bryce could be right—they could be using me for my fame. But that contradicted everything I knew about the royals, their retainers, and the way they viewed friendship, inside and outside of their game. And yet, here I was, with no memories, no Ghost, and very real memories of people telling me how shitty a person I can be because I wasn't *nice* enough. The royals and their retainers very well could hate me.

No. Don't think like that.

I wasn't the same Tack180 those other people hated, and I wouldn't let Bryce get into my head. He might think the two of us are going to Corporous, but I wouldn't thrive there, especially after dealing with the Glitch. *That* was what I should be doing right now: dealing with the Glitch and getting answers. A stupid battle bakery wasn't doing me any good. It was settling. I let Bryce talk me into settling because he made it seem like there was no other option for me. There were plenty of other options, dealing with the

Glitch and coming back here was one of them. And I wasn't waiting around for Bryce to decide for us. I needed to separate myself from him, but how?

I didn't talk as we walked the remainder of the way to the castle. I left Bryce and went to the alehouse first, where I found Eros and Nathaniel fucking around.

"T," they cheered as I entered the room. I smiled and grabbed the glass Nathaniel offered to me.

"I need this," I said.

"Nathaniel was just telling me about Fantasia's Producer." Eros pushed his glass up toward mine. They made a clinking sound as they touched, then he drank more.

"Did Bryce take over your game?" I asked.

That'd be shitty.

"No, Kaspian introduced me earlier. She's gorgeous and survived because she lives in a neighboring province of Fantasia that the Glitch didn't hit and works remotely. Since we're taking the lead in fixing issues, she's coming to join us here. She's amazing." Then he took another big sip before repeating, "She's amazing."

"That's good." I nodded. So, they had an *amazing* Producer, and I was stuck with Bryce, who made me feel like shit by solidifying every insecurity I had about myself. I was pissed. I wanted to yell, throw my drink, flip the table, or all of the above. They weren't the ones I was angry at. I didn't even know who I was angry at or if I even was angry. I just felt empty in my stomach like I was going to throw up. They wouldn't know how to get me out of Bryce's grip anyway. There were a few who could, but SmokeScreen had the most sway in gaming. I stood up, "I'm going to find Smolivia."

"Smolivia the Great," Eros and Nathaniel cheered. I tapped the table twice, then left. If not SmokeScreen, the royals would be my next bet at breaking ties with Bryce. SmokeScreen's clout, along with my own, would get anyone's attention. Seraphina and Kaspian might have connections themselves, but they seem to be playing by the rules, and Bryce, as a member of Production, *is* the rule.

"Ah, there she is," I heard Seraphina say in the distance. I looked up, and she was flanked by Olivia, Kaspian, and a woman I didn't know. Olivia frantically waved at me—just who I wanted to see. I diverted off my original course and joined them. "This is the one we were telling you about."

I crossed my arms in front of my body and stared at the woman I didn't recognize. *I felt jealous.* Her features were soft, something about her seemed calming, and she smiled with her eyes even when she wasn't smiling. She was friendly and inviting, all without saying a word. The complete opposite of Bryce. If this was their Producer, I understood why Nathaniel was so enamored with her.

"It is an honor to meet you both," she said quietly. "I'm Ingrid."

"I'm Tack180, but you can call me T."

"You are the one who forced the Glitch out of Fantasia?" She nodded at me. I thought back to the battle with the Glitch during the Council of Fantasia. Seraphina had hugged me that day and thanked me for saving Fantasia. Kaspian had mentioned I saved Fantasia, as well, and that they owed me a great deal. I didn't think I had *saved* anyone. It seemed more like luck that time than anything else.

"Well, I don't know how much I actually did, but yes, I was there," I said.

"Allow me to find some way to thank you for saving Fantasia and its surrounding games." She paused for a moment. "A typical Fantasian Ball, in honor of you, would also work to boost the morale of the people."

"I agree," Seraphina said. "A party in her honor would be most appropriate."

That sounds absolutely unbearable.

"Especially if Isabella and I can get your quest system back up and running," Ingrid said.

"Quest system? Does that mean the Game is back up?" I asked. If the Game is up and running, I'm not sure how I'll be able to separate from the Producer of *Duty Falls*, it seemed impossible. I squeezed my arms as I pulled them tighter across my body than they were before. I didn't want to be stuck again, not when I just started getting answers. Fuck, most of all, I didn't want to end up in Corporous because that's where Bryce thought we should go.

"While you still cannot *play* the Game, our quest system operates separately from the Game. Similar, I'm assuming, to the clown game you found yourselves in. That way, if a blackout were to occur, we could operate in an 'offline mode.' When the glitch first happened, there were still available quests for Players. However, without access to Production for such an extended time: no one has been making new quests on the back end. Ingrid is here to change that," Seraphina said. I didn't realize I had been holding my breath. I exhaled at the realization that the Game wasn't magically fixed, and I didn't have to leave.

"Yes, it would be quite the extravaganza. I'd love to make quests that include you." Ingrid looked at me. "For the people to celebrate."

"Quests with me?"

"Minor quests that even entry-level Players could engage in—they would be as simple as saying hello to you on the street or at the ball. Medium is the next level, so buying something from you at your store. High, with the ability to earn significant amounts of gold, EXP, and special items could include going on missions with you in their party or dancing with you at the ball."

"To be honest, I don't like people enough to dance with them." I just wanted to ask Olivia if she knew of a way to help me out, not sign up for a ball. I shifted my weight and sighed. Let's hurry up this conversation so I can talk to Olivia.

"That's what makes the levels worth it. If everyone could do it, then it wouldn't be considered hard. I can sense your hesitation," Ingrid said. "If you would prefer not to be included in this world, then we can keep you out of it."

"Now doesn't really seem like the right time for something like a ball, does it? I mean, people are dead," I answered. Seraphina cleared her throat, clearly caught off guard by the answer I gave.

"We all want to get back to normal, T," Olivia said. Her eyes were puffy and even though she acted like her normal self, she had been grieving and not hiding it well. "Your way is finding answers, but ours is to bring back something familiar and normal to our people. A ball would be just that. Sure, your opinions have changed now, but what did you want when you first came here?"

To get home. I wanted to get back to the Platform, to Ghost, to what was familiar. Yeah, it seemed a bit weird to me to be celebrating with a ball right now, but I can't blame Fantasians for wanting normalcy.

"I get it," I sighed.

"If you'd like to be included, I will need written consent and approval from your Producer." Ingrid looked at Seraphina. "Have you found lawyers yet?"

Lawyers? Yes! That's exactly what I need right now.

I uncrossed my arms and looked at Seraphina, who was quick to answer.

"Yes, we have a lawyer coming tomorrow." Then she looked at me. "He would like to speak with you and Bryce, as well."

I nodded. That was it. I would just ask to end my contract with Bryce. He was the one holding me back now. Without him, I can travel the worlds, get my revenge, and get home faster.

"I'd like to continue my tour now," she said, looking at Seraphina.

"Yes, follow me." Seraphina and Ingrid started to leave. "Kaspian, you may stay behind. You're no longer needed."

"You look like you could use a game of chess." He smiled.

"I—" I paused. Before the mention of lawyers, I could've used a game of chess. Lawyers were a game-changer; I was happier now than I was during practice with Bryce. Still, I would always enjoy playing a game of chess with him; it was relaxing, it made me at ease, and I enjoyed the way the music changed when we were together. Was that wrong? I was going to leave here as soon as I got the chance, but I feel like he was one of the reasons I wanted to come back. I felt nauseous, like I was guilty, for wanting to spend time with him.

"We don't have to talk," he offered again. Then he smiled. "I'll let you be white."

I laughed, "It's not that."

"I'm here as a friend if you need one."

"Let's go," I agreed. He was persistent, and I liked it.

"Today didn't go as planned," he said as we walked to the library. "Is that why you're upset?"

"I'm not upset," I said.

"Okay." he laughed.

"At least, not now," I clarified since he had obviously caught on.

"Everything about you during that conversation said otherwise. You were folding your arms across your chest, and you haven't done that in a while. The way you were talking to us was sharp, which makes me think you're mad at us, although I can't tell why. We left on good terms earlier today. Or did I miss something?"

"You noticed those things?" I laughed. I felt my cheeks heat up and looked out of the window we passed on our way to the library, trying to avoid making eye contact.

What are you doing, T? I asked myself.

Maybe I shouldn't be spending so much time with Kaspian. I should be looking for Ghost right now. I just got mad at Bryce for holding me back, and now I'm going to waste my time by playing chess with someone who is changing the sound of my music. I know damn well that it's the romance riff Nathaniel was teasing me about.

"Your tells are a little less obvious than someone like Olivia, but they are pretty consistent with my sister's tells. Between my mother and my sister, I was raised knowing how to spot the signs of an angry woman. Besides, as I said before, I don't like it when you're mad."

"Fuck," I sighed as we entered the library. I didn't need to hear that or anything else that would confuse me even more.

"Do you want to talk about it?"

It? Hell no, I'd rather he didn't know I was getting feelings for him right now. I could lie and bring up the lawyer situation, but why even hide it? I'm not doing anything wrong. Ghost was dead, and I will still avenge his death.

That doesn't stop me from coming back to Fantasia and starting a new life here.

"I'd rather be locked in a box full of spiders than talk about how confused I am."

"Spiders? Wouldn't have expected that."

"Everyone has their weaknesses and Character Traits."

"Fair point—needles."

"What?"

"Mine's needles."

"Bad experience?"

"Character Trait, like yours. But not a lot of experience with needles around here too often, so I'm fine."

"I'm sure you've been stabbed by swords before, and you fear needles?"

"Spiders." He raised a brow at me.

"Touché."

He didn't ask any more questions, and I didn't talk about it any further. But spending that time with Kaspian solidified that Bryce was wrong: they *were* my friends, regardless of what he thought. I was looking forward to talking with the lawyer and seeing what my options are.

***

The next morning, Bryce was waiting for me at the bakery. Eros walked with me to the bakery, so Bryce didn't start talking right away. I opened the door, Eros entered, and then Bryce stopped me before I could.

"Tack180," he started. "I want to apologize."

"Huh?"

"I don't think we ended yesterday on a good note. We are both in a place that neither of us wants to be in and it's stressing me out. What you said bothered me, and I took that stress out on you. I'm sorry."

"Oh, okay. Thank you."

"It doesn't sound like you accept it. We're all we've got. We need to work this out so that we can keep working together."

He was wrong. He was *so* wrong, and he had no idea. I had so much more to fall back on than he did, and I think he knew that. He wanted me to feel helpless so I would never leave him. I propped the doors to the bakery open. I'd listen to his bullshit, but I wouldn't believe it anymore.

"I appreciate it. As you admitted, this is hard for you, and you can tell this is hard for me, too."

"We're good?"

"Yeah." Good enough. I walked inside and brought out the sign to place in the street with our menu on it. I just had to play nice with Bryce for now. I wasn't going to be stuck with him for long. When I got the chance to talk with the lawyer, I'd like to discuss my options for traveling to other worlds for answers and retiring here, in Fantasia, when the Glitch was finally dealt with. I turned to go back into the bakery to prep and he grabbed my arm.

"Before you go in. My buddy is a lawyer who happened to be in Vampira during the glitch. He set up a meeting with your royal friends and wants to see us, too."

His buddy. Of course, it was his buddy. A weight filled my chest, but it wasn't the glitch. It was my hope of avenging Ghost and living a normal life in Fantasia dying. I nodded and turned my head away from him as I entered the bakery; I wouldn't give him the satisfaction of seeing me cry, so I climbed the ladder for a few minutes of silence. I heard someone climb the ladder after me. I quickly wiped away the tears on my face.

"Woah, it's chill," Eros said. He came up and put his arms around me. I went in for the hug and let silent tears fall down my cheeks. Bryce had control over me, just like a Player, except I didn't want to be someone's Character anymore. It was my turn to be my own Player and Character.

After working at the bakery, we all walked to the castle per Bryce's orders. Eros went in the direction of the alehouse, and I knew he was going to join Nathaniel. I looked around the castle, hoping to see a familiar face but no one was around as we went to find the lawyer in the strategy room.

"Bryce, my man," the loud lawyer yelled when we entered the room.

"Cody, glad to see you made it." Bryce clasped his hand in Cody's, they hugged, then patted each other on the back.

"Who would've thought your game would be around still," Cody said in disbelief. "You lucked out."

"You're tellin' me, man. And it was Tack180 too, not even Ghost."

"The beautiful Tack180," Cody addressed me. "So nice to meet you."

"Let's get this over with," I said, sitting down.

"Your reputation precedes you. So, I agreed to a crossover for you guys, so you can start monetizing your time here a bit better. They want to honor you all at some party tomorrow, and I said, go for it. Free alcohol and food, am I right?"

"That sounds amazing. What about our contract?"

"Fuck yeah, bro. Your contract stands as is. Nothing in here about glitches ruining the world affecting your contract. In fact, since there are clauses in here for blackout procedures, it only solidifies that the contract is in place as is."

"I'd like to discuss that further," I said.

"Sorry, Tack180. You're SOL here. You signed the contract, did you not?"

"Not that I remember."

"She chose to forget her memories, but she did," Bryce answered.

"Then the contract stands as is."

"That contract was made without any idea that something like this was possible. I feel, given the current set of circumstances, which is more than just me wanting out of a contract, we should re-evaluate things. Blackouts, as written in the contract, describe events that last, on average, less than twelve hours." I used my knowledge gained from the Council of Fantasia to help guide my argument. "Before this, the longest blackout was almost a hundred years ago when Henry Fudders still worked for Gaming Science. Besides, this isn't a typical blackout. The Platform is gone. *Ghost* is gone."

"Basically, as stated in your contract, which was signed *without* Ghost, you need to fulfill your end of the bargain and it doesn't matter how you feel about how your Producer uses your money or makes new game material for you," Cody said. "Plus, you got crossover approved so we can start working on some quests or whatever bullshit they do here."

My heart was racing. Did I lose? That meant I'd have to go back to normal, and even to Corporous when this was over to work for Bryce rather than get the answers I deserved. *Hell no.* I wasn't just going to sit there and let them win.

They don't get to determine who I become.

"I need a minute. I'm allowed one fifteen-minute break during negotiations." I stood up from the table, remembering the only thing I could about the real world.

"These aren't negotiations," Cody said.

"That's fine. Give her a break," Bryce offered.

"We are starting in fifteen with or without you."

I started a timer and left the room. Once I closed the door, I started running toward the library where I was hoping the royals kept some material on negotiations, Producers, and anything about the real world. As I turned a corner, I saw Eros standing with Nathaniel, Alton, and Kaspian.

"T," Eros said excitedly as he saw me coming. "How did it go?"

"Not well, still going, can't talk," I yelled as I ran by.

I ignored him as I turned another corner and rushed into the library. Sitting there on a computer was Isa. She looked up at me and then back to her screen, giving zero fucks about my dramatic entrance. I started scanning books to see what area of the library I was in. Fiction, not right. Non-fiction, better, but still not right.

Fuck, where was it?

"What is it you're looking for?" Isa asked.

"Did I say that out loud?"

"You didn't say anything, but it's obvious you are looking for something."

"I need as much as I can get on negotiations and fighting for my legal rights." I looked at the timer. "I have eight minutes left."

"Ah, it's negotiation day with the ass-bro-les," she sighed. "Bryce is manageable on his own, but put him in a room with Cody, and it's like we're back at a frat party."

"How can you be friends with him?" I asked. "You're so cool, and he's just... not."

"We were on assignment in Vampira. They were having technical difficulties. Bryce also serves as one of their Assistant Producers, mostly because he enjoyed his business trips there."

"That makes more sense. Ah! Here are some things."

"I highly recommend reaching out to Nia."

"Who?"

"Nia, one of the most notable lawyers in all the worlds. She's still alive. She was in Corporous when the glitch happened. No one seems to have been touched there, although there were unconfirmed sightings, which means there are actually probably a lot of other lawyers alive. They may not all be as knowledgeable in gaming as Cody, but Nia is. In fact, she would easily win any argument against him. She probably worked for your Producers but, if offered the right amount, I bet she would help you out."

"How much is the right amount?"

"That's up to her."

"Thanks. I can have Eros message her—"

"Not him." She cut me off. "Nia only works with high-level, public cases. She would only answer something from you, not Eros."

"Okay, gotta go."

I grabbed as many books as I could hold and started running back. Eros and the rest of the boys were almost to the library when I left.

"We came to help." Nathaniel waved.

"Not enough time." I started fast walking past them.

"What is that?" Alton asked, looking at the books in my hands.

"Books on negotiations and working with Producers. I'm going to need you guys to walk faster if you are going to talk to me. I have less than two minutes to get back."

"T, in that top book, there is a lot of helpful information about your rights in the legal process. Don't let them push you around." Kaspian pointed. "You are allowed to have your own legal counsel if you don't believe the ones working with you are providing fair representation. You can claim it. There is a word for it, I just can't remember."

"It's okay. I need to message Nia."

"Who?" Eros asked. "I can message them now."

"She won't respond to you. She only responds to famous people."

"Rude," Eros said. "You, that is. Lots of people like Indie games."

"That's not what I mean, Eros. I'm a high-level Character from a popular game. She will respond to me."

"It still hurts."

"Eros," Kaspian and I said at the same time.

I got to the door, and Kaspian stopped me. Thirty seconds left.

"You can do this," he said. "I believe in you." The violins started to intertwine with my music again.

"Me, too," Eros joined in. "Go in there, kick ass, break balls, and negotiate the shit out of it."

"I'm out of here." I kicked the door open, arms full of books, just as the timer went off. Cody and Bryce looked at me in surprise. "Let's negotiate, shall we?"

"Like I said before," Cody started. "This isn't a negotiation."

"Anytime a Producer, or Production representative, Character, and lawyer meet in the same room, it can be considered a negotiation and is therefore subject to following the same guidelines as all negotiations," Kaspian said loudly from the still-open door.

"What he said," I said.

"Close the door," Cody yelled at Bryce, who complied immediately.

I started opening books to their index and finding relevant pages. I wasn't going to get it resolved that day but, at least, I could buy myself more time. I felt something on my face—glasses. I sighed heavily and pulled them off, but a new pair just respawned on my face. Cody and Bryce both started snickering.

"Enough," I yelled.

"But you looked so studious, I just had to," Bryce said. "Consider the additional DLC money we could make off a 'tutor' Tack180 pack. If we are stuck here, I'm sure it would be a big moneymaker in Vampira."

"I didn't sign up to be a prostitute, and I know damn well that was not in my contract. I don't agree to a crossover in Vampira."

"Tack180, I need you to remember that *I* am a lawyer, and *you* are a Character. This is my actual job, not a game to me." Cody menacingly leaned across the table. "I was friendly earlier, but now you're pissing me off. I'm a motherfucking shark, and you're a tiny fish in an ocean full of other irrelevant fish."

Ping. It was a message that we all received because Cody stopped talking momentarily to check it. I glanced, too. The message was from Nia.

"You should not be communicating with my client when I am not present," it read.

"Who is Nia?" Bryce asked Cody, then looked at me.

"My lawyer," I said. I could barely believe it myself, but I knew she was there for me.

In your face, Bryce. I've got friends.

"I'm your lawyer," Cody said.

"No, you're a lawyer we found on the fly. I didn't hire you, and I have no intention of paying you. We didn't sign any contract to work together, and it's *very* obvious that Bryce is your client."

"Stop talking without me. All things said must now be transcribed in the group message until we have time to set up a video conference with all of us present." Nia sent another message. I quickly transcribed what had happened to her, and she immediately responded, "Thank you. Tack180, don't say anything unless I tell you."

"Can she do this?" Bryce asked Cody. I transcribed for Nia. Cody paused for a second before speaking.

"Yes," Cody said at the same time Nia sent it. "But she has no ground to stand on."

"Why do you say that?" Nia asked.

"Because, Nia, this is unprecedented. This isn't life like it was before."

That part pissed me off. I furiously typed what Cody had said, then, in a private DM to Nia, sent a period so she wouldn't immediately respond to the group chat. I gave her a brief commentary on what Cody had said to me about the contract remaining intact and why. She sent me a thumbs up.

"Ah great, so you admit that there are extenuating circumstances; this will help our argument to dismiss the contract," she sent to the group chat.

"That's not what I meant," Cody backtracked.

"I call for us to reconvene tomorrow at noon. Tack180 is legally allowed 120 minutes of prep time with her council for negotiations, which was unfairly denied to her. If you are late by even a minute to our delayed negotiations, it will immediately terminate the contract as it is written. Tack180 will be a free agent: all her assets will remain with her, and nothing, not even the past few days' salaries, will be paid out to Bryce. Understood?"

"Go fuck yourself, Nia," Cody said.

"Hardly a threat if I'd enjoy it," she replied.

"How can she do this?" Bryce asked Cody, a vein popping out his head. I continued to transcribe to Nia.

"I know the law," she replied at the same time that Cody said, "Characters have a lot of rights they fought for considering they give up so much to join the Game."

"That brings this meeting to a close," Nia sent again. "Tack180, get up and walk out of the room. They should make no other comments to you. They are not allowed to talk to you again until tomorrow's meeting. Do you understand?"

"Yes," I replied.

"I wasn't talking to you," she said. "I don't want to hear of any sneaky business. Got it, Cody?"

"Understood," he said.

I stood up and walked out of the room, just as Nia had advised me. The boys were waiting for me outside the room. I ran up to Kaspian and hugged him. I didn't deserve whatever he did to pull strings to get Nia involved.

"Thank you so much," I said. "I promise to repay you for her services."

"What happened?" Kaspian asked, hugging me back. "Why are you repaying me?"

"It wasn't you?" I pulled away from Kaspian to look at him, but for some reason, we were both still holding onto each other, and I didn't mind. I looked at Eros. "She actually responded to you?"

"You're so hurtful, T," Eros shook his head. "But I had nothing to do with it."

"Nathaniel?"

"It was me," Alton admitted.

"You?" I asked, confused. Our personalities always clashed, it didn't mean I didn't like the guy, but he just wouldn't be someone I hung out with outside of the group. He was a goody-goody rule-follower, and I was more the type to move my Character when being played by rubbish Players. Ghost would've got on with Alton; he had a similar sense of duty and liked following all codes of conduct. What Alton did for me, there was no way to thank him for that. "How? Why?"

"You have enough followers for that?" Eros asked.

"I have more followers than you, jackass," Alton retorted.

"Alton," I started, finally removing myself completely from Kaspian. "I can't thank you enough. How much do I owe you?"

"Nothing. Olivia would kill me if I didn't help you out and, I might not be trying to get in your pants like the other guys, but I still like you enough."

"Not trying to get in her pants." Eros raised his hands.

"Totally trying to get in her pants." Nathaniel raised a single hand.

"I can't let you pay for me. Please." I grabbed his shoulders. "Let me pay you back."

"She's doing this pro-bono."

"Why?"

"She's my sister, so she said she would do it."

Given Alton's personality, it would make sense that his sister was also a rule-follower and, more so, a fucking lawyer. The best lawyer. The one I needed at that exact moment in time. I finally got the featured prize in a gacha game and didn't even have to spend my money.

"Why didn't you get your sister to help us, too?" Kaspian asked.

"She is now, don't worry. I had to make sure she was alive first. And I, honestly, didn't think you would want her either."

"Why not?"

"Because she represented Rebecca."

Rebecca. Who the fuck is Rebecca?

Becca. Becky. ButtBusterBecky. Oh shit, Nia facilitated ButtBusterBecky's exit from Fantasia. I looked over at Kaspian. He was always so nonchalant about ButtBusterBecky, it was easy to tease him about it. If it did bother him, you wouldn't know–he never told us to stop. I didn't know if mentioning her hurt him, but his eyes were wide for a second, then he tilted his head before nodding.

"Then she will be good to have on our side," he said.

"Yeah, I didn't realize that Cody would be such a tool or else I would have just reached out to Nia sooner. I'm sorry, sir."

"This calls for a drink," Eros said. "To celebrate T having a successful meeting."

"Oh, it was more than successful. Nia is amazing. I feel like she'll help me get exactly what I want."

"Definitely need celebratory drinks then." Eros lifted a hand, and I high-fived him.

We celebrated like it was the first night we had gone out again. Olivia joined us at one point, and we filled her in on exactly what happened. She was unquestionably the most excited out of us to be working with Nia; it seemed like she had worked with her in the past. I wanted to ask her about it because I was genuinely curious about my friend's life, but it felt like I was snooping. As though I didn't deserve to know about it since I didn't know her at that time. Olivia didn't seem like the type to worry about that shit, but I did. I didn't like people who just wanted to know shit about me because I was Tack180 and they didn't genuinely care about me, just about my name.

Nia worked quickly; while we were out, I received a notification for "Tack180 Meeting" for seven in the morning. I tried to move it back so that I could still open up the bakery that morning, but all Nia said back was, "No. Accept the meeting invite."

"What's that face for?" Eros asked as he sat next to me.

"Just finalizing details with Nia for tomorrow."

"What's *your* plan? I'm going to ask Nia to negotiate for me to stay here," Eros said. "This is the most fun I've had as a Character, and it's actually by being a Player and Character at the same time. I could get used to this life. Plus, I don't think Nathaniel would survive without me. I'm obviously *his* best friend."

"What about me?" I was glad to hear Eros's answer. It confirmed we had actually formed a friendship in the month we'd been working together, and he wasn't just using me to go home anymore. I should never have doubted any of them.

"I thought I made it clear I was just using you," he joked.

"Yeah, well, I want to stay, too. But first, I've got some work to do. I want to search until I find answers then defeat the Glitch for good. Once I've done that, especially if there's nothing left of *Duty Falls* and no one waiting for me, I want to come back here. I want to be my own Player."

"If you left tomorrow, to roam the worlds, killing monsters on your path to creating your own RPG game exploring Fantasia and surrounding worlds, fighting the Glitch, and making friends along the way, then I would join you. It sounds like an awesome game."

"But what about Nathaniel?" I asked.

"Nathaniel isn't *my* best friend." He was grinning at me.

"You're my best friend, too," I said, putting my head on his shoulder.

***

Nia and I prepped all morning, and she was confident we would get everything we asked for, especially after Cody's slip up from the day before. I ran into Olivia on my way to the strategy room, and she wished me luck, explaining that the others were busy with Ingrid and Isa setting up the quests but that she wanted to come by anyway. That simple sentence took her about fifteen minutes of talking to get to, but it was nice to know she supported me.

I entered the strategy room, which we used as a meeting place, with one minute to spare. Bryce and Cody were already inside, waiting. I opened the video conference between all of us and informed Nia we were ready. The meeting was long, argumentative, and overly wordy. I found myself glazing over the scene as if I wasn't in it, knowing that much of it wasn't for me anyway. We agreed to consider my contract void. Bryce tried not to show emotion, but you could tell by the way he looked down when negotiations started going south for him that it hurt him on some level. Did I want to kick the guy while he was down when I was all he had? No, not really. But he was dragging me down with him, and that's where I drew the line. Still, he looked sad, almost childlike, in learning that he couldn't alter me or associate with me moving forward. I felt guilty even though I was doing the right thing for me. He still had my likeness from the *Duty Falls*, though, and anything before that point was still fair game since he still held rights to *Duty Falls* itself. So, I couldn't attend events as *Duty Fall's* Tack180, only as Tack180. Or Thea if I chose to accept the queen's name for me.

Also, we offered to give them two weeks for partial ownership; he still received his cut from me and had limited say in how I played the game for the next two weeks. Any and all production requests he wanted to make during that time needed to be done via group chat with Nia and Cody involved. Nia was the head bitch in charge, and I loved it.

I let them leave the room first and stayed inside, taking a deep breath to enjoy my newfound freedom. I pinched my fingers to get my usual tacks and then shook them away. I pulled out the throwing knives and twisted them in my hands. I threw one at the wall and watched it stick where I had thrown it. I smiled. It was like a rebirth that I didn't know I needed. The next thing I needed to do was get answers, and only Isa could help me do that. I made my way to the library, where the others were working on giving Eros a crossover patch. I walked into the room to a loud "Congratulations!"

"So, how does it feel to be free?" Olivia asked.

"Good, but I need help."

"With what?"

"Isa," I looked past Olivia.

"Yes?" She looked up from the work she was doing.

"I want answers. Sure, there's stuff you know that you can't tell me because I'm not a member of Production or whatever bullshit you want to say. But I'm asking you as a friend." I was hoping the friendship card would work on her. I knew it would work on literally anyone else in the room. "You said there are others like me. You've studied me for weeks; is there a way to use this stupid glitch to my advantage?"

She looked at the queen and they stared at each other as if they were having a mental conversation. Hell, they were probably sending DMs to each other so they didn't have to say anything out loud. *That's what I would do.*

"I don't want to get your hopes up," Isa finally said. "I have *something*, though I'm not fully sure of the effects it will have on you or your body."

"How bad can it be?" Eros asked.

"Well, I tried to reverse engineer the glitch, and I'm not sure if I was entirely successful. This is more of a hotfix while I figure out a long-term solution. I'd rather not give it to you because I don't know what it will do. It might not do anything, but my two leading theories are that it would allow you to use the glitch to manipulate the Game's code a little easier or it would heal you completely."

"Heal me completely?" I didn't know if I wanted to be healed completely. I liked this power that I'd received. Besides, if I was fully healed, that would limit my ability to find answers for Ghost. I'd be stuck here, in Fantasia, until the teleportation service was back up. *If* it ever goes live again. Would I be ok with that? In pushing myself to get more answers, better answers by traveling between worlds, I could lose the power to travel entirely. I guess I'd still get answers that way; it'd be the waiting game I'd hate, but I was already doing that right now. It'd be worth it, then, to try *something* and be stuck waiting instead of not trying anything at all. Besides, I know long term I want to end up in Fantasia anyway. I wouldn't mind being stuck with these people if that is the case.

"Well, you'd still have glitched hands," she sighed. "But they wouldn't glitch the world around you, and you wouldn't have to wear gloves. Again, I'm not sure if this is a long-term solution. It might not work at all."

"I want it," I said.

"T, maybe you should consider the larger implications," Kaspian said.

"Like what?" I asked. "If it works the way Isa wants, then I get answers. If it doesn't work, then I'm stuck here, just like I already am. At least I would have tried. I want answers, and I trust Isa's judgment."

"I would have to test it on someone sooner or later," Isa mused. "There's no way to know what will happen until we test it. While I grab it, you can get your crossover patch from Ingrid."

"Before you grab it." Olivia stopped Isa. "I need to know that it won't kill her."

"I trust my work. I can at least assure you it won't do that." Isa nodded before running off.

"Thank you again, Alton—and everyone," I said as I sat down next to Ingrid. I paused to consider how I wanted to phrase things. "Please don't take this as a slight on the hospitality you have provided me. I need to do this, but I plan to come back when I'm done."

Ingrid began typing into a tablet. She didn't look up as she started talking, "Please note that this is just a crossover patch. I have been informed that, as of this time, you are unable to fully join our game as this would require a reset."

"Got it," I said. It made sense, but it was disappointing to hear that while I might choose to stay in Fantasia, it will never be my game. I looked away from her and made eye contact with Kaspian. He smiled, and I smiled back. It didn't have to be my game to be my home. I'd already done so many great things here without a crossover or joining their game. It wouldn't change things, and it wouldn't affect how they felt about me.

"You'll like the first open quest you see on there," Eros said. "It's easy."

"Open quest?" I asked.

"Open quests are for everyone to try and participate in. They are available for twenty-four hours unless you've completed them before. You will also have personal quests that your Character can interact with for additional points. The algorithm determines the quests and points available for it. You can choose to decline a quest, so it is taken off your main view. You can always search through all your personal quests, those declined and accepted, if you want to bring it back," Ingrid said, still typing into her tablet.

Isa entered the room again, then picked a spot on the other side of me, opposite Ingrid. I blinked and, when I opened my eyes again, I could see the quests in my top left corner. The first one was "Give Me Some Skin." I raised my eyebrows and looked at Nathaniel. He must've had something to do with the name.

"Open it up," Eros laughed.

I did as he said and expanded the quest. "High-five five different people (bonus points awarded if the person is royalty)."

"A high-five?" I asked.

"You never turn down my specialty high-fives," Eros said, holding up a hand.

"There's nothing special about them." I laughed. He didn't respond, just wiggled his hand in my face.

I high-fived him, and beside the quest, a "1/5" appeared. I went over to Kaspian next and held out a hand. He met my hand with his own, and the number bumped up "2/5 +500". Next was Seraphina. I held out a hand, but she hesitated. I raised my eyebrows and shook my hand a bit; Isa grabbed Seraphina's hand and pushed it up against my own—"3/5 +1000". Seraphina looked back at Isa, who just smiled at her. Instead of getting mad, Seraphina smiled back. Sweet. Well, that was all the royals. Nathaniel nearly tackled Olivia out of the way so he could be next, then I technically ended on Olivia but followed up and gave Alton one anyway. Once my hand touched Olivia's though, the quest said "complete +1000" underneath it, flashed, and then disappeared. Next to the quests, I could see my points rise from 0 to 1250.

"Now that's done," Isa said. "I'm ready when you are, T."

"Wait," Olivia said. She stood next to me and grabbed my hand. "I'm here for you. No matter what happens. And, when you guys are finished, let's get ready for the ball together."

"Sure," I laughed. I wasn't overly worried about it until Olivia did that. I figured it would be no big deal, especially since Isa was confident in her work. But Olivia was treating it like I was about to die, and she was so damn knowledgeable on everything gaming. Isa touched my arm gently as she inserted the syringe. I looked down at my hands, a different type of weight flowed through my body; it tingled. It was how I would expect magic flowed through Kaspian's body.

"Try something," Eros encouraged me.

"Currently, no two glitched persons are reporting the same powers. T's been practicing magic, so I wouldn't be surprised if the glitch manifests like magic as it connects with the code around it. Opening portals is something connected heavily to the magical world. Why don't you try using magic?" Isa asked. This was my chance to shine: to show the others that I could control this glitch which would help us get answers. I lifted my arm and swung it in my best impression of the queen. The books that I had been aiming for went flying across the room.

Wow, that felt amazing. I feel unstoppable.

Isa took some notes and screeched, "I was right!"

"How did you do this?" I asked in awe. Was it really just great technical skills? It had to be; how else would Isa know how to control the glitch in this way?

"I'm good at what I do," she smiled. "This is really exciting for all other glitched persons, as well. If you will excuse me, this was quite the breakthrough, and I need to follow up on this immediately."

"I'll join you," Seraphina said. The two of them left together and I heard a ringing sound in my ear. A quest marked "Personal" in all red took the place of the previous quest at the top of my vision that read "Gussy Up" with the explanation that I needed to "Get ready with Olivia." That sounded right for me at that moment; celebrating with my friends at a large party for the victory over Bryce and the success with the Glitch. Today was a huge win for me. I felt like crying happy tears again, but I didn't want Ingrid to see me.

"I should be going, too," Ingrid said. Great, then I could talk about all the shit that happened today with my friends.

"Do you have a personal quest yet?" Eros asked. I nodded. "What is it?"

"I feel like I shouldn't be telling you," I said.

"It's good to keep personal quests personal." Olivia nodded in approval.

"Think of it like those inner thoughts and feelings that you have but haven't shared with others. As the algorithm gets to know you better and tracks your patterns, you may get personal quests involving love or revenge," Ingrid said. She had finished packing up the last of the things she needed. "Thank you for your time."

We waited for her to leave before anyone said anything else.

"So?" Eros asked. "What? You just use magic now?"

"I'm not sure. I'm guessing this is what it must feel like for you?" I looked at Kaspian.

"I'd certainly like to help you learn about your powers; it definitely looks more like magic than it did before." He nodded. "We could discuss this more now if you have time."

"No." Olivia grabbed onto my arm and started to drag me from the room. "We're leaving, too. We need to get ready. We'll see you boys tonight."

Olivia treated me as though I was the queen as we got ready. Instead of getting ready together, she put me through a whole make-over, claiming that I wouldn't do it right myself. Not like I'd tell her, but it was surprisingly fun, so I let it happen. We talked a lot about my next steps. I wasn't surprised that everyone was curious if I was going to leave them, and the answer was yes, but not forever. They were always more than welcome to come with me on my journey, but it was a journey I needed to make no matter what. When I finally got the answers that Ghost and I deserved, I'd come home to them.

There was another big step I needed to take once I got answers, and I wanted them to be a part of it. I would want Eros, Olivia, and Kaspian by my side when I finally confronted my past. With a broken contract, I could pursue my family, whoever they were, without legal ramifications. I'd still have no memories of them, but I didn't need Production's approval to search for them. *If* they wanted to see me, too, that was. I wasn't even sure I definitely wanted to meet them. The thought was terrifying: what if they *hated* me and that was why I left? I didn't want to be alone when I tackled that battle. I had found my version of Olivia's best team, and I needed my team with me when I searched for my family.

I looked at the two of us in the mirror when she was finally done; long, plum-colored dresses, gold-accented jewelry, and curled hair. We matched the colors of Fantasia, purple and gold, perfectly. Well thought out by Olivia—or Seraphina, if we were being forced to wear these dresses. We, then, went to the queen's private quarters to help her get dressed. Her gown was large and extravagant: gold and highlighted with purple hues. Her long blonde hair was still straight as the tops lightly grazed the floor. The finishing touch was placing her heavy crown on the top of her head.

"I know you declined the offer to be my retainer," Seraphina said as we started leaving her room. "However, the offer still stands. Whenever you are ready."

"Thank you," I said, giving her a bow.

"Follow me, Olivia. It's almost time for our grand introduction."

Olivia waved as she left with the queen. Alton peeked out of the next room over, where the boys had been getting ready, and then called back in, "Okay, the queen started—we can go now. Eros, T's right here, so you don't have to look for her." I stayed where I was, knowing Eros and the others were coming based on what I heard.

"You look so royal," Eros said when he saw me.

"Is that a compliment?" I asked.

"It means you look beautiful," Nathaniel joined in.

I looked over at Kaspian and Alton, the only guys who hadn't inflated my ego yet. "I'm waiting."

"You look good, but no one can beat Olivia," Alton said while grinning.

"Such a kiss ass, and she's not even here to appreciate it," I said.

"That's love for you," Alton said. We heard trumpets in the distance, and Alton looked back, "Prince Kaspian, you ready?"

I looked at Kaspian, looking more royal than I did. He was wearing a military outfit for the special occasion, medals adorning his lapel. I made eye contact with him and realized I had been staring a little too much. My cheeks heated, I smiled, and he smiled back.

"I think you're missing something," Kaspian said.

"Don't worry," I said, pulling up the slit in my dress to reveal a garter with knives. "I came prepared."

"T!" I heard Olivia's voice as she came back. She grabbed my dress and pulled it back down. "I forget one thing, and this is what I come back to."

"That's not what I was talking about anyway." Kaspian shook it off. "Olivia, can you get her something for me?"

"What?" she asked, but it sounded like she had an idea.

"The purple one," he said.

"I was hoping you would say that one." She squealed and jumped in more excitement than usual, then ran off.

"Let's go," Kaspian said as the group started walking past Eros and me. Kaspian stopped briefly next to me. The light sound of the violins intertwined with the castle's music. "Save me a dance."

"Who said I want to dance with you?" I laughed.

"Well, I guess I don't *need* the EXP for 'Dance with a Newcomer.' "

"No, wait," I tried again.

"Prince Kaspian," Alton called.

"I'll find you later." He winked before walking away.

"Eros?" I said, watching them walk away.

"Yeah?"

"I think I like him."

"You know, I could help you two out tonight. You can just call me cupid, literally."

"You think I need help?" I raised a brow at his insinuation.

"Not at all, just letting you know that if you need a wingman, I make a good one."

"Not as good as me," Olivia said from behind us, smiling knowingly. "Voila!"

"What's that?" I asked, staring at the fancy circlet in her hands. I had seen that exact same one once before, and I was wearing it when I saw it through Seraphina's eyes.

"The perfect accessory for you." She placed it on my head. "Especially if Prince Kaspian thinks it would look good on you. It is, technically, the crown of a princess."

"The what now?" Eros asked.

"This crown is meant for the princess, literally. See mine? It's not as fancy because I'm just a retainer. But this crown, this is actually meant for the future princess."

"If I had an arrow, I'd shoot it." Eros motioned as if he was shooting a pretend arrow from a bow and then looked at me. "Are you smiling?"

"And blushing," Olivia added.

"I'm not doing either of those," I said, even though my body betrayed me.

We could hear the sound of trumpets in the background, and Olivia looked past us toward the ballroom.

"Gotta go, but I will see you guys later!" She ran off before either of us could say anything.

"Shall we?" Eros held out an arm.

"We shall."

I grabbed his arm, and we started toward the ballroom at the other end of the castle. Except, unlike the others, we walked to the front of the ballroom to enter with all the other people. It was like we belonged.

"Ah, there you are," a soldier said as she came up to us. "We're ready to announce you."

"You're ready to what?" Eros asked.

"Announce you; you are the guests of honor. Follow me."

We followed her to an area hidden behind long curtains. She pushed us to the edge of it, then nodded at a different soldier.

"Now presenting, Eros from the game, *Gods of Mercy*," the man announced as the female soldier pushed Eros through the curtain. There was a polite clap as he entered. I took a step forward, playing the role, and the man yelled down again, "He is escorting the guest of honor for the night, Miss Tack180 from the game, *Duty Falls*."

I took a step out of the curtains, and the same polite clap echoed in the room. I scanned the ball and found my people, all of them entertaining and engaging with people I had never seen before. The ballroom was filled, completely, by more people than just Castle Town. People from all over Fantasia were there, including guests from Vampira, such as Ambrosio and Hawthorn, who were unsurprisingly close to Bryce and Cody. But Bryce seemed to be schmoozing more than just the king of the sex den; there were plenty of people surrounding him. I wondered if one of them would be his next Character. After the announcement, the ballroom quieted down then people were staring at me. I looked over and, at the top of the stairs, Eros was waiting for me. He held out an arm, and I grabbed it.

"Miss Tack180 is honored here tonight for saving the Kingdom of Fantasia at the Battle of Blackburn." The crowd erupted and I saw a proud smile on Seraphina's face, she was standing next to Isa and Ingrid.

Did they name my battle? I couldn't stop smiling. *Of course, they did because I'm a badass and they like me. They actually like me, not just because I'm Tack180.*

A tingling sounded in my ears, and the quests at the top corner of my vision altered slightly. "Dance with a Newcomer" was on there, and so was "Dance with a Royal." But the one I didn't want to see was "Dance with the Guest of Honor." Since I was both a newcomer and the guest of honor, I was worth extra points, not to mention that "Dance with the Guest of Honor" was worth 20k as a hard-level quest. I sighed.

I don't want to interact with people. Well, not with people who weren't *my* people.

"Eros," I said as we started walking down the stairs. My eyes scanned the room, and I could see people heading toward me already, their eyes locked on me like prey. Except, I wasn't as vulnerable as they expected. "I don't want to socialize."

"Got it."

When we made it to the bottom of the stairs, Eros immediately grabbed my hand and brought me to the dance floor, effectively claiming the first dance. Not exactly what I had in mind, but we both needed the EXP, especially with the long-term goal of staying in Fantasia. Everyone turned away as we started dancing.

"Sorry, dibs," Eros said, looking behind me. I turned around to see someone about to tap me on the shoulder. It continued like that for a couple of songs in a row, with Eros finding new and creative ways to turn down would-be dance partners:

"I'll kill you if you get any closer."

"She smells; you don't want to dance with her."

"Worst dancer in the world. I'm saving you, buddy."

"It's mine," he said to the last one. Then he grabbed my face and licked my cheek. "I licked it. So, you can't have it."

"Oh my god, Eros." I wiped away the saliva on my face. "That was disgusting."

"Do I get to lick you now?" Nathaniel asked from behind me.

"No, no one gets to lick me." I turned around to see Nathaniel, Alton, and Kaspian. "What are you guys all doing here?"

"We just wanted to add our names to the list of guys *and* girls that want to dance with you," Nathaniel said.

"Sure," I said. I scanned the room and saw that Olivia was talking someone's ear off by the wine table. "Let me guess. Alton, she got distracted, so you get a break from dancing. Nathaniel, Ingrid didn't want *anything* to do with you. And you, Kaspian, you have been waiting so patiently to dance with me but had to suck up to other important people all night. But, since you're done schmoozing, you've finally come to take Eros's place."

"She turned me down." Nathaniel sighed dramatically.

"Sounds right to me," Eros laughed. "You come on too strong. Come with me; we'll just join their group and talk to them, like *normal* people."

Eros and Nathaniel walked away, leaving the three of us. Kaspian and I both gave Alton a look, he quickly turned on his heels and walked toward Olivia. Kaspian held out a hand.

"So, I was right?" I asked as I grabbed his hand.

"Dancing with you is much more enjoyable than sucking up to royalty from other provinces in Fantasia," he admitted. I smiled. "I guess it wouldn't hurt for you to talk to them, as well. You may be more interested in joining other provinces within Fantasia. It's a large world."

"I've already decided I'm staying with you." With those words, the blush tried to work its way back up my neck. "Well, I mean, here in Fantasia proper. I obviously have some stuff to do first, and then I'll come back. Eros wants to stay here, too. Although, I'm pretty sure he's joining me on my journey first."

He smiled down at me, his gaze roaming over my face. "I'm happy you're staying."

The music, our proximity, and the butterflies in my stomach almost made me feel nauseous again, only this time, it was in a good way. I wanted to reach for him and close the gap between us. I stopped myself, being in public view and knowing that Bryce was somewhere watching me, I couldn't do it.

"Well," I changed the subject. "I have to thank you."

"For what?"

"This crown. I know you left before I had the chance to decline it. It's too beautiful, too royal."

"Well, it looks good on you."

"Yes, but it's not my style. It's not me."

"Coming from the girl who, when she first got here, acted like she would never consider living in a world like Fantasia. Now you're going to try and stay here."

"Touché. I guess it does look good on me. You know, if I have to wear it."

"You don't have to wear it. I could call Olivia over here to take it back."

"No, it's fine. It's already on my head. It would be a hassle to take it off now."

"An absolute hassle. I'd need to call in the guards."

"We don't need to waste precious resources. So, it's stuck on me now."

"It will help keep random strangers away from you, too. Although, there will always be those who want the EXP enough to try anyway."

"How?" I asked with a laugh.

"Because that's the crown of the future princess. Not the one my sister wore growing up, but the one that goes to my future wife."

"So, people will think we are together, got it." *Butterflies.* I enjoyed my time with Kaspian and the way my music changed. It was new and exciting, yet I *still* felt guilty. I thought maybe since I got the patch for Fantasia, the guilt would go away, but it hasn't. I don't think it ever will. Ghost was such a large part, well, the only part of my life. I built my life around him. I can't just move on to someone new, but I did feel overwhelmingly real emotions when I was around Kaspian. "Well, just so you know, Eros has been doing a really good job of turning people down before they got to me. If you are taking over his position, then you can't let go of me for the rest of the night."

It sounded like he said "I wasn't planning on it" but I couldn't tell. I didn't want to ask him because what if he didn't? I wanted it to be what he had said, so I decided it was and just soaked in the moment, riding the high of successful negotiations and violins. Of course, it didn't really work out that way. Being the prince meant he actually had to interact with other people and was called away momentarily by his sister. I felt hundreds of eyes on me. Men and women started to make their move; a few of them called out to me as "Blessed Tack180." I was open, and all my people were taken; Olivia with Alton, Eros with Isa, and Nathaniel finally got his chance with Ingrid. I folded my arms across my body, lifted my head to show off the crown a little better, and dared someone to ask me to dance with my defensive stance and death glare. I looked about as welcoming as the Glitch. People looked at me then quickly looked away. I had enough friends now; I didn't feel like making any more.

"You really hate people, T," Eros said. He and Isa finally joined me after the song ended. "I don't know how we even became friends."

"You tried to kill me, then you just started following me around," I reminded him.

"I believe you stepped in when I was fighting with Medusa. But who's keeping track?"

"It's a shock that you've created such a home here, T," Isa acknowledged.

"I wasn't trying," I joked. "But Olivia can be pretty pushy."

"Excuse me," Seraphina interrupted. She and Kaspian joined us again. Then she stuck out a hand toward Isa. "Would you like to dance?"

"I've been waiting all night." Isa took Seraphina's hand, and they left us.

Ping.

"Did you guys get a message?" I asked, looking at the red notification at the top of my view. Kaspian and Eros shook their heads. I opened my messages, found the unread one, and quickly skimmed. "It's from Nia. Bryce wants me to complete a quest."

That's shitty timing.

Now that I could use my powers so easily, I wanted to capitalize on it; I wanted to travel, not just do stupid quests for Bryce for another two weeks. I knew it was a compromise and a much better alternative, but it felt like a waste of time.

"It's a quick way to make a large sum of money," Kaspian acknowledged. "Bryce is exploiting that before his two weeks run out. We'll fight with you; they are rather enjoyable."

"If Kaspian thinks they are fun, then I'm in." Eros put his arm around my shoulder.

"Who says I'm inviting you?" I joked.

"Hey, I need to raise my EXP, too."

"Fine. I'll accept."

With the quick acceptance, I received a flurry of even more messages back and forth in a group chat between myself, Nia, Bryce, and Cody, with Nia and Cody being the only ones communicating.

"She accepts."

"We pick the quest."

"Depending on experience."

"It will be a quest that any level can complete. It will change to match her current level and EXP."

"She gets to pick her team."

"No royals."

"No royalty, but their retainers are fair game."

"She has to start tomorrow."

"We accept."

"So do we."

"Okay, so, given the current circumstances, I pick Eros, Olivia, and Nathaniel. Sorry, Kaspian," I said, after recapping the conversation to them.

"It's okay. We can check in with you after you complete the quest. I'm certain Nathaniel and Olivia, in fact, Olivia, can provide great insight and strategy. Think of it as a training exercise on how to be a better Player," he suggested.

"When's it going to be?" Eros asked.

"Sounds like it's tomorrow. We'll have to put a sign up on the bakery that we're closed again, and we should probably get some rest."

"I'm just going to stay up a little longer." Eros looked at me and then back at Nathaniel, who was off to the side with Ingrid. He walked up to Nathaniel and pretended to shoot him with guns from his fingers. Nathaniel fell back as though he had been hit before nudging Eros back.

"I should get some rest. I'll see you tomorrow before we head out?" I asked Kaspian as I started in the direction of my room.

"Wait," he started following me. "I'll walk you to your room."

"I'm perfectly capable of walking myself. Or is this just a way for you to spend more time with me?" I teased.

"I wouldn't want you to get lost."

"Yeah, I wouldn't want to accidentally get lost and end up in your room."

"I don't know. Your room's a little small already. I don't think two people would fit. So, I think my room would be a great place to get lost."

"Fair point," I laughed. We were back in the main halls of the castle, close to my room. "We could—"

"Guys!" Olivia said excitedly as she and Alton rounded the corner from where the rooms were. "What are you doing here?"

"Kaspian was walking me back to my room."

"You're already done partying? You can't be!" She grabbed my arm like she wanted to pull me back to the ballroom.

"I need to sleep before the quest. I haven't gotten more than four hours since opening the bakery." I resisted her pull.

"Quest?" Olivia asked.

"Bryce wants me to complete a quest. No royals on my team, but I can have you. So, it's going to be us, Eros and Nathaniel."

"What about me?" Alton asked.

"I can only have four people."

"But I'm better with a sword than Eros."

"He needs the EXP," Olivia said. "And Nathaniel uses a spear. She doesn't need two swords. It makes a lot of sense. Nice thinking, T!"

"Are we going with them?" Alton asked Kaspian.

"We'll recap when they're done," Kaspian responded.

"Fine," Alton sighed. Kaspian nodded at me, and I nodded back. I tried to mask the disappointment of being interrupted. Although it might have been for the best, I still felt this immense guilt, which wasn't going away, and that was no way to start something new with Kaspian.

I turned around and left the others to head back to my room. I changed out of the hot dress into my usual outfit and jumped into bed, ready for the opportunity to complete a legitimate quest, and not just for the EXP. It sounded like a lot of fun.

I was up early prepping for the quest when I heard people talking outside my door. I finished putting two spare potions in my tactical belt before opening the door. It was the whole group outside, Isa included.

"T, I'm glad I caught you," Isa said.

"Is there something you needed?" I asked her.

"Well, after our breakthrough yesterday, I was doing some research into the effect the glitch has had on the worlds. When we turned on comms, there were a lot of significant effects, but there was an important aspect that we overlooked, time. I was working with Ingrid when we realized that before the comms came up and reset our clocks to be consistent with the rest of the world, our time was off—like, way off. Basically, you didn't time travel when you went into that clown game. The world stayed frozen until you came back to unfreeze it. Anytime that you have used that power it has frozen our time."

"You just lost some cool points," Eros whispered to me. "I thought you could time travel."

"Okay, I guess that makes a lot of sense," I said, ignoring Eros.

"Again, this is very consistent with magic. Although, I'm curious to see if this is a requirement for you to make portals, which is not consistent with magic. I know you're heading out today, but I'd like to test a portal to another world when you get back."

"I'm down," I agreed. Isa didn't have to convince me. I had already wanted it.

"Great, now that things are easier for you, I'm wondering if that side effect will go away completely. Or what other things we might see if—"

"Isa," Seraphina said.

"Of course, sorry, I got sidetracked. What's important is that right now, there's still much for us to learn, and I need to confirm if my hotfix can remain in place as a permanent patch or if I will have to adjust it. We've lost a few more games since communications have been back up, so the sooner that we can all get answers to the glitch, the better it will be for all the worlds."

Had they lost more games? I guess I knew just because we didn't see the Glitch. It didn't mean he wasn't still around, causing mayhem elsewhere. It was stupid to feel so comfortable just because he wasn't affecting me. I felt guilty I'd partied the night before when other people were experiencing the same pain I had that first night.

I knew it was a terrible idea to have a ball right now.

"Patch?" Kaspian asked.

"Yes, it would act as a firewall for a virus and treat the glitch as such. Think of it as a vaccination, except it goes into the Game code. It should keep the Glitch out of anywhere it's not already in. What I used for T was created in the process of making this long-term patch."

"That's promising," Olivia said.

Too promising. It had only been two months; how would Isa have something ready to take care of such a big glitch? I guess I wasn't surprised that the Production team would have the safeguards for it; however, Production wasn't able to get comms back up. That was us. At the same time, Isa was quick in getting me the hotfix or whatever she called it. Maybe it wasn't far off to have a glitch-blocking patch. I sure as hell don't know shit about IT or how feasible that would be.

"Well, I won't keep you all waiting. Have fun on your quest," Isa said. She waved and the queen bowed slightly, then the two of them walked off together.

"Message us when you're done," Kaspian said. "We'll await your results."

"Thanks, guys." I smiled.

I grabbed my stuff and we all headed off. The quest was to defeat the monster in Hallow Point Cave. The journey to Hallow Point Cave was a day trip, or two days round trip if we didn't want to tackle traveling back tonight. Since I wasn't allowed to use royals or their benefits, I couldn't ask Kaspian to open us a portal. I was tempted to open one myself, but I resisted. Bryce and Cody didn't know about whatever Isa injected me with, and I didn't want them to know. Hell, they'd find a way to use it against me these next two weeks, so I figured it was better to keep it a secret instead.

We made it to our destination without any problems. The areas surrounding Fantasia leading to the cave were forests filled with wolves and mist. The enemies weren't scary or hard to battle, but the sounds were terrifying. When not in battle, it was silent, and that silence was only broken up by the sound of screams. I wanted to assume those screams were other Players in battle because, when I didn't hear screaming, sometimes I heard children laughing instead. The sounds were so different and the mist so thick that if I weren't traveling with the others, I'd be confused and turn back around. It was a great way to keep some Players out of the area and attract the attention of thrill seekers.

Traveling with the group again felt similar to when we were stuck in the clown game, with the addition of Eros. At times we worked well together, and, at other times, we wanted to kill each other because others weren't listening. There were a few times Olivia threatened not to heal Eros because he didn't listen to her, although she threatened me with the same thing way more often than him. And if I learned nothing else from this game, the most important thing was to never fuck with your healer.

Hallow Point Cave was nothing special, and by the time we had made it there, we were at level twenty, which wasn't perfect but gave us extra stat boosts that we would appreciate in battle.

"Alright," I said when we got to the front of the cave. Eros and I took a step forward, away from the others. "We got this."

"Just remember," Olivia said. "I'm recording, so try to avoid using magic because it's being sent to Bryce."

"That won't be hard. I believe in our team."

Who the fuck am I? If Ghost could hear me now, he'd absolutely make fun of me.

"Let's go, T," Eros said.

"Hey, don't forget us." Olivia followed after us.

"Yeah, but if you're not there, Oliva, then *we* get all the money and EXP," Eros pushed her back.

"Don't push me, Eros. You need a healer, and you'll appreciate having mine and Nathaniel's skills and knowledge."

"Liv, can you just, not?" Eros tried again.

"Sure, I won't heal you. But I'm still coming along," she agreed a little too cheerfully.

"Let it happen, Eros," Nathaniel said. "I've already learned that lesson."

"Fine, you aren't getting healed either, Nathaniel. I'm only taking care of T in there. I hope you both have to respawn."

"Okay, before Olivia starts throwing punches, can we head inside?" I asked.

The cave glowed a light-blue hue as we entered. There was nothing waiting for us inside. It was a wide-open cave, rounded and *empty*. I looked at Olivia and she nodded. Since she was a streamer, she was in charge of recording the video to send to Bryce upon completion. Actual live streams still weren't available, or maybe Isa purposefully blocked them to avoid mass panic. Nia offered to make Bryce be present for the battle, but the little dick decided he was too scared to be there. Well, that's not what he said. He simply declined, but in my head, it was because he was chickenshit.

"I don't understand," Eros said. "Where's the monster?"

"Just wait," Nathaniel said. "This is a common tactic."

"What exactly is the tactic?" I asked.

Just as I asked it, there was a sound that echoed in the cave. Nathaniel pointed toward the sound like that answered my question. We all looked in different directions for what made the noise. A dark shadow, haze-like, emerged from the end of the cave. As it made its way to the middle, with a puff of smoke, it changed its form into a spider. It wasn't just any spider, in actual fact, it wasn't just one spider either; there were multiple spiders, all much larger than the size of an average SUV. I didn't want to look at them, but I couldn't turn away. The spiders were colorful with electric blue legs and a brown bottom. Their beady eyes stared at me while the fangs looked to be dripping a purple poison. If they weren't ugly enough like that, their bodies were hairy and with how large they were, every strand of hair was long enough to match the length of my forearm.

Nathaniel and Olivia took a step back. I stood, frozen, staring at my worst nightmare, which was clearly what Bryce had wanted. My thoughts about him being too scared were gone. I only wondered why he didn't want to see my fear for himself. Maybe the fact that Nia would call him out for purposefully giving me a quest that involved my Character's written fear. *Plausible deniability.* I couldn't prove he knew it would be a spider. Either that, or it was because he knew if I made it out of this, he would be next on my hit list.

"T," Olivia said calmly. "This monster changes its level based on who it's fighting. Nathaniel and I will stay back so you don't have to take on a level ninety-nine. I know this one is going to be hard for you."

"Hard for me?" I asked with a laugh. "This is literally a living hell for me."

"Just keep a level head. You are the only one who can't respawn without actually dying. So, protect yourself, and I'll watch out for Eros. The two of you can do this together."

"Olivia," I felt my voice tremble. "They're spiders."

"Yes, I know. But you're Tack180. You're badass. You're working on bettering yourself and breaking out of your assumed Character and Character traits by joining our game. Make this your next step. Come on, Lady Thea, kick some ass."

I watched their long legs move quickly as the spiders charged. Eros took two of them head-on, protecting me like he said he always would. My legs stayed firmly planted where I was, and I felt the adrenaline kick in, the heavy feeling that was so familiar from the glitch. I almost let it take over until I felt a nudge from behind me. I looked back, and Nathaniel pointed with his spear at the third spider making its way over to me.

"This is *your* quest, T. You have to battle, but you don't have to be the one to kill it. Go dodge that shit, throw a couple of knives, and I'll go in for the kill at the end," he said as he pushed me closer.

The spider turned to me as I got closer to it. They were right and, if this was some test, I was going to prove to Bryce that he couldn't control me. The spider scurried toward me, shaking the ground beneath it. I slid out of the way of its charge, then backflipped to gain further distance. Instead of turning, the spider shot webs out of its ugly ass in unnatural patches, trying to hit me and stick me to the closest solid object it could. It was easy to dodge, flip, spin, and roll out of the way. I looked back at Nathaniel and Olivia, who heavily focused their attention on Eros. He was struck by a web and trying to get himself loose. The two spiders that were zeroed in on him were preparing to charge.

"Fuck," I whispered under my breath. I took out a knife and threw it, gaining the attention of one of the spiders targeting Eros.

"T, don't," Eros yelled as he got pegged by a web from the other spider.

I dodged another web attack from the first spider targeting me as the other began to circle. I caught a glimpse of Eros getting tied up in a web while Nathaniel and Olivia were trying to give him instructions without getting too close. My vision blurred with fresh, warm tears as I continued to fight. I screamed as I charged my original spider, knife ready. Just as I reached the front of the spider, I flipped over its body. As if time froze, I looked below me and threw the knife, just like I would have thrown my trusty tacks. Bullseye. I landed on my feet and turned around to target the spider again. Minimal to no damage.

I needed a sword; I turned and ran toward Eros, Nathaniel, and Olivia. Eros had freed himself and plunged his sword into the spider, killing it. We made eye contact; spider guts continued to drip from his sword as he ran to meet me. When he reached me, I turned to face the two spiders in front of us.

"I'm proud of you," he said as he swatted his sword at oncoming web shots.

"I don't like this."

"I can tell," he nodded at my face, and I wiped at the tears. "Just remember, I can respawn, you can't—now, let's finish them off."

The spiders screeched as millions of normal-sized spiders began descending on the room. *Fuck.* I tried to shake them off as they crawled onto me. Eros chose to charge on, even as they tried to crawl on him. It was when I tried to move that I realized what was happening. The millions of normal-sized spiders were wrapping us up with webbing. I flinched, feeling the heaviness and trying to push it away. I continued to shake the spiders off of me as I felt them wrap my legs. Eros sliced the webbing around him with his sword only to have the spiders immediately make new webs. I followed suit and hacked at them with my dagger.

"... healer." I heard. It was Nathaniel yelling at me. "Save your healer."

Olivia was almost covered in webs, her ability to provide health to Nathaniel quashed. They were both fighting level ninety-nine enemies, who were biting them while they wrapped them up. Nathaniel had some hope with his spear at slicing the webbing, but it was just enough to keep himself afloat, not enough to save Olivia. While Nathaniel was busy fighting spiders, he wouldn't be able to revive Olivia, who then wouldn't respawn until the quest was complete. Without Olivia to provide me with healing when I was low, I would legit die. I needed to save my fucking healer.

"Go," Eros yelled. "I got it here."

I ran back to Olivia and sliced a dagger through the webbing that surrounded her. Spiders crawled all over my body and began biting me; Olivia immediately healed me so I never felt the drain on my health, but I felt every painful bite.

"I can't help you and Eros," Olivia said. I looked back to Eros, who was wrapped up in webbing as the two spiders circled him. He was screwed. I felt the heaviness and let it take over. The feeling was so fluid now as it rushed through my body. "Don't," she said and gave me a knowing look, "he's going to be alright."

I held onto the heavy feeling and watched a spider lift its front legs and then lower its body to feast on Eros. I couldn't do it. I couldn't look, and I couldn't just stand there. Eros would feel everything. I angled my body, so I covered Olivia's view; she wouldn't see it, which meant Bryce wouldn't get it in the recording. I forced my hands forward and used the glitch against her wishes; Eros was wrapped in that same protective shield that had surrounded me in the Platform. I smiled at my handiwork. Things were going to be a hell of a lot easier moving forward. The spider tried again, but my shield held on.

"Go help him," Nathaniel yelled.

I ran up to him, slid across the baby spiders, and slashed the webbing. Eros shoved his sword past me and stabbed the spider who had been attempting to eat him. Another one down. The one that was left stared at us, bared his fangs, and raised his front legs. A spear shot through the air and injured the last spider to the brink of death. Nathaniel fulfilled his promise. I grabbed Eros's sword out of his hand as he bent down and held his hands together for me to step on. As I stepped on his hands, he boosted me into the air, straight above the final spider. At the crest of the jump, I made sure the sword was angled directly above the spider, then let myself fall, stabbing the final blow into the spider's back. With the last spider dead, all of the mini spiders disappeared. Any anxiety I had felt was immediately relieved by the sensation of Olivia's staff.

"Quest Complete" showed up in front of my face, followed by "+10000 EXP" and then "+4000G."

"4,000 gold? That's it?" I handed Eros back to his sword.

"But we leveled up," he tried to be positive.

"Motherfucker," I cursed.

"Let's focus on keeping the healer safe next time, sound good?" Nathaniel offered. "Other than that, you did us proud."

"Whatever," I groaned as I walked away.

I followed a path from the cave entrance and down a trail that led me to a pond surrounded by the woods. A treasure chest was waiting at the end of the path in front of a log. I opened the chest, and all it gave me was a seed of dexterity as if I needed to raise my dexterity. I sat down on the log and faced the water, tempted to throw the damn seed into the pond but chose to eat it anyway. It was huge, kind of like an acorn, but ended up tasting like a peanut, which was weird.

Fucking seed.

Except, I knew I wasn't angry at the seed. I was angry at Bryce, the quest, and how he got away with using my fears against me. I sat by myself for a few minutes before I heard footsteps behind me. I turned and found Kaspian standing over me.

"Can I sit here?" he asked.

"Sure." I scooted over to make room for him. He sat right next to me anyway. I rested my head on his shoulder. He put his arm around me and squeezed my shoulder.

"Long day?"

"The longest," I laughed.

"I know that wasn't expected and Bryce probably knew what he was doing, but you honestly did an amazing job. You're amazing."

"I don't feel amazing."

"Are you kidding? Liv showed me your video. You did great out there. I like how you adapted to change with the addition of the smaller spiders. The only thing you will need to work on is ensuring your healer's safety, but that's not something we've had to discuss in training before, so I'm not surprised you didn't automatically consider it."

"You make it sound like I genuinely did do a good job, but I barely got any EXP and a stupid seed of dexterity." He laughed at me. I started laughing, too. "Okay, well, it would've been better if you were there."

"I'll always be there. If you were really in trouble, I wouldn't have hesitated." He squeezed me again and then kissed the top of my head.

"You really shouldn't say things like that. It can give a girl the wrong idea."

"What if it's giving her the right idea?"

"I think I'd like that."

"Me, too."

"Let's just stay here for a bit."

"We can do that."

And we sat there for a while, just like that. His arm around my shoulder, my head resting on his shoulder, mostly in silence. The silence was never awkward. Instead, it was relaxing, like crossing off the last thing on your to-do list. I liked it. *I did.* Not my Character; it wasn't in my code—it was real, actual feelings. Our bodies radiated heat. Kaspian flicked his finger, and in the distance, a lightning bolt struck an enemy that didn't even see us in the dark across the pond. I pointed at another monster that spawned in the distance, and a bolt of lightning took it out quickly.

"T!" We heard Olivia yell.

"Ignore her for now," I said.

"Sounds good."

"Let them be," I heard Eros say.

"Let me by, Eros. I want to talk to T."

"T!" I looked over to where I heard Olivia's voice. She was in Eros's arms as she was trying to fight her way past him while Alton tried to grab her out of Eros's grip. Eros, who apparently had way too much faith in Alton, let Olivia go once Alton had her. Alton, forever faithful to his pesky girlfriend, also let her go. Once she was free, she ran at us. "Nia sent the video of proof to Bryce. You're officially free for the night, and I also sent a picture to a few news outlets. Everyone loves a good comeback story, and yours is blowing up. You're gaining a huge following right now."

"Jesus, Oliva, you're squirmy," Eros, clearly frustrated, said as he caught up with her.

"You shouldn't underestimate her," Alton said. "I taught her well."

"I don't think you had anything to do with it," Nathaniel said. "Olivia's always been sassy, even before you came around."

"Nathaniel is right," Olivia said enthusiastically. "I took self-defense classes with SquatsWithSteve before he was even known as SquatsWithSteve."

"I'd like to hear more about that," I said with almost just as much excitement. "Was it before or after he started seeing ButtBusterBecky?"

"I don't think anyone wants to hear about that, T." Kaspian tried to playfully cover my mouth.

"It was before. As a matter of fact, ButtBusterBecky and I took the class together in the back. You know, before I became SmokeScreen and before I knew who she actually was," Olivia said. *Interesting.*

"What?" I laughed, trying to get more information about Olivia and Kaspian's past.

"I know! So. Much. Drama. It's fine to look back at it now, but I wouldn't want to go back to that time in my life." Olivia's voice started in its typical perky manner, but halfway through the thought, it changed. She was quieter. Kaspian's hand had slowly slipped away from my mouth. There was pain in what Olivia said; I could hear it in her voice and the way she phrased it. Alton grabbed her hand and squeezed it. She shook her head. "Ah, the past is the past. I'm not going to dwell on it."

"Let's head home," Alton suggested. Kaspian nodded and opened a portal to the castle. I needed a drink, so as soon as we stepped through, I started in the direction of the alehouse, but Isa messaged me before we made it there. I tapped Eros on the shoulder, and he stopped walking.

"I'm gonna check in with Isa," I said.

"I'll come along." He nodded.

"What?" Olivia yelled. "You can't leave!"

"After?" I smiled.

"You better."

"We'll be back," I called as Eros and I ran off to find Isa.

Isa was the most helpful person to have on my side. With every new adjustment, if others were required, I could imagine getting better and better at using the glitch to my advantage, which meant finally getting answers to how the Glitch came about, who created it, and how I could get my revenge. She was waiting for us in the strategy room. Her tablet was face-up on the table, and a 3D model of my body, stats, and health meter popped up.

"Welcome." She smiled. "Looking at your body, you seem to be thriving since you got the patch. This is *great* news."

I smiled back. I didn't know what to look for in the 3D model, but I took her word for it. I was excited anytime I was around her; with how much she had progressed our world during the glitched time and the powers she had given me, she held more power than the queen herself. I never knew when she was going to give more good news or updates. She was more addictive than slot machines.

"So," I started. "What does this mean for my options?"

"Well, I'd say your real limitation is that you can't go out there and stop the Glitch yourself. I know that doesn't deter you, but you have no way to stop it." She sighed.

"You're right; that doesn't matter to me. I'll destroy the Glitch. I'm sure you'll help me find a way." I needed to encourage her. If she felt like she had done the most she could, then she might stop trying. She didn't seem like the type to give up. But I didn't want to risk it. Although, I did question my ability to stop the Glitch. I had no idea what to do, but I had to do something.

"I *might* have a way."

That's what I want to hear.

"Just like you *might* have had a fix for T, and it worked out?" Eros asked.

"Exactly. It's just a more concentrated dose of what I gave T. Knowing that it works on T, I'd be hopeful that it works on the Glitch. Though, again, the only way to test it would be to actually try it on the Glitch." She seemed to be guiding us in the way she spoke. I would hope by now she knew my answer, but if I needed to say it again, I would.

"I'll do whatever it takes. I need to do this," I said. "For Ghost."

She nodded, took two vials out of her pocket, and handed one to each of us.

"Why two?" Eros asked.

"In order for my test to be accurate, at least one of you needs to get the job done. Can you handle that for me?"

"I can do it." I nodded.

"I don't know what this will do to it," she said. "I need you to know that beforehand."

"Why? You haven't been wrong so far."

"I've tested you for months. I might not have *known*, but I had a damn good estimate based on the science. With you, it's not a guess. While I'm familiar with how the glitch operates, I don't know who created the Glitch, if there are safeguards in place, nor how it's using the saved files of lost

Players. If Ghost is alive and a part of the Glitch, this could kill him or bring him back. I don't know which one it would be."

"It's okay." My voice shook as I spoke. I wasn't certain it was okay. I couldn't be the one to kill Ghost. Isa was confident when she gave the patch to me, and that confidence was what helped me make my decision. Her lack of assurance now worried me about what could happen. I had assumed Ghost was dead; I'd given him a gravestone, and I was finally starting to accept it. Though I still believed, more than the fact that he was alive and being used by the Glitch, I couldn't be the one to use the patch on him and kill him. I stood up, ready to leave and be alone.

"Before you go," she said. "I wanted to know if you felt like traveling."

THIRTEEN

"What?" I sat back down. "You mean between worlds, right?"

"Yes, that's precisely what I meant." She smiled. "Like we discussed before you left."

"That's what I've wanted to do since I arrived here."

"The Glitch is on the move and, while things are much slower than that initial day, we are losing at least one game per week. He's not consistently sticking to worlds he has and hasn't been to. I was hoping to send this patch out tonight, but I'm afraid of the implications of doing so. If I know that you can keep us and others safe by opening portals between worlds with ease, then I will feel more comfortable using the patch. That way, if he decides to come back to Fantasia, you can send its inhabitants to a location covered by the patch in which he hasn't been to yet."

"Yes," I agreed. Isa was right; if the Glitch is limited to the worlds it can travel to with the patch, then he might come back for Fantasia. I need to ensure that I can keep Kaspian, Olivia, and all of my friends safe if that were to happen. "Where should we go?"

"Let's try my home," Eros said. "Didn't seem like anyone has seen the Glitch yet. I'm familiar with the world too and have a safe house there. People know me; we'd be good."

"I like that idea. Although I was hoping for somewhere else, like Corporous," she said. "It'd be a more direct route to Production."

"I'm not going to Corporous." I shook my head. I looked over at Eros. It'd probably be good for him to see his game again. I wish I could see mine—*It's been so long.* I felt like I was about to cry, so I said the next part quickly, "We're going to Eros's world."

"Might as well bring Medusa with us," he suggested.

"I'll message Kaspian about it."

"Then I'll message the queen," Isa offered. "She'll want to know what's happening."

I took a minute to open up my messages with Kaspian and decided on a simple "I'd like to send Medusa home" as my message. I didn't get a response from Kaspian. Instead, he had opened a portal into the strategy room and both royals came through it.

"What's going on here?" Seraphina asked.

"I've been working with the Producers for the past few hours," Isa said. "We lost another game. I want to send my patch out, but I need a way to keep you safe if he comes back here. I'd like to know how easy it would be for T to travel between worlds now."

"Another game?" Seraphina quietly asked the question, but she didn't really ask it to hear a response from Isa. The act was more as if she had been shocked to hear it. "And what does Production have to say on the matter?"

"They wanted me to send it an hour ago. But that's easy for a bunch of people in Corporous, where he hasn't been yet, to say. No restarts are required, and it should keep the Glitch out of any world, and subsequent games or locations within the world, that he hasn't been. For example, he has already been into the world of Fantasia. However, as far as I have been made aware, he hasn't been in Vampira yet. So, any area considered part of Vampira, he will not be able to enter if the patch works."

"That's wonderful," Kaspian said. "Why exactly are you concerned about sending this out?"

"He can, and, most likely, will come back to the Castle Town and a few of the surrounding areas as he's been here before. Once his area is limited, he might try to look for other ways in, which may include backdoors from places he's already been. Based on his behavior so far with T, despite him being something of a technical simulation, he seems to hold an oddly personal and humanistic grudge. When his ability to destroy all worlds is limited, he will be angry, and I am confident he would come here again, then Fantasia will be in danger of being destroyed. I don't want you to lose your home and game that your family has built for years. I don't want to lose you."

Seraphina stared blankly at the wall ahead of her. She didn't say anything for a minute, but she started crying.

"I don't know what's going on," she finally said. "I haven't been able to see it since I shared that vision with T. I can see other things, but I feel like I'm being blocked from seeing the Glitch. I don't know what's going to happen. How am I supposed to keep my people safe if I can't see the next step? I don't know the answer. I've been hoping that I'll get some sort of vision, but nothing comes."

I felt for the queen. She was used to being a strong ruler because she knew what was coming next. Not knowing now didn't make her any less of a queen, but it did shake her confidence. I felt even worse when I thought I might be the reason she couldn't see the Glitch or glitch-related visions anymore. If I had done it, I hadn't meant to. I didn't even want to see the vision of the future that I saw.

"I'd like to ensure that we can protect our people, as well," Kaspian agreed with Isa's sentiment. "We should let T travel. It's something she would like, too."

"We can do it," I said to Seraphina. "I *know* I will be successful. We are going to go to Eros's world and will return Medusa as a trial run."

"Which world do they belong to?" Seraphina asked me. "Many games span across several worlds that are based on Greek mythology. Do you know if their world is safe?"

"Olympus," Eros answered. Kaspian nodded with a smile. Olympus was the most popular and most accurate Greek mythology world, and *every* game inside it was themed for it. The games based on Greek mythology in other worlds *wished* they were in Olympus. His little indie game was more popular than he let on if it was in Olympus.

"Is there a way to confirm if he has been to Olympus yet?" Kaspian asked Isa.

Isa typed furiously on her computer before answering. "No reported sightings."

"Alright," Seraphina sighed. "We must determine all ways to ensure the safety of Fantasia. T, I humbly thank you for all you have done for our world."

"Don't thank me. I need to find a way to keep you all safe for selfish reasons, too. This is my new home, after all."

"This world may be frozen while we're gone," Kaspian said to his sister.

"Don't worry about that," Isa said, not looking up from her computer. "If T still freezes worlds while traveling, I can set up an away message that we are doing work in Fantasia in order to rebuild and communications may be delayed."

"I'll summon Olivia," Seraphina said.

"Olivia won't be very helpful," Isa declined.

"She's the most helpful person to travel with," I rebutted. From her knowledge of gaming to her healing ability, Olivia was *the* most important person to have travel with me.

"It's just that none of you have a crossover with any games in Olympus. Your powers set for Fantasia won't work."

"They've worked just fine before," Kaspian defended Olivia's abilities.

"Places like the Platform and games like the clown game do not have game-specific powers. You are *meant* to be able to use all of your powers in the Platform or as a Player in the clown game. Olympus has its own healing Players or items, and a healer from Fantasia is not one of them. Since the game is not active, you will not be given similar powers to those you already possess as you once would have. Also, her code is not written into the game as a Healer class there, so given that everything but comms are still down, she won't be helpful. Neither will you, Kaspian. But everyone will still have their physical attacks; sending in Players known for physical attacks would be the most beneficial option."

"But Medusa can use her powers," I countered.

"She had a crossover with a game here." Eros shook his head.

"Is there any way to change this?" Kaspian asked, sounding desperate. "Olivia is an essential component of keeping T alive when she uses the glitch, and I need—I would like to be there, as well."

"I could reach out to the developers of the game, but they would need access to you guys for a full crossover. I guess I could go with you guys and write you into the code myself once we get there."

"I will go then," Seraphina said. "I need to keep you safe."

Isa smiled.

"This group is getting too big," I declined.

"You're right," Seraphina said. "Kaspian, you and your retainers will stay here to protect the kingdom. The prince and queen shouldn't both be gone from the kingdom when there is an imminent threat to the public's safety."

"You can't just tell me what to do," Kaspian sassed his sister.

"As your queen, yes, I can," she retorted in a queenly way. Although, I'm sure part of it was the 'I'm older than you' type of way, too. "You will stay here."

"Eros and I will go grab Medusa," I said. I wanted to get away from the confrontation because it made me feel awkward.

"We'll be waiting for you," Kaspian said.

"Yes—myself, Olivia, and Isa," Seraphina said just as quickly.

I left without responding, but I could hear the siblings yelling at each other while Eros and I ran through the hallways. Eros and I shared a look that said "that's siblings for you." The stairs to the dungeons were on the far end of the castle behind a guarded door. The steps were made of stone and there was water dripping from above, which seemed simply cosmetic and added to the eerie aura. I nodded as we got to the door. Eros nodded back before we opened it.

Roughly twenty frozen guards were blocking the way. I weaved through them, avoiding direct eye contact with Medusa until we made it to her. Medusa was lucky neither of the royals saw what she had done down there. If they had, she probably wouldn't be going home right now. *They'd be pissed.*

"Eros, too? I get to kill you both tonight? I'm so lucky." By the way she said it I could tell she was smiling.

"You're not killing anyone," I countered.

"I'm here because of Eros," she said. "I'd be happy to take him out for personal reasons if no one else."

"Medusa," Eros said. He looked over and grinned at me. "You're not actually upset about what we did in Vampira. You're just upset that we got stuck here. What if we weren't stuck here? Would you honestly be *that* upset with me?"

"I'll let you know when we get back home," Medusa laughed.

"Eros, you sly devil," I smiled. "Medusa?"

"I'm the god of love, T. No one wants to turn me down."

"You two a thing, or can I send her back where she belongs?" I asked.

"By all means, you can totally send her back. We're typically just a once every couple of months hook up when no one else is available."

"Once every couple of months?" Medusa laughed. "Try once a month. Sometimes a few days in a row."

"You can kill her if you like," Eros suggested.

"I don't know. I think I want to hear more about how desperate you are."

"Nah," he laughed. "Let's head back to Olympus."

"What?" Medusa asked. I looked back at Medusa, and she looked childlike as if she was asking, begging, for clarity.

"We're sending you home," I answered.

"Seriously?" she asked in disbelief. "You can really make this happen?"

"It's a give and take." I looked around at the frozen guards. Within a moment, all the soldiers were moving freely again. I nodded at Medusa to thank her. Eros stopped a guard and had him open up Medusa's door. "Follow us."

When we got back to the strategy room, all the retainers were waiting with the royals. I wondered how that argument played out. There was no way to tell just by looking at them, and I wasn't about to ask and cause another fight. So, we entered the room and waited to be addressed.

"Eros," Olivia said. "I didn't realize your game was in Olympus! You're always telling us how you're an indie game, but Olympus is huge."

"There are a lot of games there, Liv. I *am* from an indie game. Our budget isn't as great as *War Gods* or some other games you find in Olympus. But *Gods of Mercy* is well-known. It's one of the biggest past times in Olympus."

"Take these with you." Nathaniel handed me a few vials. "It should keep you alive in case Olivia can't."

"So, are we actually going to leave, or are we just going to talk about it some more?" Medusa asked, making herself known. Seraphina's eyes glowed purple as she stared at Medusa.

"We can go now," Seraphina said. "T?"

I took a deep breath and felt the heavy wave easily flow through me. I tried to separate the two abilities, but I couldn't just open a portal. I had to freeze Fantasia first but, when I did, the world around me froze faster than it ever had before.

This is helpful.

I reached over and touched Kaspian; I wanted him to share my excitement, to see how easy it was becoming for me.

"Look how quick that was," I said as I touched him. "Thanks for being a great teacher."

"You did it," he acknowledged. "Now you just have to make it home safely. I'm not going to be joining you."

"Oh. Well, don't worry, I'll make it back." I winked. "I can't die before you've had the chance to ask me out."

I touched everyone else, closed my eyes, took a deep breath, and knew I had done it. Opening a portal was just as easy. Isa raised a finger and quickly typed something on her computer before closing it and grabbing her tablet. Medusa rushed through first without a second thought. Seraphina and Isa held hands as they walked through, and Olivia and Eros waited for me so we could walk through at the same time. The streets were bustling in a different way than Castle Town; the people moved through the market in colorful robes, statues of gods and goddesses were found throughout the streets, and white decorative pillars were in the front of every building. I didn't have to worry about Medusa once we walked through the portal because she immediately left us. Isa held up a hand and stopped all of us before she started typing on her tablet. People around the area looked at us, acknowledged Eros, then knew they weren't in any danger. But there was still a commotion around us.

"It's done," Isa said. "Everyone should be able to use their powers. I'd like to test some things before we leave. Is there a good place to do that, Eros?"

"Follow me," Eros said. "I've got a place near the Parthenon where we can recap."

We followed Eros, and a group of people started following us, trying to see what was going on. Some people began cheering Eros's name and giving him high-fives. He really was well-loved here. Did he miss being treated like royalty? He always complained about money, but he'd never really needed any when he was with us. But this? He knows we love him, but the people of Fantasia didn't treat him the same way they treated Kaspian and Seraphina. I didn't want him to miss being here.

I don't want to lose him.

Eros continued to lead us through the streets while Kaspian messaged me about how weird it was being stuck in a world that was frozen. I had unfrozen his retainers before leaving so he wouldn't be *that* mad at me, but I'm sure it was still a weird situation. Still, they would make for great test subjects for Isa when we returned. I messaged him back that someone needed to protect Fantasia while we were gone with a smiley face.

"Hey," someone yelled from the group following us. "Why haven't you helped us?"

Eros stopped rather abruptly at the odd message. People around us began whispering to each other. He turned around.

"Eros?" I asked.

"It's okay," he whispered back. "They think I ghosted them and that's why they haven't seen me."

"I haven't been here," Eros addressed the crowd. "I was stuck in another world."

"Please, don't leave again, Eros," someone else from the crowd yelled. "Help us."

"It's the pankration," the original person who asked for help spoke again. "They're in *your* stadium."

"The Panathenaic?" I had never heard Eros so offended before. "Who is there? What are they doing?"

"They're taking people left behind and forcing them to engage in pankration," the guy answered for her.

"What's pankration?" I asked; my Ancient Greek knowledge was more than a little rusty.

"It's a hand-to-hand tournament–there's pretty much no rules," Isa filled me in.

I looked at Eros, who looked back at me. I knew we couldn't leave, whatever it was; it was his domain, his name attached to it, his people that he needed to protect. He nodded to the people, grabbed my hand, and began leading us down some alleyways. I looked back, and Olivia was following me, holding Seraphina's hand with Seraphina also holding Isa's hand. We made a long train as we kept making sweeps through different alleys. He barely slowed down as he turned a corner and entered a door. The room was simple, with nothing more than a bed, toilet, fireplace, and some provisions.

"I insist you tell us what is going on," Seraphina demanded. She was out of breath, not used to battle and definitely not used to training and running in the same manner that Eros and I were.

"This is my safe house if I'm ever in *Gods of Mercy* overnight. We have time to talk. You can do whatever it was you wanted here while I go figure out what's going on at the stadium."

"What's so important about the stadium?" Olivia asked.

"*She* made it." He looked down. "I won't let them destroy something she worked so hard on."

"Who?" I asked. He couldn't make eye contact with me, which had never been an issue before, even when he talked about his dad. He continued to stare at the ground.

"Cordie," he whispered.

"Who's Cordie?" Olivia asked. I wondered the same thing, but I could tell he didn't want to talk about it. The day he told me about his dad, he wanted to tell me about something else and stopped himself. I wonder if Cordie was the other thing and, if she was, who was she to him?

"I'll be back." He ignored Olivia's question. He started for the door, but a gust of wind swayed him backward.

"You will explain what is going on," Seraphina demanded.

"Okay," Eros grumbled. "So, *Gods of Mercy* is an indie game, but it actually became really famous as a 2D fighting game, reminiscent of original arcade games. My—Cordie created it, and she helped me get a role as a Character for one of the gods in the game to be closer to my dad. We battle in the Panathenaic Stadium, which alludes to an actual stadium in ancient times. Pankration is the type of battle we use."

"I thought you were a mercenary," I said.

"I am in the world of Olympus, just not in *Gods of Mercy*," he corrected. "People started to bet on the outcomes of the games, things got rowdy, and our world was never the same. For a little side hustle, I got paid by the Olympian gods to keep everyone in check. Except, I didn't often kill, since, you know, people usually just respawned. So, it was my job to take them to the brink of death and leave them there as a warning."

"You are so much darker than I expected," Olivia looked at him with wide eyes.

"I never meant to hide it from anyone; we all know I met T because I tried to kill her, so," he trailed off.

"I'm not scared. Just utterly surprised that such a sweet cinnamon roll like yourself is so dark."

"Cinnamon roll? Me?" he asked.

"Move on," Seraphina interrupted.

"Right, so I need to find out what's going on. This is my game, *my legacy*, and *hers,* too. I can't let them ruin it, even if I don't plan on staying. I'll be back, but I need you guys to stay here. If a single person even attempts to come through this door, you kill them, even if it's me. I'll respawn."

"I'll do it," Seraphina said.

"Thank you, Queenie."

"Some respect, Eros?" Olivia asked.

"*Queenie Seraphina,*" Eros said before he gave me a quick nod and reached for the door.

"I'll help." I started after him.

"No." He turned around and held out a hand.

"What?" I felt sick to my stomach hearing him refuse me. He'd helped me through so much already. I tried using his own words against him. "You've helped me. Now, let me return the favor."

"I need to do this on my own. I need to gain their trust if I want to get answers. I love you, but I can't have you with me now."

"Okay." I looked away so he wouldn't see me cry. I heard the door shut and assumed he'd left. I walked into the corner of the room and sat down, my body facing the wall, so I didn't have to communicate with the other people stuck in the room with me. I understood; I did. But I wanted to help him just like he had helped me, and it pissed me off that I couldn't. It was stupid and irrational, but I felt unwanted by my friend, even though that's not remotely what he said. Olivia came and sat next to me after a few minutes. She didn't say anything but just sat there quietly. Her silent comfort was more supportive than she realized.

After a few hours, there was a bang against the door as it started to open. Seraphina readied herself as the door opened; she used her powers to whisk the person against the wall. I ran to the door, shut, and locked it to make sure no one else entered. Seraphina was about to hit him with the kill shot when she froze, realizing it was Eros.

"Eros?" Olivia looked at the bloodied body in front of us. "Want some help?"

"Please," he said as he spat out blood.

"Eros," I examined the face of the obvious loser in battle in front of me as Olivia waved her staff, slowly healing him. There was no way he got the information he wanted. He took a hell of a beating. "Who did this to you?"

"I wasn't strong enough."

"You weren't strong enough?" Olivia asked. "But isn't this your game?"

"I'm wildly average." He laughed lightly. "I've got moderate stats in an indie game that blew up overnight. But my adorable personality has made me well-loved and respected by my people."

"I could've helped you," I sighed. "You're lucky you're loveable."

"How can you hate the god of love?"

"So, did you get what you wanted?"

"Exactly what I wanted." He took a deep breath. "That help you offered earlier. I could use it now."

"What's the plan?"

"I'm not exactly sure. Strategy isn't really a part of *Gods of Mercy*."

"I usually just follow the dots," I said.

"This sounds like something Olivia can help with," Seraphina said.

"Me?" Olivia asked. "I'm not sure it's appropriate for me to guide people in their game, especially if it's not my own."

"You should never have let the opinion of *that* man, or any man, make you feel that way." Seraphina and Olivia shared a looked. Then, there was a quiet moment as Olivia looked down at her nails and started picking at them. The queen stopped her habit with a firm, "Olivia."

"Right." She nodded. "Eros, what else can you tell me?"

"Some sinister group of people I've never met before has captured people stuck outside of their game. They're selling battles with them at a bar not too far from here. There's one going on tonight."

"Selling battles?" Isa asked.

"*Gods of Mercy* was about battling in the stadium, right? Well, the stadium is still there and operational. This is all the people know. So, they kept battling. But, without actual Players and loot, it isn't as much fun. They tried to get people back into the game by upping the stakes, battling people from other games that are stuck here. It's a fight to the death, well, respawn. The better known the Character, the more the battles cost to join and the higher the rewards. Even people who aren't Characters are betting their ways into games."

"They have found a way to keep their economy alive," Seraphina sighed. "Regardless of how unethical it is."

"Well, not on my watch." Eros, finally fully recovered from Olivia's healing magic, stood up and pointed out a window. He patted the top of my head like I was a child. "I need to do this for myself and Cordie, just like you are still doing things for Ghost."

"Is she dead?" I asked. No, she couldn't be; he wouldn't have known if the Glitch got her when he talked about his father in the forest. Then, again, when he said no one seemed hurt when comms went back up.

"No." He smiled. "But a love lost, nonetheless. Anyway, let's get back to the business at hand. What are we doing, Liv? Are we sending T in undercover?"

"No," Olivia interrupted. "I have a better plan."

FOURTEEN

"Just be yourself. It will work out, all right?" Olivia said.

"I mean, none of us really know if this will work," I said pessimistically.

"But, Olivia, I'm impressed. I underestimated you," Eros admitted.

We stood in front of a dark overbearing door that Eros said was the entrance to a bar. It wasn't friendly or welcoming like everything in Fantasia. But, if I had learned anything from my time outside of *Duty Falls*, it was that each world had its own expectations for reality versus Game. Fantasia, the largest MMORPG world, really delved into the world of the Game. Even though it was a modern version of some medieval world, they never truly had to tough it out as they would've in medieval times. They had also declined applications from chain suppliers to build in their world. While other worlds, like The Platform, had Game aspects and reality aspects. I was used to coffee shops, stores, and fast food everywhere, while Kaspian was used to fresh eggs in the morning. Eros pounded on the door three times, pulling me back to my current reality. A man wearing a robe with a hood and a white mask opened the door. The man nodded at Eros and let us in.

Seraphina and Isa had entered ahead of us, both wearing tunics to blend in with the people of this world. The rest of us wore our normal clothes, which for Eros *was* blending in, but Olivia and I purposefully stood out. There were murmurs as we entered. We just kept walking, found Seraphina and Isa, and purposefully sat a table away from them.

"Sold," a man at the front yelled as they escorted a large burly man the size of Hawthorn off the stage. "And now, our reigning champion, not even from our game, N0F@ce."

The people in the crowd started cheering. I hadn't heard of NOF@ce before but judging by the saliva forming at Olivia's mouth and the excited gleam in her eye, NOF@ce was from a popular game and a celebrity in their own right. The person they brought on the stage literally had no face, although maybe BlurryF@ce would have been a better name. It was like a haze was where their face was supposed to be, and they had a petite figure, covered in black spandex. Everything was covered in the material except for the white light that emanated from the blurry face. Their hands were handcuffed.

"Olivia?" I asked.

"Huh, what?" She looked at me. "Oh shit, yes, now is an excellent time."

"I heard you want a battle," I yelled, standing up so everyone could see me. The crowd turned around to look at the interruption.

"How did you get here?" someone yelled. "You're supposed to be in Fantasia."

"You want to battle the strongest person, don't you?" I asked, ignoring the question.

"Ladies and gentlemen," the announcer started, excited by the energy in the room. "We have a challenger."

"You've gotta pay, just like everyone else," the guy next to me muttered. I looked down at him, he grabbed my arm and yelled, "Sit the fuck down."

Asshole.

"Let them go," I said to the announcer as I kicked the asshole who grabbed me with my foot.

"I don't think NOF@ce needs your help," the announcer laughed, and the crowd followed.

"Does NOF@ce want to battle? Do any of these people? Let them all go."

"You're ruining our fun." The asshole next to me was irritated. He tried to yank me down by grabbing my arm again, but, instead, I got a hold of his, twisted it, and shoved his face into the table. I held it there while I stared at the announcer.

"Take her down," the announcer yelled. "The first one to take her down will be the first to have a go at her in the stadium."

I let go of the asshole and jumped onto a table to get a better view of my surroundings. The same asshole was the first to lunge at me. I kicked him in the face before he even had a chance to get close to me. Another fighter grabbed my leg from behind and pulled me down. I drew my knife and stabbed the fighter in the leg. They fell in pain, and I used their body as a shield while the asshole punched at me. I didn't feel a thing, not even reverberation through the other guy's body. It was almost as though he sucked at fighting. I pushed off the ground and stood back up to see the whole bar was fighting. Eros was protecting Olivia in the corner, and Seraphina was protecting Isa in another corner.

I dodged my way to the front of the bar where NOF@ce was fighting with the announcer. I threw a knife, and it stuck straight through the announcer's right eye. His hands instinctively grabbed at it as blood poured down his face. NOF@ce looked at me, I think, then searched the announcer's body for the keys to the handcuffs. While NOF@ce looked for the keys, I avoided another attack from the asshole again. I grabbed the hand of another fighter as he tried to stab me with a knife and shoved it into the asshole's chest. The guy who stabbed him said, "Oh shit," as the asshole just laughed.

"T, it's a buff," I heard Olivia yell as the asshole, with his buffed-up power, barely slapped me and I flew back. The entire crowd stopped fighting and watched us.

"Hit me," he laughed.

"Hell no." I dodged another lunge by him. Someone else stabbed him, increasing his strength, and the crowd started cheering as he came at me again. I took a deep breath and let the heavy feeling flow through my body as I froze time.

I'm done.

The people around me froze, but it was different this time because they weren't actually frozen. I slowly walked by people whose eyes watched me as I walked while I went to unfreeze Olivia and Eros.

"T, I was awake. I could see you," Olivia said as I unfroze her.

"Yeah, something's not right."

"Get Isa," Eros said.

We snaked our way through the crowd of frozen fighters. Isa started talking as soon as I unfroze her. "What an unexpected twist. I don't think this has anything to do with the patch before you ask. I think since Fantasia is still frozen, your powers are not at one hundred percent; therefore, the people here aren't fully frozen. My answer is only reinforced by the fact that neither Kaspian, Nathaniel, nor Alton messaged me like I asked them to if Fantasia became unfrozen at any point."

"But, if the only reason I'm in Fantasia is that I used my powers to get there, then wouldn't The Platform be frozen and Fantasia not frozen all the way?" I asked.

"We can't actually confirm you sent yourself to Fantasia, just that your powers and thoughts while hearing Olivia's voice *might* have guided the portal you went through."

"The clown game tried to start moving again in the end, didn't it?" Olivia asked.

"I think it did." I thought back to the day where a giant clown foot almost squashed me, then shook my head, knowing better than to get distracted. I looked at Eros. "Who should we be unfreezing?"

"We could always talk to my old man," he whispered. "Well, not my old man exactly, but he's pretty well connected."

"I'm so ready for this," Olivia said excitedly. "Is your dad Zeus?"

"No, Hermes," he sighed. "Follow me."

"Ah, Zeus. Lovely." I could tell by Seraphina's voice that she and Zeus had some sort of history; it didn't seem to be positive.

"You know him?" Eros asked.

"For many years," she confirmed.

"Then, I'll bring you there, but I can't face my dad. Not right now. I'm not in a good headspace, and I don't think seeing him is the best decision."

I wanted to ask him why he didn't want to see his dad, but I couldn't make myself do it—as much as I wanted to know the answer, I also didn't. I knew he loved him; he'd told me that before. So, why not face him? If there were other reasons, did that mean there was a chance that my own family wouldn't want to see me?

"Fair enough." Seraphina nodded.

Eros brought us to the base of a very tall mountain. I could hear Olivia curse him under her breath as we took a long look up to the top. Eros laughed then walked through a fake part in the mountain to an elevator. He pressed the button as we all awkwardly waited for the doors to open. When it finally arrived, we filed in, and Eros stayed outside and smiled at me. Olivia waved at him as the doors closed. We heard the ding to tell us we had stopped and emptied out into a fancy chamber that was a different type of elegance than the castle. Where Fantasia was ornate and slightly over the top, Olympus was clean and white; pristine marble with intricate designs adorning the room. Twelve people, frozen in place, were seated on thrones facing the entrance to the temple. Their eyes followed us as we moved.

"Zeus is in charge." Seraphina nodded at a young guy only slightly older than her in the middle. He was probably the same age as Eros, if I had to guess, though Zeus' game, as the ruler of Olympus, was more established than Eros's.

I touched Zeus; he quickly took a deep breath then immediately pointed at me. Lightning struck down from above as I jumped back to avoid it. I threw two knives that cut through both of his hands, keeping them stuck to his throne, unless he wanted to feel the pain of ripping them out.

"Don't make me freeze you again, dude," I threatened.

"Who are you?" he asked.

"My name is Tack180. Eros, who is from your world, is waiting outside and can vouch for me. So can Queen Seraphina." I nodded back at her. "I'm here to help you and your people, regardless of how it currently looks."

"I'll take over from here, T." Seraphina came up to me and put a hand on my shoulder, tapping me out.

"Queen Seraphina," Zeus hummed. "I almost didn't recognize you in the clothes of my people. They suit you. What brings you here?"

I ripped my two knives from his hands. He hissed through the pain, trying to act all godlike about it. I wiped off the blood from the knives and turned to face the rest of the group. I backed up and let Seraphina do her thing while examining the group of Olympians. I didn't need to ask Zeus which one Hermes was. It was easy to spot him, being the spitting image of Eros and all. I finally got why Eros dyed his hair blue; if he hadn't, it would have been far too obvious they were related.

"Zeus, we seem to have found ourselves in your game and in need of assistance," Seraphina said. "It would behoove us to discuss the current situation our worlds find ourselves in after we resolve this matter. As a fellow ruler of your world and member of the Gaming Summit, it is our duty to protect the worlds as a whole."

"Always straight to the point, Your Majesty." Zeus smiled. "I hope you understand that I must do only what I believe to be the best course of action for my people."

I didn't care for the political banter that was about to happen, so I walked over to Hermes, where Olivia joined me. I was tempted to touch him, to ask him questions that I didn't have the answers to myself. Did he regret getting rid of his memories? Did I regret doing it? Did that change the Character he became or the person he truly was? Maybe if I just touched him, I could get another opinion. Ghost and I had talked about it before, and I had talked to others who chose not to keep their memories, as well. But now, in the middle of a Production blackout and crisis across all worlds, did that change the way others felt about their families? I'd thought about my family more in the past two months than I had in the past seven years.

"T," Olivia sounded shocked as she grabbed my arm, pulling it away from Hermes. "What are you doing?"

"He's like me," I said. "I want to know if he regrets it." Hermes' eyes tracked my movements.

"What are you talking about?"

"Losing his memories."

"Is it bothering you?" She pulled me away from him.

"If the roles were reversed, and Ghost survived the Glitch, and you never met me. In that scenario, do you think anyone would care that I died other than Ghost? I'm not talking about followers or people who care about me as a celebrity. I mean *really* care. I'm the only one that cares about Ghost; that I know of. I have no one to reach out to, to notify them of what happened if he *does* have family still out there."

"T." Her eyes watered as she placed her hand on my arm.

"If it were Ghost standing here, instead of me, you would love him the same way you do me right now. I know that. But you wouldn't love me like you do now; you'd be helping him get answers for his dead partner and I'd just be a celebrity you liked before the Glitch hit."

"But you can't take it back—your lost memories are not only lost; they're gone. So, what do you want?"

"I don't know." I felt my eyes start to water. This wasn't really the time or place, but I couldn't help it. "I don't know who I am anymore. Without Ghost. Without my weapons. I'm becoming someone else entirely, and that's terrifying. But, this person I'm becoming, is this who I was all along? I want to know. I want to meet the people who knew me before I joined the Game. They're my family. But when will I have time to do something like that?"

"You can take time for yourself, too."

No. That's selfish.

I can't take time for myself when we have a Game-altering, life-shattering, and existence-ending Glitch on the loose. How could I ever think it would be okay to take time for myself? I already felt guilty for not having done more earlier.

"So, Zeus." I looked back at the sound of Seraphina's voice. "Will you come with us?"

"That bar is technically under Hades' control. However, all subjects of Olympus are under my control. After confirming the happenings at the bar, I will discuss with my people what to do from there. I don't usually get involved in the affairs of *mortals*."

"Dude," Olivia muttered under her breath. "You're not a real god."

"I will determine what's fair and it may not be what you like," he continued, not hearing Olivia.

"You will respect the autonomy of *all* people, including those not in your game," Seraphina fumed. Her magic began radiating around her body. "Or do you not remember our pact as world leaders?"

"I will determine what is fair," Zeus' voice boomed. Lightning flickered over his body in the same way Seraphina's magic did.

"This is not a repeat of school-aged Model Gaming Summit. This is the real deal; the longest blackout in history, and I would appreciate you listening to my requests rather than assuming you know better than everyone," Seraphina said.

"I shouldn't have to remind you that neither of us are Producers. We only have control over our own worlds. You have no right to come into mine and tell me that I'm doing a poor job."

"When I became queen, I made a choice to protect not only my people but *all* people. That is where our leadership skills differ, Zeus. You're not doing a poor job for your people; you're doing a poor job for those in your care who are *not* your people."

"Always the bitch, aren't you, Seraphina?"

"Zeus, if I may," Isa diplomatically interrupted. "Since we haven't found a secure and consistent way of getting people back to their games, those who are stuck in your game should be considered 'your people' as they may now live here until the end of time if this doesn't get resolved. That being said, while you and the queen were talking, I took it upon myself to give anyone living in this game, who was not already a part of this game or with an active crossover, the powers of their game. I'm sure this will contribute to helping find a solution that all members may be happy with. If not, well, I do wish you luck when NOF@ce gets their hands on you."

"Now, who's this bitch?" Zeus asked.

"A Producer," Seraphina answered. "And you will treat her with more respect."

"Challenge me one more time, Queen Seraphina." Zeus' voice was laced with menace. "You have come into my game, harming my people with your freezing powers, and trying to disrupt the peace. You have proven to be nothing but a nuisance committing acts of war that should be punished."

"Wait a minute," Olivia interrupted. "None of this was meant to be an act of war against the gods. We're just trying to help the people. Eros demanded that we stay as these are also *his* people. He's outside if you want to talk to him before we all go home."

"He's not staying?" Zeus asked.

"He found a new home." Olivia folded her arms.

"If looking into this will make Eros reconsider, then I will join you." Zeus stared at Seraphina.

What a jackass. I rolled my eyes.

Zeus followed us back down in the elevator and gave Eros a handshake when they saw each other. Eros filled him in on game-specifics while we headed back to the bar. Zeus was like a completely different person in front of Eros; he put on the charm like a true salesman. Eros kept to the facts, though, and focused on the issue at the bar rather than why he wanted to leave. People's gazes followed us as we entered the bar, but no one moved, still frozen in time as they had been before we left. Zeus looked around, unsure of where to begin. Seraphina pointed to the announcer. I walked up and touched him, he immediately knelt in front of Zeus.

"What's going on here?" Zeus asked. His eyes were fixated on the chains around NOF@ce's hands.

"M-my lord," he stuttered, letting his guilt show. "We are having battles in the stadium, as we usually would in the game. People are making bets on the outcome, as always. This is business as usual without the actual Game mechanics in place."

Zeus nodded at NOF@ce. I touched them, and Zeus started talking again, "Explain yourself."

"I was captured and forced to battle with the highest bidder."

"Lord Zeus, this is an extreme exaggeration—" the announcer started.

Zeus briefly looked over at Seraphina. She nodded, and it seemed like they shared a moment of understanding because neither of them showed any signs of anger.

"Did you consent?" Zeus asked.

"No, but I would have if asked," NOF@ce replied. "I enjoy the battle."

"Reform is needed," Zeus acknowledged. Then lightning formed around his hand as he punched the announcer in the chest and then shoved his fist through his body. The announcer respawned on the spot. "NOF@ce, I'd like you to work with this asshole on creating a project that this world can be proud of. The entertainment of a game and revenue for our world can have positive benefits for all people. Gambling on the outcomes should be open to all, exclusive front-row seats reserved for paparazzi who pay, stories written for and sold to news stations to publish. When done right, this could benefit more than just the wealthy. Are you willing to help build a world worth living in?"

NOF@ce tilted their head at Zeus. I'm assuming it was thoughtfully, but honestly, I had no idea. They had no fucking face.

"Yes," NOF@ce answered.

"I'm sure you can feel it, but your powers have been returned to you for a fairer fight," Zeus acknowledged.

NOF@ce bobbed their head in acknowledgment.

"Does everyone in this room understand?" Zeus looked around. "If you fuck up again, I will make sure you are dealt with appropriately. Unfreeze them."

I unfroze everyone while Olivia continued to hold her staff over me. Zeus stared at the room, daring anyone to go against his ruling. No one moved, as though they were still frozen. Zeus nodded in satisfaction and began to leave the room. He stopped to grab and kiss Seraphina's hand.

"Once again, you come out on top," Zeus said.

"This was never about first or second place, Zeus. Only about the people." Seraphina bowed to him as a sign of respect.

"One more for the road?" Zeus asked.

"Surely you've taken enough losses for the day?" Seraphina smiled.

"I have. That's why I deserve a win with home-field advantage."

"We should be getting back," Seraphina declined.

"My Queen, I recommend you take up my offer. We find ourselves in uncertain times, and it would benefit Fantasia to know that they have an ally in Olympus."

"Are we not already aligned?" she retorted.

"We will be if you do not threaten my rule. We will battle once before you go. You are a visitor in my kingdom and will follow my rules."

"Alright then." Seraphina's eyes glowed purple and, although she was pissed, she wasn't the queen of Olympus and she had to focus on cross-world relations. "I accept."

Zeus held out an arm, and Seraphina grabbed it. Zeus and Eros brought us to the stadium and got us set up for battle. Even though gaming wasn't functioning, the Game mechanics still worked automatically. Eros moved as he explained to all of us that movement was only toward or away from your battle partner. Seraphina couldn't move her body in any other direction that was non-linear. Eros grabbed me as an example and placed me so I was facing him. I took a few steps toward him, and I could move just fine. I moved a few steps away, and it was the same result.

"Hey, yo." We heard a yell from the stands in the stadium. Medusa took a front-row seat next to Seraphina, who glared at her. "I owe you, Eros. Call me up next time you're in town."

"I think I'll stay down here," Eros acknowledged, deciding not to return to his seat. "I might be more helpful to the queen here than from the sidelines."

Seraphina stood up and removed herself from Medusa's presence. She and Zeus joined us in the ring.

"Are we battling or not?" Medusa yelled from the stadium, where she was still sitting by herself. She started clapping and cheering.

"Ladies first." Zeus bowed, and the rest of us stepped away while Zeus and Seraphina readied themselves for battle.

"Before we battle," Seraphina said. "I just want to confirm that we have an ally in Olympus regardless of the challenging road ahead. Rebuilding the Game and lost worlds will take time and having you on our side will be most helpful."

Zeus laughed. "Yes, Seraphina, you can count on Olympus as an ally."

"I hope that is still your answer after you lose."

Seraphina smirked as she took the first shot; badass was a good look on her. They went back and forth for a while before Zeus finally landed a lightning-infused punch to Seraphina's chest. I thought it would be the end, draining most of her HP in one hit, but she rallied back. Her eyes glowed purple as Zeus was pushed all the way back to the edge of the arena. She continued to fling her arms in a non-stop barrage of hits on Zeus, forcing him down and incapacitating him. It was clear she had been holding back because she extended both arms, and purple darkness swirled above her before striking down on Zeus ferociously. He was blown out of the arena and into the stadium seats.

"Game over" rang out from some unseen sound system.

"I would've had you," Zeus grumbled as Seraphina ran over to him. She held out a hand to help him up.

"Hardly, Zeus." She waved her hand to a podium for first and second to stand on. "I believe you're familiar with your position?"

"That's my queen," Olivia cheered.

"Thank you for a good fight." Zeus waved his hand as if he was done talking to us. Give Nathaniel my best. It's been a while since I've seen my favorite of your retainers."

"I certainly will." She smiled.

"Nathaniel was your retainer?" I asked Seraphina.

"Yes, for five years until I turned twenty-three. He and Kaspian were friends the whole time if that was what you were curious about?"

"No, I guess I just assumed he always worked with Kaspian."

"He was a general retainer to the royal family. Our fathers were friends; prior to my father becoming king, they were both just young men in the same guild trying to make a name for themselves."

"Next stupid question," Eros said. "Your dad wasn't always the king?"

"No." Seraphina shook her head. "My mother was the princess and, in a classic story, was kidnapped and needed to be saved. Or so it was intended. She practiced magic and fought her way out of the kidnappers' grasp at the same time my father and Nathaniel's father made it to save her. So, she joined their guild and traveled with them for a year before returning to the castle. For bringing my mother back, they were both given a place in the knight's guard."

"So romantic," Olivia sighed.

Ping.

I opened my DMs to a message from Kaspian. It read, "He's here."

FIFTEEN

"We need to go," I said. Kaspian's message was quick and concise. It was sent to let us know they needed backup, and they needed it now. We couldn't waste any time with pleasantries. "The Glitch is in Fantasia."

I froze the world, touched my crew, and opened the portal back home. The portal opened to the coordinates Kaspian's next message gave us. We were only a couple hundred yards from Castle Town's walls. The Glitch was standing in front of Kaspian and his retainers, staring past them at Castle Town.

He will not destroy my new home.

"Don't engage," I said to everyone. Olivia snorted at that, clearly remembering the last time I had said it before instantly going against my own advice.

Kaspian didn't turn around, but I could tell he heard me because his posture relaxed slightly. They weren't alone; we were here to help.

"I need to protect my people," Kaspian answered.

"I'm already glitched. You have no reason to get too close." I ran up next to him.

"I don't want you touching it either."

"Neither of you should touch it," Olivia interrupted.

The Glitch turned his attention from Castle Town to me. He tilted his head as he looked at us.

"You bother me," it said.

"Yeah, the feelings mutual," I answered. He pulled out Ghost's gun and pointed it at me. I swung my arm, and the gun went flying.

"I have information on you," the Glitch said. "I've been downloading your code."

I took a step forward but felt a hand holding me back. I quickly looked at the hand, realizing it belonged to Nathaniel. I shook him off. The Glitch pulled out Ghost's gun again and started firing. I set up a shield to block the people around me. I pinched my fingers and began throwing tacks at the target in the distance. He disappeared, and I dodged as I turned around, knowing he would show up behind me, given that's how he battled in the past. I repositioned the shield around my people and watched them fly back as if the wind pushed them. Kaspian nodded at me, helping in any way he could.

I tried to avoid touching the Glitch, knowing the consequences if I did, and used my shield to block actual swings if I couldn't dodge him in time. I had no way to defeat him, so I was keeping him from touching me, which was his only way of defeating me; therefore, we were at a standstill.

That didn't stop us from destroying the whole area around us in a one-on-one battle. I froze everything, trying to take some time to think about what to do. I had the vial Isa gave me, and I knew she was watching the battle, waiting for me to pull it out, but I couldn't risk killing Ghost. The Glitch started moving slowly as if he was only half frozen like the people of Olympus. *He was learning.* Isa mentioned he would, with every time I used a move, he would learn and adapt. I unfroze things, not wanting him to learn how to use my power against me. I wasn't sure I would be able to unfreeze myself if he *could*. As though he could read the fear on my face, he started walking to me without any weapons, like he was going to negotiate an end to the fight.

Lightning struck in between us, but it didn't stop the Glitch from coming closer. Nathaniel, Alton, and Eros were running in our direction, but I blocked them with a shield.

"T, what are you doing?" Olivia yelled.

Keeping you all safe.

"T," Isa yelled. She didn't need to say anymore. I wouldn't either. I didn't want him to hear what she had planned. Still, I wasn't going to use it.

"They were right," the Glitch said.

"Who was right?" I asked, sounding more frantic than I wanted to.

"Those who made a deal with me in order to save their world."

"Who made a deal with you?" I asked.

More importantly, since when was that an option?

"They told me the way to win against you was to use," he paused, raising his hand and then closing it to make a fist. Olivia went flying into the air in a shield, one that I didn't create for her. The Glitch had new powers. Or maybe he copied mine. "Your friends."

"Put her down." I hissed as I stared him down. It took every ounce of self-control I had to drown out her screams as she called out to Alton. I didn't want him to see my weakness and, if the worst-case scenario happened, I couldn't watch as another friend died. I saw Alton running at us in my peripheral vision. Eros tackled him, knowing that Alton couldn't do anything. He didn't respond, so I yelled again, "Put her down."

"Why would they help me?" he asked. He pulled Olivia, still in the shield, closer to him. She was only an arm's distance away. All he needed to do was reach over and grab her, making her disappear just like Ghost.

"If this is some kind of rhetorical question, then I really don't care."

"I," he paused. His face showed a minuscule amount of emotion that I hadn't seen before. "Care."

"Let her go, please." I tried to capitalize on the odd weakness he showed me.

Come on, man, show me some empathy.

"Why wouldn't they try to stop me?" he yelled. I jumped in fear, not expecting that extreme answer. I allowed myself to look at Olivia, floating in the shield. She was scratching at the side farthest from the Glitch, trying to get out, her hands starting to bleed. Then, quietly, he asked, "Why do I care?"

"I don't know who you're talking about," I tried. I briefly glanced around; Kaspian and Nathaniel were holding Alton back from trying to get to Olivia, and Seraphina was looking over Isa's shoulder as she typed quickly on her tablet. "But if you tell me, then maybe I can answer you."

"They know so much about you," the Glitch said to himself. "They told me on their own."

"Was it Bryce?" I asked. "Did he make you, too?"

"Who is Bryce?" The Glitch thought for a second before replying, "I have a creator, yes. Though I do not know who it is."

"Of course not," I groaned.

"Why do I care?" he yelled again as he charged me, both arms outstretched as if to reach around my neck. I froze him, just him, and a slow smile showed up on his face. He continued to fight against my powers as my HP drained heavily without Olivia's support. I fumbled for a potion as he finally set himself free. I took a step back and he disappeared. I figured he would show up behind me but, instead, he was standing next to Olivia. His hand plunged through the shield as she pushed her body against the far end of it, attempting to avoid his grasp. I charged him as he grabbed onto her by the skirt of her dress.

"No, no, no," she cried, but her dress color didn't change. The material was organic. *Thank God.* He looked to see why it didn't work, not realizing that he hadn't touched her because he was too focused on me. When he turned back, I was ready to engage him in battle. He disappeared, and I knew he would show up behind me, but I didn't have the energy to turn. I felt a body slam into mine and I waited for the shooting pain of the glitch, but it didn't happen. I opened my eyes to see Eros's body on top of me. On top of him was the Glitch, but he wasn't dark anymore. Eros pulled a syringe out of the Glitch's body.

"Get off." I struggled against Eros, who pushed the Glitch off then rolled off of me.

I watched as Ghost, my Ghost, skin-colored and normal, had taken the place of the Glitch.

"Ghost?"

"Tack," he replied. Ghost was the only one who called me Tack.

"It's not really him," Eros pleaded. "You know that, T. The real Ghost is gone."

"I'm alive?" he asked.

"How do I know it's you?" I asked.

He raised a hand to touch my face, and I didn't pull back. A spear shot through the air, cutting Ghost's hand before he could touch me. He pulled his hand back and blood formed at the gash; fresh, red, blood. I know I should've looked at Ghost again, but I didn't. I instinctively searched for Kaspian. I wanted, no *needed*, his support. Ghost's hands grabbed at my face, pulling my gaze back to him. Our eyes locked and his thumb slowly rubbed against my cheek.

"It's you." I reached out and hugged him.

"T, get me out of here," Olivia sobbed.

"Let her out," I said as Eros pulled me out of Ghost's arms.

"What?" he asked. I watched Ghost's color flicker, covered in darkness momentarily.

"She's my friend. You need to let her out, please."

"Friend? Please. Who are you?" Ghost tilted his head like he didn't believe me. "I'm not alive, am I? This is some sick joke."

"No, that's not it."

I've changed, but I'm still you're Tack180.

I reached out for him, but Eros pulled me further away. Ghost's body glitched again briefly before returning to its normal color.

"We need to kill him," Eros said.

"Fuck *you*," Ghost said to us. Regardless of if he was saying it to Eros specifically or both of us, it hurt. His color flashed away again, faster this time. He looked at Olivia and started walking toward her. He touched the shield but didn't undo it. I don't even know if he knew how.

What are you doing, Ghost?

I looked at his flickering body and then Olivia. She showed no fear with the spiders because she knew she would respawn. But the way she looked at Ghost, *my* Ghost; she was terrified. Her eyes were wide, hands bloodied from scratching at the shield, and her already small frame looked frail in comparison to Ghost's tall posture. He looked back at me before saying, "You keep getting in the way."

"T," Olivia yelled. "It's not him!"

"I don't think this stuff is long-lasting," Eros said.

"Ghost?" I asked. I couldn't give up on him. I had done everything I could since the glitch first happened to get him back, to save him or get revenge. Now, here he was, standing in front of me. I couldn't just *kill* him like they wanted. Except, in that shield was one of my best friends. She'd kept me sane and safe since I wound up in this world that was so different from my own. I *needed* to kill him to keep her safe, right?

Every second I spent thinking about it was a second wasted in taking action, and I was already out of time. Eros decided for me; he aimed his sword at Ghost. I kicked my foot up, knocking it out of his hand. Alton began charging toward Ghost. I ran forward to stop him; I couldn't let him take Ghost away again. *Not yet.* I haven't told him I love him. I haven't said goodbye. He doesn't know that I will do everything I can to avenge him. There was so much I wanted and needed to tell him. Eros's arms were firmly wrapped around me, pulling me away. I tried to fight him, but he kept pulling me. I searched for Kaspian—I needed his help. If anyone could convince the others to give up, it would be him. But, when my gaze finally found him, he was staring back at me.

"Let him go." I don't know if Kaspian mouthed it; if the words came out of his mouth, I didn't hear it. I didn't want to. I can't let him go.

"Let me go, Eros," I yelled.

"I can't," he replied. "You know we have to do this."

"I'll find you again." I pulled against Eros as I yelled to Ghost. He made eye contact with me. "I'll fix this. I promise I will help—"

I stopped as I watched Ghost freeze into ice before getting pierced by Alton's sword. I thrashed against Eros as I watched Ghost unfreeze and begin to bleed. Alton pulled his sword out as Ghost's color drained, his body returning to the glitched color. The shield around Olivia flashed a few times, and Nathaniel ran to her aide as it finally disintegrated. The Glitch stood up, looked at his body, and then disappeared. Eros pulled me back to the group as I continued to fight against him, reaching for the area where Ghost's blood, not the Glitch, laid pooled on the ground. *It was him.*

I could hear them tending to Olivia, but it didn't faze me. The thing that did was a firm slap across my face. I looked up to see Olivia staring at me, crying. She didn't say anything as she started to walk away.

"Wait, Olivia, I didn't choose him over you. I just needed to let him know that I would find him again. I just needed a few more minutes. You weren't in any real danger. Ghost wouldn't hurt you like the Glitch."

Olivia stopped walking and fell to the ground crying at my answer. Alton wrapped her in his arms.

"That wasn't Ghost," Eros said. "You know it wasn't really him."

"Do I? Because he looked fucking real to me."

"He wasn't real; it was whatever Isa gave me to inject him with."

"Why did you kill him?" I demanded of Alton.

"Talk to me when you're not upset, T," Alton ignored me. "It's obviously not the right time."

"You killed him."

"Fuck, T, so did Kaspian. You've got such a hard-on for the prince that you didn't see it or didn't care. Alton can't freeze people," Olivia said. "Ghost is dead. What you saw was something that made the Glitch weak, and if they hadn't done that, then the Glitch would've killed me, too. I wouldn't be here right now—no respawning. You know how we are all worried you might actually die? Yeah, that would've happened to me, but you seem more preoccupied that your dead boyfriend looked sentient for a hot second in between his attempts to kill me."

"Let her see for herself," Seraphina said.

Eros let me go, and I raced to the area where Ghost was stabbed. Just as I was about to reach for the blood to prove I was correct; it turned into a hazy purple ooze-like substance. Was it Ghost or a good copy? But he called me Tack, and only Ghost called me Tack. He knew me well enough to know I'd changed. He was still in there, somewhere, and we can reach him. I walked back to the group, tears falling down my face as I processed the loss all over again.

"No, T. You don't get my sympathy this time," Olivia said. "Why do people I put my trust in always let me down? Prince Kaspian, open a portal. I want to go home."

Kaspian opened a portal to the throne room, and we walked through. Olivia left the room without saying another word, but the rest of us stayed where we were.

"Was it him?" I asked Isa.

"Just like a computer with a virus can recover some files, I think Ghost could be recovered, as well. Nothing is guaranteed, though," Isa answered. "What you saw was the short-term effect of a possible antivirus shoved into the Glitch, courtesy of Eros. It very well could have been a remnant file of Ghost projected since he is taking Ghost's form. However, no, that did not seem to be Ghost. I'm sorry."

I trusted Isa's response. She was the most knowledgeable after months of studying me. Hell, she knew how to help me control the glitch better within my own body. I could only assume that she would know whether or not it really was Ghost. So, after all that, I risked Olivia's life to save Ghost, *and it wasn't him?* I felt like such a bitch. I dropped to the ground and covered my face. How was I supposed to know what to do at that moment? It all happened so fast.

"Send out the patch," Seraphina commanded. "It's time."

"On it," Isa said. "Let's control where he can go a little bit, shall we?"

"Come on." Eros helped me to my feet. "Let's take a break. It's been a long day and night."

"That's a smart idea," Isa said. "While we seem to have worried him enough that he retreated, we still aren't sure how he'll respond."

Eros brought me back to my room. Kaspian joined and stayed, briefly. I didn't know how to apologize to him, either, just like Olivia. I wasn't sorry for trying to save Ghost and I would do it again if I could. I was sorry because I felt guilty that I was trying to move on with Kaspian and I still loved, or was still programmed to love, Ghost. So much so that I couldn't even kill someone that looked like him. I didn't know if it bothered Kaspian, but it bothered me as I cared for him, and it wasn't fair to him. I ignored them both, hid in bed, and cried.

***

Eros and I woke up early the next morning and started prep at the bakery as if nothing had happened. To the citizens of Fantasia, nothing did happen. They were frozen for most of it and, when they unfroze, we engaged the Glitch in battle and kept him away from Castle Town. After everything that happened the day before, it was hard to wake up and get out of bed. So, I was later than I wanted and rushed there to meet Eros.

I saw I had notifications and DMs, but I didn't have the time to bother with them. Not until I had a few minutes before opening. I sat down on the counter while Eros washed dishes and opened my notifications. A flurry of messages continued to rush in, and I tried to focus on one just to read what it was about while new messages kept pushing the old messages down at an alarming speed. I saw Nia's name, but the barrage of messages continued to flow in. I put myself in do-not-disturb mode, but the damage was already done. I tried to scan through the messages to find Nia's, but I couldn't. Every single message that showed up wanted the same thing from me.

"Fuck," I said out loud.

"What?" Eros asked.

"We need to get back to the castle." We both looked toward the doors, and through the window, we could see one of the largest crowds we'd had waiting outside the door. It seemed like the group outside the windows started chanting once I made eye contact with them. "Without passing by those people."

"That won't be easy."

A portal opened inside the bakery, and I grabbed one of my throwing knives, ready to fight. Eros followed my lead and stood in front of me with his sword ready, even though he still didn't fully know what was going on. On the other side of the portal, I saw Kaspian, Seraphina, and Isa in the strategy room. Eros looked back at me, and I nodded. No one was going to be getting any baked goods today. We ran through the portal, and I could hear pounding on the bakery door as Kaspian closed the portal. I didn't know how my trip to Olympus became viral, but those bitches better not destroy my bakery over it.

"Nia, are you still with us?" Seraphina asked. "We have Tack180 and Eros safely on castle grounds."

"Yes, thanks for conferencing me in and taking the time to discuss this so early. Tack180, Production is offering you the deal of a lifetime," Nia said.

"What?" I asked. "I'm not in trouble?"

"Quite the opposite," Seraphina said. "Zeus praised your work in Olympus to members of Production. Headlines for all major news outlets are singing your praises for traveling between worlds."

"And Production wants to capitalize on that. In fact, some news articles are stating that you were able to travel under Production's instructions and control. So, I wouldn't be surprised if they are claiming it themselves," Nia said. "Regardless; the deal is fantastic."

I mean, they weren't wrong. I was traveling under Isa's guidance; whether she told Production or not was her choice.

"Well, what's the deal?" I asked. "Are they going to give me answers?"

"Well, there's nothing they know that I don't already know." Isa laughed.

Isa was smarter than I had originally given her credit for, and I already gave her a lot of credit. With Isa's sway in Production and Seraphina's sway as queen, the two held a lot of power. Hell, they were both guaranteed spots at world summits, given their position, to help keep all of the worlds in

"Peace and Prosperity" or some stupid tagline like that. Fantasia was popular before, but at this moment, with the political and Production influence, it was holding the power to become the next Platform if the current one couldn't be salvaged. Bryce had mentioned the spot would go to Corporous, which was a contender, but Production was still running ideas through Isa, who was in Fantasia. Still, how did Isa know so much? Or rather, how were we lucky enough to have the smartest member of IT visiting Vampira when the glitch broke out?

Was it luck?

"Safety, actually," Nia said.

"From the Glitch?" I asked. "Can they do that?"

"No, it's safety from a reset. Many people are calling for a reset of your game, claiming it may be the last missing piece to restoring the worlds to what they used to be prior to the glitch," Nia answered.

"But that would kill me."

"*Potentially,*" Isa said. "It also has the potential to do what they think it will do. Turn it off and then back on again, type of thing. It's a decades-old concept, but it really does work, which is why people always recommend it."

"If you offer to help Production, they've allowed Isa to encrypt your code. For every person claiming that resetting you can restore your game, there are another twenty calling you a god with the powers you have; the next Henry Fudders. Help return people to their games, and in exchange, no one is *allowed* to reset you."

"Can't you encrypt her code on the down-low?" Eros asked Isa.

"Right now, her code is already encrypted, and Bryce is the only one with access," Isa said. "Now, he's not *supposed* to touch T's code anymore. However, he can share that access if he wants by sharing the decryption key. Then, he *technically* wouldn't be touching T's code. Agreeing to Production's terms and conditions would allow for me to add my own layer of protection that not even Bryce could bypass."

"So, T would be guaranteed safety from a reset, accidental or otherwise," Eros thought aloud.

"I agree," I said. Why wouldn't I guarantee safety with Isa? Besides, traveling through the worlds is exactly what I wanted to do. There won't be anyone there to stop me from returning people and getting the answers I wanted while I'm in those other worlds. Sure, maybe I'd be stuck traveling to their specific world first, but it opened up literal worlds of possibilities.

"Great, we'll agree to your teleportation services," Nia said. "Next, we'll need to discuss additional protections for you, such as frequency of trips and so forth."

"I trust your judgment," I said. I didn't want to deal with this anymore. I wanted Nia to fix it. Whatever it was, she could agree to it for me and resolve it. Thinking about all of this was added stress, and if another person asked me a question or told me something else I needed to attend, I might lose it. I was feeling burnt out and needed a break. Except, heroes didn't get breaks, and I'd somehow become the hero type, even though it wasn't in my Character Profile.

"If the small details don't bother you, I can negotiate on the back-end and send you the final deal?"

"Sure, just know that long-term, I want to stay here in Fantasia," I added.

"I also want to be a part of the package," Eros said. "Wherever she goes, whenever she goes, I will go with her to make sure nothing shady happens."

"Nia, I'd like to continue discussing this further with you," Seraphina said. "Tack180 is my subject and very well-liked by my family and retainers. I'd like to ensure she is safe in her travels, as well, which may require parting with a retainer every so often."

"I'd like to be present for this conversation, as well," Kaspian said.

"Sure. Tack180, if you couldn't tell already, don't leave the castle grounds, got it?" Nia asked.

"Sure."

"Then, you are excused." Seraphina nodded.

Eros and I left the room and looked at each other. I raised a hand, and he high-fived me. Safety and the ability to travel? There was nothing wrong with the deal; I felt confident, like I was finally going to get answers from the people I needed them from; Production.

"Hey, what's going on in there?" Alton asked. He, Nathaniel, and Olivia were barely a few feet away. Olivia looked at me and then away.

I'm sorry. It's not hard to say. I can do this.

"You didn't hear?" Eros questioned.

"It all happened rather quickly." Nathaniel shook his head, yawning. "And so early."

"Production found out about our trip to Olympus," Eros answered for me while I stared at Olivia. I was waiting for the right time to apologize. It would be to all of them, but mostly to her. "Zeus sends his best."

"Ah, Zeus. We had some delightful trysts with the ladies when—"

"I'm sorry," I interrupted him. "Olivia, I'm so sorry."

"I know," she answered. "It doesn't mean it doesn't hurt. With Odin visiting, I was already on edge and snapped."

Odin?

"Who is O—" I started, but Nathaniel nudged me. "Anyway, I'm sorry. I didn't think it would be so hard to stop him, and I didn't think he would use you. He knew it would bother me because I love you guys."

"I know," she said again.

"Anyway," Alton segued. "What's Production going to do now that they know you can travel?"

"They are offering protection from a reset—the internet's going crazy over it," I said. "They'll let Isa encrypt my code once it's finalized."

"The internet can love you one second and cancel you the next," Olivia said. "Production loves you right now because the internet does. We need to go make sure that doesn't change until your contract is signed. I need to go do damage control as SmokeScreen. Alton, a little help would be nice. We'll find you guys later." She ran off with Alton and I stood there slightly stunned by her reaction. She was the knowledgeable one; people loved me, there was no way it could change so quickly. I looked at Nathaniel and Eros for answers, but they didn't seem to have any.

"You'll be fine." Eros waved a hand in front of his face. "Check your DMs. Mine all say the people love you."

I did as he said and opened my DMs. I had put myself in Do Not Disturb mode, so there weren't any new DMs from strangers. But the most recent DM at the top was the one that shocked me.

It was from Cap.

I tried to open it, but no matter what I did, it wouldn't open. It had to mean that he was alive, right? There was no other way I could get a message from him. If Cap, who was presumed dead, was able to message me, regardless of what it said, then he had to be alive.

"Eros," I said his name quickly. I didn't want false hope and RPG positivity. I wasn't even sure if I could tell Eros, but I needed to figure it out. "I want to wait somewhere a little more private."

He nodded and we left Nathaniel to wait for the prince.

"Excuse me." We heard as we were walking down the hallway. We turned around, and a soldier was behind us. "Can I speak with you in private?"

I looked at Eros. He shook his head. "After that talk, I'm going to be a part of whatever conversation you have."

"That's not a problem," the soldier said. He opened a nearby door to a random room within the castle. It looked like a sitting room, which the castle probably had ten of, with a fancy couch, decorative flowers, and, of course, a painting of the royal family. The picture was from before the queen's mother had Seraphina, probably only a month before because she looked ready to pop.

"What do you need?" I asked.

"Tack180," the soldier started. "I want you to kill me."

What the fuck?

"I want you to kill me," he started crying. "I lost my wife and son when the Glitch came to our town of Blackburn. I don't want to live without them. I *can't* live without them. You're the only one with the power to end my suffering. I just want the pain to end."

A warm tear fell down my cheek. I knew how he felt; the pain and the loneliness. I had grappled with Ghost's death for a while, but I chose revenge. This man chose defeat.

"You're out of line," Eros said. He stuck out his hand and pushed me back toward the door. I wanted to help the man, I did, but I also couldn't *kill* him. My hands were shaking as I continued to back up.

"I'm begging you, Tack180," the soldier yelled as I opened the door.

In the hallway, another group of soldiers walked by. They immediately knelt on the floor as if I was the queen.

What the hell is happening?

Eros closed the door, leaving the other guard in the room, and turned to face our new friends.

"Oh, for fuck's sake," he sighed.

"Blessed Tack180, we are not worthy of being in the same room as you. We humbly apologize and ask for forgiveness," one of them said. I knew she would be fast, but what did Olivia do? No, this wasn't just from SmokeScreen's intervention. I had heard this before, even during the battle bakery, but it had never been this obvious.

"Don't worry about it," I said. *What are they even apologizing for?* I whispered to Eros, "We need to get out of here."

Eros nodded, then followed me to the library, where I sat at the chess table as he stood guard by the door, making sure no one else came looking for us. I message Isa, but she didn't respond. If anyone knew how to open a corrupt DM, it would be Isa. If not Isa, then maybe Bryce, since he was my producer. My right leg began to shake as I stared at the chessboard without making any moves.

"T," I heard Kaspian's voice from the other side of the door. "Are you in here?"

"Is it just you guys?" Eros asked. "People are acting crazy right now."

"It's just us," Alton answered. Eros moved from the door, and the prince and his retainers entered.

"Leave us alone," Kaspian said Eros.

"I'll be outside with the others." Eros nodded in my direction before leaving.

"Are you alright?" Kaspian sat down across from me and picked up a pawn. He moved it forward, then looked at me. I grabbed a pawn and moved it forward.

"I thought you were supposed to give me the advantage when I'm in a crappy mood." I smiled.

"We can switch spots." He stood. I laughed and shook my head.

"Did you know some guy just asked me to kill him?"

"Eros messaged me."

So that's why he was here.

"I don't even know how to respond to something like that. I'm here, stuck in the unknown of whether or not this glitch on my hands will kill me, or if people will reset me, when I don't even want to die. And this man comes up and says he wants me to kill him." I paused, taking in my real feelings and trying to make sense of everything before I said, "I just don't want to lose everything I have and everyone I love."

"You won't," he said, his voice firm.

"I have a message from Cap in my DMs that I can't open," I said. I needed Kaspian's support, his ideas, or even just to tell me it was ok. A lot of random shit just happened that I wasn't prepared for. My popularity, already high, just skyrocketed, I had the chance to hear from Cap, who should be dead, and some random dude I didn't even know asked me to kill him. I had no idea how to feel, or the ability to figure out which pawn to move next. None of that felt like it mattered with Kaspian around.

"Cap." He thought about the name.

"He's the leader of my world. My version of Seraphina."

"What do you think it means?"

"I want to be excited, but I feel like that's foolish. It could be a glitch, especially since I can't open it. I don't know what to do."

"I think we should ask Isa," he said after a moment of silence.

"I've already tried." I nodded. "There's a lot going on right now. It's hard waiting for a response."

I looked up at him as he stared at the table, analyzing his next move. I had apologized to Olivia, but Kaspian was just as important, and I probably hurt him just as much. If the roles were reversed, I'd be mad. He didn't seem too bothered, but he always had a good poker face, especially when we teased him about ButtBusterBecky. I had no idea if what happened bothered him, but I needed to apologize if it did.

"I'm sorry," I said. "For what happened with Ghost."

He sighed as he continued to stare at the chessboard. "Do I remind you of him?"

"Ghost? No, you two aren't alike at all. Nathaniel reminds me of him, actually." I knew why he asked. It seemed like I chose Ghost as if I had just been using Kaspian because I was lonely, but that wasn't really how I felt. "I have to save Ghost; he's written into my code. But, with you? Well, right now, playing chess with you and listening to the music has become one of my favorite things."

His eyes widened with that confession, then he smiled, "I enjoy listening to the relaxing sound of the violins, as well."

He reached over and grabbed my hand. I listened to my music, the light violins playing within the main melody. *He heard them too,* and they were more beautiful than ever. Nothing seemed to matter anymore. Not at that moment. What mattered was that Kaspian, who wasn't programmed to do so, stopped what he was doing to be with me when I needed it. We played chess until I finally received a message from Seraphina asking that I return to the strategy room.

"I'll come along," Kaspian offered. I nodded. Eros was waiting just outside the door for us and followed along.

We knocked on the door to enter the strategy room, and the door flung open on its own. Seraphina's eyes glowed purple briefly before returning to their natural color. In front of her were champagne flutes and a bottle. *Really? That's a little much.* But I realized that was my answer and they were happy for me, even if it wasn't a way I would celebrate.

I got what I wanted, and Isa could encrypt my code. My life was easier knowing that I wouldn't be reset, not that I had worried about it much before Production got involved, but the thought that others believed it would work was terrifying and I didn't leave off on the best terms with Bryce. Still, everything was falling into place, and I didn't have to choose between my old life and my new one. I didn't have to let anyone down with my decisions. Getting revenge on the Glitch and their creator was the best I could do, and I was going to do a damn good job of it.

"We thought you'd want to celebrate." Seraphina smiled widely at me.

"I do." I smiled at the offer.

"T—" Seraphina started, but Nia was calling me. I held up a finger as politely as you could to a queen and answered her. "Hello?"

"I have good news," she said.

"Yeah, I already know. Seraphina and Isa told me."

"The very popular live-streamer, SmokeScreen, was going to bat for you." I could tell by the way she phrased it that she might have known something was going on and who SmokeScreen really was. "So did N0F@ce, a few other prominent figures in the gaming community. Well, with that, we also have our first return set up. You will be compensated for your time, of course. Bryce and Cody want to go back to Corporous. Production would also like one of their well-known Producers and lawyers back in Corporous, as well. I've negotiated that, in addition to your base pay for this return, the remainder of your contract will end immediately."

"All I have to do is send them back?" I asked. "No catch?"

"No catch."

"Let's do it," I agreed. "I want to be done with them."

"I'll send you the details now."

I messaged Olivia to meet us at the strategy room because, even though I loved the support from others, she was the only one I really needed when using the glitch. While we waited for her, I explained the situation thoroughly to the others and read up on Nia's details on the Returns. Every other week, until the end of the glitch, or everyone had been returned, whichever came first, I would be returning people to different worlds. Nia and Isa negotiated for more time due to the unknown nature that the Returns would have on my body, so I had a full week to complete one Return and a full week in between each Return. I would be paid *enough*; it wasn't my salary from *Duty Falls*, but it made up for the lost income from that week at the bakery. While I did the hard work, Production will try to group people together on the back-end so that we could be more efficient during each Return. Everything, I mean *everything*, was legit. Nia wrote the agreement so clearly that there was nothing out of place in the offer.

Olivia showed up soon after we finished discussing everything in detail. Before we headed out, I tried to talk to Isa regarding Cap's DM, but she said she'd look at my messages later. I knew she was busy, but I wanted answers, and it was hard to walk away from it and act like I didn't have a life-altering DM waiting for me.

The meeting place was in the forest, just on the outskirts of the town, so it seemed like overkill to have Kaspian open a portal there. We went through a side entrance to the castle and out an obscure path through Castle Town that I hadn't been on before. I could see Castle Town's side entrance when I heard it, a cheer within the crowd.

"Save us, Tack180," someone yelled.

"We believe in you! Protect us!"

"Grace us with your powers. We are forever unworthy of your holy light as it shines from above, but we will fight to live a life in which you will continue to protect us from the Glitch." I focused on one person as people started crying and reaching for me as I walked through the streets. Eros and

Olivia tried to keep them off at first, but we became overpowered by a mob. The voice I focused on kept talking, "You slay the fallen angel. You open heavenly paths to places unreachable. We are unworthy of your love and protection. Grant me divinity. Grant me power as you touch me with your hands."

The person reached for my glitched hands, and Eros pushed them away. We continued to push through. We were so close to the gates. People continued to cheer, beg for my help, and praise me as a god as they outstretched their arms past one another, just to touch a single strand of my hair. I focused on the gates because I didn't know how to feel, but I was feeling something. I wanted to cry and be ignored. I didn't want to be their god. I just wanted to be me; Tack180. I didn't let my eyes wander to the people approaching us; they all looked so sad, like the man from earlier.

Just focus on the gate. I repeated it to myself. *Just a little closer.*

When we were almost to the castle gates, the guards helped us push our way through and blocked the crowd from following us just long enough for Kaspian to show up with backup. The new soldiers assisted in pushing the crowd back as he opened a portal the rest of the way to ensure distance between us and my horde of followers.

"What the hell is going on with people?" Eros asked.

"Well, like I said. One minute the internet can hate you, and the next, they love you. They were already calling T the next Henry Fudders because he was the last person who held so much individual power before the Production teams were put in place," Olivia said. "But they really do love you, T. Your new followers are calling themselves Tackticians."

"Oh god," I groaned.

"That's what they're saying." Eros laughed.

"I don't want this." I shook my head. "I didn't want to be glitched, and I don't want to be the next Henry Fudders."

"We can keep you safe on castle grounds," Kaspian said. "Though I'm not sure about when you travel to other worlds."

"Let's just get this Return over with and then we can discuss it more. I don't want to be out in the open any longer than I have to," I said.

Everyone nodded in agreement, and we walked the remaining way to the meeting point to find Bryce and Cody, with nothing more than a few bags. The two of them stopped talking when we got close. I set up a video conference on my comms with Nia so she could see and hear everything that was happening as if she was in my body.

"Tack180," Cody said. "Beautiful as always."

I didn't answer. I just rolled my eyes at his complete 180 since our last meeting, then added Cody and Bryce to the conference with Nia.

"Alright then," Nia said. "Tack180 is completing this Return, therefore the remainder of your relationship with Bryce, as the Producer of your game, will be terminated. Bryce will remain as the Producer for *Duty Falls*, but he will not have production rights over anything you do moving forward. You will no longer be a Character for the game *Duty Falls*. Are you ready?"

"Yes."

I waited a moment before acting. I had wanted this moment for almost as long as I had known Bryce, but it was still a bittersweet feeling. Holding onto Bryce was holding onto the last remnant of *Duty Falls*. Sending him home meant I was ready to start my new life. As weird as it was, I was excited about the change. I took a deep breath, clenched my hands into fists, and let the weight take over, freezing the world around me.

"Well, that was interesting to watch," I heard Nia say.

"You're still here?"

"You froze Fantasia, not Corporous."

"I guess that makes sense. You're in for a show then." I walked up to Olivia, Kaspian, and Eros first. Then I unfroze Bryce and Cody at the same time. "You two ready?"

"Thank you, Tack180. I appreciate your support in getting us home to the safety of our own world," Cody said with a sly smirk on his face that made me want to punch him even more than I already did.

"I'm sorry things turned out the way they did," Bryce said to me.

"Me, too." But I wasn't really. I just said it as one final pleasantry before I was done with him and his annoying lawyer.

"Have you heard from anyone since the comms came back up?" He asked. I didn't know what to say; it seemed oddly timed that he would ask about communications after I got a message from Cap that I couldn't open. I didn't feel comfortable telling him, even if he could help me.

"No." I shook my head.

"Well, take care, Tack," Bryce said, then they grabbed their things and walked through the portal without any further farewells or fighting.

"That's it, Tack180, but you can reach out to me if you need anything. You and my brother both know how to contact me. I'll call you before your next Return. Until then, don't get up to anything stupid."

"I'll try," I laughed. As she hung up, I let the world around us unfreeze and took a deep breath of well-deserved freedom.

"I've talked to Ingrid. The crossover you two received is still in effect," Kaspian said to Eros and me. "No further action is required until you choose to officially join our game. After you deal with the Glitch, that is."

"I'm free," I said with a smile. Eros held up a hand and I met it with my own.

I am my own Player.

I wrapped my arms around Kaspian, feeling the warmth of his chest as I pressed my body to his. I took a deep breath, smelling the mixture of leather and metals used to create the outfit he wore. He wrapped his arms around me and trailed his fingers lightly up and down my back.

"Want to play some chess?" he asked.

"Yes," I whispered.

"Let's head back."

Kaspian opened a portal back to the library and everyone stepped through. Olivia left us to meet with the queen. Eros, on the other hand, no matter what I said, refused to leave my side, citing safety concerns. Kaspian assured him that no outside visitors were allowed on castle grounds, but Eros didn't care, and Kaspian didn't push him on the issue either. So, Eros sat around staring out the windows as Kaspian and I played chess.

"I know some weird shit has happened today," I said and smiled at the prince sitting across from me. "Thank you for being there with me. I'm happy with the outcome of today's events."

"I'm just as happy." He beamed and grabbed my hand from across the table.

"Are you falling for me, Kaspian?" I laughed.

"I like my music better when you're around."

"I do, too."

We played chess until late into the night, when I instinctively stopped to get some rest before having to get up to bake in the morning. Except, everything I had built at the bakery was a wash; without Bryce, I wasn't going to continue the battle bakery and, with the way people were acting, I didn't feel comfortable leaving the castle walls. The last thing I wanted was to be serving cake while people tried to grab me. I couldn't go back to the bakery until I knew it was safe to do so. It hurt to see my hard work destroyed before I had the chance to truly enjoy it, but that didn't mean I had to stop baking. I could always use one of the castle's kitchens.

Kaspian talked about other safety concerns as well; he didn't trust the Tackticians. I didn't either, but even though people could sneak onto castle grounds, the royals and retainers always said that no one could make it *that* far into the castle. If that was true, why would I need a backup plan? Kaspian was firm in the matter; even Eros, Seraphina, and Olivia got involved. At the end of the night, a backup plan was created, even though I doubted we'd need it.

Kaspian walked me back to my room, hugged me, and, just as he was about to leave, I grabbed his hand and stopped him. Kaspian looked down the hall in both directions before entering my room and shutting the door. Once inside, he held me in his arms and put his head against mine; his gaze shooting between my lips and my eyes. I closed my eyes and enjoyed the feeling of being so close to him with the violins playing beautifully in the background.

I was free to make all of my own decisions and there was one I had been waiting to act on. I pushed my body closer to his. His arms trailed slowly from my back up to my face before pulling me into a kiss. I pushed him towards the bed to keep the night going. Sex with Kaspian checked off a few more personal quests from my list, increasing my experience and endorphins. It was a win-win situation and it felt amazing, too.

The next morning, I stretched in bed and rolled over to see Kaspian, still sleeping next to me. It was great for a moment, and then I thought about the last time it happened with Ghost; it had felt like just a normal day before Ghost was taken from me. I scooted my body closer to Kaspian's, feeling his warmth and not wanting to leave. I couldn't lose him, and I wouldn't. I would do everything in my power to make sure that he was protected from that Glitch.

When he woke up, Kaspian waited in my room until Eros was awake before leaving. Only as he was leaving did he tell me that his guards reported thirty attempted intruders overnight, all of whom attempted to get to the servant's quarters. It didn't stop all day. Frequent Tackticians attempted to climb the castle walls.

I told them when I got here that was a stupid mechanism, EXP or not.

Eros and I stayed out of sight and set up camp in a kitchen on the opposite side of the castle where I baked, and Eros ate. Isa was too busy to look into Cap's surprise message, or maybe she didn't care enough, and I was starting to regret not telling Bryce about the message. Cap's life mattered to Bryce, just as much as mine previously had. Though we didn't have the same rationale, we wanted the same outcome.

The sound of yelling in the courtyard pulled our attention away from the cakes in front of us and we looked out of the window in the kitchen. There was fighting on the castle grounds as a familiar fallen angel type was battling the guards. I grabbed a knife, knowing that he was a tough opponent.

"T?" There was a knock on the door as Kaspian called my name. "I'd like to implement the backup plan. We need to get you out of here and to a safer location."

"Where's the castle's defense?" Eros asked.

"We have over a thousand people storming Castle Town's gates as we speak," Kaspian snapped. "We must protect our people. Freya will keep you safe."

"What do they want?" I asked.

"They're chanting nonsense phrases about your divinity. While I don't think they'll hurt *you*, they are engaging in acts of war to get to you. I don't trust what they will do if they storm the castle. Pack your things."

As I packed, I could hear the chants of people begging to go home, to see me, or to be placed on a list for the Returns. While we fought with the Glitch, someone had taken a video of my one-on-one fight with him. Tales of my battle and abilities had spread throughout the worlds, solidifying a *need* for me rather than a reset and confirming my god status across the worlds. The hordes of people, calling themselves the Tackticians, continued to march through Castle Town in an attempt to reach me.

After packing, Kaspian joined Eros and me in the strategy room. He opened a portal to an open field filled with fierce-looking soldiers. A woman was standing behind them in front of a giant ship, which seemed out of place in the middle of an open field. Kaspian said Freya would keep me safe. The only time I'd ever heard the name Freya before was in relation to games dedicated to Norse mythology, which I didn't know enough about, but that made sense as to why Olivia said Odin's name. I at least knew he was a typical Norse god Character as well. Freya was familiar; she was one of the members of the council of Fantasia, the one who cried golden tears next to the one with the crow, who I assumed was Odin. Except nothing else about the scene was familiar. Soldiers, with deadly wounds still visible, crawled from the ground, joining the woman as if they were being commanded to battle. Contrary to the ferocity of the warriors, the ship was covered in flowers almost like a scene from a painting. She beckoned us forward with a reassuring smile while a golden tear rolled down her cheek. And still, even in her beauty, she exuded power as the soldiers turned to her, waiting for a command.

Where was Kaspian sending me?

Eros put a hand on my shoulder. I looked over at him and he nodded to me. I wasn't sure what was going to happen next or what this meant for me, but if it was anything like the adventure I had had since joining Fantasia, then I was ready to start my next RPG.

Thank you for reading!

Go to 5310PUBLISHING.COM
for more great books you can read today!

If you enjoyed this book, please review it!

Connect with us on social media!
@5310publishing on Twitter and Instagram

Subscribe to our mailing list to get exclusive
offers, news, updates, and discounts for our
future book releases and our authors!

You might also like...
HONEY BEAUMONT

Once upon a time, an unlikely hero was born out of servitude. Honey Beaumont, our hero, strived to do right by everyone and see justice prevail no matter the consequence. He dreamt of the intrepid Adventurer's Guild and helping those who can't help themselves.

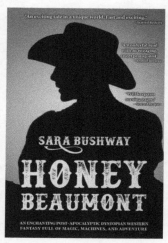

Every day Honey persevered the wrath of Byron, his owner. Helping those around him doesn't fill Byron's pockets, bringing out anger in his boss. One day, Byron brutally attacks Honey after a wealthy client offers to help Honey leave the life of servitude and be free. After the attack, Honey was scarred, disfigured, and with a grudge. He begrudgingly left his home and the love of his life behind to move into a new and luxurious home.

Honey mingles amongst those in the new house and learns about the world's inequalities, especially between the nobodies and humans. But with his new owner forbidding him from being independent, Honey has no other choice but to leave this new luxurious life behind.

Freedom for Honey meant joining the Adventure's Guild, becoming a hero, and helping his family leave the horrible place he used to call home. Will Honey be strong enough to take on Byron? Only time will tell.

Embarking on a journey of a lifetime, being a hero is harder than Honey ever imagined, but at least he has his friends by his side to help him save the day.

SCAN ME

You might also like...
MAGIC OF LIES

Princess Eirian Altira has always walked on a knife's edge with flowers chasing her footsteps. Born with magic, she struggles to balance her ability to give life with the desire to kill. Raised by mages, the day comes when she must return home to a kingdom she left as a child, and a father she has not seen in 20 years. Surrounded by a strange court with expectations she was not prepared for, Eirian hides her magic until she's faced with the choice between becoming queen or returning to the mages.

With secrets around every corner and war with a neighboring kingdom on the horizon, Eirian discovers her power means more than she realized. As does her long-standing friendship with the crown prince of the elven nation they've been allied with for generations. But the whispers in her mind and the rumors spreading through her court threaten everything Eirian holds dear, and she will do anything to protect the ones she loves.

"You don't know what I'm capable of or what I'm willing to do.
Don't underestimate me. You might regret it."

When Eirian Altira returned home after decades away, she thought it would be a fresh start. Raised a mage in a distant city, she struggles to adjust to life as a princess in a court where magic is undesired. Caught between two thrones, she knows where her duty lies. With assassination attempts and rumors of war, Eirian proves to those around her that she is not one to hide from confrontation. Even when it risks her life.

Torn between her love for a man sent far from her side, her attraction to the captain of her guards, and the best friend she has always needed, Eirian refuses to bow to the demands of her advisors. Determined to be the queen

her kingdom needs her to be in the face of war, Eirian seeks the truth behind who she is and why the enigmatic land they have never had dealings with is seeking an alliance. But the answer may not be what she expected, and the repercussions could cost her the very throne she must defend.

SCAN ME

You might also like...
A KISS TO WAKE ME

"A high school romance full of love—and turbulence. The novel highlights different family dynamics that readers may resonate with... [a] story of trust, love, and family." — Kirkus Reviews

A Kiss to Wake Me is a modern-day love story between Jamie and Cara. When the two first lock eyes in the high school cafeteria, "love at first sight" is no longer just a cliché to either of them. Their romance takes off at record speed but just as quickly crashes into a wall of disbelief when a figurative bomb is dropped into their lives, upending the world as they knew it: Cara is pregnant, even though she believed she was a virgin.

When these unforeseen circumstances threaten the couple's future together, everything comes into question. Is Jamie the father of her baby? Will he still love her and the baby if he's not? How did Cara even get pregnant? How could she possibly cope without him and his family, whom she has grown to love and depend on? Will Jamie and Cara's love endure the hardships thrust so harshly upon them? *Fans of romantic first love and those who desire to see first love withstand seemingly insurmountable obstacles will enjoy this sweet yet intense novel.*

Three days before high school graduation, 18-year-old Cara mysteriously delivers a premature baby boy at home in her bathroom. The novel begins with her frantic 911 call and flashes back to unfold the beautiful and romantic first-love story between Cara and Jamie, the new tall and handsome student from California. They are two clever, level-headed teens who strive to do the right things but make one big mistake leading to dire consequences.

Faith and morality hang in the balance between choices made and the tiny miracle baby they've all grown to love. The couple's hope of a happily-ever-after is further at stake as the ensuing police investigation uncovers secrets, lies, and the answers they have all been holding their breaths to receive to move forward.

SCAN ME

You might also like...
THE ART OF BECOMING A TRAITOR

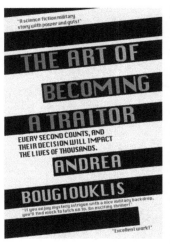

Eleri is the only one with the ability to destroy the world around her... Now she needs to save it.

She had always loved being used as the weapon, being both the arrow and the target. But when Eleri learns the truth about the impact of their pasts and all the chaos that they have created, they are tasked with the impossible: to undo the damage they have caused.

Fyodor and Eleri know that they are strong and influential, but will their power be enough to alter the course of history forever?

A young woman with a larger than life legacy and an incredible sense of self truly believed that what she was doing was right. With all of her being, she thought that she was helping to serve a long-overdue justice.

When Eleri learns that she had been used as a pawn in a larger, evil plot, she has to find it in herself to right her wrongs - even if it means going against everything and everyone she ever loved. The war had been raging since she was a young child, and she had never thought to question it.

When Eleri and her best friend Fyodor discover that their leaders have been doctoring and altering history and are planning to disintegrate an entire population, they realize that they may be the only two who can prevent this atrocity. **In a race against time, power, and their own morals, they can only hope that their willpower and strength are enough to overturn a war that has already begun.**

SCAN ME

Lightning Source UK Ltd.
Milton Keynes UK
UKHW010348150223
417035UK00006B/20